CHOOSING LOVERS FOR JUSTINE

'I must have her, Julia,' she said. 'I will have this girl tonight or I shall die.'

But Julia shook her head. 'I'm sorry, Celia. She is not available. She is spoken for.'

'Is that so?' Celia stepped back from the bed. 'Then pay them off,' she said abruptly. 'Let them take one of the others.' Suddenly, she took hold of Justine's face in both hands and pushed it down and back and stared into it while Justine trembled on her knees. 'Know it – I will have you, whatever Julia says. And when I have you I shall punish you. I will punish till you beg for more.'

'Celia!' Julia was affronted. But the feeling had already come to Justine: the awful, luscious sinking feeling down between her legs.

By the same author:

THE SLAVE OF LIDIR
THE DUNGEONS OF LIDIR
THE FOREST OF BONDAGE
PLEASURE ISLAND
THE HANDMAIDENS
CITADEL OF SERVITUDE

Other Nexus Classics:

THE IMAGE
THE INSTITUTE   April 1999
AGONY AUNT   May 1999
THE HANDMAIDENS   June 1999

A NEXUS CLASSIC

CHOOSING LOVERS FOR JUSTINE

Aran Ashe

This book is a work of fiction.
In real life, make sure you practise safe sex.

First published in 1993 by
Nexus
Thames Wharf Studios
Rainville Road
London W6 9HT

Reprinted 1994, 1995

This Nexus Classic edition 1999

PhotoTypeset by Intype, London

Printed and bound by
Cox & Wyman Ltd, Reading, Berks

ISBN 0 352 33351 0

Contents

1 An Escort for a Gentleman   1
2 The Top Floor Room   4
3 A Schooling in Submission   16
4 The Escritoire   27
5 Sharing Roxanne   43
6 A Nymph for Celia   55
7 Elizabeth Learning   70
8 The Letter   88
9 The Coldness of Snow   105
10 A Change in Leasehold   120
11 The Stemple   136
12 The Mare in Harness   149
13 The Preparation of the Bride   172
14 A String of Beads   190
15 The Pleasure-pangs of Giving   200
16 A Study in Arousal   213
17 The Club   227
18 Beware Her Needs   254

1: AN ESCORT FOR A GENTLEMAN

On the eve of his betrothal to an intelligent, personable and well-connected woman twenty-seven years his junior, Philip Clement stood at one of the first-floor windows of his comfortable private office. He was watching the progress of the single motor car marooned in the press of carriages that were shuffling round the gas-lit square. Behind him, the room was silent apart from the slow tick of a clock. The time was already seven-thirty. The hansom cab that had been sent to collect him waited below, its horse pawing the cobbles, its driver rubbing his hands together and drawing his collar up against the cold. But Philip had business to attend to; that was why he would be late. Charlotte would understand.

In the centre of the carved leather surface of his desk, a letter lay open, a large pale pink sheet, faintly perfumed with attar of roses. He walked across and picked it up again. Its tone seemed more circumspect with each rereading:

21st. November

Sir,

Our mutual acquaintance, Mr Lawrence Jesber, has conveyed to me – in confidence – the substance of the business matter which you wish to contract.

By an accident of good fortune, satisfactory completion may now be possible rather sooner than expected. However, in view of the delicate nature of the subject, and in order to avoid embarrassment to either party, I propose not to entrust the details to the post nor to suggest a meeting at this stage, but rather to communicate with you by telephone tomorrow evening (Friday).

1

I shall do this after office hours. Should you then decide not to proceed, I should understand and trouble you no further.
In this matter, sir, I am your faithful servant,
Julia Norwood

Then the telephone rang; the strident screech of the operator was replaced after a short delay by an altogether smoother voice:

'Mr Clement?'

'Yes.'

'It's Julia Norwood, Mr Clement. Are you free to speak?'

'Ah, Miss Norwood. I was expecting to hear from you; thank you for your letter – '

'You may call me Julia.' Her tone seemed quite different from that of her letter.

Philip lifted the telephone from the desk, then settled into his chesterfield chair, drawing the gold cigarette casket towards him. 'Miss Norwood – Julia. Yes, we can speak frankly. Please go ahead with what you have to tell me.' The desk lighter was just beyond his reach. He started to get up again but stopped when the woman simply said:

'I have her. She is perfect.'

He sank back down again. The hard cylinder of the cigarette rolled between his fingers. He examined the monogram, then tapped the end of the cigarette lightly on the casket. 'Go on.'

The voice spoke slowly: 'Slim – willowy. Long legs. Blonde, short hair.'

'Short hair? How short?'

'Very short; short like a boy's.'

His chin lifted and his eyes focused on a point in front of him, about four feet away and five feet in the air, while the voice continued: 'Large breasts – noticeable.'

'How old?' he said quietly.

'Nineteen.'

Again, the voice waited a decent interval, during which his forefinger had time to lift and slide up and down across his lip, then move down to join with the thumb to remove

2

a pure grey hair that disturbed the symmetry of the fine stripes on his immaculately tailored suit.

'But she has had a sheltered upbringing: she was schooled in a seminary.' There was a further pause. 'It seems they were very strict with her . . .'

'Regarding men? Liaisons? Surely that is only to be expected?'

'I mean that they were strict with her body, Mr Clement. We still do not know the full story of what happened there.' Again, the woman waited. 'But it left its mark, if I may put it so. You may perhaps have come across the writings of von Sacher-Masoch? Anyway, she is a most extraordinary girl.' When there was still no reply, she said, 'I shall be in touch again.'

He suddenly realised she was about to hang up. 'Wait – she has a name?'

'Justine – Miss Justine Lambert. I believe her mother was French.'

The connection was cut off with a soft click.

Ten minutes later, the cab still waited and Philip still sat in the same chair, staring at that same spot in the air. The tip of his cigarette was now linked to it by slowly sliding coils of thin grey smoke.

2: THE TOP FLOOR ROOM

In the old heart of the city was an upstairs restaurant known only to the few. Overlooking the hubbub of the streets below, it retained an atmosphere of intimacy and of opulent discretion. Above it was a suite of rooms.

It was no accident that a young woman of around nineteen was sitting in the restaurant on a particular Wednesday evening in late November. She sat there by design, but not through choice: she did as she was told. Had you been there – if you could have seen her, as the waiter did – you would have thought that she was perfect. She sat primly and straight, but with eyes cast down to the table. Her hair was blonde and very short and was shaved at the back and shaped. She had the kind of slim, wan beauty that can frighten. It made the waiter look away and close his eyes and imagine the fine coalescing lines of pale down at the nape of her neck descending into her spine.

The table at which she sat was in an alcove more secluded than the rest. When he looked back, she was again lifting the heavy glass of pale yellow wine. With a solid chink, it caught the edge of the dinner plate on which the silver knife and fork lay crossed above the barely touched food – the vegetables entire, the sauce an undisturbed pool of glaze about the wedge of bleeding meat – and the conversation stopped. Six eyes turned to watch her drink, as they had watched her every minimal movement since the dinner began; six eyes which were her guardians, or her gaolers. Her lips closed about the deep rim of the glass, her head tilted back and she drank. Her neck was now exposed above the high-collared russet jacket, which appeared to have

4

been tailored faithfully to her shape. It was buttoned closely down the front, fitting tightly. It clung to the fullness of her breasts, outlining them accurately and individually. And it constricted her waist, where a tongue of the material was drawn across to make a short, secure belt. The sleeves clung, extending to cover her wrists. Thin, looped straps of the same russet material stretched from the wrists and slipped between the forefinger and second finger, giving the illusion of a child's mitten support, and reinforcing the impression of constraint.

She placed the glass down unsteadily, and the movement was accompanied by another chink. Already there was a dark stain of moisture on the smooth clean cloth. By sliding the glass to try to cover it, she only drew attention to it. And in doing so, she had turned the glass, so the marks left by her lips on the rim could be seen by the others at the table. Her large blue eyes suddenly expanded as they fixed upon the lip-marked glass. They lifted, flickered, then retreated from each of the other three pairs of eyes which watched in cool fascination as the looped hand rose above the glass and the slim thumb slipped inside and made contact with the smear. The glass tilted, the hand tried to catch it but it toppled over her plate. The perfection there was destroyed. Red blood mixed haphazardly and unwillingly with sweet yellow wine. At her catch of breath, their eyes moved upon her face again until the waiter intervened and the plate was swept away.

'I shall replace it,' he whispered, to her alone.

'No!' Then she said quietly, 'Thank you. I had finished.'

'Madam.' He retreated.

Her pure blue gaze fell down to the blank cloth before her, with its small surface spatterings of brown and red and the thicker blotches of moisture beneath. She remained with shorn head bowed and pale eyelashes unmoving while the others took their time and spoke of things she did not hear.

'Justine is very quiet. Do you not think so, Philip?' Julia spoke in the coquettish, tantalising way which she manufactured for the purpose of throwing men off their guard. She had addressed the older man, and pronounced the name in the French way, with a soft 'J'. Justine looked up at the man she had never seen before tonight; he had not been caught off balance, either by her gaze or by the question, and his stare outfaced Justine.

But it was the younger man sitting beside him who replied to Julia. 'Does she understand the arrangement?' He had pale blond hair, much paler than Justine's, and his voice had an edge of arrogance which made Justine look away. She had met him only twice before, but he was cold for one so young – cold and frightening in the way he used the girls, not seeking his satisfaction with them, but searching out their fear.

There was laughter far away in the background, at the other tables, but Justine was slowly drowning. Her collar was tight. She could feel the looped constraints which pressed against the skin between her fingers, and the pressure around her breasts. *I want your breasts and arms and hands imprisoned* – this was what Julia had said. That afternoon, she had made her wear nothing but this tightly fitting jacket; Justine had remained naked below the waist while Julia had used her, and the blond man had held her so she could not move.

'The arrangement has not been made,' Julia said, and her dark eyes turned to the older man, who looked again at Justine before reaching into his inside jacket pocket and removing an envelope. He placed it quickly and precisely down on to the cloth, then laced his fingers together, resting his elbows on the table edge and his chin upon his fists. He stared at Justine from under his eyebrows. A faint smirk crossed the blond man's lips as Julia's hand slid over the cloth and drew the envelope towards her. She took up a small knife which had escaped the efficiency of the waiter and she slit open the envelope along two adjacent sides then turned the corner back. The notes were crisp, unused and of large denomination.

The waiter had returned with an accomplice, and with a fresh cloth over his arm. They would now re-lay the table.

'That will not be necessary,' said Julia.

She whispered to the waiter, who looked at Justine, then quickly corrected his error by forcing his eyes to defocus before he whispered discreetly in return, 'Yes, there is a private room upstairs.'

The room was warm, the ceiling was magenta, the walls were pale cerise. Chandeliers sparkled above and to each side of the bed, which was almost in the middle of the room. The man called Philip stood by the door. He was to be the watcher, Justine knew. She was kneeling on the quilt, in a room into which she had never been before and for a man she did not know.

Button followed button, freed, as Julia's hand moved upwards. Justine's hands were behind her back. The looped straps that crossed her palms and fitted between her fingers were gripped in the younger man's hand. Nobody as yet had spoken his name, but it was Lawrence. Justine knew it. And she knew what he liked to do to girls. Each time Julia's fingers freed a button, the jacket opened further and the pressure was in part released from Justine's breasts, which were gradually slipping free.

Philip gazed; Justine wore no chemise. Completely covering Justine's breasts and stomach were fine hairs, which could be rendered visible as blonde in a certain play of the light, or as darker lines when Justine's breasts were oiled. They made branching, fern-like patterns on the centre line of her stomach. They were also present on her back, between her shoulders and just above her buttocks. Julia liked to comb these fine hairs and she liked to make Justine stand sideways against the light while she brushed them with her tongue. She made Justine do many kinds of things which were playing upon Justine's mind now as the final button was freed. Justine was frightened, but nevertheless she felt secure in Julia's presence.

Julia lifted up Justine's breasts so that Philip could see them properly; he had not moved from the door. She held them while she rubbed the nipples with the tips of her fingers. Julia was used to playing with Justine; she knew what to do. Whatever she did was right and was acceptable

7

to Justine. She formed her fingers into loops to trap the nipples and squeeze them. Justine's breasts were even larger than usual because her period would soon be due; her nipples were more sensitive. Julia pinched them, not playfully, but so that it hurt. She watched Philip's expression while she was doing this and she listened to Justine's mumurs; Philip's expression was controlled by Justine's murmurs and by the way her head turned gently away to the side whenever she closed her eyes.

Lawrence held Justine's arms behind her back, pinning them at the elbows while he held the looped straps crossing her palms. He lifted the jacket back from Justine's breasts.

Julia could see the fine blonde hair on Justine's breasts picked out as golden curving strands which were raised because the skin of Justine's breasts was now so tight. It made Julia want to comb this hair into flowing circular patterns. It was hair that was strong; not thick, but strong, so that it showed up in the light and had to be wetted with the tongue to make it softer. Justine's body was slim, and it appeared frail. She was ribby, but her breasts were over-full and tight. Her hair had been shorn. It had been long until yesterday, but Lawrence had said that Philip wanted a girl whose hair was short, so Julia had had it cut off and hadn't told Justine it was going to happen. She had waited until it was done. 'I wanted to see your expression when you saw yourself in the mirror,' she had said afterwards. Justine had thought that it would only be a trim. And now she looked like a boy.

Julia went to get the cane from the case she had entrusted to the waiter when they had arrived. It was an old school cane which she had found in a junk shop two days after Justine had first told her about the housemistress. The cane had a hooked handle, and a shaft which was crooked from use and thinned to wickedness at the tip. It was a cane for punishment, and it would have been useless for any other purpose. She had used it on Justine that same night, with Justine face down on the bed, and Justine had subsequently blacked-out when she came. Julia now placed it on the bed and Justine flinched.

Philip folded his arms; his eyes had never moved from Justine and his face had no expression beyond this concentrated gaze. Then Julia opened the case again and asked him to select. His eyes lowered briefly. He whispered in reply, then his gaze returned to Justine. Beside the cane in front of Justine, Julia placed a small white dildo, then a stiff quill-feather, and Justine flinched again.

Justine's skirt buttoned up the side. Julia carefully unbuttoned it, working upwards again, so the bare thigh with its down of golden, brushable hair kept peeping out before the skirt could finally be taken away. Justine wore knickers which were very brief and cream and clinging. Julia called them 'panties'. She doubted that Philip would have seen such things before. Julia pulled the panties down to Justine's knees. With Justine's arms still pinned behind her back, the jacket was drawn open – Justine's breasts prevented it from closing. Her legs were edged apart as far as the constraint of the panties round her knees would permit. Her arms remained fully sleeved. Philip now walked to the bed and the other two retreated.

Justine kept her hands behind her back, pressed together at the wrists. Philip whispered something in her ear; his thin lips briefly touched her burning ear lobe; they did not kiss it, but touched it accidentally as he spoke. Her back straightened, then hollowed deeply, her breasts trembling as she strained to push them out. Her stomach, so flat before, bulged to make a belly. Philip stood back and looked – at her short blonde hair which could not reach the collar of her russet jacket; at her thin-skinned breasts which forced the jacket open; at her smoothly bulging belly; and below it, at the panties round her knees, which edged a little further out across the quilt, drawing the panties tighter.

He walked around behind her and looked at her buttocks, which were pale and tight and projected roundly below the line of her jacket. The muscles on the backs and insides of her thighs were slim but still visible as muscles; they had a form which made one want to touch. He moved further back and saw that the inside muscles narrowed where they rooted at the top of her leg, leaving a gap which was not completely filled by the downbulge of her cunt. He would have this part of her in due course; he would hold it in his hand first, but he would want to take it from behind, so he could feel her buttocks moving against him as she squeezed.

The backs of her legs were entirely covered in fine, pale gold hair. The soles of her feet looked soft; her toes were long – his lips would fit around them individually. He moved closer to look at her wrists, which remained pressed together behind her back, against her russet jacket. He touched her fingers, which trembled and jerked away at first then moved only very slightly while he continued touching. Three times nineteen was fifty-seven: the arithmetic was neat. Young skin was so soft; slim fingers were so delightful. He touched the loop which separated her forefinger from the rest, then slid his finger underneath it, touching the separating skin, and she shivered.

Philip returned to the front, where he waited until Julia provided him with a wooden chair, which he turned and sat astride. The other two were waiting. He nodded. His mouth began to open but his lips had sealed together and did not want to part, so the words followed later and the sound was hollow when it came. 'Do it,' he said.

Julia gave the cane to Lawrence, who had to put it down again while he removed his jacket and placed it on the table. He removed the cuff from his right sleeve and rolled it up. Justine stiffened. She was not ready; she had known it was going to happen, but she was not ready. It made no difference. In one swift movement he was behind her, bracing himself with one knee on the bed, slipping his fingers through the loops across her palm and lifting them out of the way. She heard the terrifying swish, and with the first hot narrow lash across her bottom, the breath burst out of her. Her breasts jerked forwards, bulging through the gap in her jacket, but the curvature of her back and belly could not save her from the blows as the cane kept coming. It could only add to the pleasure of watching the blur that whipped across the tight nude buttocks while the defenceless breasts and belly kept thrusting so provocatively out and upwards, strongly upwards, in rhythmic jerks, through the gap in the short russet jacket. Blow followed blow so quickly that she had no time to breathe: that was the intention. Her waist was so narrow, her buttocks were so exposed and round, and they kept dancing as she wriggled. In order to keep all the lashes in the same place, Lawrence had to lift her arms and hook his forearm underneath them and across her back to steady her while he whipped her bottom.

Justine tried to close her legs. She had to keep them open; she had to keep her buttocks still. She knew this but could not do it. The cane kept whipping, aiming for the same place, where the cheeks were most sensitive, not whipping her anywhere else. Her breath was sucked in quickly, only in now, as her belly pushed out in front to try to make the strokes fall above or below that punished place, but he seemed to know what she was doing and eased a little back and aimed the whipping in precisely the same place every time. With Justine's breasts continuously poking out now, Julia pinched the nipples up while Philip watched and Lawrence whipped more quickly. Justine could not breathe. Her lungs were full; her breasts were bursting; her bottom was burning. But in her belly was a heavy warmth and in her throat a craving that was sweet.

The whipping stopped. Justine was gasping, her legs still open, her panties stretched between them. Dull throbbing pains searched upwards through the cheeks of her bottom: they made her shiver when they touched her spine; they licked upon it like a lover. She wanted Julia to suck her nipples and nip her between her open legs and make her come.

There were fine droplets of sweat which no one could see, but Justine could feel, in the creases at the tops of her thighs; there were damp patches which were quite visible in the cloth of the jacket under her arms. Julia lifted the jacket back and smoothed her hand over Justine's belly, which stayed curved and felt slightly sticky from the sweat. But the hairs upon it were soft now.

11

'This time,' Philip said, 'keep her chin up. I want to see her face.'

And with each stroke, the panties trembled as they stretched between her knees. Justine's small tight belly pushed into Julia's palm and Julia's finger and thumb kept pinching the broad surrounds of Justine's nipples. Justine felt swollen hard between her legs now; dulled points of thickened pain probed up inside the cheeks of her bottom; her head tilted forwards.

'Keep your chin up, Justine,' Julia warned, and she lifted it on her palm. For a second, Justine saw the pupils of her dark eyes turn completely black. Then she saw Philip still sitting astride his chair, and the awful gnawing sexual feeling was like a hand pushing up inside her throat.

'Enough,' said Philip. The cheeks of Justine's bottom shuddered one last time, but her long slim inner thighs still trembled. He glanced towards the items lying on the bed.

Julia took up the small white dildo, which had a bevelled point. 'Lawrence,' she said. He was needed on the bed again, to hold Justine while she was masturbated. During masturbation, Justine was normally kept restrained. This was to be a continuation of the process that had begun that afternoon, when Julia had masturbated Justine, with Justine held in position on a chair like Philip's, while Julia explained that she would be caned for a man who had expressed an interest in her and would pay for the privilege of watching. Julia had not at that time finished what she had started with Justine. She might not even finish it now; she might leave Justine aroused. The treatment might be taken up again, later in the night. Justine could never predict when, or in what ways, she might be used. Julia had said it was better that way. Justine trusted her: Julia provided all the love and physical affection that she needed.

Lawrence now pinned Justine's arms back and secured her hands together with a finger slipped through the loops which separated her fingers. He pulled the jacket back from her breasts, pulling it round and under her arms and up her back, so that the narrowness of her waist and the bulging melon shapes of her breasts could now be seen

12

extraordinarily clearly. Philip edged forward in the chair until it tilted.

There was no sound, there was no breathing, while the smooth, white, rounded shape slid up Justine's labia, which were swelling pink, and pushed them to the side. It burrowed through the soft wet hairs, moving down then up again. It seemed in no hurry. A pure white shining tube now held the inner lips apart. It did not enter, but it prevented the lips from closing. It moved up a little and the lips bulged round it. Everything was still, except this slightly moving dildo and Justine's belly, which was changing shape as the muscles rippled beneath the skin. And then came the murmurs, very faint, as the dildo slowly turned. Suddenly, the bevelled tip touched something electric in Justine. Her legs jerked open; her panties trembled – but the rubbing tip probed deeper. Her head bowed forward while her belly tried to pull away. A hand came up to support her.

'Chin up, Justine,' said Julia, while Justine gasped and shuddered and the bevelled tip found again that sweet electric place.

'Stop,' Philip said softly, and the bevelled tip was withdrawn, shiny with her liquid. He stood up. His eyes were fixed on Justine's. To him, her eyes were very young and trusting. To her, his eyes were grey and cool. She offered her eyes to him – for love, and for the coolness in his eyes to turn to warmth. 'Cane her,' he said.

Her bottom was caned in that same place until her legs would not stop shaking; then she was caned again for tears. Caning for tears was the cruellest caning. Even Julia did it only sometimes. It was not the pain that brought the tears but the hopeless drowning feeling that came to Justine when she knew there was no escape and they would just keep punishing her until they decided to stop. Tonight the punishment was to whip her in the selfsame place, torturing a narrow band across her bottom while she was offering herself in trust, aching to be loved, wanting only to be held and kissed.

'There . . .' Julia said gently. The blinding tears had

13

come at last. Julia held the trembling chin up while the tears ran down into her palm and wet Justine's neck.

And when the dildo was reapplied, her clitoris formed an even harder ball against its bevelled surface. Her panties, stretched in tension, were working upwards from her knees. Julia held them while she carefully twisted the dildo up and down and from side to side. It worked around the clitoris until it stood out from the junction of the lips. Justine was about to climax: Julia could tell from her breathing and from the tremulous panties stretched above her knees. She pressed the soft cream crotch of the panties down on to the bed. Justine was coming. Lawrence held her tightly. She had to be held in climax, restrained. She had to want to fight towards it, to want to move, but to be unable to do so. Philip was now by the bed. 'Kiss her,' Julia said softly. She knew that the tenderness of kisses was important at this time. She eased the dildo to the side of the clitoris, which was left erect and exposed, then picked up the stiff quill-feather. Justine's head was drawn back and held, and she was shuddering. 'She needs you, Philip – kiss her.'

He cupped her head in his hand, and held her beneath the chin, supporting her in this way because she was drowning as the tip of the feather touched and brushed and plucked her pulsing clitoris. His fingers stretched around her head of short blonde hair. Her mouth was opened wide. He sucked her tongue, sucking hard enough to bruise it, to make it swell. It felt hot within his mouth. She shuddered, but he held her, his lips a tight band round her tongue. Between her legs, the feather continued plucking. Quill-feathers are harsh and sweet and strong enough when wet. Justine tried to gasp. Julia eased the rubbing tip away and held the soft wet labia open with her fingers, then touched the stiff point of the feather carefully to the tip of the clitoris and pressed and gently twisted. Lawrence's hand came between the legs in time to pin the tightly stretched knickers down to the bed before Justine's climax was triggered. She was held so she could not move – her

14

labia stretched open, her distended clitoris stabbed by the wetly flicking feather.

The tongue pushing deep into Philip's mouth became rigid; Justine whimpered through her nose. Her body, so tense, turned limp in his arms. He kissed her eyelids, kissed her lips, ran his fingers through her short blonde hair. Philip was in love with Justine. Justine was drowned in the floods of sweet submission.

Julia laid her on the bed and covered her with the quilt. She immediately fell asleep, but Philip did not want to leave her. He sat beside her, watching over her, and barely listening while Julia arranged the terms.

'Be aware of her needs, pay heed to them, and she will love you,' Julia told him. 'Her needs are met for now; it is better that you go.' But she suggested that Philip might bestow some little gift upon Justine that Justine might like to wear and that Julia would help him choose.

Philip was engaged to Charlotte, that was only proper; it was Justine's body that he craved. He dreamed about her that night; the next night, a message came, but in a form he could never have expected.

3: A SCHOOLING IN SUBMISSION

Justine was in the shower-bath in Julia's bathroom. Julia had let her sleep late, telling her that she would not be needed during the day.

'About last night,' Julia had said when they met on the stairs. 'I was pleased with you, Justine.' She had even said it in front of Krisha and the others, adding: 'Oh, and you may use my bathroom.' It was a special favour.

Justine's showers were always long these days; she took showers that drained a tank. And Julia's shower-bath was large. It reminded Justine of the ones in the school where she had spent two years, and it reminded her of her lover who was dead.

It was the hollowness of the sounds, the echoes in her ears, the high fall of the water, and the bumping in the coarse brass pipes which reminded her of that place. Memories can be as sweet, as real and as terror-fraught as life. Her back slid down the faded pattern on the tiles, just as it had done on that day four years ago. In the sound of the falling water, she could almost hear again the voices and the laughter from the changing rooms. She could feel her heartbeat; she could hear again the footsteps on the wet, tiled floor. She closed her eyes and knew they came. She could remember every detail – slow footsteps pausing, then the sigh, but no movement, no movement even when Justine looked up. *Eyes of frightened longing* – that was the way she had seen Justine, but she had told her that only much later. That day, Justine had no way of knowing for certain.

'Justine, you are still here.' It was a statement; there was no pretence of surprise in the housemistress's expression

16

and no hint in her eyes that the incident of the day before had ever taken place.

The knot in the pit of Justine's stomach tightened. She felt sick. She hadn't eaten breakfast or lunch; she hadn't eaten properly for days – since the kiss. One kiss, but the first kiss ever of that kind, and the first kiss, you remember. Afterwards, Justine could think of nothing else; over and over, she kept saying that one name, 'Rachel,' that she was not supposed to speak in public. 'Rachel,' she whispered it like a prayer.

She was the youngest teacher in the school; she was athletic and attractive. Justine never thought of herself that way. The mirror told her she was awkward and gangly; she had breasts that felt too large and a belly like a ball. That was why she wasn't eating. So, once that first kiss had been taken, long and lingering and sweet, Justine had thought of nothing but the next one. Gradually, she had become afraid that the next might never come. There were signs – chance meetings of eyes – but nothing more. And for the last two days, Rachel had ignored her. Then, last night, she had stopped her on the stairs and pushed her to the wall and stared hard into her face, before moving close, as if to kiss her. Justine had closed her eyes – waited – but the kiss never came. When she had opened them again, Rachel was still staring at her. Then she had left her, trembling, on the stairs. And now, as she sat in the pool of lukewarm water, she was trembling again. Her hair was plastered down her shoulders and her foot was over the drain. With the trapped water lapping between her legs, Justine waited again.

Rachel's arm reached through the spray above her and twisted the unwieldy tap. The last heavy drips splashed on Justine's breasts. Her foot had moved and the water was draining, pulling at the hairs between her legs and lapping at her bottom. A door banged in the changing rooms; the last of the class were leaving and Justine would now be late. But Rachel stood at the mouth of the cubicle, her hand resting on the wall, her feet planted apart, blocking the way. Now that the shower had stopped, the cold

17

draught sweeping along the shower room was sucked into the cubicle. Justine started to shiver as her body cooled. In her stomach, the knot was harder and still twisting.

Rachel waited until everyone had gone, then walked down the length of the shower room, closed the door properly and took the keys from her skirt pocket. Justine heard the door being locked.

Then Rachel walked back. She wound a handle on the wall, which opened the skylight vent. 'Get up, Miss Lambert.'

Justine's back slid up the tiles and her legs straightened. The drops of water on her skin turned chill in the cold moving air; the goose bumps rose and the skin hairs lifted. Her stomach was flat because she hadn't eaten; now it was rendered concave by the way she held it in. Her breasts were already larger than the housemistress's and they lifted with her breathing.

Rachel reached past her and turned the silvered brass pointer down, all the way down, to cold. Justine pressed her back against the cubicle wall.

'Stand in the middle, Miss Lambert, please. Put your hands at your sides.' Then Rachel seemed to have second thoughts. 'No. Put your arms up.' The sleeve of her cotton blouse touched Justine's bare wet skin as she arranged her with her palms upturned above her head, then moved her legs apart. And the feeling that Justine experienced when Rachel's hands touched her naked wet legs was as intense as if Rachel had done something to the place between them. But she had only touched her legs. Then she reached behind and turned the freezing water fully on. Pausing only to place her fingertip across Justine's lips to seal the shuddering gasps within, then to shake the water from her sleeve, Rachel left her.

Justine never moved her feet, but every other part of her shook, violently at first but then more slowly as the warmth of her body was gradually sucked away in the freezing, gushing water. There was no one there to witness it, or to know when to call a halt. She became afraid that Rachel would not come back, but still she did not move. She closed

18

her eyes and waited, telling herself it was a test and that the last test, on the stairs, she must have failed. Then the fear turned to an awful calm in which she could hear only the running water and feel only the cold, like a numbing sheath around her; but it did not frighten her any longer. In order to pass that test, she would have waited until the warmth of life had ebbed away.

Rachel returned ten minutes later, turned the tap off and took her out of the shower. Her teeth began chattering; her skin had turned a blotchy purple-pink; the veins beneath looked deep blue. Rachel made her stand against the wall while the shivers started, then became uncontrollable as the water ran down her legs. Then Rachel took a short phial from her breast pocket. In it was a thermometer. She took it out and shook the mercury down. 'Turn around, Miss Lambert,' she said. 'Open your legs.'

Because the shudders were so violent, the bulb could not be introduced until Justine's stomach was pinned against the wall. Then she felt the short glass tube slipping upwards through the tight ring muscle.

While Rachel waited, she began to dry Justine's back. She made her keep her legs wide and her arms out, with her hands pressed to the wall. The towel was moved from under her arms to her shoulders and down her back. It wiped her buttocks and the backs of her legs; then it returned to the split of her cheeks. Rachel held them open. Justine felt a finger-end pushing through the towel and slowly brushing the skin which squeezed around the glass tube of the thermometer. When the thermometer was pulled, the ring did not release it willingly and she felt the muscle pouting when the glass slipped out.

Rachel made her turn round. She wiped the thermometer on the towel and examined it. She nodded. 'You're not dead yet, Miss Lambert.' And she smiled. Then she put the thermometer away. She examined Justine's breasts, which were still dripping. Her hair was saturated. She began to dry it and Justine's skin began to warm. She made her keep her legs apart and kept pressing a hand against her stomach. 'You're very skinny,' she said. 'Very skinny.

19

We shall have to feed you up.' She began to dry very gently between her legs and the feeling of arousal came strongly to Justine. 'Look at me, Justine. Tonight, I want you to eat all your supper. Will you do that?'

'Yes,' Justine whispered weakly, knowing she never could. The towel-covered hand moved up and pressed firmly against her stomach and she felt nauseous.

'And afterwards, I want you in my study.' Then Rachel kissed her, and this kiss was much deeper than the first and the feelings that it stirred were more intense.

For Justine, there was an excitement that always came with crossing an empty schoolyard when lessons were in full swing. The sounds drifted down now – singing, ringing bells, windows being opened, thumping feet. And there was the feeling of vulnerability, too, the feeling that someone was sure to see her, that Sister Margaret was aware . . . And suddenly her invisible presence high up on the third floor struck down at Justine and curtailed her plan of taking wide sweeping circuits round the yard, and made her run through the doors and up the stairs, to arrive at last with an involuntary breathlessness in her chest and with a tall tale on her tongue. And for the rest of the afternoon, Justine was dreaming of the housemistress and what she would do to Justine when she got her in the sanctum of her study, and Justine's knickers were wet already with the thinking . . .

'Justine?' called Sister Margaret.

'*Amo, amas, amamus –* '

'No!' cried Sister Margaret.

'Yes . . .' whispered Justine.

That night, Justine still sat at table when all the others were gone. She stared into the half-full bowl in which the custard had formed a skin. Her stomach was bursting; she wanted to heave. Rachel was watching her, standing guard. But she could not finish; she pushed it away. Rachel strolled across and whispered, 'If you can't eat it, you needn't bother coming to my rooms; you needn't bother me again,' then walked away and stood by the doors. She watched Justine forcing the last thick spoonful down, then she left.

The study was large but, full of ancient cupboards and bookcases, it looked cluttered. Rachel was sitting on an armchair which had a towel thrown over the back. The carpet under Justine's feet had threadbare patches. A racket in a press lay on the table; on the walls were photographs of Alpine scenes. There was a pair of skis propped behind the door. The room was a strange mixture of the old and the new. Rachel was a contradiction.

Beyond the armchair, Justine could see the door to the bedroom: it stood ajar. Her heart was thumping. The heavy, sour-edged smell of old books mixed with the sickly smell of warm milk. The mug was on the table next to her. Her knickers were already untied and rolled down to the tops of her legs, where they hung loosely, threatening to fall. Rachel had turned her sideways and lifted her skirt so her small distended belly was exposed. She pressed a hand against it. Justine murmured because the touch hurt. Rachel pressed more firmly and Justine wanted to retch. But she still felt excited by this slow undressing. Rachel took Justine's skirt off, leaving the blouse extending to her navel. She unfastened the bottom few buttons and parted it, then made Justine turn to face her. She rolled the knickers a little further down until a gap appeared, then slipped her hand into it and touched Justine. It was the first time anyone else's naked hand had touched her there. She was frightened but excited by these different feelings coming so quickly, and she was terrified by the thought that she might smell.

While Justine gasped softly and closed her eyes and Rachel touched this place between her legs, Rachel told her she must call it 'cunny'. She made Justine repeat the word. Justine could only whisper it, but Rachel made her say it loudly, until it echoed in the stillness of the room. And while one hand still pressed against her swollen belly, the other continued to rub and stroke the lips that were so unused to this treatment, until the lips turned wet. When

Justine's eyes opened, her gaze fell again upon the polished oak table and the cup of chocolate milk. There was melted butter floating in it.

'Pick it up,' said Rachel. When Justine did not move, she turned her, slipping one hand under her buttocks while continuing to play with her cunny. 'I want you to drink it.' Justine could never do it; her belly was already bursting. But other hands, other explorations, you cannot predict; they control you in curious ways. Anxiety and pleasure can be interlinked. And Justine had never been touched in such ways by anyone before that night.

Rachel asked Justine the name for what she was doing. Justine thought it was 'fornication'. Rachel put her right. 'Plant your legs apart,' she said. She opened the pulpy lips and began to rub the edges while the backs of her fingers rustled against the inside of the knickers. While Justine's legs shook, Rachel explained that this was 'masturbation', that her fingertips turning wet was right, and that it had to take time. 'Let your stomach expand. Let it out.' She drew the blouse apart and held it back while she watched and touched the slippy lips and kept them swelling wetly. 'Now, pick your chocolate up and drink it – slowly.'

In the mirror, Justine saw a gangly girl with long blonde hair and a belly that was ballooning so hard it seemed to have split her blouse wide open. Her legs appeared to be tied together by the knickers round her knees and she was being masturbated very slowly by a young woman who was watching her through the mirror. The loose ribbons of her knickers gently trembled from her knees. Justine reached for the mug of milk and raised it to her lips.

'Slowly,' Rachel whispered.

Justine closed her eyes and felt sick. Her upper lip touched the melted butter and the thick warm skin beneath it stuck against her lip. She tilted the mug and tried to swallow continuously, to be rid of the awful thickness. The drink was lukewarm, cloying, coating her tongue and slipping like sweet mud down her throat.

'Slowly . . .' Rachel whispered. The mug tilted more steeply; the belly bulged. 'Smoothly. Drink it all.' Rachel waited until the mug was empty and the hand holding it fell limply away. Then she spread her fingertips around the belly and squeezed. The belly contracted. Justine swallowed, then groaned and clapped her hand across her mouth. 'Shh . . . Not yet,' said Rachel, and those words terrified Justine.

Rachel took the mug from her, turned her round to face her and pulled her knickers down to her ankles, took her shoes off and pulled the knickers over her feet. Then she stood up, took the blouse completely off Justine and unlaced the short linen bodice which Justine always fastened so tightly. 'I don't want you to hide them,' she told Justine as she took her breasts out and looked at her in the mirror – standing her sideways, so her distended belly looked disproportionately large. Then she led her in her stockinged feet to the bathroom, where she raised the toilet seat and made her kneel with the cold enamel pressing against the top of her stomach. She lifted her hair out of the way and spread open her bodice, pushing her forwards so her hands gripped the bowl and her breasts hung down against the inside surface. Then she held the swollen stomach in her hand and squeezed it firmly. There was a choking cough. 'Shhh . . .' said Rachel. 'There . . .' And she steadied Justine's forehead and the hand that held the belly just kept squeezing.

When the hollow, wrenching, retching sounds had ceased, Rachel flushed the toilet. She turned Justine's head and asked her to open her mouth. There were beads of perspiration on her forehead. Rachel pushed her fingers deep inside Justine's mouth and directed her head into the bowl. The hollow sounds came again, and a cry of cramping pain this time, because the stomach was by now almost empty. 'Open your mouth,' Rachel said again. This time, nothing was delivered and the cramps continued for the greater part of a minute.

Justine was drenched with sweat when Rachel finally lifted her up. She wiped her with a towel and gave her a glass of water with which to gargle. Then she helped her to the bed, where she removed her bodice, but kept her in

23

her stockings and played with her again until she became wet. Progressively, she tried to stretch her. Justine, of course, was tight. Even one finger, pushed in deeply, hurt her.

Rachel turned her on her side and tried it from behind. She said, 'Relax,' but Justine was shivering and sweating at the same time. The feeling of the warm finger, so close against her, sticking to her stretching inner skin, moving inside, made her nauseous. Rachel's middle finger stayed inside her, pushing until the stretched skin gave and the wave of nausea struck again. Keeping her finger still now, Rachel sat up slowly and looked down at Justine's face, which was paler than the sheets. She stroked her breasts, which were again wet with sweat, and pressed her fist gently into the small sunken empty belly, then unrolled the stockings to the ankles. She did all of this with her middle finger still inside Justine.

When Justine was naked to her feet, Rachel used the flat of her hand to rub the soft parts of Justine. She rolled her on to her other side, with her finger still inside her, so that they faced each other, then she pulled down the pillow for Justine's head. She arranged Justine's hair so it flowed out behind her and left her neck bare. She made her lift her leg and hold it, then she pushed the finger on and up inside her until it touched the nose of her womb. Justine moaned; the beads of sweat were coalescing; Rachel rubbed her free hand over the soft wet parts. She turned Justine on her back but kept the finger against her womb, keeping Justine sweating and weak and terrified that the finger might be dragged out quickly.

Rachel was in no hurry with her. She opened out the lips of her cunny and masturbated her by wetting a finger and rubbing it around the small projecting tip between them; she called this place the 'clitoris' and asked Justine if she knew what it was for. Justine swallowed and shook her head. Rachel probably knew that she lied. When Justine began to respond, she tugged the finger that was still inside and Justine became still while Rachel continued the slow masturbation. The film of sweat appeared again and Rachel

24

smoothed it up and down the nipples, which were very erect in the cold, but were slippy. She made Justine hold herself open while she drew her finger out and carefully licked it.

Rachel pulled all the sheets and blankets from underneath Justine and off the bed. Then she pulled the stockings off her feet, using one to bind Justine's wrists behind her back and the other to tie her ankles. She placed her on her side with her knees tucked up and again attempted to stretch her, pushing two fingers up inside her, to her womb. The fingers tried to nip the small nose, then tried to open out inside her. Justine moaned; her upper knee tried to lift to accommodate the hand while her ankles were tied together. Rachel reached round and pushed two fingers into her mouth. Justine was shaking, she was gagging against the hand and her body was hot with sweat. When the third finger entered her cunny, she cried out.

But Rachel completed the stretching, then played with her until her legs began to tremble, when she warned her to keep still. She lifted Justine's legs, then pressed her knees together as tightly as her ankles, making her cunny squeeze out behind, and she touched her clitoris in this position while Justine could not move. She kept wetting it and rubbing it gently as it projected between the lips. Then Rachel left her on her side, uncovered, and went out, closing the bedroom door. She returned an hour later and turned Justine on to her other side. Justine's teeth began to chatter when the cold mattress touched her and her warmer lower side was exposed to the air.

'Pout it out,' said Rachel. Justine did not know what she meant at first. Then she felt the thermometer sliding up her bottom. Rachel came very close behind her and smoothed her hair and kissed her. While she kissed her she held her clitoris. She kept Justine's knees tucked up and reached round from behind to hold it. Justine had to twist her head round to present her lips for kissing. It was a feeling like no other that she had experienced. Rachel's lips felt very warm; her breath was strangely scented.

Justine was eventually to discover what that scent was:

it was the scent of girl, and the taste of it was always on the housemistress's lips after each time she finished her rounds. But that night, Justine was aware only of the warmth of muskiness dabbing softly on her lips and the fingertips playing gently upon her clitoris till it ached. When Rachel took the thermometer out of Justine, the slim glass rod slipped smoothly. Rachel looked at it then shook it down.

She took her clothes off and lay beside Justine, but drew the covers over only one side of the bed, over only herself. She left Justine uncovered and tied.

In the night, Justine's eyes opened. There was light in the room, but she did not know where she was. Her body felt heavy and very tired and she felt cold, a numbing cold, but she did not shiver any more. She felt something sliding out of her.

Rachel held the thermometer up, then stared steadily at Justine.

Justine felt the knots being loosened from her wrists and feet. The fingers felt hot where they touched her skin. Then the warmth of the covers flooded over her. Rachel's bare and burning body was pressed against her freezing naked-ness and it held her while her shivers came back, while her shivers subsided, while the love welled up inside Justine to drug her into sleep.

The shower tap was turned off; the tank was drained; Julia stood above her. Justine sat in a pool of cold water, as cold as her lover who had burned her and was dead.

4: THE ESCRITOIRE

'Philip has sent you this. He wants you to wear it for him.'
Julia placed it in Justine's lap and continued to dry her hair
with the towel, taking the time and care that she would
have done if Justine's hair had still been long. But Justine's
hair was short now; it was just that Julia liked to dry Justine
and talk to her while she dried her.

Julia was in her dressing room, sitting on her small sofa,
with Justine below her, on the floor in front of the fire.
Justine was wearing a white silk blouse which had a blue
and green dragon embroidered on the back. Julia had given
it to her for her nineteenth birthday; Julia had embroidered
it herself and she liked to see Justine wearing it after her
shower. Only the bottom three buttons were fastened.
When Julia looked down, she could see Justine's breasts
inside it; they were full but swollen more than usual because
she was due. At the onset of her period, Justine could
become very aroused when her nipples were wetted and
gently sucked. The sucking could be prolonged, but it had
to be gentle, because Justine's breasts were so tender then.
Julia found Justine to be particularly sexual at this time.
Her belly became slightly swollen too. Julia could not see
it now because it was hidden under the folds of the blouse,
but she could see Justine's slim nude thighs as she sat with
one knee drawn up alongside her on the Chinese carpet. In
the well between her heel and stomach, sitting on the
bottom corner of the white silk blouse, was the leather G-
string that Julia had helped Philip to choose. It rested
where it had fallen, over the fingers of Justine's right hand,

27

which had not moved, although her fingertips curled slightly towards it rather than stretching open and away.

'Will you wear it – for him?'

There was a pause, during which Justine's fingers curled over until the tip of the middle one touched the thick part of the string, the part that would separate her, hold her open. Because she would never refuse: the request was made out of politeness and consideration.

'I will wear it, for you.' Justine's head turned. Her full lips, gently protuberant, pressed against the web of skin between Julia's thumb and forefinger. Justine sucked it gently, her mouth gradually opening wider, the moistness of her lips gradually enveloping the skin.

Julia held Justine's head of short blonde hair while she sucked. 'He wants to meet you, Justine.' She cradled the head as if it were a baby that she suckled.

'He has met me.' Justine looked into the fire.

Julia continued to smooth her hair. 'No. He wants to meet you alone. Just the two of you.'

Justine's eyes opened so wide that Julia wanted to kiss their perfect blueness. 'No!' She tried to pull away when Julia extended a hand to touch her hair.

She was frightened. She was not used to men. No man had ever taken satisfaction with her in that way. Men were there to watch her; they were there to hold her so she could not move while soft tongues licked her, while slim hands touched her, stretched her, used her. She preferred the thought of slim smooth hands and the fullness of a distension that could only come about with perfect understanding. Julia held her close now, her fingertips brushing upwards over the close-shaven hair above the nape of Justine's neck.

'It was Philip who wanted your hair like this, you know.'

Justine turned to stone. Julia continued the fingertip brushing. Slowly, Justine looked up again. 'But I thought that it was you. . .' The expression in her eyes told that her world was coming apart. Julia's reply was to kiss her gently until the kiss became deep and open-mouthed. Justine's mouth stayed wide open, so wide it hurt her. Julia had taught her that this was the way she wished to be kissed. Justine must never break away from a kiss; she must keep her mouth so wide it hurt her, while Julia's lips and tongue explored within it. Julia's tongue pushed deeper; Justine tried to swallow it, then Julia pulled away.

'Keep open,' Julia said. Justine's head was back and her eyes were closed and her mouth was open wide but she was trembling.

Julia bunched the fingers of her right hand together and slowly pushed them in, over the tongue and down. When they reached the knuckles, Justine gagged, but Julia held the chin cupped in the palm of her left hand so it could not lower and the smooth sweep of neck remained unbroken. She pushed Justine's tongue down and slipped her fingers deeper. 'Suck,' she said. The lips closed round her fingers and Julia closed her eyes. The hand beneath Justine's chin began sliding gently up and down her neck, squeezing softly at intervals, while the saliva welled inside Justine's mouth, and her tongue, so passive at first, began to slip between Julia's fingers and to make them slippery wet. Julia now withdrew her fingers and held them, wet and slightly spread apart, above Justine's mouth. Justine took one finger at a time and slowly sucked it dry. Her lips sealed round it at the web of skin at the base and pulled downwards, opening and closing in warm sucking contractions that squeezed around each joint while the waiting fingers drew lines of glistening wetness across her cheek.

'I know that Philip will like you. I know that you will please him.' Julia's left hand slipped down the blouse and caressed the swollen nipples. 'Look at me,' she said, and she squeezed them until Justine murmured. 'I want to squeeze them hard, to make them hurt,' said Julia. Justine did not answer, but her head bowed forward as her breasts swelled down and her lips kissed the bare arm gently as the fingers rolled and squeezed her nipples until she could not bear the pain. But she did bear it, and Julia pulled her head back, kissed the proffered neck and squeezed the hard hot nipples and knew that Justine would do anything she told her to do.

29

Julia stood up and drew Justine to her feet. She would take her to the Yellow Bedroom. But first, she stood back to look at her in her blouse and nothing else. There was a perfection about Justine: it was in the sculpting of her figure and in the fine strong blonde down that formed a sward upon her bottom and her legs, which Julia liked to keep bare. She kept her house very warm and very thickly carpeted with Persian rugs and Chinese mats so that Justine would be comfortable being bare below the waist and Julia would have the pleasure of the downy belly and sculpted bottom and slim smooth legs throughout the day as well as in the night. Julia preferred Justine to be only partially bare, but she was particular about the distribution of this nudity. She had no objection to Justine's arms and neck and even her breasts being covered. She liked the look of any clothing that would convey an impression of constraint about the upper body; she liked jewellery in moderation – mainly neckbands fitted closely to the skin; and she liked to see a definite line around the stomach and above the navel, below which Justine was entirely bare.

Julia liked at times to bandage Justine's arms, working the bandages carefully between the fingers to form fingerless gloves and bandaging tightly up the arms, under the armpits and round the torso above the breasts for one or two turns, then down the other arm, so that Justine's arms were stiff and her breasts were made pear-shaped by the pressure from above and Justine was completely nude below these pushed out, pear-shaped breasts with very swollen nipples.

Now that Justine had stood up, the blouse, although short, annoyed Julia because it still extended below the navel and it was loose. She secured the strap fastenings at the cuffs. She undid the lower buttons and fastened the ones at the neck. Then she pulled the sides up and over the tops of Justine's breasts, drew the cloth tightly round the back and tied the ends together across Justine's shoulder blades. Justine's breasts projected, but her arms were now completely covered to the neck and Julia wanted to kiss her nipples. Her nipples were engorged because Julia had been squeezing them and because Justine was due. She was very regular – twenty-six days – and she was usually quite heavy and she would probably start tomorrow or the day after; tomorrow would be more convenient because it was Friday.

When Nettie came in, Justine became agitated; her eyes darted round. Even after all this time, she would always become upset when the servants came into the room unexpectedly, and she would still feel embarrassed to be kept naked in the afternoons. But Julia continued sucking her nipples as she stood sideways before the tall cheval glass, and Nettie, with an 'Excuse me, Ma'am,' turned again to go.

'It's quite all right, Nettie,' Julia said and began again sucking the nipples up to a polish that looked painful, while Nettie curtsied briefly and began filling the drawers with blouses and chemises.

Julia picked up the leather G-string. 'Justine – I'm expecting guests for tea this afternoon,' she said and Justine looked at her again with frightened eyes. 'But I want you to stay up here and work. Krisha will amuse them.' Justine's gaze descended to the G-string. The supporting belt was narrow and very finely crafted: it had an inner skim of softer leather which would lie against the skin, and the outer surface was carved to the shapes of interlinked loops. But the part of it that would fit between her legs was not shaped so as to contain her; it was shaped to split her and to keep her so. 'He needs to know that this part of you is separated,' Julia said. 'Therefore, you shall wear this most of the time.' The single thin leather rope descender had a finer strand wound round it repeatedly at the front to make a large bulge that would hold her labia open. Because it had been oiled, it looked like a length of soft clay which had been rolled out by hand to leave this smooth bulge in the middle. Julia fitted the belt snugly around Justine's belly. Before she fitted the separator, she made Justine plant her feet apart. And with Nettie still tidying-up around the room, Julia slapped Justine.

The slaps sounded softly because they were gentle; they were intended to arouse. Justine was easily aroused by this means at this stage of her cycle. Julia used these gentle slaps while Justine stood as Julia had taught her, with her legs apart and her belly pushed out and her hands behind her neck and her face turned so she could see herself in the long cheval mirror. Her breasts, exposed beneath the tightness of the knotted blouse, shook gently as Julia slapped her belly. She used a cupped palm, not to hurt, but to make the soft sensitive places tremble, to induce feelings of pleasure between the legs. She slapped the insides of the thighs, then pulled the labia down to make them warmer and distended, then slapped the belly again. While she slapped, she talked to Nettie about the arrangements for tea. There were to be two ladies and a gentleman, and Krisha was to remain in attendance all the while. Julia's hands were warm and smooth; her fingers were long and slim. Justine liked them. Julia could use these long slim fingers in many ways that would bring about submission.

When she split the lips, the inner surfaces were moist and fresh and clean and the faint scent of sexuality was stronger through arousal; the clitoris was already hard. She fitted the bulge in the leather rope against the lips; when it was tightened, they opened and held it, smooth oil against slippy warm inner skin. In time, the rope would absorb her moisture and swell; it would keep her lips aware; it would give them something thick to grip; where it narrowed upwards, it would press against her clitoris. Julia had explained all of these things to Philip. She had explained how Justine should be made to sit – that she should be made to sit forwards – and she had explained about prolonged arousal and its relationship to pain, although she had not as yet mentioned Justine's period. But she had asked him if he might make himself available at the weekend. And she had arranged that a message would get to him to tell him that his gift was fitted.

On the first landing of the upper stairs that led to the Yellow Bedroom, Julia stopped Justine and turned her against the wall to examine her: Julia had discovered that the stairs held some special significance for Justine. The cheeks of Justine's buttocks were divided so deeply that

32

the rope could not be seen until Justine arched her legs open as she leant against the wall. Then Julia could see the mount protruding down, and the labia, thickened by her touching, split and held apart by the elliptical bulge in the rope. Justine's mount was large and low-slung; it was readily visible from behind. She could, when sufficiently excited, bring herself to orgasm standing up, merely by squeezing her thighs together, even without prior application of the cane. Julia wanted her to do it now, on the stairs, with her pubic lips astride the rope and slipping against it when they tried to grip, and with her clitoris squeezing against the leather. She wanted to see how long it would take her and how effective the rope would prove in getting her there.

'Stand up,' she said, 'and squeeze.' Justine seemed not to want to do it. Julia turned her round, so she faced away from the wall, then stood on the step above her, held her chin and said, 'Bring your legs together slowly.' Justine did it. The rope passing down over her belly disappeared between her legs. 'Now tighten.' Julia cupped her hand across the belly. 'Keep doing it.' And Julia could feel it, the slow, rhythmic tensing, through her fingers. 'Open your mouth, Justine. Breathe deeply.' The tensing and relaxing continued steadily; the cupped hand pressed; the back of the head touched the wall. Then the breathing changed: it stopped, then started, then suddenly stopped again. It became a gasp. The legs became unsteady; tiny tremors shook the knees; the head began to force itself back and the tongue slipped through the open mouth. 'Stay still,' Julia whispered. 'Open your legs, now – gently. Slide your feet apart.' They were shaking. 'No, don't stop. Keep contracting it,' she said. Julia wanted to train Justine to come, like this, with her legs apart. She waited till the toes were pointed outwards and away across the dense pile of the carpet. Then she touched the outside of the lips, where they were spread about the rope. 'Not yet,' said Julia gently, for it was the time of toying.

Justine knew that whatever might be done to her, she must never come during the toying; she must never come until Julia gave permission. And Julia toyed with her gently and long, and she kissed her. The lips that she toyed with felt hot; there were little gasps of pleasure delivered into her mouth. When Justine began to gurgle, Julia stood away from her a little, because she liked to watch the way she moved when self-control was in the balance.

She rubbed the side of her forefinger at the top of the right leg, at the crease. The knees started to bend, to press the crease against the finger. Julia stopped. Justine's legs turned outwards; her knees stayed bent and her split lips protruded downwards. Julia watched them shake each time she smacked the insides of the thighs. She continued this smacking accompanied by the gasps until Justine's back had slipped so far down the wall that her split swollen cunny was sitting on the landing floor. Then Julia helped her up again and led her up the last few stairs. But she would not let her close her legs.

When they reached the Yellow Bedroom, she made her kneel on the carpet while she took the cane from the drawer. Then she laid her face downwards on the bed, with her legs drawn apart so the split bulge was visible in between, and she whipped her quickly – one stroke only, but the buttocks jerked. 'Keep still, Justine,' she said. She whipped again, but the trembling could still be seen. Julia put the cane down, turned Justine's head to the side, drew her legs wide apart across the bed and whipped again, whipping at the tops of the legs, so the bulge of the cunny was caught with the thin tip of the cane. Then she went round to the other side and whipped again. She whipped the cane down six more times and Justine never murmured. But there were streaks of wet across the cheeks upon the counterpane. They were salty to the taste. Her mouth was open and her lips were hot; Julia's lips pushed inside them, took the tongue and sucked it.

Julia opened the split between the cheeks of Justine's buttocks, touched the rope, lifted it up and touched the firm warm well of the anus. It was sensitive, but it remained still and firm and tense while Julia touched it. It had not learnt to open voluntarily to the pressure of her thumb.

34

Her fingers lay along the outer lips, swollen and reddened where the cane had caught them. The bulge in the rope was already moist. The thumb pressed and the anus tightened. Julia slipped the cane under the rope at the base of Justine's spine and lifted it and twisted. Justine gasped as the rope beneath was drawn up between the lips of her cunny, whose edges now projected as the anus was exposed. Bending forwards, Julia pushed the tip of her tongue under the lifted rope and licked the anus slowly. Then she applied her wetted middle finger. Justine gasped again. Her hips pushed down into the bed but her anus opened and the finger pushed in to the first joint, then to the second, then to the knuckle. Julia gently bedded it while Justine squirmed with her legs wide open. 'The sweetest ring a finger may wear,' Julia whispered and she took the cane away, turned Justine over with her finger still inside her and kissed her. Then she stood up and whipped the cane across the front of Justine's legs, which remained open for the duration of this whipping.

Justine had wanted Julia's finger to stay inside her while her legs were caned; she had wanted her bottom distended; she had wanted it to grip. And now she wanted Julia to turn her over and lick her there again, to use her in the ways that Rachel had used her, to play with her and to use liniments and toys. But Julia only lifted her from the bed and led her to the desk – the escritoire, as she called it – and made Justine sit on the hard cushioned seat with her bare legs apart and wrapped around the long chair legs and her feet not touching the floor. She made her sit forwards so the cushion pushed the thick wet rope up into the down-bulge of her cunny and she feathered her swollen nipples with a quill. She kept touching her naked belly and between her legs, then she retied the blouse in a high knot round the front to make her breasts swell downwards. She made Justine place her elbows on the desk, then she stood to the side and feathered her breasts again. She said, 'Celia would like these. She would beat them – smack them hard,' which frightened Justine because she didn't know who Celia was and her breasts were already so sore. But Julia did not smack them; all she did was to turn them out to the sides and wet them, nip them, and feather them with the quill. And when Justine was quite ready, Julia took the sheets of vellum from the drawer and placed them before Justine. She ensured the inkpot was full and the walnut pen had a new gold nib. 'Today, I want you to write down the things that Rachel used to do to you. Shh . . .' She placed a finger across Justine's lips. 'I want you to do it; it will help you, Justine. I want to know exactly what you felt.'

'But those things, Julia – how could I ever begin to write them down?'

'Begin with the table.'

Justine's eyes implored her. 'But some of those things I could not even tell . . .'

'Then why did you do them? Why did you let her do them to you?' There was a restrained passion in Julia's voice.

'Because I loved her. She wanted it.'

Julia's dark eyes met Justine's. 'I want this. I want it . . .' She kissed Justine's upturned face; she squeezed her nipples till they ached.

Later, Justine looked up from the writing, in which she had become totally absorbed, to see a gentleman of mature years watching her from the door of the Yellow Bedroom. She recognised him: he was dressed for visiting and he still carried his grey kid gloves and his black lacquered cane which had a gold boss at the end. Last week he had come in the evening and had brought with him a lady, exacting in her manner, who appeared to be his wife. They had asked to see the girls and had selected Justine. While the man looked on, the lady had examined her. After a brief discussion with Julia, the couple had then departed suddenly, leaving Justine afraid that they were unsatisfied with her. But Julia never discussed the incident further.

And now, the man stared at her again while Julia came in and checked that Justine was still sitting as she had been placed, with her legs reaching down and the split bulge of her cunny pressed against the front edge of the seat. Justine's gaze returned to the page and she carried on working,

36

but she could feel the man's eyes on her until Julia escorted him away. A few minutes after that, Julia came back unaccompanied.

'Come,' she said. 'I want you to look at Krisha.'

The small tea party had retired to the upstairs drawing room, because Krisha was only partially clothed. Accompanying the gentleman was the same stern lady who had examined Justine the previous week, and also a much younger lady of about thirty-five. They were dressed in elaborate gowns of blue and yellow brocade and they still wore their hats. Krisha did not wear a hat; she wore no blouse or bodice of any kind and her nipples had been deeply rouged. She wore only her skirts, and even her boots had been removed. She was being chaired while the gentleman looked on, his hands twined across the gold top of his cane and his chin resting on them. Everything was very quiet.

Julia crept in with Justine so as not to interrupt and placed Justine beside the man on the settee. She felt vulnerable, with her blouse tied up across her breasts and with her legs and belly bare. But the man had eyes only for Krisha now. Krisha had eyes for no one – they were closed. Her skirt and petticoats had been pulled up; her bare bottom rested on the chair and she sat in a slumped position, her hips pushed forwards. Her lips were moving as her head arched back. The ladies that knelt beside her wearing their hats were whispering to each other; the younger one referred to the older as 'Mama'. They ignored everyone else and attended only to Krisha's needs. Justine wanted to be Krisha at that moment; that was why Julia had brought her down – to let her see.

Krisha was moaning; her breasts bulged out each time she breathed and her bright, rouged nipples swelled as if reaching for someone to burst them like ripe morello cherries. Her legs were open and her white thighs shook; her toes curled into the carpet; the fingers that had been inside her carefully withdrew and Krisha stayed open. Her curls were black. They were wet and the flesh inside her was redder than her nipples. The tip of a finger began to rub

37

her clitoris again and Krisha gasped. Her pure white thighs began to close until this was prevented by her feet being taken back and locked round the chair legs. The daughter held her belly while the mother began smacking the wet, red lips. She used her fingers; in between the smacking, she whispered to the daughter, whose fingertips tightened to keep the lips of Krisha's cunny open and protruding for the smacking. Every so often, the lady would stop and examine Krisha's clitoris, in the way she had done with Justine. She would press it with her finger, and Justine would shudder, but Krisha would moan and her bottom would slide a little further towards the front edge of the seat. Then the lady would smack again. And all the time, the breasts, capped by the swollen rouged ignored nipples, would be heaving.

The lady who had been smacking Krisha stopped again and took one of the large ivory hairpins from Krisha's head, then another; Krisha's hair cascaded down behind the chair. Her legs were unlocked from the chair and lifted. Krisha shuddered and grunted as the hairpins were slipped into place along the lips between her legs, one pin gripping each lip, and the two pins touching at the top, directly above her clitoris. Two fingers slid up into her and the thumb eased the noses of the pins aside and rubbed against her clitoris. Her belly jerked upwards. 'Her breasts, Lydia,' said the lady whose fingers Krisha moved against. 'Quickly girl – some milk here. Wipe her nipples; suck them.' And Krisha writhed against those words and against the pins that nipped her labia so tightly. The lady took her fingers out, held apart the heads of the pins and wiped Krisha's wetness slowly upwards across her clitoris. The daughter poured milk into a fluted china cup; she dipped the corner of her handkerchief inside and began to wipe the rouge from Krisha's nipples. But even as she wiped her, Krisha came with sobbing gasps; her labia were kept open while her clitoris pulsed and the pinkened milk ran down her breasts and underneath her arms.

At this point, the ladies broke for tea; the gentleman, who had remained immobile, donned his goatskin gloves and began stroking the boss of his cane whilst looking at Justine. He did not move any closer to her, but beckoned to Julia, who sprang forward to attend to him, then summoned her butler and gave him the instructions. Justine waited, the two ladies watching her now while they sipped their tea, and Krisha sitting quietly on her chair. The footman brought the round baize table and placed it before the settee, but by the time Caroline arrived, late and a little flustered, curtsying quickly to the ladies and the gentleman, Krisha had been stripped and turned. She had been placed, almost kneeling on the floor, with her belly on the cushioned seat of the chair. Her breasts pressed against the bars of the chair back and her nipples pushed through the gaps. The ladies were arranging her so that her knees were bent and her feet rested on the bars between the chair legs, and the part that extended furthest down and behind her was her cunny, with which the ladies now began to play, with the hairpins still attached to it. There was a short interval pervaded by Krisha's murmurs, before Julia said, 'Justine . . .'

Justine sat bolt upright. The eyes were upon her again, and as she stood up, the awful feeling of nakedness came. She saw Julia nodding to Caroline, and Justine knew then that nobody would be holding her and she would have to take the pleasure unrestrained. But she displayed herself at the green baize table in the way that Julia had taught her. She could feel her skin tingling, her nipples tightening, the gentleman's gaze sweeping up her body, and in the background, she saw Julia watching and saw that she was pleased. Justine moved slowly therefore, leaning further back against the table and arching her body until her elbows rested on its surface. Her breasts rolled outwards, to the sides. The man would see her heartbeat thumping through her chest, and he would see her nipples trembling. She opened her mouth and spread her legs. She heard the rustle of skirts as Caroline knelt in front of her. She heard Caroline undressing, exposing her breasts. Justine balanced on her toes, in the way that Julia had instructed her to do on these occasions, so that the tremors in her thighs would be magnified and could more easily be seen. She felt Caroline's bare breasts touch her skin and stroke her as Caroline moved. Justine's hips projected forwards; the separated lips of her cunny protruded around the leather, waiting for the suck.

'Justine,' whispered Julia – because Justine had forgotten. Justine's eyes opened, her head turned and she looked at the man. She had to keep her eyes upon the man because it had been his request that she be given pleasure in this way. She had to offer her eyes to him, keeping them open while Caroline's lips moved upwards, planting soft, moist kisses inside her thighs, then taking fully into her mouth that hot wet place while Justine listened to the slaps and Krisha's groans and tried to push her cunny forwards, tried to push it into Caroline's mouth, tried to thrust the leather against Caroline's tongue while the man watched unperturbed and Krisha's crying sobs spilled out a second time as the quick slaps of the ladies' fingers sounded against her cunny. Justine trembled open-legged with the pleasure, and the tips of her toes balanced on the floor. Then the feelings came, welling, surging, making her drown: the feeling that she wanted to beg to be allowed to come; the wet, tight pressure of the leather against her and the memories of the things that Rachel had done to her over and over again to try to make her lose control and pee. And Caroline just kept sucking her and the gentleman's eyes stared blankly and the ladies began readjusting Krisha once more in the chair.

Suddenly, the end of the lacquered cane knocked three times on the carpet. Caroline stopped; Julia sent her away. Justine, abandoned, shivered on the round baize table. The ladies took Krisha to the settee and placed her on her back beside the man. He stared between her legs. His fingers closed about the boss of the cane, then loosened; he removed his gloves. Then Julia led Justine away and put her once more to her writing. About a quarter of an hour later, Justine heard the ladies' urgent whispers and for the first time, the man's voice. Then she heard Krisha's sobbing moans.

Julia came in to her and stood beside her. 'Sit forward,' she said. 'Continue writing.' Julia was reading over her shoulder. While she read, she touched Justine. She rolled her nipples between her fingers and Justine closed her eyes. 'Open your legs.' Justine did as she was told. Then she felt her feet being gripped. She opened her eyes; the ladies were in the room. So was the man; he was sitting on the bed, resting his chin upon his hands upon his cane. Krisha was not there; Caroline was. The ladies had fastened Justine's ankles to the chair legs. Julia had moved away; she had left the room and abandoned her. Justine was drowning.

'Keep writing, my dear,' said the older lady. 'Edge forwards, edge it over – there.' The lady had to rest her weight against the back of the chair to prevent it tilting forwards. Caroline was kneeling on the floor, between Justine's legs and under the desk, kissing her cunny, drinking her wet. 'Keep writing,' said the lady, then, 'Lydia . . .' The younger lady supported Justine and gently pulled her nipples. Caroline licked and sucked the warm distended lips; Justine pushed to feed her and the old lady urged her from behind but Caroline could not reach the clitoris, sealed behind the rope. 'Up,' said the lady. 'Stand.' And Justine's legs were bowed out, shaking as she balanced on the footrest with her toes pointing out and her ankles tied to the chair legs and her fingers gripping hard about the walnut pen while Caroline craned up to suck her. 'Your nib is dry,' said the lady, 'dip it in the pot.' As Justine's shaking fingers reached out, Caroline's wet tongue smeared the lips of her cunny with spittle and the lady pulled the rope aside and wormed a bone-dry finger up her anus. Justine fell forwards; her fingertips turned rigid; the nib broke and its ink burst across the paper. But the finger inside her kept worming; the wet lips kept sucking her. No permission was asked for, or given, but her climax kept coming. Only when the pleasure turned painful did the rough dry finger relinquish its claim upon the tender gripping ring.

The lady lifted up the sheet that Justine had blotted. There were two lines of writing at the top. 'It seems her little love note is cut short, George,' she said, 'and she has omitted to sign . . .' She placed it on the seat between Justine's legs. 'Sit,' she said, then levered out the inkpot from the desk and poured its contents down Justine's belly until it seeped between her legs.

Then she called Julia in and thanked her for the excellent tea but chastised her for her protégée's lack of control, before the assembled party left.

Julia dismissed Caroline and remained with Justine. She had to take the G-string off her. While Justine took a bath, Julia leafed through the sheets that had been written. She dried the last one very carefully. Once Justine was clean again, she kept her in the Yellow Bedroom. She did not punish her for the unsanctioned climax; she washed the G-string and oiled it, although she did not replace it, preferring to keep Justine entirely nude, in the anticipation that she would take the time to further her self-control. She had not intended that Celia would find her – she had no reason to expect that Celia would be calling so late in the afternoon – but, had she known in advance, she might have locked the bedroom door.

5: SHARING ROXANNE

While Justine was sitting at the escritoire in the Yellow Bedroom, wearing the leather G-string that Philip had selected, and composing the letter that was destined to be delivered into his hand, Philip was taking his leave of Charlotte, his fiancée. He had escorted her to her uncle's, where, through a change of plan, she would now spend the evening without him, because Philip had unexpected business to attend to at the office. Unfortunately, Charlotte's uncle and aunt were out, although expected shortly. Charlotte decided she would wait, but Philip was reluctant to leave her on her own. She stroked his cheek and told him he must go.

'Can you forgive me?' he asked as he took her gently in his arms.

'I can forgive very little,' she replied demurely. But her face was radiant when she looked at him again. 'So be gone, sir, before I change my mind . . .'

Philip touched her dark, curling hair, slipping it through his fingers, and Charlotte smiled. She knew herself to be a sensible woman, but these small demonstrations of love could make her smile – 'Keep it long; let it grow, it is beautiful,' he had once said to her, and now she grew her hair for him. His eyes had done it – she did not care about his age – he had eyes which had captured her from the start. 'I shall collect you before midnight.' And he was considerate, the most considerate man she had ever met.

'No – I shall take a cab. Or uncle will lend his carriage.'

'You are sure?'

She kissed him. 'Go. You mustn't work too late, Philip. Telephone me at Papa's before you go to bed. Promise?'

She still called it that – 'Papa's' – even though everything would pass to her in less than two months' time. But for the present, the trustees would not grant her even the upkeep of a carriage. Charlotte was long-suffering, she was undemanding, and Philip loved her for this. He strode off into the wet November night.

Ten minutes later, the hansom had dropped him, not at his office, but at the mews, and the small flat that Charlotte had no inkling existed. The rain was turning to sleet. He tried the key in the door, but found it unlocked; Jesber was already there. He had the girl. But when Philip crossed the threshold of the parlour, then turned and saw her properly, he stopped in his tracks. She looked nothing like a streetwalker. She looked like a young society lady. In that first glance, she reminded him of Charlotte; her hair was longer than Charlotte's and her skin was darker – she had an almost Latin look – but apart from this, she might have passed as Charlotte's younger sister. And that resemblance made the prospect even more exciting. He took off his hat and gloves.

'Philip . . . Fine whisky.' Jesber was standing by the fire, cradling a glass in his hand and nodding appreciatively.

Philip gave a slight bow. 'Lawrence . . . A cold night; I might join you.' He stepped towards the cabinet, began to pour, then looked again at the girl sitting on the couch with her eyes downcast. Her eyelids lifted, and suddenly Philip was looking into eyes so dark-brown that they merged with the width of the pupils and looked black. He raised the tumbler and drank the measure. When he spoke, his voice was laced with the rich roundness of fine old malt. 'And shall you introduce the young lady?'

'Mr Philip Clement,' said Jesber with a flourish, 'I present to you – Roxanne.' And he lifted her chin, which had lowered as she gazed back to the floor. 'But I understand she bears a message, from a friend.' Jesber's eyes sparkled. He moved back to the fire and took up his glass. The light reflected palely from the side of his oiled blond hair.

Philip frowned. 'A message? From whom?' He stepped closer, and again noted that the eyes below him seemed

44

very wide and black. He looked at Jesber, who shrugged. Then the girl spoke. Her voice was smooth; she began speaking without a trace of an accent, reciting the words slowly, as if she had been made to memorise them accurately. 'She is thinking of you.'

His frown deepened. 'Who? Who is?'

'She wants to meet you. The gift is fitted.' His eyes widened, then looked away, then returned. He opened his mouth to speak, but she continued, 'Miss Julia will arrange the meeting.'

The room was silent; she was looking at him. 'When?' he asked at last.

'I do not know. Miss Julia did not . . . I do not know the one she speaks of. That was the message. But, sir?'

She had fine eyes, exceedingly black eyes. 'What?'

'Sir – Miss Julia sent me. She said that you would . . .'

'I would what?'

Her voice was shaking. 'That you – the two gentlemen . . .' Her eyelids flickered and lowered and her voice could barely be heard. '. . . would share me.' A dark silk lock of hair fell forwards, across her cheek. Her upper lip shivered; he could see it shivering, and the lock of silk trembling where it touched it. Her hair had been drawn back above one ear; the ear was exposed; the lobe was soft and vulnerable. Her skin was faintly dark, faintly Mediterranean. He wanted to kiss it – the warm skin, behind and beneath the lobe.

'Lawrence?' Philip said, turning on him. 'What do you know of this?'

Jesber shrugged again. 'I was asked to collect her and to bring her to you. That much, I have done.' But his eyes, too, returned to her.

Philip dropped on one knee in front of her. He lifted away the trembling lock of hair and his fingertip touched the warmth of her lips. Her head stayed down, but her eyelids lifted and her lips parted as she looked up at him. 'Share me,' Roxanne whispered.

When a room is quiet, when movements are slow, when

45

time is immaterial, the senses are enhanced, imagination can take flight. The mind's eye can float above the room and look down upon the couch where the two clothed men tend the nude young body, which seethes with the slowness of the salt-saturated oily sea on sultry summer days. The sexuality of a woman aroused is the most perfect, the most pervasive pleasure that a man can ever know. It fills his mind, blotting out all else; it bathes his careworn eyes; it drifts into his nostrils. She is warm to the touch; the feel of her skin is smoothness, tightness, roundness, softness; her hair is silk. She has the centre line, the divide which, when she breathes, pushes her breasts out and away, so they appear like separate crowns on her ribcage.

Philip knelt beside the couch, watching Roxanne breathing. Her nipples were stalked; they were almost as brown as her eyes. And even above her navel, her dividing line was already dark with soft hair. Her legs were slim, so long, so smoothly thin. When she had stood and faced him, with her dress around her ankles, a gap had been there between the tops of her thighs, the gap that had taken the width of three fingers, pressing upwards, cupping, capturing the warm projecting inner lips, and holding her while her legs gave and her belly slowly sank into his hand.

But now her slim legs struggled slowly, against something from within. They were bent; they pressed against the surface of the couch and slipped, her left leg horizontally, her right leg upwards, the foot crawling up the back of the seat. She was like a creature pinned on its back, but nobody restrained her. Between her open, tucked up legs, her hips and buttocks moved, sliding with a heavy slowness from side to side across the smooth plush of the seat. Her feet were tucked up so far that her buttocks formed two small haunches which fitted into Lawrence's hands, and the dark centre line became an open oval split, which Lawrence's thumbs encouraged in its openness by gently stroking the youthful labia outwards. This was the only action that he performed; the support of her buttocks and the smooth upwards and outwards stroke against the resilience of her labia, which opened in a slow, rhythmic bulge as if an oiled, invisible object were being inserted and then expelled. There was a smooth narrow gap, bare of any pubic hair, around the labia themselves. They were brown; the skin still looked slightly wrinkled, though it was already swollen. When the thumbs stroked slowly upwards and the lips out-turned, individual strong shiny black hairs, curving rather than curling, reached across the lips and touched the inner pinkness. The thumbs pressed into the lips just below their junction and the clitoris extruded moistly from its prepuce of swollen skin. It looked like a small blind penis. Her knees were knotted with tension; her breathing stopped; her lower belly looked distended. She was pushing down and holding, pushing her clitoris out against the pressure of the thumbs. Her legs became very still. Lawrence bent, pursed his lips and blew a slow stream of cold air until the vulva contracted. Then he licked it, once. The vulva contracted again.

'Hold her knees up, right up; press them back until they touch the seat,' he said. Her split haunches lifted, the small dark wrinkled ring could now be seen, and the labia stayed open unassisted. When he pressed his thumbs against her this time, her clitoris distended to a shiny pip. 'We should find a way to keep it out,' Lawrence said. 'It would be good if it could be kept so – when she sits. Or you could touch her even underneath her clothes and know she was excited. It might need a clip of some kind.' He studied the pip intently, pressing his thumbs against the rim of flesh in which it was bedded, making it project. Then he bent forwards again, pouted his lips and fitted them to the pink stud in between his thumbs. It disappeared. His cheeks sank deeply as he sucked. Roxanne groaned with pleasure. Philip held her knees down but he watched her face. Her eyes were closed; her mouth was open and her lips were moving. He wanted to kiss them. She gasped, then grunted. Her knees began to push against his hands, trying to lift. Her breathing thrust her breasts out; the nipples touched the sleeve of his jacket.

'No,' said Philip. Lawrence stopped. 'I want her kept like this. I want her . . . Look – ' He stroked her hair, her neck, then lifted her breasts and rubbed his thumb across her turgid nipples. 'She is beautiful, so beautiful,' he murmured. Her mouth lay open. Philip touched it with his thumb. She turned; she kissed it, sucked it.

'Share me,' Roxanne whispered.

She lay on her back again, one leg hooked over the back of the couch, the other horizontal. Her hips had been placed on a cushion, to lift them and to keep her open and exposed. Her labia were thick now, thick from the sucking, warm from the blood drawn into them, and fringed by the curving shiny hairs.

Her clitoris was hidden. Lawrence pushed the prepuce back to make it stand out. 'We must do something about this, Philip,' he said again. 'There must be some way of keeping it out. We need to be able to tell straight away when she's erect – to see it, or touch it and quickly know.' Philip looked at the small swollen saddle of sheltering skin while Lawrence spoke. 'She could be displayed in this condition. You could take her out walking when she's aroused – and have her touched by strangers.' Lawrence wetted the tip of a finger and gently rubbed it in a circle round the clitoris. He placed the pad of his thumb against the mouth of her anus. The slim legs that were angled out so wide became tense and the muscles stood out.

'Keep her like that,' Philip whispered. 'Just like that . . .' The thumb was stiff, gently pressing, but it did not move; the wetted fingertip, too, kept still. But her belly looked swollen; she had that look, that very sexual look, of slim legs reaching up so high towards her body that her belly appeared between them rather than above them and it looked round, like a small potbelly, because it was held in this pushed-out, pushed-down state against the fingertip and thumb. She looked like an artist's pencil study of a nude, in which the shapes, the changes of curve, were emphasised in the bunchings of fine dark lines of shadow. And Philip wanted to touch her. The innermost muscle of her thigh was so long and hard and tight and rooted so high up against the side of her cunt that he wanted to bite it where it rooted. He wanted to suck her pubic lips till

48

they stood out hard. He wanted to make her kneel with her head down to the floor and her cunt pushed out so far behind that he could smack it, only it, with a flexible wooden rule.

'Make her come,' said Philip. 'But slowly, Lawrence – take it slowly.' He got up, walked to the cabinet and poured himself a drink. He stayed there and watched the younger man's hands moving, two hands now, between her legs, which were splayed, with the knees bent and the feet again beginning to slip. He watched the head move down to join the hands and the lips push into her open cunt to suck inside and drink. The head of blond, straight hair moved in gently thrusting circles above the sparse dark strong shiny curls; the lips sucked the hot slippy places that Philip would have liked to kiss. They kept the labia firm; they sucked the clitoris erect; they coaxed the entrance to her anus. Her knees tensed open and she gasped. Lawrence stopped. The girl whispered to him urgently.

Lawrence looked at Philip. 'She wants you, too,' he said.

Her eyes were as wide as saucers when Philip looked at them; her hair was as smooth and dark as Charlotte's. He knelt beside her, kissed her, then kept his face so close to hers that he could feel her breath across his lips. 'Let him suck you,' Philip whispered. Her head arched back, her tongue slipped out from between her lips and licked him. Her tongue was hot and wet.

'Share me,' she replied. Her hand slipped across the couch and opened his trousers. He did not try to stop her. He watched her face. She took his cock out; it rested on the couch, thick but not erect. Her cheek moved across the seat; her lips were close and he could feel her warm breath on him. Her tongue pushed out and licked the gather of foreskin hanging from the tip of his cock. She slipped two fingers loosely round the stem and masturbated him slowly. The tip of her tongue pushed through the tube of foreskin, touched the mouth of his cock and forced it open. Then she groaned and became still. Her legs were still wide. Lawrence's fingers held the prepuce back; his wetted thumb had entered her anus and was pushing down. Her teeth nipped the foreskin closed; her fingers masturbated. When Lawrence kissed her clitoris, with his thumb still inside her, pushing down, her teeth opened to a moan, and the bulge of the cock slipped through its foreskin to the warm wet of her mouth. The cock swelled quickly, pushed deeply.

Philip touched her breasts – one nipple, then the other, lightly squeezing. Roxanne shuddered; her mouth and fingers became very still. Philip continued squeezing her nipples, one by one. 'There . . . Let it come,' said Philip. He distended his cock fully by tightening the muscles deep inside. Then he maintained it in this state, not pushing deeply, but keeping her lips held open by the strength of his distension until there was a delicious, shuddering, muffled groan. Her nostrils flared, her breathing burst, but her lips held him tightly and her fingertips squeezed convulsively at the base of his cock. Her head kept still, as if she were terrified he would come inside her mouth, and yet her lips stayed sealed about him and the tips of her fingers, rubbing underneath him, tried to make him start to pump.

Philip took his cock out of her mouth and kissed her. He lifted her, sat down and placed her head on his lap. She lay between the two men, on the couch. Philip would not let her suck him. He toyed with her nipples and touched her hair; Lawrence played with her feet. They discussed the question of erection again – whether it would be feasible to keep a woman sexually aroused, visibly erect, all the time. By reference to a man, they thought it might be possible – at least for all the waking hours and to some degree, perhaps, in sleep. Although Roxanne was there to overhear their ideas, they did not discuss the question with her. It did not occur to them to do so, any more than it might occur to a horseman to discuss with his mount the method of its grooming.

This question, along with other related ones, was considered further during the time that Roxanne was masturbated in front of the fire, in a kneeling, then a standing position. Philip, in his armchair, watched while he smoked a cigarette of fine Latakia. He looked at the clock; it said ten. He looked at Roxanne; she was trembling. She stood, in half profile, facing the fire, with her long hair drawn round and over her opposite shoulder, leaving her neck bare. Lawrence was kneeling behind her. She was trembling because of what he was doing, and because what he was doing required that her legs stayed apart and her knees remained slightly bent.

It was at times such as this that Philip wished he were a painter. He wished he had the skill to capture sensuality on canvas. And if he were a painter, he would capture her arousal in shades of pinkness for her skin, edged with silver-white for depth, pencil marked for roundness, her lips and nipples berry-brown and her labia full crimson. Her labia would project. They would be seen in profile, below the curve of her belly, which, like her breasts, would look as if she were carrying a small child. Which is to say, the breasts would look as if they were distended to the brown projecting tips with milk, and the belly would be low-slung but tight and very round, with many criss-cross markings of the lines of pencil shading. A silver-white edge could represent the reflection of the fire, but the bright red glow in the double curve of her distended labia would come from within. It would represent the flow of blood; it would represent arousal. The picture would contain no representation of pubic hair because her arousal would need to be at all times visible. That would be the purpose of the picture, to permit her sexuality to be seen. Philip stared into the fire. But its glow was orange, not silver-white. He stared at the girl. She was wrong – delicious, but wrong for his picture anyway. She had not short blonde hair.

Lawrence murmured to her, and again she trembled as her knees bent out a little further. The instrument that made her tremble was a fingertip dipped in brandy. The glass was on the floor between her legs. Lawrence's broad left hand held the cheeks of her buttocks open; the middle finger of his right hand was wetted in the glass. 'Still,' Lawrence whispered. The middle finger, hooking upwards, touched. Her breath was drawn in quickly. The middle finger painted the small brown ring, slowly straightened,

51

pushed in to the first joint, then withdrew. But it was the vision at the instant of penetration that remained in Philip's mind – the vision of the nude woman on the tip of the man's middle finger, her body arched as if balanced, her breasts and belly pushed out and away, her legs bowed out in trembling sexual tension. It was a vision of perfect domination and of perfect response – perfect because she was aroused.

The wetted fingertip opened her a second time. 'Keep it in her,' said Philip. He cast his cigarette into the fire, then stood before her. The fire being warm, he removed his jacket. She was on her toes. Beneath the small distended belly were the thighs which opened outwards to reveal the hard long trembling muscle which extended to her cunt. Again, he wanted to bite it – the muscle itself and the lips of the cunt. But he opened them. Her clitoris looked hard; it felt hard too. He kept her open; he kept her on her toes and touched her, and his fingertips became wet. Suddenly, she whimpered. 'Keep up,' said Philip, and she moaned again, because the tongue had now entered her from behind. Philip knelt in front of her. 'Cross your arms above your breasts.' Under that squeezing pressure, her nipples and their surrounds were sucked. He tried to take as much of her breast into his mouth as he could and he kept her labia open while she suckled him. He kept her clitoris projecting. Then he left her nipples wet and he sucked her cunt, taking the lips in their entirety into his mouth and sucking and, at the same time, nipping the tops of each long thigh muscle between thumb and index finger. With each thigh muscle trapped, he simply held her cunt in suction in his mouth, and he waited. Her orgasm was induced from behind, by the slow wet thrusting of a hard hot tongue through the ring muscle of her anus. Her toes no longer held her up; she was balanced upon the two places of suction, the two pressure points on that long hard muscle, and the two tongues that tried to touch each other from inside her, back and front.

At a quarter to midnight, Philip telephoned Charlotte. Roxanne had been lifted up from the bed and she lay across his lap. His hand lay on her belly. Her labia were moist and puffy. He stretched one finger down between her legs and drew the prepuce back. Her clitoris was still erect. There were flecks and strings of half-dried semen resting on her sparse shiny pubic hairs; she smelt of semen rather than of cunt. Charlotte answered; she was home. Her uncle had taken her. She had missed Philip. Philip took hold of Roxanne's left hand and placed it where his own had been, holding back the swollen skin surround, then he wetted his fingertip. Lawrence held her feet with one hand. Philip's fingertip touched the clitoris and moved gently in a circle. Yes – Charlotte's uncle was fine. The hips began to move though the feet were pinned together. Two of Lawrence's fingers entered. 'Just a minute, darling,' said Philip and covered the receiver. 'Hold it back – hold the skin back tight,' he hissed at Roxanne, then he held his finger up. 'No sound!' His finger now returned to circle; the hips began to writhe as Philip rubbed and pinched the clitoris. 'I'm sorry, darling, what were you saying?' Roxanne's free hand went to her mouth; there was a wrenching, muffled grunt. 'Good, Charlotte, good – I'm very pleased . . . Elizabeth? Yes. Where? But will you be meeting her there?' The clitoris turned thicker, softer. Philip's fingertip pushed and rubbed; he could feel Lawrence's finger-thrusts up inside Roxanne. Then everything at his fingertips turned liquid. Roxanne's teeth sank into the skin between her forefinger and thumb; she whimpered; her hips thrust; her head lifted up; he could feel the pulsing contractions of her clitoris through the tip of his finger. They kept coming; they would not stop nor slow. Why was his heartbeat steady? 'Darling just one thing: I love you . . . I know . . . Yes. See you tomorrow for lunch. Shhh . . . And you too.'

He put the receiver down. He waited a second or two, staring at the wall, then took Roxanne up in his arms, with her young bare breasts pressed against the grey hairs on his chest, and he kissed her. Despite her dark, long hair, he kissed her long and deep and held her in the way that would be reserved for a person from whom you had been separated for a long, long time, when in your heart and soul you wanted her to take you with her, you wanted her to take you home. And the personage that Philip sought was love, but he sought it so very badly. And he sought it not in the shape of Charlotte or Roxanne, but in the perfection of Justine.

6: A NYMPH FOR CELIA

A whirlwind tumbled up the stairs, the doors of the Yellow Bedroom burst open and Celia Delamere was in the room, making less than ladylike haste across the amber carpet to the naked frightened figure kneeling on the quilted bed.

'But Julia, she is gorgeous. How could you hide her? The servants told me – you can't possibly keep her all to yourself. Come to Celia, little one.' Celia's wicked, bright eyes flashed. Her fingers tugged open the button loops on her green bolero jacket. Justine remained frozen in position on the bed. In the mirror, her breasts stood out in fear, in profile and in the perfect fullness of relief.

Julia smiled her knowing smile. 'Oh, Celia, don't exaggerate, you make it sound like a conspiracy. I haven't been hiding her; why on earth would I do that?'

Celia's eyelids half closed as she looked sidelong at Julia, then they widened again to drink in Justine. 'Mmmm . . .' Her voice turned deeper, her head moved gently from side to side and she murmured, 'Come to Celia . . . Mmmmmm.' But Justine did not move. Her eyes stayed fixed on Julia. 'Tell her, Julia,' said Celia at last, stabbing the carpet with the point of her umbrella.

'Justine,' said Julia sharply. Justine's body jerked; she edged across the bed. Her eyes looked downwards when Celia took her chin and lifted it.

'There . . .' said Celia gently. She lifted the chin higher and put the umbrella down carefully.

'Justine . . .' whispered Julia. Justine's shoulders slid dutifully back and her breasts pushed out before her.

'Good,' said Celia. Then she crooned, 'Oh, but she is

gorgeous.' Her right hand lifted and its fingers spread. 'Look up. Look at me, Justine.' The hand lifted higher; Justine looked up into eyes that seemed to be staring through her. Then the hand dropped, with all the force that a determined woman could muster.

Smack!

Justine screamed with the shock; she gulped for air. The side of her left breast, from the underarm to the nipple, was bathed in waves of fire which kept coming although the hand had moved away. It replaced the left hand under her chin. And now the left hand lifted. 'Shoulders . . . Look up . . .' Justine was shuddering.

Smack!

She screamed again; she continued crying. Both breasts were consumed in liquid flames and there was a deep throbbing ache below the surface of the skin. Celia held her chin and watched the tears slide down her face and the breath being drawn down in sobbing gulps.

'I must have her, Julia,' she said. 'I will have this girl tonight or I shall die.'

But Julia shook her head. 'I'm sorry, Celia. She is not available. She is spoken for.'

'Is that so?' Celia stepped back from the bed. 'Then pay them off,' she said abruptly. 'Let them take one of the others.' Suddenly, she took hold of Justine's face in both hands and pushed it down and back and stared into it while Justine trembled on her knees. 'Know it – I will have you – whatever Julia says. And when I have you I shall punish you. I shall punish you till you beg for more.'

'Celia!' Julia was affronted. But the feeling had already come to Justine: the awful, luscious sinking feeling down between her legs.

'Know it . . .' Celia whispered to her. Then she pushed her away and raised her hand. And the feeling came again to Justine. It took her breath away more sweetly than a climax could, and she had not experienced pleasure like this since Rachel. She lay on the quilt, gasping, shaking, waiting to be hit, her breasts pulsing out, uplifted. Celia smiled triumphantly. She turned to Julia. Julia was staring at Justine. Celia looked around the room, then she walked over to the escritoire. 'Ah . . .' said Celia, picking up the large pink envelope that Julia had sealed. She examined the name written on it.

Her voice projected across the room to single out Justine. 'You prefer a man above my attentions?'

'She – '

'Hush, Julia. Let her answer.' Celia did not move but her gaze struck across the room.

Justine could not look to Julia for protection from the drowning feeling in her heart. 'No . . . I do not, no,' she answered, but in a whisper so soft that it hung like gossamer on the quiet air. The echoes of its meaning refused to sink and disappear.

Julia folded her arms and studied the ceiling. Then her gaze returned to Justine, who would not look at her after this admission. 'She must be back by noon tomorrow,' Julia said.

'Or she will turn into a pumpkin!' Celia was exuberant now that she had her way. She ran across the room and sat on the bed. She still looked tall; she had a strong nose. She tried to ruffle Justine's short hair. 'And will you let them do it – men? Turn you into a little pumpkin? Plant their wicked seed and let it swell inside and burst you? Destroy you as a woman?'

'Celia!'

Justine looked at Celia. She was frightened by her. She did not know where Celia would take her, or what she would do with her, but she knew that Celia would be attentive. And there was a pleasure for Justine in the thought of each of these things, especially in the last one. Celia could hurt her, could make her breasts burn, as long as she remained attentive, and there was a fire in Celia's eyes which said that she understood.

Justine was hurried, naked, down the stairs. Celia did not wait for the servant; she flung the front door wide. It was raining lightly and the rain had a sluggishness that spoke of snow. Julia's was a town house and, even in the dark, its porch scarcely afforded protection from the casual

57

eyes of anyone passing in the street. Yet Celia proposed to take her acquisition, barefoot and bare-breasted, out to her carriage.

'You're not doing it, Celia. I won't allow it. She'll freeze to death. And my name will be mud. What if people see her?'

'Julia – you're such a fuss.' While the argument continued, cold points of pleasure drifted through the open door and settled on Justine's naked skin. Then Celia ran across the pavement to the carriage and returned with the driver's cape. Justine's skin was cool now, and the leather cape was damp. It hung over her buttocks and breasts and chilled her nipples up to bumps where it touched; the damp November air played lover with her naked thighs. She shivered and the cape shook and Celia stopped speaking. There was a look in her eye, a look that Justine would come to know so well.

Suddenly, Celia forced her against the porch wall and the cold cape touched her belly, making her shiver all over again, making Celia whisper, 'Oh, God . . . How I will spank them. Kiss me . . .' Her tongue was warm and probing; Justine yielded. Celia's hand slipped under the cape. The hand was warm; the tips of Justine's nipples were cold. Her breasts were hot on the outsides, where they had been smacked, and her tongue was touching Celia's.

Then Celia wrenched her lips away. 'To the brougham – run!' she cried before she even took breath. And she smacked the pale round buttocks with the hardest, flattest crack she could delivery, then watched them peep in turn below the cape to connect through the quick long thighs to the tender feet that splashed across the murky November pavement.

There was a sensuality about that journey in Celia's carriage through the dark, cobbled streets. The cape lay on the floor now. Justine was naked on her back. Celia had stripped her. Everywhere that Justine's body touched was cold, aromatic, studded leather that slipped against her skin. The light from the street lamps slid through the carriage windows and stroked across her body. When the carriage jolted, the substance of her breasts shook, but her nipples remained as still and stiff as if they were pinned between invisible fingers.

Celia said, 'Turn round.' She wanted her across the seat. 'Stay on your back and put your head over the side. Let it hang down. Now straighten out your legs.' They extended slowly up the back of the seat until her body formed a right angle, with her head upside down. Bands of yellow light kept sweeping up to her toes and disappearing across the ceiling. 'Open your legs. Take them right out.' Justine spread them to a wide, shallow vee. 'Now push against the backrest. Keep pushing with your heels.' Her body slid across the seat and arched until she was frightened she might fall. She did not know what Celia wanted, but she kept pushing. Then the weight of her breasts moved over the edge. 'No – keep your head down. Push . . . Ah, yesss . . .' Justine's breasts hung upside down, curving out and away from the narrowness of her ribcage, the nipples drawn down as if pulled. They rolled with the carriage; they shook with every juddering bump, they were so full. Justine felt she was falling.

'Shhh . . . Oooh, yes. Stay still – still, now.' Celia leaned towards her and Justine felt the bobbing wet tugs of Celia's moistened fingers, then she felt her breasts being thickly smeared with spittle, then the soft wet pumping of her nipples again. It caused a throbbing ache between her legs, a wanting in her cunny. 'Hold your breath . . .' The wet hand lifted high. The sinking pleasure came, and the hot searing smacks followed quickly and kept smacking downwards on those weighted, upside down aching curves, smacking until the wetness was burned dry, smacking until she was driven downwards to the floor, her bowed-out belly never touched, her cunny lips ignored.

Then Celia lifted her and made her lie face down on the seat, so her swollen breasts were soothed against the coldness of the leather. 'We must save them,' whispered Celia gently and she opened Justine's legs until the warm moist lips between them touched a bulge in the leather quilting. As the carriage bumped and rolled, the lips progressively opened out to kiss lightly, not fully, but with a repeated, tremulous inner-lip kiss against the polished, aromatic leather.

The noises of the street lessened; the lamps became fewer, then smaller as the carriage advanced up a curving private drive. Justine glimpsed a large house with a columned frontage. When the brougham stopped, she could hear the horses of another carriage in front of the portico steps. Then her carriage door was opened by a footman. Celia threw the cape round Justine and hurried her up the steps and past a butler waiting at the door. His eyebrows lifted when he saw Justine, and she turned her head away while Celia spoke to him.

The house was very large. There, in the entrance hall, even whispers seemed to carry. At the back of the hall were a lady and a gentleman who had been talking to a plumpish, middle-aged man. He had been about to lead the couple into a reception room, but had stopped in mid-sentence, with his fingers on the door handle, when he saw the figure standing at the foot of the broad stairs, quivering in her short cold cape. At the front, it extended only half-way down her thighs, and at the back, it barely hid her bottom. Her feet were wet and there were splashes of mud up the backs of her legs. The couple turned and stared; the butler coughed lightly and the cough echoed as a whisper which seemed to come down from above.

'Get upstairs and wait,' Celia said tersely. Justine just stood there, disorientated and confused. 'Run!' Celia shouted. 'Run!' She held up the flat of her hand and Justine ran; she did not know where she was going, but she ran, taking the wide, shallow steps sometimes two at a time, the cape flying out behind her, the trio at the back of the hall awed to silence, craning their necks to follow the progress of the figure fleeing up the curving stairway and disappearing down the corridor to the first-floor bedrooms. 'Bare those breasts in readiness!' Celia shouted after her. 'I shall deal with them quite soon.'

She laughed defiantly at the critical glances, then walked across to kiss Robin quickly and slightly on the cheek and

60

to chide the Langhams in the manner she reserved for her intimate friends. 'You are early, Elizabeth – and you shall pay for it dearly. I shall leave you entirely to Robin's tender mercies until the others arrive.' Elizabeth groaned and Robin beamed like a schoolboy with a tin of plum-and-raisin cake. 'He can tell you some of his stories about his exploits in the Far East.' Her eyes rolled upwards, then closed, only to open again like the slit eyes of a cat. 'While I deal with that gorgeous little bitch upstairs . . . Now, doesn't that make you jealous?'

'Oh – *Celia!* You're terrible, you really are. But where on earth did you find her?'

'James,' Celia said sternly, 'did you hear this sly little vixen you so innocently took as your wife and friend?' But James had heard nothing; he had seen nothing since that length of slim pale leg, flashing at him through the gaps in the balusters and extending up through the split in the cape, all the way from the stair carpet to the navel.

Justine stopped running when she reached the corridor. Her head was reeling, her breathing coming in shuddering gulps, her heart pounding. And lurking in her mind was the illicit fear, the delicious one, the fear of sexual punishment. She tried to walk on, but her legs were shaking. She kept thinking of that kind of punishment, and the ways that Rachel had used to control her, and the words that Celia had shouted. When she reached the corner, she stopped completely and looked about with frightened eyes, then started.

A footman walking towards her hesitated, looking at the shaking figure in the leather cape. He stared at her naked, mud-spattered legs, then turned the corner and continued about his business without saying or doing anything else.

Then Celia appeared behind her. 'Quickly,' she flung the cape open, 'breathe deeply. Hold your breath . . .' The feeling was coming. Justine stood, eyes closed, leaning against the wall, naked from her neckline down. Her breasts felt hard and full and round; she could feel the beat of her pulse in the tips of her swollen nipples. 'Let me look at them. Quick. Arch your belly. Arch it out.' Her belly turned hard as it curved out from the wall. She could feel the pulse there too, in the tight skin in the well of her navel, which pushed to make a stretched shallow oval dish like a fingertip scoop through butter. 'Gorgeous bitch,' whispered Celia, pushing the cape back. 'You gorgeous little fucking bitch.' Justine's eyes opened wide. The footman had reappeared. He hovered at the end of the corridor, but Celia ignored him. She clasped her hands round the narrowest part of Justine's back and jerked her belly forwards, making her breasts shudder. 'I will smack these gorgeous tits of yours until you cannot breathe.' So saying, she took her by the ear, ran her gasping and crying along the corridor, with the cape drawn back behind her and her breasts and belly naked; ran her through the double doorway of a large bedroom opposite some stairs and flung her to the floor.

'Get up,' she said. 'Kneel up. Kneel up and face me.' Celia sat on a low dressing-chair. 'Oh, but you are beautiful,' she said, unfastening the cape and throwing it to the floor. She looked at Justine, then smiled, then laughed and her hands slipped round the back of Justine's head and over the short hair, smoothing it then holding the head as if it were a precious vase. 'Now – put your hands behind your back.' And the merest line of moisture overflowed from the outer corners of the eyelids as the head fell back submissively into Celia's hands and the nipple-pointed breasts pushed out for punishment. 'Ooooh . . . Breathe deeply,' Celia murmured. 'Fill those precious lungs.' And she watched the delicious breasts expanding. 'Keep breathing, fast and deep.' And the eyes began to glaze. She supported the head in her left hand; it felt heavy as it hung back. She wanted to kiss the lips, to sip the tears, to drink them, but as yet the tears were insufficient.

'Now hold your breath. Hold it in.' The right hand came up, slightly cupped, then smacked down hard upon the left breast. The first smack forced the breath to burst out, the second one forced a snagged scream, the third one forced shuddering drowning gulps, only ingulps, so the breast reinflated. The hands quickly changed over; the right hand cupped the head, the left smacked down; the right breast took the full force. The breathing burst again and with each continued smack, the breasts quickly reinflated. Celia smacked each breast, in that same manner, six times more, smacking only when the breast was fully inflated.

Then she took away the hand supporting Justine's head and Justine collapsed to the floor. But she collapsed backwards; her body was so supple, her backbone so flexible that her knees still stayed tucked under her. They were splayed, and she lay on a slightly diagonal line with her belly as the highest point on her upcurved body, and her breasts, half swathed in scarlet skin now, pointing up and out to the sides as if invisible incubi sucked there. Her lips lay open; they had the redness of blood and they were moving as if she were whispering the kinds of silent afterwords that follow the release of fully sexual love. It was the most sweetly perfect pose of submission that Celia had seen. Justine's breathing was becoming slower but it remained deep; it lifted her belly and gently thrust the tips of her breasts to feed those invisible mouths that sucked her. The backs of her hands lay on the carpet, her fingers curling slightly upwards but remaining open as if she had not the strength nor resistance to squeeze them shut. And Celia understood the kind of pleasure that Justine was experiencing, and she knew that she had delivered it with the spanking of her breasts. Justine's eyes were closed. Lines of tears shone down one side of her nose and down her other cheek. Her tongue could be seen moving inside her mouth; they were not silent words she spoke, but sweet invisible kisses.

At the door, which was slightly ajar, stood Robin, as quietly as his namesake that sits upon a bough, with his glowing red cheeks and black dinner jacket and white stuffed shirt and tie. He watched his wife leave the young girl on the carpet and go to get the jug and washing bowl. She had her bathroom, but she liked her bowl.

She brought the jug to him. 'Refill it, dear – this water is aired. It needs to be fresh and cool.' The girl had opened her eyes; she saw him, but she remained in that same position of wantonness while Celia returned and sat upon her chair. Robin took the jug and walked stiffly away.

When he came back, he heard the smacks sounding again through the open door, and he heard the shuddering gasps and whimpers. He waited until the smacking stopped and he could hear instead the comforting murmurs, the words of encouragement, the tender tones that told that Celia was pleased with her new toy. Then he went in with the jug. His wife was sitting on the chair and talking to the girl in a very low voice. The girl was kneeling up again, her breasts in Celia's hands, which were cupping them and rubbing the bright red skin at the sides and touching the dark red nipples. Celia's eyes sparkled as she spoke, as her fingertips kept rubbing, as the sobs ebbed gently away. 'My saddler will make me a leather,' she was saying. 'It will have a brass-ferruled handle. It will have a soft long tongue that will smack across your breasts and lick across your cunt. I shall dress you like a mare and I shall whip you.' Then she edged forwards and drank the tears that trickled down the cheeks. 'We have so little time now for all the things I want to do to you, all the ways I want to punish you. But for the present, you shall rest . . . Robin, thank you. Bring the bowl.'

Justine was bent over it while Celia bathed her breasts in the pure cold water. When the cold porcelain touched the undersides of her breasts, she fell into a sickly faint. 'Hold her, Robin,' said Celia, because Justine was fainting – with the freezing cold of the water washing over and round and under her breasts and the tightening of the burning skin and the hardness in her nipples and the memory of Rachel holding her head down, pressing a fist against her stomach, while the cold enamel of the toilet bowl squeezed beneath her breasts.

Justine was deathly pale when her dripping breasts were taken in the towel and dabbed dry. But her feet were still filthy when Celia put her into the bed. 'Robin,' she said, 'you'd better go down while I get dressed. Your guests are waiting.' And Robin grunted some response before shuffling from the room.

Cool cotton sheets are kinder than cold water from the tank. Celia pulled only the lowest one up over Justine's body to make the contact an awareness rather than a weight. She parted Justine's legs and allowed the ruffles of cloth to fall between them. She lifted her breasts over the top of the sheet and drew it carefully round them and up, lightly to cover Justine's face, so that the only parts of her that were visible above the sheet were her breasts, which Celia could watch moving gently with her breathing as Celia dressed. She could have spanked them like that, caught with the sheet slung round them, but she didn't.

She lifted the sheets from the perfect face. In her hand was a small glass decanter of hand lotion perfumed with oil of peach. She tipped it, then withdrew the stopper and applied the glass tip of it to each nipple. Then she worked the lotion into them and stretched them one by one, pushing back the skin with the fingers of one hand and pulling the nipple out with the other until it necked. Then she rubbed it in a sucking motion until it filled with fluid. When she pulled next time, Justine cried out, but Celia continued to work the nipples and slowly to stretch the skin. 'The skin will stretch; it must be stretched,' she said. 'Tomorrow there will be little stretch-marks here. Your nipples will be more sensitive and will bulb more fully for the suck.' Finally the nipples were shiny red balls and Justine's body was trying desperately but in vain to minimise the stretching by arching up from the bed.

Before she left, Celia kissed her and promised she would be back. The kiss left a warm inner glow in Justine's body and a soft calm in her soul. Her breasts ached, her nipples throbbed and the stretched skin felt like it was burning. She lay as she had been put, with her legs open and her toes turned out, so the soft cool weight of the sheet was against her swollen vulva. Her breasts had been smacked, the lips of her cunny had not, but Celia had promised she would smack them too, and so the lips of her cunny were swollen. She tried to move against the sheet; it brushed the

65

swollen lips, but the touch was too soft. She wanted to touch them, to split them with her fingertip and to masturbate very slowly, in the way that she had done for Rachel. But how could she do it with nobody there to watch, and without permission?

She thought again about the man – the watcher – in the restaurant. Julia had addressed the envelope to him. He would find out the things that had happened. Justine was frightened of him, of his grey eyes, of the way that he had put his money down and stared at her. She was frightened of the things that he would do to her, of the ways he would possess her, and of the leather string she would have to wear. She was frightened of the way that he had kissed her after she was caned. She knew that he was cruel enough to hurt her and not care – Celia cared, and Julia, too. Julia had always protected her. But what if Julia were to let the watcher take her away? He was a man, and this was what frightened her most of all.

When the door opened silently, she still lay in the position in which Celia had left her, with her legs open and her naked body outlined beneath the sheet, and her arms and breasts exposed. She heard breathing, then a sigh. Her head jerked round: Robin was leaning his weight slowly against the door. Beside him was the other man she had seen in the hall. Justine sat up, her heart pounding. The door clicked shut. The younger man removed his dinner jacket, and now she was terrified. Robin locked the door and pocketed the key. 'Shh . . . It's all right. Shhhh!' he whispered anxiously when she began moving back across the bed and pulling the sheet around her. 'Celia sent us to see if you're all right. Nobody's going to hurt you. Shhh.'

'No . . . *No!*'

But Robin was far more agile than he looked, and far more determined than he had ever been in Celia's presence. In three strides he was by the bed. He clapped a chubby hand over Justine's mouth. 'Lie down. Shhh . . . I told you, nobody's going to hurt you. Put your arms down. Put them under the sheet. James, give me a hand. There . . .'

She was seizing up with fright, but on the inside she was frantic. Her body began to tremble violently.

'What's the matter with her?' James was turning nervous.

'My boy – she's short of something. Can't you tell? And now she's going to get it.' Justine's eyes opened wide in terror, causing Robin to hold a chubby finger up. 'Now don't take on so. Nobody's going to do anything you won't like.'

But James was now distinctly uneasy. 'Robin, I thought – '

Robin turned on him. 'Thought what? Come on – get on with it, man. I'll hold her; you can have first go. But watch her knees.'

Justine bucked, and screamed against his hand, but Robin pinched her nose and stopped her breathing. 'Shut up, you pathetic little fricatrice. Now suffocate or keep still, girl. Make your mind up. Which is it to be?'

'Spoken like a true missionary for the cause!'

'*Celia!*'

She stood at the door, waving her key in the air. James stood up quickly, moved away, leaving Robin the sticky-fingered boy caught stealing all the sweets.

'Elizabeth – look at them. Who would have them?' Celia declared. Elizabeth shrugged. 'Robin,' continued Celia, 'get out. I shall deal with Robin later,' she explained to Elizabeth, adding in a whisper delivered behind the shelter of her hand: 'A good stiff birching should calm him down.' Then she said in a loud voice, 'James, of course, can stay – he's a guest. Ill-behaved, perhaps, but young enough to learn. Wait,' she said, as Robin slunk past her. 'The spare key . . . Thank you.' Then she whispered to Elizabeth, 'I didn't even know he had it in him. A woman's not safe, these days, from bothersome irritations! He's a boil on the bum, but I wouldn't pop him, not for the world.' And Elizabeth laughed.

Celia took Robin's place on the bed. She kissed Justine, then she held her head. She stationed Elizabeth on the other side, with the hand lotion, and she instructed James by means of small whispered asides while keeping her attention at all times on Justine.

The gas mantles had been turned down, and Justine's long legs appeared even longer and slimmer in the uneven light, which came predominantly from one direction. The sheet had been folded up to leave her legs exposed and to form a ruffled waistband, with the ladies sitting upon it at each side, giving a feeling of constriction which was enhanced when Justine was made to sit up against its pressure while Celia supported her slim, pale shoulders and arms and Elizabeth performed the necessary stretching of her nipples, until Justine's head fell back and Celia's tongue could slip into her mouth to take away the murmurs so the stretching might progress. But with Justine's vulva being positioned relatively far back between her legs, James was unable to touch it extensively while she was in this fully sitting position. He had to be content with touching the insides of her legs; her stomach, with its pushed-out, shallow navel just above the edge of the sheet; and the tip of her clitoris, which could be felt, rather than seen, beneath the junction of the swollen lips, as a hot wet stub which, when pressed or rubbed, contributed to her murmurs.

But Celia would not permit much stimulation of this stub. She preferred Justine's sexual arousal to be more dispersed – into the stretching of her nipples, followed by their wiping free of skin lotion, then slow suction by Elizabeth's lips and tongue, delivered in the way that only a woman understands, with Justine leaning forwards, keeping the fluid weight of her breasts feeding to the tips, but with her head back and her mouth fully open to Celia's tongue, and her legs apart, her belly thrust forward, the weight of her body, though slight, bearing down through the swelling vulva that pressed into the firmness of the bed beneath her legs, while James held her ankles and carefully oiled and stretched her toes by wrapping his thumb and first two fingers round each one and pulling it like a teat. In this way, her toes, which had been muddy, became clean, and her nipples, which had been hard, became softer and more engorged, and her cunny, which had been oily moist, with its lips stuck together, became open, and, since the absorbency of the sheet was soon used up, the lips of her cunny stayed wet. As Justine's arousal became fuller, Celia began to look around the room for things that she might use as toys to stimulate her further.

Justine was a nymph, a delicious lesbian nymph for Celia and her friends to play with, and the time that Celia had at her disposal was all of that night and half of the next day.

7: ELIZABETH LEARNING

'Put her to bed,' Elizabeth chided. 'Put the girl to bed now, Celia. You have a dinner party to attend to.'

But neither Celia nor James, who was watching silently, was disposed to leave. Justine moaned and Celia slowed the stimulation and eased her forwards. She had almost climaxed, sitting with her legs astride the long pink stool. It was the lowest stool that Celia could find, and she had had it brought in from an adjacent bedroom. It was like a long, low footstool. Justine's feet were flat to the floor, but because the stool was so low, her knees were bent so sharply that they touched the sides of her breasts. And she sat forwards – always forwards. Celia wanted her to sit between the stimulations, so she was sitting on her vulva.

'Celia – what about your guests?' said Elizabeth again.

'Let them go hang – how can I leave her? She needs me, don't you, little darling?' She raised Justine's heels and made her balance on her toes, then she lifted the breasts over the knees and tucked the knees together while she slipped her fingers underneath and opened out the pubic lips. 'It's hard. You're hard, my little baby . . . It's so hard, this little bone between these little fishy lips. Oh, that's good,' she whispered. 'Let me touch it. Oooh – it's so gooood. Does it feel good? Elizabeth – quickly! Her nipples. Ooooh! Let.it come. Open your mouth, my baby. Shhh . . . Put your head back. Lean forwards. There . . . Let it lie upon the fur. Sit on it . . . Sit,' she said. 'Ride. Keep your head back. Ride it. Ride this little cunny. Oooh!' and she held the quaking belly in the cupped palm of her

70

hand. 'Faster. Ride it. Rub it. Push . . . Breathe. Breathe in. In . . .'

Justine's breath snagged; her legs began to shudder. 'Quickly – her legs, Elizabeth – lift them! Take her foot. Lift it. Get her legs up. Higher. As high as you can. Quick – she's almost . . . Oh, God. Keep them up! Keep her still, now. Shhh . . . Very still, Justine. Oh, but she is beautiful . . .'

Celia rubbed the muscle high up on the leg that she held; she carefully touched the swollen labia that she had caused to be lifted up and away from the dense pink plush before the climax had been triggered, and she looked at the image in the large mirror that she had placed beyond the end of the stool. Even in the mirror, and even through the soft veil of yellow-blonde pubic hair, the labia looked swollen, and their skin, more velvety than the skin of Justine's legs, looked that shade of warmest pink which almost verges on red. 'Elizabeth, open my drawer, please – that one.'

Justine could not see its contents. 'Lie back,' said Celia. 'Lie down.' The stool was only large enough to take her torso. Her head overhung the end and her arms overhung the sides and fell to the floor, drawing her breasts outwards, so their weight rolled down. But it felt good, that pulling. She could see the man – James – watching her, looking at her breasts: desiring her, she knew. He had not spoken. He leaned against the wall. It sent a shiver through her body – that he watched her in silence, that he watched her being used. That desire – people watching – it nurtured her arousal; she wanted her arousal to go on and on. 'Bend your legs, Justine. Put your feet up. Tuck them up.' And she wanted to be used this way, by women. She liked to be made to do things – to be directed – while she was aroused. The feelings such usage induced were sweet. There was a pervasive sensation, as if cold water were trickling down her back while her belly was bursting to pee, and every threat, every promise of sexual torment, was like a freezing needle being pushed into the warm wet folds of skin.

Her feet kept slipping because the stool was too narrow.

71

Each time a foot slipped, her breasts shook. Justine kept doing it. She could see the man watching. Her breasts kept shaking, her nipples kept pushing; they were tingling from the stretching, sore with erection, tight beneath the film of dried saliva. 'Get some knickers,' Celia said to Elizabeth. When they were brought, she looped one leg of them over Justine's right foot, round the instep, twisted the material then looped it over the left one. The knickers, stretched across the seat, acted like stirrups for her feet. Celia pushed them back along the seat until Justine's buttocks opened. James stirred from his quiet vantage point, then froze. Celia had something in her hand.

Justine moaned. It was thick and round and shaped like a bullet and it distended Justine's anus wide. Her belly lifted, her feet pushed down and the twisted knickers formed a rag rope stretched between them. But Celia completed the insertion. And she did it with the lips of Justine's cunny sealed. She had forced the anus open after closing the lips then holding them sealed while she pushed. The lips had lifted in response to the intrusion and the anus was now kept open by this thick polished plug. Celia sat down on the end of the stool. 'Spread your legs – and spread them fully,' she whispered.

She smacked the insides of Justine's thighs with her bare right hand, whilst the anus was stretched round this smooth plug, which resembled a child's spinning top and was in truth too large for Justine's anus. It intruded very visibly; it kept the ring held wide. When her legs fell fully open from the knees, the cheeks of her buttocks could not press together but were forced to mould around its shape. But it was not there for any visible effect: Celia had put it there to hurt Justine, as she had promised to do. And hurt Justine it did. Each time a scalding smack descended on her inside leg, the muscle of her anus contracted in a spasm against the solid, polished wood, and Celia saw it jump. She smacked until she heard the low whimpers from the head that she could not see, because it hung down. Then she smacked until her right hand hurt, at which point she changed to the left. She kept smacking in the same two places, the tops of the thighs, that had looked so white against the darker pink of the cunny.

She watched the breasts and belly heaving all this while, and she listened to the sobs of pain, but she kept smacking. She did not care that her hands were throbbing, that her fingers were turning numb; she smacked to win a young girl's sexual love. How could she stop until she had won it? She smacked, beyond the point where James had begun to look uncomfortable: his eyes, so fixed upon that scene, had started to slink away now. Elizabeth was left to watch, at first, then to kneel beside Justine, touching her breasts – anxiously touching the shiny nipples which reached up to be kiss-stroked by the nervous fingertip skin – then whispering to her, lifting her head, kissing her hot lips, sipping her teardrop trickles: Elizabeth learning a kind of love she had not known; Justine slowly drowning in submission. Elizabeth took her tongue and kissed it, used it, nipped it with her teeth; her fingertips toyed with Justine's nipples.

And Celia smacked until the anus would no longer relax after each contraction but remained in spasm. Then she pulled Justine up and made her kneel in front of the mirror. The tops of her legs were no longer white: they were redder than her vulva, which glowed, swollen-lipped and deep pink, beneath its wispy yellow hair. She kept her in this position while she removed the plug of wood.

'We'll take her downstairs,' said Celia, unwrapping the knickers from round Justine's feet.

'Like that, in front of everybody – naked?'

'Yes. She can amuse them.' Celia's eyes suddenly sparkled wide. '*Yes!* Naked – deliciously nude – and blindfolded. Would you like that, darling? To be played with? To be passed around like a toy?' She squeezed the nipples that bulbed so warmly; she rubbed the swollen belly and the bright red legs; she slipped her finger down the side of the labia, which felt hot, hotter than the nipples. She felt the shudder coming there, against the side of her finger. She took the heat of the vulva in her hand and held it while she kissed Justine. 'Get the blindfold. Tie her hands behind her back. She must not be able to interfere.' She placed the cunny-warmed finger over Justine's lips. 'And she shall not protest, or she will be gagged.'

Justine was trembling; her lips moved, she wanted to speak, but she did not. She wanted to tell about men: there were men down there; did Celia know that Justine had never . . . ? That she could not . . . ? That the feeling of horror struck down inside? She would be sick if she were made to do it; her body would freeze.

Her wrists were tied with strips of cloth, like cuffs, not tightly, but with a short length in between them, so they were still free to move. The cloth stretched above the swell of her buttocks; her hands faced back, leaving her fingers free and available to touch whatever might be placed against them from behind. Celia explained this to her. But her hands could not protect her breasts, or any part below them; frontally, she remained nude, a free temptation. Her thighs were at all times to remain sufficiently far apart that two fingers placed side by side might have unhindered access to the soft re-entrant between the bright red punished skin and the downbulge of her cunny, which was aching to be kissed and sucked. Celia told her, 'I want them to be able to feel this gap and know that you need to come.'

The blindfold was complete, and tight, but still it was her friend. It blotted out the world; it was her own velvet night; it heightened her feelings. Her skin came more alive than ever; the fine hairs bristled with every slight touch, every sound. And it made her dependence absolute.

They made her try to walk to the bedroom door. She took two halting steps: the carpet felt like a living thing, like an animal whose soft pelt slipped between her toes. She could not use her arms; she could not balance properly – if she fell forward, what then? Her persecutors had moved away from her; they were keeping silent. She tried to remember the distance to the door. She took another step, then another. The door opened with a click. Step followed tentative step. Had she reached the doorway? Her head was swimming. Then the voice came, from the side. 'Keep your thighs open.' But her right thigh touched something cold and she froze. 'Go on.' She tried to move to the left. She could hear distant voices that seemed to be in front of her and below. Something cold touched her belly. She cried out. Her knees banged against something hard. But there was nothing above her; her breasts were in emptiness. There were voices beneath her, gasps. She had reached the balustrade. 'Go forward – go!' But she was falling. She tried to bring her hands forwards and the balustrade collapsed. She screamed; nobody moved to save her as she toppled forwards. Then the floor smacked up against her knees, jarring her spine: she was still in the bedroom, sobbing, pleading, with her back hunched and her breasts touching the carpet. 'Legs apart,' whispered Celia.

Elizabeth ran to help Justine. 'Leave her!' ordered Celia. 'Leave her. Let her be . . . Legs apart,' she repeated.

Celia held the wooden chair that she had placed in Justine's path and then had pulled away at the last second. 'Elizabeth – go down and tell them she is on her way. James – stay with us. This may take some little time.'

Celia watched the nude slim figure on the carpet; she watched the curvature of the backbone tighten as the deep, sobbing shudders came again. She walked across and edged the upturned feet wider apart until she could see the gap and the swollen cunny. 'They need to see it in this state, so they can know what she is feeling,' she whispered. She watched the toes tense, then the belly lift, then push with every shudder. She looked across at James, who stood transfixed. But she touched only the fine, barely visible hair at the base of Justine's spine. She touched it and the spine curved downwards and away, and the buttocks edged submissively apart. The breathing was heavy, the tears had stopped, and the tip of the finger moved down – ever so gently, ever so slowly. The knees splayed out across the carpet; the submission was perfect; the breathing stopped. 'Kneel up, Justine. James – come here. Hold her . . . Hold her so she cannot move.'

Even the words were enough. Justine's belly and cunny melted. James knelt before her and reached round her waist. She turned her face away as her bare breasts brushed against his clothes. His knees, between hers, held them open. His broad hands tightened across her lower spine, forcing the curve, forcing her buttocks to open so the tight brown ring would show, forcing her nipples into her breasts, which flattened against her ribcage. Then Celia's finger touched her anus. It was the tightness in her body, the strength of the hands, the feeling that she could not move, that overpowered Justine. But it was the lightness of the touching of her anus – light tickles forcing hard contractions that Celia controlled – that squeezed the sexual liquid drop by precious drop from a cunny that was aching.

Celia did not touch it. She allowed the drops to gather and to drip to the floor. 'Sweet bitch,' she murmured, touching the brown-pink ring very lightly, very persistently and gently until the contraction came again. 'I shall keep you thus, in heat.' She had James lift Justine's breasts out while she touched the nipples projecting to the sides; she pulled and wetted each one until it had assumed the shape of a glans. 'Ring for Bostock,' said Celia to James. 'Have him bring me a collar and leash.'

Standing at the top of the main stairway was Celia, in all her stateliness, with her bitch-in-heat, reined-in at heel. James watched from a few steps down. Elizabeth and the others looked up in wonderment from the foot of the stairs. 'Go,' said Celia again to her bitch. 'Go on down.' The girl was still blindfolded, James was close enough to hear her terrified breathing. She had stopped when her knees reached the edge and now she cowered down, crouching on her heels, her wrists fastened behind her back, and her knees apart. Suddenly, Celia yanked the collar back. The breasts thrust out and Celia smacked them with her bare hand. The smacks echoed from the high vault of the ceiling; they were followed by the softness of the whimpers. Then she dragged the girl forward over the edge. With her hands tied behind her, she could not break her fall. There were gasps from below, and from above, a piercing scream. But James caught her as she toppled forwards, with her body arched back away from the drop and her punished breasts thrust out towards him. Her breasts and belly pressed, warm and pink, against the cool white of his shirt. For a second, his hands enfolded again the narrow part of her back, and he held her in his arms. It was a feeling that he would remember. The broad blades of his fingertips slipped and fitted between the bumps of her spine as if it had been shaped by nature to that very purpose. And for James, that single second of time was stretched. Her body slipped down him slowly, the yellow-blonde curls around her cunny scratched against his starched shirt-front, but her pubic lips slid silently, oiled by the liquid that was softly expressed. James lowered her breasts and belly gently to the stair carpet.

The stairs were broad and their rake was shallow. Celia guided her bitch, controlling her with the leash as she slid on her belly down the staircase. When they reached the bottom, James was still standing near the top. He watched Celia draw the girl's head back until she was forced to kneel, then whisper something to her, then lead her on her knees into the drawing room. When he looked down, there was a short silver trail down the centre of his shirt-front. He did not move to wipe it away, but stood silently, then walked slowly down the stairs.

There was no sound coming from the drawing room. He peered round the door. The male guests were spread about the room. He saw Robin on the couch. He heard the crackle of the fire, then he heard her breathing. She was on the chair; the women attended her while the men looked on. It was a cane chair with an open back, and she sat astride the seat, still blindfolded, facing backwards, her hands still tied. She still wore the collar and leash. Her breasts had been lifted over the backrest, which, being curved into a hoop, directed them outwards, twisted them slightly and turned their nipples to the sides. Two of the women took their suck. Her belly was pushed out through the gap in the back of the chair and her buttocks were straining to urge it forwards. Celia was instructing her. The smooth inner half-loop of cane pushed into the tops of her thighs.

Her knees were opened so wide that both legs lay in the same plane; her toes arched and pushed against the floor. Those were the toes that James had massaged with sweetly scented body lotion until they were spotlessly clean. His wife sat on the floor between the girl's legs. She was brushing the blonde curls back to leave a smooth gap around the swollen pubic lips that had touched his shirt with their silver trail. The lips still glistened wet; they were pursed together, but were weeping from their junction. Elizabeth was not touching them; she was only brushing the hairs away from them to leave a naked gap.

The butler slid past James and into the room. He carried a pale red china bowl which he placed by Celia on the table. Next to it he placed a brush which had a short round handle and a very long cylindrical head of golden hair which tapered to a point. Celia smoothed and shaped this golden hair, which was so long that it slid like heavy liquid through her fingers. Her eyes lifted when she heard a gasp; for a second, they stared at James – bright green eyes that had the liquidity of a cat's. James glanced at Elizabeth; she was intent on the girl; her head had never lifted. Elizabeth was drifting away from him, James knew it.

He looked again at Celia. Celia smiled and James felt a gnawing emptiness inside. The girl gasped again. The gasp made him draw closer, yet Elizabeth did not know he was there. The women were lifting the girl's breasts, holding each weight cupped in the palm and tugging the wetted nipple slowly. Each nipple had a hard stalk with a softer bulb at the end and this bulb bulged each time the women tugged, and the stalk was necked between their fingers. Another soft gasp came and the belly pushed through the back of the chair. The pubic lips stood out as hard dark pink ridges which had the sheen of silk; in the gap of bareness round it, the skin looked polished. Elizabeth was stroking this skin, and pressing it with the tips of her fingers. The pressure made the liquid weep to form an oily droplet. When she tapped the lips, they shook, and the droplet ran and dangled from their lower end. The tip of Elizabeth's tongue reached for it, caught it, then stroked

78

against the resilience of the lips, up one side, then up the other. The gasp became a moan, the vulva contracted, and the pubic lips pulsated, pulling away then pushing out to touch the tongue that tantalised them.

'Elizabeth,' said Celia. Elizabeth moved away and Celia took her place. The women urged Justine's buttocks forward again, to make the insides of her thighs more exposed for Celia to smack them while the women continued to play with her nipples. She smacked the thighs flat-handed, hard and alternately, and each smack made the pubic lips shake as effectively as the tongue had done. Elizabeth slid across the floor and sat by James's feet. She leaned her head against his thigh. She looked up at him and touched his leg, high up on the inside, and found that he was hard. She touched him all the while that Justine whimpered; she touched him while Justine's cunny went into spasm a second time and her labia pulsed and bulged against nothing but the warm air; she touched him while the labia wept and, with no tongue to take those oily tears, no fingertips to wipe them, no starched shirt-front for them to smear against, they became heavily filmed and shiny with their weepings. Then she lifted her head and whispered, 'Celia wants me to stay the night.' Her eyes were shining. He just stared at them; her eyes were beautiful. 'May I? On my own?'

How can a heart be heavy and glad? When he kissed her lips, so tentatively reaching, James knew. He knew that she was drifting away, but he knew she loved him, in her way. Elizabeth's rapture made him glad.

Through the blackness of Justine's blindfold, each smack was a droplet of pure white light which burst across her eyes. Warm hands held her breasts up throughout the smacking, pulled her nipples, milked them. The back of the chair pushed into the creases of her thighs, making her cunny swell and ache. She wanted to be licked there. But all they did was to brush the hairs back again and lay the lips bare and smack her while she trickled.

Suddenly, she was lifted up and carried through the air and placed astride a pair of trousered legs. Her knees sank

79

into the softness of a large chair or a couch. She could feel warm breath against her back. The clothes smelt slightly stale and smoky. Thick fingers touched her nipples, making her gasp and try to jerk away. But her collar was grasped, while the same thick fingers touched between her legs, touched the bare, polished skin, and wiped against the oily film on the thick lips of her cunny. And she could not get away from this prying touch. There were women's voices round her: she felt other hands between her legs, to front and back. The trousers were being unbuttoned. She struggled; the man lifted her up; her thighs were opened and she felt his bare hairy legs touch her. The women pressed her down – they would make her do it. She began to cry, to gasp. Her hands, tied behind her back, began to writhe. They touched something hot and stiff. She screamed; the skin felt damp and alive. Even Julia had never made her touch one. But these women took her fingers and closed them around the head and round the shaft. Justine's tears streamed through the blindfold and down her cheeks. A clammy hand clapped over her mouth.

They made her sit against the base of the shaft; she could feel it in the crease of her buttocks, and between her legs she could feel the balls. The head began to move between her fingers. The hand still gagged her and the thighs began to jerk her body up and down; other hands held her breasts and wetted her nipples. She heard a gasp; her fingers squeezed around the cock and the gasp became a growling grunt. Slim hands touched her between the legs: gentle fingers – too gentle – touching her labia, smearing her liquid down, separating the lips, lifting the balls and trying to push them in her cunny. And then she felt it coming – a pulsing where the cheeks of her bottom were squeezed around the shaft, then the thick, hot semen jumping, splashing against her back and running over her fingers and down between the cheeks.

She squeezed the cock as hard as she could, but it kept pulsing like a cunny and its head kept slipping through its skin like a powdered foot through a rolled-up stocking. Justine thrust the skin down hard and made him scream.

And she knew from the scream that the man was Robin. With his semen running down her back and plastered between her fingers, and the smell of it burning her nostrils, she thrust his foreskin down again and bit his hand clamped over her mouth and Robin squealed like a pig.

A woman's lips took her mouth and kissed her urgently, sucking her bottom lip then saying, 'My precious little bitch – you have a vicious streak after all. Shhh . . . It is good. And it is still so hot and hard – let me tease it.'

Justine cried out, but her clitoris remained erect for the duration of the teasing. She was kept tied and blindfolded.

James watched her being masturbated by Celia and the other women. When she was gasping, they lifted her on to the table. They made her kneel over the pale red china bowl, into which they dropped the long-stranded, golden-haired brush. While it soaked and softened, Celia explained to an older woman, who had shown a particular interest: 'My dear Hilary, I have only borrowed her – tomorrow, she goes to be used by a man. But before that I shall leave my mark.'

She separated Justine's knees until the edge of the bowl between them touched the places where the tops of her thighs became the sides of her cunny. Justine's labia pouted down and almost touched the surface of the oil. 'It is attention that counts,' Celia said. 'Men never know it.' She took hold of the collar and pulled it back and Justine's belly arched up and her elbows touched the table behind her. Then Celia masturbated her with the soft brush and the oil. 'I will have you back,' she whispered, while she painted the oil up the sides of the hard pouting lips – in the bare, polished gap that Elizabeth had formed by her prolonged outward brushing. And as she continued painting, the knees moved apart of their own accord until the thin sides of the bowl cut into the creases at the top of Justine's legs, but the labia opened and the heavy, oiled swath of brush-hair painted deep inside and slid up to the clitoris.

'I will have you back with me,' crooned Celia as she watched Elizabeth open Justine's mouth to take the foot-man's stiffly proffered cock as he knelt above her on the

81

table. Celia watched it touch, then push between the wetted lips and at that instant, between the cheeks of Justine's bottom, she felt the thick ring of the anus open to the small round head of the brush that she steadily introduced until the anus swallowed it and closed. She watched the lips sucking about the thick cock; she lifted the oily strands up and laid them along the centre line of the open cunny. Then she dripped oil upon it with her hand and watched the golden swath slowly slipping as the belly bulged upwards and the cunny gradually lifted. She watched the lips stop sucking the cock, and the mouth try to shed it in gasps – gasp upon stifled gasp as the oiled swath slowly slipped across the clitoris. But Elizabeth stepped forward and held the cock in place, its underside touching Justine's upper lip. She pulled the foreskin steadily back; when it reached a polished tightness, the cock began pumping. Elizabeth held it as it pumped; she kept the skin back, but she did not force the pace. The footman groaned, as the pouted lip touched lightly below the glans. Justine's mouth stayed open, gasping. The swath of brush slipped free; her cunny contracted; Celia dripped oil into it; it kept contracting. Her head tipped back; her upper lip supported the glans, but her mouth stayed open as the semen, thick and white, bubbled smoothly over her teeth. Her mouth did not close; her head turned to the side and the semen slid down her cheek and on to the table. Then her lips shut tightly and her breasts heaved and her nostrils flared like a punished mare's. Celia checked her clitoris. It was still hard and the whole area around it was swollen.

In the bedroom once again, they removed her blindfold and smacked her seated on a low pink stool. They used the polished plug of wood to distend her. Celia said it was needed. She removed it afterwards.

'James – help us get her to the bed.' They put her on her back, then crossed her ankles and tied them using strips of cloth, so her knees remained bent and her legs remained open. Celia found a narrow sheet which was as thin as gauze but was soft and heavy against the skin. Lacking the crispness of starch, it flowed. She drew the sheet up between Justine's legs and as far as her breasts, then pulled the hem of the sheet under them, into the tuck between breast and ribcage, and around her back, leaving Justine's stomach covered, but her arms and breasts exposed. She touched the pubic lips through the thinness of the sheet, which she arranged so that the shape of the lips could be seen through it. Then she opened them through the sheet. She watched Justine's face, as Justine's belly readjusted to the fingertips and lifted. Then she felt her fingers suddenly becoming warm, with a damp warmth, and the warmth slipping along them as she pushed. She looked at the sheet, pure white, so smooth between the bright, smacked thighs, and at the dark cleft that was now slipped about her fingers like a glove. Then she removed her fingers gently, and the glove remained in place inside Justine. She stretched the sheet carefully until the belly was outlined as a round swell, then she touched the breasts, squeezed the nipples, pulling them to make them larger. Again, Celia was reluctant to leave Justine.

'Your guests . . .' Elizabeth began faintly, but Celia's fingers, sliding down the roundness of the belly, found the outline of the pubic glove, toyed with it, then slipped into the warm again, and Elizabeth never finished.

'Quickly – your hand Elizabeth, your fingers. Feel . . .'

Justine's knees turned outwards on the bed. Cool fingers touched her labia through the silkiness; cool fingers slipped up, deep inside her cunny; cool fingers used her gently. Justine moaned softly, deeply, open-mouthed.

'Elizabeth, is she not sweet? Is she not bonny? Look.' And between the open pubic lips, the clitoris was outlined through the silk.

Elizabeth touched it gently; she coaxed it, coaxing from Justine the feeling of swollenness, the feeling of wanting to pee. She kept smoothing the silk around the pushed-back prepuce, making it a nose, which became wet, with a hard round pimple at the tip, pushing through the thin material, throbbing like a heartbeat, aching. When the hardness was fullest and the belly was roundest, Elizabeth waited. She pressed her hands against the glowing thighs. She opened the glove again and slipped her fingers into Justine's body; the belly became harder and Justine moaned. Then Elizabeth slid a hand beneath the sheet and tested the mouth of the anus, which was hot and swollen too. She touched it tentatively, and Justine gasped. Elizabeth was learning.

And having touched this special part of Justine, her fingertips returned, gently to mould the nose, to keep the whole of that area swollen, not simply the clitoris, but the whole of its surround, to irritate it gently, wetly through the silk, until it had the shape and the turgidity of a nipple. Then she played with it as if this nipple could yield milk. Justine mewled and her thigh muscles bulged as her bottom lifted. Elizabeth reached underneath again and split the cheeks and touched the hot hole of the anus. She touched it while she kept the prepuce pushed back and while she squeezed the sexual nipple. And with each squeeze, Justine seemed wetter, as if this nipple were squirting, and her anus kissed the lightly rubbing finger. Elizabeth was learning. She showed Celia her handiwork, and that her handiwork stayed erect.

They left Justine tied, frog-legged, open, her cunny lined with silk, and this small wet nose with its bone-hard pimple pushing out between her legs, and they returned to their dinner party, which would progress well into the early hours. But the small wet nose remained hot and swollen, awaiting their return.

They returned with the other guests, in ones and twos. Celia particularly wanted to display Justine in this state and to make it clear that she would spend the night in Celia's bed. She talked freely of the ways that she would use her, and the ways that she would dress her – like a mare – she said this many times. 'I will whip you,' Celia whispered in front of her guests and she kissed Justine and lifted her breasts and touched her nipples tenderly, while Justine lay tied defencelessly. While the women sitting on the bed watched, Celia opened the silk-lined pocket and slipped her fingers in and Justine's belly swelled to take them, the moist warm nose bulged beneath the wetted sheet, and Justine moaned softly.

One of the women examined her toes. It was the same woman, the older one, Hilary, that she had heard downstairs. She had grey hair; she looked tall and distinguished. She lifted the lower part of the sheet aside and touched Justine's toes. Even though the touching tickled, Justine could not move because her feet were crossed and tied at the ankles. 'Her toes are long,' said the woman. Her fingers slipped between them, tickling the separating skin, then pulling them very gently, rubbing the joints, sliding the skin up and down each toe as if it were a penis that she was masturbating. Celia, sitting beside Justine, held her breast and slid her fingertips up and down the nipple. She wetted it with her tongue. Then she pulled it through her wetted fingers, shaping it to a glans. Justine's lips moved, although her mouth stayed open. The woman playing with her feet worked slowly. She selected a toe – the longest, slimmest toe, the second one – and drew the other toes away from it to isolate it fully, then her wetted lips pushed down it to the base. The tip of her tongue slid up and down the underside. Then her lips slipped off it and her teeth nipped it – the bulge of the pad at the tip, the small bulge of its belly. The point of her tongue licked around the base of the toe. She licked the toe clean, then she sucked it again and held it in her mouth.

When at last her head lifted, she said, 'Why do you smack her breasts and legs?' The skin was still glowing on each side of the hour-glass shape of the gathered sheet that lay between Justine's thighs.

'It is what she needs,' said Celia.

'You smack her nowhere else?' The woman slid the sheet down Justine's belly. She turned it back from the labia, laying their outer sides bare. The sheet adhered to the junction. The woman teased it away from the swelling at the top, which glistened like an open flap of slit skin with a raw pink bud in the centre. The woman twisted the sheet and Justine felt it turn inside her, then she felt it sliding out. Her pubic lips stayed open. The woman's soft pale eyes watched Justine. Celia toyed with her nipple. 'Have you smacked her – tied, I mean, with her legs like this?' The woman turned to Celia. 'And does she climax when you smack her? You should try to make her. Smack her again,' she whispered. Celia nodded to Elizabeth, who went to get the plug.

It was difficult to insert with Justine's feet crossed and tied together, so the women raised her hips on to a pillow. Then her fastened feet were pushed under it, to stretch her thighs and tighten the skin, and keep the cunny slightly open. Her buttocks overhung the pillow, allowing freer access. But the entrance ring was tight. Although the plug of wood was still the same, the entrance ring had shrunk. Celia remarked upon it. 'It is swollen,' Elizabeth whispered. 'She is still swollen – look . . .' But the accommodation was in time effected and the distension made complete.

Then Celia smacked Justine. 'Look,' she said, pointing out the consequent pulse which lifted up the plug. After a dozen smacks or so, the pulse became double: she would smack the inside leg, the anus would contract, the thick round plug would lift then lower and almost immediately there would be a second small contraction.

The old lady smiled knowingly. 'Hold her belly when you smack her,' she said. 'Stretch the skin up a little. There . . .' And at the very next smack, the anus went into spasm about the wood. It remained in spasm. 'Touch her now,' said the lady. 'Keep touching round her knob. And kiss her.' Elizabeth stretched out on the other side of the bed. They shared her lips – she and Celia – while her lips stayed open and still. Her breathing became strained as the small soft kisses touched her. Celia kept her hand on Justine's belly, feeling it rising. Elizabeth wetted her fingertips and pushed the prepuce back. 'Slowly,' said the lady. 'Avoid her knob directly . . . Just keep pushing the skin back. Wet it when you hear her moan. But keep pushing it, just keep pushing. La . . .' The women changed hands. They kept working the swelling wetly and pushing back the skin. Justine's mouth opened wider. Two tongues delved within it, but the fingertips kept pushing the soft distended nose of flesh as if it were a nipple. The lady took hold of Justine's second toe and began separating the skin in preparation. 'Push,' she said. 'Just keep pushing, it will come.' And when the lady rubbed a wetted fingertip round the base of her toe, Justine screamed with the bursting pleasure of the tightness in her untouched clitty and the pain of the contraction of her anus round the plug.

The fingertips kept the fleshy surround of her clitoris pushed back until all her cries had softened to murmurs of sensuality in the women's mouths and all the contractions that her anus needed had been taken and were gone.

In the early hours, Celia got up and looked out of the window. It was the stillness that had made her rise. Soft heavy flakes of pure white snow were falling; there was no wind and the snow fell quickly. She returned to the lovers on the bed. Justine was sleeping. Elizabeth lay behind her, stroking her short blonde hair. 'Tomorrow, we shall take her walking in the woods,' Celia whispered. 'She will need suitable apparel. Boots – if long enough – should, I think, suffice.'

8: THE LETTER

Before one o'clock, Philip left his retreat and returned home, as was his custom. But he took Roxanne with him. He rarely retired before two and he would send her away before then. The risk in any case was slight; most of the servants would be in bed, and Goodson valued his position sufficiently to turn a blind eye, and to rein in any careless tongues below stairs. On the night of his engagement, Philip had felt it wise to call Goodson in and obtain an undertaking on this matter: 'The staff have shown me personal loyalty, Goodson. Can I expect this personal loyalty to continue once I am wed – and we move to a grander house?'

'Without question, sir,' was Goodson's answer. And there the matter rested. Nothing further needed to be said.

At one o'clock, then, Philip took Roxanne to his study, where he placed her in his chair while he turned the lights up and poured himself a nightcap. He often spent the last part of his waking hours with a book, which helped him to unwind. The house was quiet, the fire was dying, the nightcap was relaxing. Roxanne was staring nervously round the room; she seemed to be made ill at ease by the stillness. Her complexion looked darker in this light, and her hair looked black. There was no doubt that she was attractive. Automatically, Philip's eyes followed hers. Then he saw the letter, sitting in a silver salver on the small table by his chair.

Roxanne's gaze moved on, but the effect on Philip was electrifying. He stood, stock still, and watched the letter as if he expected it to move. Then he looked round the room

– studying the curtains of the French windows to the balcony, then the door to the small adjoining room, then the larger items of furniture in turn, as if he expected someone else to be there in the study unannounced. He did these things although he knew that Goodson must have placed the letter there to await his return. Then he approached the letter cautiously. Its significance had escaped Roxanne, who stared at him strangely. He lifted the letter by the corner and turned it over: it was heavy; the envelope was again pink; it bore no stamp, but the seal was untampered with. He held it up to the light to check; there were several sheets inside. He sniffed it; even when he inhaled deeply, he could smell nothing. All of these precautions and tests he completed before he opened it, but from the start, he had known from whom it had come – he had known it from the electrifying feeling in his heart. He sniffed it again – there was no smell, no scent of any kind. Philip slit the envelope carefully. He urged Roxanne aside, on to the arm of the chair, then he sank into it and removed the folded sheets. His heart was thumping steadily when he opened them. An observer might have found it strange that he opened the letter out in the presence of the girl, who might easily be able to read its contents. But that was what he did. 'Undress,' he whispered absent-mindedly. 'Leave your top. Take off everything below the waist.'

He scanned the top sheet quickly, then slid it aside. There were several sheets and each one was covered in a precise italic script, perfectly spaced, with almost no variations, but on the last page was a large ink blot and the letter was unsigned. He turned to the front sheet again but, leafing through, found himself looking at the writing – the shapes of the letters – rather than the sense of the words. The hand looked confident. Then one word registered – 'pierced'. It stopped him. His eyes lifted and he stared at the wall. Then he placed the sheets on the other arm of the chair and began to read again slowly, for meaning, starting from the beginning, which nevertheless read as if it were a continuation. But now Roxanne's petticoats lay on the floor and she was nude below the navel as she perched on the arm of his chair. The reflection of the firelight on her naked, dark-haired belly was a temptation to his hand. He smoothed this place for reassurance. He rubbed her open thighs many times during the course of the reading. Repeatedly, he touched her where she was hottest. But he was distracted from his reading only at those times when his fingertips had coaxed an audible change in Roxanne's breathing, when, becoming conscious of her needs, he would push her bodice up, using two hands to gather her breasts and lift them and thus expose her ribcage and her belly for his lips to kiss, while the warm place between her open legs pushed itself gently against the arm of his chair. Then he would make her turn and lean against the back of the chair while he continued to touch her with one hand and with the other he progressively lifted the leaves of the letter which read as follows:

They told me that I was upset, that I was young and that Rachel had taken advantage – that she had done it with other girls and she was evil and not to be trusted – but I knew that they were worse. They never cared. Every feeling that was good, they said was wrongful. And because I loved Rachel, I was punished.

After that first night we spent together, I was summoned by the headmistress. She had her deputy with her. My bed hadn't been slept in and they wanted to know where I had been. But I kept quiet; I wouldn't betray her; I didn't say a thing. The more they shouted, the more certain I became that they would never get to know. They said they would give me until that night to come to my senses – after that, it would be the cane. It would be the cane every night until I told them where I had been. Perhaps they suspected even then. They found out in the end, of course, but not that way. I never told them. I went away and cried, but I didn't know why I cried, because their threats hadn't frightened me. I cried the rest of the morning and into the afternoon. And that night, they kept their promise. There were two of them there, always two each time, although not always the same two. They asked me again and when I wouldn't speak, they called me names and accused me of terrible things. They tried to trick me into admitting where I'd been. Then they caned me. They made me lift my skirt and bend across the arm of a chair. They took it in turns: while one caned me, the other watched her doing it. Then they quizzed me again – they even asked about my mother, trying to make me feel worse – and then the other one caned me. It hurt me – how it hurt – but I never cried for them. When they had finished, I left them none the wiser. 'Remember – tomorrow night, the same,' they said. 'And every night, until you choose to tell us. And make no mistake, you will tell us.'

I went out into the night – we weren't supposed to go outside after dark even to cross the yard – and I cried then, when I was certain none of them would hear. When I looked up, I could see the light from Rachel's room, and her silhouette on the curtain. I went up there, making sure that nobody saw me. Her door was unlocked and I crept in. And when I closed the door behind me, I felt afraid – that she might reject me now. I couldn't move. She was working at her table. She looked up, then threw her pen down and ran across the room, then suddenly stopped. And it was obvious that she knew. There were tears running down my cheeks again. They wouldn't stop. Rachel touched them. 'You didn't tell them?' I tried to swallow, shook my head, but could not answer. She checked the corridor, then locked the door and took hold of me. 'I knew that you wouldn't . . . I knew . . . Hushhh . . .' She turned me round and lifted the hem of my skirt. 'Oh,' she said. 'Oh – what have they done to you?' Her tenderness made my tears keep coming. They hardly stopped that night.

She unfastened the ribbon and my knickers fell to the floor. She took my skirt off; she was kneeling at my feet and I was still crying. She kept touching the backs of my legs and buttocks where the cane had marked me, and whispering, 'Oh – what have they done?' And I just stood there, trembling. Every time she touched me, I shivered – and I loved it, even though the tears were running down my cheeks. It made it worth all the punishment in the world, just to have her touch me and whisper these things to me. No one else had ever shown me such concern, and no one else had ever touched me in the way that she did.

91

From that moment on, she owned me. I would have done anything she asked, anything at all.

She turned me round and pressed her cheek against my stomach. Then she kissed it. I kept shivering all the time. She kissed my legs; she asked me to open them. I thought that she was going to touch me there; I was aching for her to touch me between the legs and to possess me with her fingers in the way she had done the previous night. I closed my eyes and waited. But it was her lips which touched me; she just kissed it. She took it into her mouth and kissed it, and I was terrified. She kept kissing me there, and I kept shaking and wanting to pull away. It was an awful feeling, that first time – the sweetness of it, and the shame, giving way to the terrible fear that something dreadful was going to happen, that she was pushing me towards something that I could not control. And suddenly it came. I had never had it happen before. I did not even know what it was. I thought that I had wet myself. I stood there, shuddering, with my legs apart, trying to pull back, to lift up on my toes while Rachel kept it in her mouth and touched it with her tongue. I thought that I had peed into her mouth, and Rachel just keep kissing.

But when it was over, I felt so good. I told her what they had said about punishing me again. 'Then come to me,' she said, 'and I shall make the pain go away again.' She unfastened my bodice and touched my nipples. I wanted her to put me into bed again and hold me – even let me freeze, so I could feel her against me, warming me again – but she wouldn't. She said it would be too dangerous now, that we might be found out. She must have seen the look in my eyes – even then, after so short a time together, I was terrified of losing her – because she said to me, 'We will take our chances as they come. Whenever they punish you, come to me.'

And I did. And when I look back on it, that was what made it so exciting: the secrecy and the way that Rachel made those short times last. The next night, when they punished me again, every cut of the cane pushed the feelings of longing up through my belly and to the back of my throat, because I knew that every weal would be caressed by the tip of Rachel's finger. The more marks I had across my bottom, the more concern she would *show and the sweeter would be her kisses. Before they had finished caning me, there was a damp patch in my knickers. Half an hour later, I was in Rachel's room, with my bottom bare and my bodice open and my nipples tingling while she knelt between my legs again and kissed me in that special way. She made me hold her head while she kissed me there. She kept kissing it and sucking it, making wet sounds and touching it with her tongue. Then the feeling came on harder than before. I pulled my hand away from her and bit it to stifle my cries.*

'Why did you do that?' she asked me. 'I wanted you to hold me when you came. I wanted you to hold my head and press it between your legs. I wanted you to take my mouth and fuck it with your cunny.' Then she laughed because I was embarrassed. But those first few nights, she was kind almost all the time.

On the third night, she made me go naked under my skirt when I went for my caning. I was terrified of what they would think, but I did it. And while I waited to go in, it suddenly occurred to me that they might examine me when I was naked. It became fixed in my mind that this would happen, and the feelings I experienced then were overpowering. The arousal was so intense that it scared me. I stood shaking, with the frightened feelings washing up between my legs: I was swollen and they would see it swollen, but I couldn't help it – and they might touch me. And the feeling was there between my legs, the feeling of wanting to pee. But it was another kind of wetness seeping out of me, and it felt luscious but shamefully wrong.

When I bent across the chair, my heart was racing. They ordered me to pull my skirts up. I heard their gasps; my face was burning, but I felt secure because my face was buried under my arms and against the seat. They called me all the wicked things in the world, all the wicked names they could think of. But they did not make me get up, and they lashed me harder than ever. When they finally let up, the middle part of the cane was shiny and there were splashes of wet on the backs of my legs. But that was the last time it ever happened that way. They never called me back and I never told them anything. They only found out when it was too late.

When Rachel saw how sharply the cane had marked me, she

became very excited. She undressed me to my bodice, then kept me standing while she licked my skin. Then she opened my legs and touched me from the back, between my buttocks, just stroking the skin very lightly while I kept my legs apart. She would not let me lie down. Her fingertips kept coming back to the throbbing ridges on my legs and buttocks. She moved to my front and unfastened me. My nipples were hard, but she didn't touch them; she lifted my bodice open so they stood out and she looked at them in the mirror. Then she knelt in front of me, pushed the tip of her tongue into my navel and played with me between the legs until her fingers were wet to the knuckles. She knew what I wanted, but she would not give it; after those first two times, that was always the nature of Rachel's love, to teach me how to plead. Not that night though, because I was too shy to speak things out loud. But over the next few days, I learned.

When I was wettest, she made me dress and she sent me away with a warning: I was not to touch myself. 'I shall take charge of you, now, Justine. I shall play with you. And I shall decide whether you will come and when and where and how.' She made me kneel and promise. She said that if she were ever to discover, or even suspect, that I had done anything like that, she would never let me see her again. That was the threat, and it was more than enough. 'You can come to me again tomorrow night,' she said: that was the promise that made her threat so sweet a burden to bear. 'But keep your bottom naked for the caning.' I hadn't told her that the punishments were over – I had been afraid to do that in case it might have meant an end to our meetings – but this way, if I kept quiet and did as I was told, our meetings might continue. That was all that counted.

When I lay in bed in the dormitory that night with my legs open and my nightdress rolled up above my breasts, I was imagining her tongue still licking inside my navel, her hand upon my belly, stretching the skin, and the warmth of her lips gradually moving down, toying with me, gently pulling the wetness in between my legs until the ache became a hurt. But when she did her rounds, she ignored me. I could hear her whispering to one of the girls; I saw the sheet move. When the girl started to murmur, Rachel's hand moved across her mouth, and there were no more sounds. But the sheet still moved and

94

Rachel stayed with the girl until she fell asleep. Then she came to me. She moved the cover down, exposing my breasts to the cold air, and pulled my nightdress down across their tops to trap them, because that was how she liked to see them, tight and exposed. Then she pushed her fingers into my mouth and made me suck them. I could taste the girl and it aroused me. I spread my legs for her, but she wouldn't touch me there. She pulled the covers partly back to leave my breasts exposed. I fell asleep that way. When I woke, she was gone: my breasts were frozen, my legs were still apart and I was hot there and swollen. I felt sticky.

In the morning, when I washed myself, I was afraid that Rachel might disapprove of even this touching. Even the slightest brush of the moist flannel against my skin, I found arousing. It was as if the fingertips touching me were no longer mine.

In the evening, I had to remove my knickers before going into her room. I stood at her door and dropped them. I had never felt so aroused – she picked them up and pressed them to her lips and my legs were quaking – but I was frightened, too, because I had no new marks: all that she would see would be the faint remaining ones from yesterday's caning. I began to tremble when she got me inside and her hand moved up my skirt and her fingers started searching my skin. 'Oh,' she whispered. 'Have you no hurts today that I can tend with kisses? Then why have you come to me without your knickers? You do not need me any more. Perhaps you should go.'

Perhaps she was playing games with me, but it did not seem so then. I began to weep. I pleaded with her not to send me away. She never replied to any of my entreaties, but stood there, looking at me and smoothing her hand over the bareness of my bottom. 'Have you touched yourself?' she asked suddenly.

'No. No!' But the question had taken me unawares and I felt guilty – because I was so aroused and she would be able to tell this if she examined me.

She stared at me as if she didn't believe me, then she undressed me to my bodice, which she left open again, and she made me stand with my legs apart. She went into her bedroom, returned with a cane and flexed it, then whipped it through the air several times. My heart was racing. She kept whipping the

95

cane through the air in front of me. Then she stared round the room impatiently. Her gaze fell on the table. It was a heavy black table with rounded corners and a top which had been polished to a mirror finish. She swept to one side the things that were on it. The table was very large. 'Get on,' she said. 'Lie on it.' She made me bend, face down across it, with my bodice open. But she made me stretch out my arms and bend my knees, so my feet lifted from the floor. Then she caned my bottom, while my hands and breasts and belly pressed and slid against the polished table and the weight of my hips and legs gradually pulled me to the floor. She kept whipping me while I slipped, and she made me keep my legs open. She didn't seem to care where the cane strokes fell. When my knees touched the floor she lifted me up and it began again. She wanted my legs kept wide, she said, so she could see between them – see my cunny tighten when she whipped me. She used that word and reminded me that I was to call it by that name. She made me say it every time the cane whipped down, and she kept caning while I slid until my breasts were balanced on the table and my knees were on the floor. Then she made me stand and turn round while she touched me. She pushed three fingers into me and they came out wet. She made me lick them. While I licked that hand, the other one held me open and played with my cunny, then used the wet to smear about my nipples. Then she sucked them. Then she said that she would cane me in a new way.

She moved me round and showed me the corner of the table, but I did not follow what she meant. Then I saw that the black polish showed a paler stain there, a small oval patch where a cup might have spilled. She said one word – 'Veronica' – and she touched the stain upon the surface of the wood, and smiled, and I was frightened. She said that she wanted me to understand the meaning of that mark. When I looked at her, she put her finger across my lips. Then she turned me so I faced away from her and made me sit astride the corner of the table, with my thighs kept open by the two diverging edges. I had to balance with my arms locked behind my back and my knees bent and the soles of my feet together under the table. I had to balance on my cunny while she whipped me. She whipped only my buttocks, whipping one at first, then switching to the other.

Each lash made my legs jerk open. She stood to the side, so she could watch it. 'You cane better than she does,' she said, whipping the cane down swiftly. 'Come on . . . Come on, Justine. Let it open, let it kiss.'

I groaned; my feet pressed hard together and my cunny opened; I felt the lips push out and slip against the polished wood and kiss the image that was bleached into the grain. Rachel suddenly pushed me forwards, holding my arms pinned behind me. With my feet still pressed together at the soles, she touched me in between the cheeks of my bottom, touching the entrance, pinching it lightly, and telling me the things she would do with it when next I came to her. She explained that she wanted it kept at all times clean and ready – to be opened, kissed or licked, or filled, as she might choose. Then she made me keep my feet together while she showed me what she would use.

She put a heavy silver serving spoon on the table in front of me. She stood behind me and made me sit up as straight as I could. Then she lifted the open lips of my cunny from the table and took the tip of my clitoris in her fingers. She kept hold of it while she picked up the spoon by its bowl, turned it upside down, wetted the smooth crown of the handle and pressed it against the mouth of my bottom. She began rubbing my clitoris. My legs began to open but she made me keep my feet together while the smooth knob of silver pressed. My clitoris was poking out between her fingers and it kept slipping against her skin. She made me hold my head back. There was a sudden tightness from my belly to my breasts and the feeling came – when the handle tried to enter – that I wanted to pee, and I could not stop this feeling. My bottom opened and the handle of the spoon went in. It felt cold and it kept coming. The feeling kept coming too, like the feeling when she sucked me; my cunny just kept slipping, and my clitoris came wet between her fingers. She made me cry out when the feeling peaked. Then she would not let my clitoris retract. She kept rubbing it while my belly wriggled, but she wouldn't release it. She said that she could feel my arousal through the movements of the spoon. When I gasped, she held my clitoris still while she pressed the handle of the spoon against the front wall from inside. When the feeling came this second time, she held the spoon pressed against me, but kept it still, so the feeling came on slowly, but it came much deeper and it lasted much longer. And I remember that I reached behind and touched her, and her blouse was open and there was naked skin and a nipple that I squeezed and Rachel murmured.

She lifted me down and laid me on the table, on my back, with the spoon still inside me. She placed my feet flat to the polished surface, took the spoon out, turned it upside down and slid the handle up my cunny. Then she sucked me with the spoon in place, with the curve of its handle fitted to my shape. She rocked it very slightly against the front wall of my cunny. The smooth crown pressed against me. When my legs began to move, she slowed the pace of the rocking and she stopped sucking. She made me look at her and move my hips. She lifted the flaps of my bodice aside and touched my nipples. She made me wet them for her first. Then she kissed me again between the legs and the feeling started coming on so strongly that it hurt. My legs collapsed open. Rachel's lips released me. She tried to slow me. She held my cunny lips open for a few seconds, then she licked them. She touched my clitoris with the underside of her tongue; she lifted the spoon against me and I jumped. My legs tried to open wider. I wanted to push my cunny down her throat. When the tip of her tongue touched me again, the feelings took me in overpowering waves. She held the upturned bowl of the spoon and lifted it, and my body tried to snatch it from her fingers. When she slid it out of me, I whimpered; she had made me sore. The table was wet where my lower back had pressed against it.

Rachel lifted me up and held me in her arms. Then she told me I had to go. 'We must be careful,' she said and kissed me. I told her I loved her – how I loved her: she had given me sweet and dreadful feelings that I had never known before.

After that, we always met in secret. We dared not spend too long in one place, least of all in Rachel's study. But our lovemaking evolved to suit: after a short while, it would be suspended. Rachel would use that word: 'It is suspended,' she would say, and my bottom would be burning, my cunny liquefying, my nipples aching for more. She would touch me very

98

gently, then dress me and I would have to go. And she would warn me not to touch myself, but to keep myself in readiness for the continuation, which might come the next day, or I might have to wait longer, and pray for chance encounters. When these encounters happened, I would already be swollen and aroused, and I would be wet before she touched me. She would devise elaborate games to keep me that way.

On Sundays, she used to make me go without my knickers to mass and sit on the cold stone pew. She would have already caned me and the hot aches would be throbbing across my bottom. And I would have to lift my skirt and move the cushion out of the way and sit on the bare stone seat. Rachel would be behind me to make sure that I opened my legs and made my burning cunny kiss against the freezing seat. Then she would whisper to me where she wanted us to meet. After mass, in her room or in the grounds, she would play with me to keep me aroused. If I climaxed, she would always spank me; I would become aroused very quickly and the cycle would begin again.

On that first Sunday, she left mass so early that people noticed. Afterwards, I ran to her room and found her waiting, but she seemed edgy and excited. She looked at the clock on the mantelpiece, then checked her fob watch – she used that watch many times. She used to frown when she looked at it; in the middle of our lovemaking, she would stop and use it to check my pulse, and I would be gasping, groaning, while she counted; whenever she looked at it, it caused a shiver of expectation to run between my legs. 'We have nine minutes,' she said, 'before they get here to find out why I left.'

I couldn't see how she knew that, but I believed her, and it made it doubly exciting. 'Take your clothes off – everything.' She sat in the chair and watched me until I was naked. 'Seven minutes. Now stand at the window.' I was terrified because it overlooked the quadrangle. For the first time, her hands were actually trembling when she touched me. 'Stand up to it – against it – and stretch out.'

I was shaking as my arms reached up. My nipples touched the glass. Rachel was behind me, watching the scene from over my shoulder. I wanted to look up. 'Look out there,' she said. We were very high up. Two tiny, darkly draped figures moved below; they were joined by several more. A face looked up. 'Stand still,' said Rachel. 'Five minutes.' Then the awful feeling came between my legs; Rachel's hand had slipped between them from behind, supporting the cross that my body made, and her fingers held me open. The middle finger began masturbating me. 'Four minutes.' It kept sliding up and down between my cunny lips; my cunny lips kept sucking it and my open body moved. I lifted up on tiptoes. 'Three minutes . . .' My cunny was wet; it was dripping. Rachel used two hands and my legs bowed out. 'Two minutes – come on . . .' I tried to masturbate myself against her hands. 'One minute.' And it was coming, and I was gasping. But she counted the seconds down slowly, with small wet smacks of her fingers against the side of my cunny lips, until my belly jerked against the glass. Then she took my clitoris in hand and gently rubbed it. When I cried out, she suddenly spun me round, pushed my head down and lifted me on tiptoes, then forced me back until my open cunny pulsed against the coldness of the glass. And she finished me in this position, with my clitoris protruding down between my legs and the lips of my cunny suckered to the glass.

When the knock came at the door, she hid me, naked, in the wardrobe. When they had gone away again, she showed me the marble egg.

Afterwards, at breakfast, it was as if nothing had happened. Rachel sat at the top table. I watched her and felt warm all over; the waves of warmth kept coming. She glanced across at me and again the feeling came. I wanted to touch myself, but could not. When I moved, I could feel the polished marble egg that she had put into my cunny. 'It will keep you swollen,' she had told me. She made me keep it in all that day and it was still inside me that night, when she told me it was time to have me in her bed again.

She made me kneel up with my hips in the air and my breasts on the bed. She spent a long time touching me. She used her thumbs to massage the swelling around my cunny, then she probed me with her fingers. She said she wanted to feel the shape of the egg inside me. But the more she touched, the more I tightened, and it hurt. She wanted me to deliver the egg into her hand while she masturbated me. But every time she touched

100

my clitoris, I contracted and the egg stayed fast. Eventually, she used oil, applying it thickly around the whole area, opening the lips and dripping it in then rubbing it between the cheeks of my bottom. She kept rubbing the entrance to my bottom with her thumb. She made me squeeze it while she masturbated me. She oiled her fingers and pushed them down into my bottom and coaxed the egg from inside. I felt it begin to slide. She used her thumb to stop it at the entrance, then made me tuck my knees up and squeeze my legs together. Then she took her fingers out of me, oiled her hand again and just kept rubbing it gently from side to side across the protruding egg, across my clitoris, across my cunny lips until my climax came and the force of the contractions squeezed the egg into her hand.

She spread my knees out across the bed. Then I felt my bottom being oiled again. She oiled it and it kept contracting. Rachel smacked it. Then she held the egg against it and pushed. 'There . . .' she said. 'There . . .' while I murmured and cried and the egg kept slipping endlessly through the ring, with Rachel whispering, 'There,' and my belly shuddering as she rubbed my dangling lips around my clitoris until the mouth of my bottom had closed around her thumb and the egg was now a heavy weight inside me. She turned me over and lifted my legs in the air and I could feel it moving, sliding down inside me. She wanted me to suck her.

It was the first time that she had let me do it to her, but even then, she controlled me. She put my head on the pillow and she knelt over my face. She pulled her drawers down to her knees then over my head, so my head was captured between her legs. Then she made love to my mouth. There was a small stud earring fastened to her cunny; she kept pushing it between my lips and begging me to lick it, to make it move and to bite it. She promised she would fit one to mine, that she would use a needle and a cork to do it, and that when I was pierced, she would play with me and whip me, with the lip of my cunny fastened.

Philip looked at the page. The last lines were scrawled shakily and the rest was a smudge. Then he realised there was a pattern there – two round bulges with wispy outlines,

101

the bulges separated by a narrow gap and, down the centre, a thick straight line. He knew now what it represented.

Roxanne murmured. Her belly moved against his fingers. He wetted them and pressed them up between her legs and suddenly felt them slip. She groaned as they disappeared. She felt hot in there and good, and moist. When he took his fingers out again, he could smell her on his skin. He got up, made her stand, then lifted her on to the large walnut table. Its surface was smooth against her naked skin. He pushed her knees up, placing her feet beside her narrow buttocks and flat to the table surface. Young women were flexible. The distended lips of her cunt projected over the table edge. Her toes curled to the roundness of its bevel, as if gripping. In the half light, she seemed a primeval creature. Her scent was strong, primeval too. Her hair was dark, like Charlotte's. Philip gathered her body slowly. He spread his hands around her waist – he had hands that were strong; they were not too bony yet to touch a young girl up to pleasure, he prided himself on that – and he gathered her, sliding his hands up, lifting her breasts, easing her weight up, until he supported her under the arms, then lowering her body again gently. He was searching for something, an intimacy between her body and the smooth top of the table. And he wanted to make it clear to her, by the single-mindedness of his actions, that he would indeed bring about this intimacy – that this intimacy was what he required. Her buttocks spread, her breathing changed, but no, it was not there, not quite. He pushed his hands under her bodice again and rubbed the tips of her nipples. Young girls always felt good, so very good: their skin was so soft, their breasts so smooth and warm and their nipples so resilient.

He looked down while he worked her breasts and he listened to her breathing. Her body moved, attempting to co-operate, guided by the urgings of his hands, and her projecting cunt lips pouted, opening and closing like a moving, breathing mouth. And the exhalations of that mouth he found primeval and exciting. He touched it briefly, opening it fully with his fingers and tickling the thick small protruding sticky tongue. Then he took her round the waist again and his hands slid down to complete his purpose. They spread about her buttocks and gently pulled the cheeks apart, forcing her toes to crawl sideways, out along the table. Roxanne gasped; a shudder rippled through her and he knew that she had opened and that her anus touched the wood. He pressed her hips down to make her anus kiss against it like a small round sucker.

He became aware of a noise on the landing outside, but he chose to ignore it. There was only one thing that mattered now – this intimacy. 'Push it out, let it kiss,' he whispered to Roxanne. She moaned while he touched the sticky tongue that lolled so sweetly between the split lips of her cunt. Her breathing had reached that stage of quickness in which she was oblivious of all else. She groaned and tried to push herself against him when his cock touched her naked cunt. It bathed its head against the thick lips, then it thrust and she gave a small half-stifled cry. He held her hips down, hard against the table and thrust up into her again. And this time, he reached the hilt. His balls hung down, suspended against the bevel of the table and between the curling toes that tried to claw a purchase round the edge. He pushed her bodice up, bared her breasts and thrust deep again, deep so that the sticky-tongued clitoris touched his body. And he held her while she whimpered her arousal. He opened her buttocks and held her down and thrust. The small sobbing cries kept coming and his balls were turning wet with her secretions. He held her tightly against him, took her hair and wrapped it round his hand. He kissed her face and ears.

And at the door, his man, who had been roused by the sounds – thinking his master might require something – now watched his master moving against the flexible figure balanced on the table, her belly pushing out between her doubled-up knees, her belly thrusting. He watched the kisses, the caresses and the lifting of her breasts. And he saw the strange and distant expression that was on his master's face throughout the gentle but deliberate twisting of the long dark hair.

103

The slender figure gasped; the master took his erect cock out of her and knelt. Then he kissed the part of her that pouted most strongly between her doubled thighs. But while he kissed it, he held her round the waist, holding her waist down, hanging on it, pressing her haunches against the table until she screamed. But he kept kissing the pouting place in small quick kisses as it reached out over the edge. At this point, the observer crept away to consider the scene at his leisure in the kitchen.

Philip pushed Roxanne back until she was lying on the table. He stood above her, rubbing her belly, the creases of her legs and the place above her cunt, but he was not looking at her now. His gaze was fixed upon the small moist round mark ingrained into the perfection of the polished surface close to the table edge.

Roxanne was good. Of that there was no doubt. But her hair was long and it was dark, not blonde. And Roxanne was too willing.

He read the letter again when Roxanne was gone, and then again the next morning. He reread the last two sentences many times. But in all those readings he never thought to check the envelope thoroughly. There was a small slip of paper still inside. Eventually, it fell out. It said:

You may take Justine tomorrow night, though you might care to postpone: I fear her time of indisposition is imminent. But she is a good girl, and I know that you would treat her with consideration at such a time. I leave the decision to yourself. Meanwhile, I shall see to it that she makes herself available, should she be required. – J.N.

9: THE COLDNESS OF SNOW

Elizabeth woke to the sound of smacking. She looked up at the ceiling; the light was bright, the gilding on the pale blue cornicing glowed. It magnified the morning sunshine. The faces painted there were cherubs, with chubby hands clutching bugles and darts. Celia's bedroom had tall windows facing south; her curtains glided effortlessly, hung perfectly. Outside was a greater brightness – the intensity of snow and the fine china blue of frosty air. Inside, it was warm, with the kind of even, fresh warmth that made you want to languish, coverless, on the sumptuous pink bed. Celia had the kind of lifestyle to which Elizabeth aspired. Her house had grounds; beyond the grounds was woodland, and above the woods was a hill. Celia owned the lot – or rather, Robin did, which was to all intents the same.

The smacking sounds came again. They were the sounds of breasts being smacked, Elizabeth knew; the sound of thighs was different. She had learnt that much already. But what was the sound of cunt?

Elizabeth blushed – she hated herself for thinking these things. She rolled over and closed her eyes. But the smell of it was still on her face, and its taste was on her lips. The night that she had just spent was unlike any other; it had been heaven. James had called her an angel before he left. 'My sweet, seduced angel,' he had said. But Elizabeth was a minx. Behind the smacks now, she could hear sobs, sweet sobs of hopelessness. Elizabeth turned and watched through languorous eyes behind lazily curving lashes.

The breasts kept bouncing. Celia kept smacking them, then kissing the girl, offering her tongue, which the girl took and sucked until Celia decided she would smack her breasts again. The smacks were hurting – Elizabeth could tell that from the whimpers – but still the girl would throw her shoulders back each time that Celia asked her. Her breasts would thrust out from the slimness of her ribs and Celia would smack and the breasts would bounce. The nipples were enlarged. Celia kept pulling them gently while she kissed the girl. Celia's hands were wet. The girl was kneeling astride a bowl of water and Celia was washing her and kissing her but smacking her while she washed her and the water was running down the girl's legs.

Elizabeth became interested in these curious proceedings. She slid off the bed and crept over to the window. Celia did not appear to see her at first. The girl did, but seemed frightened to turn her head. Her eyes were fixed on Celia's, which seemed to mesmerise her as they stared down. The girl's cheeks were wet with tears. Her breathing was coming quickly, her heavy breasts lifting up and pulsing. Celia brushed her short hair back; she used two hands to do it. Her gaze was loving.

'Celia, perhaps you should not smack her, not quite so hard. They must be tender.'

'Oh yes, they are tender,' said Celia softly. 'Why else would I smack them?' Then she looked up. 'Elizabeth – can you stay?'

Elizabeth nodded. 'I'm supposed to be meeting Charlotte after lunch.'

'Charlotte? Do I know her?' Celia continued to touch the girl.

'I think you know her uncle – George Lessing.'

'You mean Charlotte Lessing – the heiress? I hear she's engaged to be married now.'

'That's right. She's kept it all very quiet. I haven't even met him – something in the city, so they say.'

'Not after her money, is he?'

'I shouldn't think so. Charlotte may be a quiet one, but she isn't silly.'

There was a soft moan. Elizabeth watched. 'Mmmm,' said Celia, then: 'You'll have to bring her over some time

– preferably without her fiancé. She's rather attractive, as I recall. I like the quiet ones.'

'Celia!' But Elizabeth's cheeks suffused with colour as she watched the water being trickled down the skin.

All that Justine could see were Celia's eyes, rich green in the bright light. She could feel many things – Celia's hands returning from the bowl to smooth her hair back and touch her ears as delicately and gently as she had touched her breasts after each time she had smacked them; she could feel the warmth there, an aching warmth under her skin, and the coolness of the water trickling down them. Celia kept wiping them to cool them in between the smacks, and she used the cloth repeatedly to dab Justine between the legs, where she burned hotter than any smacking could have made her. Celia also used her bare fingertips to touch Justine; she wetted them and opened her and ran her wetted fingertip inside.

'A pixie,' said Celia, brushing Justine's hair back once more, tilting her head and exposing her ear, touching the warm bare patch of skin behind it, bending forwards and kissing the lobe.

Elizabeth chuckled softly. 'A pixie? With breasts so large as those?'

But Celia kept smiling. Her voice was gentle. 'Elizabeth, you do not know . . .' As she spoke, and looked at Justine, there was a sparkle in her eyes – a film of wet. 'Look at her face – so small. Her ears. See how slimly bodied she is. And pixies do have large breasts. Pixie breasts are over-full; they have upturned pixie nipples. And look – give me your hand, Elizabeth, your fingers . . . Feel. Pixies are full here too.'

Celia guided her. Justine gasped. Elizabeth's warmer, slimmer fingers brushed the fold of hot skin back and touched her clitoris. 'They are full here all the time. They cannot help it.' The fingertips closed expertly around her clitoris and held it, rubbing it gently as it remained exposed. 'When a pixie goes out walking, she cannot close her legs, her cunny is so swollen. Her cunny lips can never hide her clitty – it projects.' Celia's hand slid into the water; her fingertips splashed cool droplets up into the open cup of Justine's cunny until the water dripped back down. 'When she crouches in the grass, the dew drops tickle her . . .' The fingertips collected the drips and rubbed gentle, moist swirls around the mouth of Justine's anus, then held her labia gently open while the moistening continued and the fingertips of the slimmer hand teased her clitoris in fits and starts, in time with Justine's little gasps and trembles.

'But Celia – a pixie cannot go out walking on a day like this.'

'On a day like this, she will need her boots . . . To keep her legs warm while these hot, protruding cunny lips burrow deep into the snow.'

They dried Justine's legs and dabbed her swollen cunny very lightly, in a way that would keep her aroused. Then they stimulated her clitoris – 'To keep it projecting,' Celia said. She used a thin cylinder of polished wood, like a pencil, only thicker. She used it lightly on the clitoris and the moist inner surface of the lips, until the feelings of arousal came on strongly and Justine's legs were trembling. Then the cylinder was pressed instead against the outside of her lips, sliding and rolling against the smooth bare skin, its gentle pressure against her swelling cunny seducing the inner lips to openness then keeping them apart.

Celia continued using it on Justine while the maid was called and the long, brushed-leather boots were brought. They had loops at the back which helped with their fitting, and they had straps, so the tops of the boots snugly gripped the tops of her thighs. Then Justine was placed on her back on the bed and she was masturbated with her legs wide open. Elizabeth and the maid each took a foot and held it lifted. Celia used her fingers on Justine, gently at first then roughly, until Justine's legs were shaking and the booted feet wrestled with the hands that held them open. Then Celia used a soft brush on Justine's belly, directing the pubic hairs upwards and away while she rolled the cylinder alongside the isolated naked labia until Justine felt her clitoris pulse. She wanted Celia to touch it with the tip of the pencil. Celia watched it pulsing and projecting. Then she asked that Justine's legs be brought together and laid straight. When the boots touched each other from ankle to thigh, there remained a narrow gap at the top into which the pouch of Justine's cunny projected, and from this pouch her inner lips protruded, and from the top of the inner lips, her clitoris stood out like a tiny swollen tongue which was pulsing as if in want of water. But the tongue was wet, not dry.

Her outer lips felt smooth and appeared sensitive when touched. Celia pushed the cylinder into the gap alongside the pouch – against the sensitive skin – and twisted it. Then she pushed it into the gap on the other side. She kept touching Justine very lightly with the cylinder, and tapping her clitoris, but not firmly enough to bring her on. But when they opened her legs and sat her up, then brought her legs together quickly, she almost came, because her cunny had extruded down to press against the bed.

Celia forced her head back and made her take deep breaths. She held her arms back but pushed her shoulders forwards, so her breasts hung down. Elizabeth sat upon the bed and touched her nipples. Then they moved her legs apart again, across the bed. Celia pushed her until her belly rolled forwards and her cunny pressed deep into the sheets. The pressure of her breathing kept her on the brink of coming. Celia kept her head back, made her breathe deep and hard, and Justine could feel it coming – the light-headedness – because she knew that she could never escape their games, that the sexual teasing would just keep going on, and that they would never relent.

'Aaah! No!' she gasped through lips held so open, so wide. 'Oh – please. Aaah . . . ,' as her legs were spread still wider apart, while the smooth cylinder of wood was used repeatedly to tease the labia open and Elizabeth's moist mouth tried to close about her nipples which bobbed thickly and invitingly with every gulp of breath she took.

They made her stand up. They slipped a short fur coat around her naked body. The smoothness of its lining brushed against her nipples and belly and bottom. The coat had a high collar which covered her cheeks and ears and cupped the back of her head. It made her features appear even finer. 'You really do look like a pixie,' Celia said. She opened the coat below Justine's belly and took the fullness of her cunny in her hand and squeezed it. She felt the clitoris touch her palm. 'You feel like a pixie, too,' she said.

'A brisk walk should do us good,' Celia said to Elizabeth. 'We will take her up to the retreat.' And through the window, she pointed out where she meant. There was a tiny building above the wood on the side of the hill. Wisps of smoke issued from its chimney. 'It should be quiet enough up there. We can put her through her paces.'

They did just that. The two women, muffled warmly against the sharpness of the bright blue air, took the other out into the sunlit snow. She was naked beneath her short fur coat and above the tight lips of her leather boots. Her neck and legs stayed warm; her cheeks glowed with the briskness of the pace; her body slipped freely against the silk-lined fur; the downbulge of her cunny brushed the tops of her naked thighs and her clitoris stayed excited. They ran with her, kicking up the snow in flurries, up the steep slope behind the house, stopping, breathless, at the edge of the wood. Justine could feel its stillness as a presence behind her, the dark branches of the trees laden heavily with white. When she looked down, she could see the kicked-up snowflakes sticking to the suede of her boots, thickly round her calves and extending as a thinner dusting up above her knees. But her toes felt warm; her body felt warm beneath her coat. Behind her, the sky was growing darker and the morning sun was more focused as it slanted through the trees.

'Another storm,' said Celia. But there was no wind, only a darkening and thickening of the sky behind the hill. 'Can you feel it coming?' Her hand slipped out of its foxfur muff and under Justine's coat and found the smoothness of her belly. Justine shuddered, although it was warm against warmth. Celia's fingers were soft and quick, sliding down to gather the bulge of Justine's cunny. Her thumb, gently slipping from side to side, opened the pouting lips. She did

110

not touch the clitoris, but it was erect, and the legs beneath the coat began to open. Icy draughts of air swept up between them, but the outer fingers held the cunny cupped and warm, while the thumb kept stroking. Quick shudders of the leather-clad thighs shed fluffy snowflakes to the ground. There was that perfect silence that comes before a heavy fall of snow.

'Elizabeth . . .' Celia whispered, and Justine felt her coat being lifted at the back. She felt the freezing air sweep down across her naked bottom. She felt Elizabeth's hand, warm against the coldness, cupped, rubbing the tightness of the tensed cheeks, urging them open, making their inner faces slip – so smoothly, in the cold – while Celia's thumb kept rubbing her cunny lips open, from side to side, and the hot tongue of her clitoris pushed. She felt Elizabeth touch her anus, holding the cheeks open to the cold and rubbing it with the smooth warm tip of a pointed finger. She felt her legs bowing open; she heard herself gasp. Celia took hold of the thick fold of skin above her clitoris and pushed it firmly back and Elizabeth touched her anus, tapped it, made it pulse. Then Celia opened Justine's coat, exposed her breasts and belly and played with them while she touched her with the cylinder of wood, rolling it upwards to the sides of her labia, pressing it into the seam at the tops of her legs, keeping her clitoris pushed out hard, making her cunny ache. Then she gave the cylinder to Elizabeth, who opened Justine's bottom cheeks and pressed the rounded tip against the pouted mouth of Justine's anus. Elizabeth rotated the cylinder and the muscle contracted hard. But the cold air made the entrance smooth, so the round tip slipped against it.

'Wait,' said Celia. She used two fingers and a thumb to surround the clitoris, but not to touch it, and she pressed the fold of skin until it was doubled back, and the whole area around the clitoris now felt hard. 'Push it,' said Celia, 'push it into her.' And it felt to Celia that the cylinder had not only slid through the muscular ring but had pushed right through to distend the area around the clitoris from behind. It was almost as if she could feel the rod, sleeved in hot skin, pushing between her fingers as Elizabeth moved it from behind and Justine's belly heaved and shuddered. 'The storm is coming,' Celia said again. 'Leave it in her. We must run.'

And as they ran her through the trees, she had two protrusions, one at the front, of flesh, and one at the back, of wood. The wood was not wide, but it was bedded firmly and it slipped against the cheeks of her bottom, against the sensitive facing skin. Each time the muscle tightened, the hard tip of the cylinder pressed against her from inside.

As soon as they had got above the trees, the snow descended in a wall. Celia stopped Justine, stood behind her, opened her coat, pulled it back and faced her into the wind. The shower of flakes pricked icy tickles up her breasts and belly. Her nipples gathered to the cold. Celia opened Justine's legs and the snowflakes caught in her pubic hair. Then she masturbated her, fully, pulling back the hood of skin and rubbing the clitoris in deep circular strokes. When Justine started to gasp, Celia took her fingertips away. She brushed the snowflakes back from the hairs on Justine's cunny. She bared the area around the lips, and she masturbated her again until her belly quivered on the verge of coming. Then, with one hand, she turned the rod that was inside Justine and with the other she held her open while the warm moist surfaces inside her cunny were pricked by icy needles of melting snow that had been collected on Elizabeth's fingers then stuck against the inner skin. With each touch of cold, Justine's clitoris pulsed and Celia felt a tiny nervous tug upon the rod between her fingers. Then she took the rod out, brushed the melting snowflakes from the breasts and legs and warm red pubic lips and fastened Justine's coat. She stripped a thin branchlet from a birch and took it with her and they ran for the refuge of the shelter.

Inside, it was warm: a fire had been lit and there were rugs in front of it. It was a small place which seemed almost empty; their boots sounded hollowly across the wooden floor. They took Justine's coat off, brushed the snow from her boots, dried her down and placed her on the rug by the fire. There were provisions – eggs, bread, ham and tea, and a small flask of brandy, which they drank. They put a pot on the fire for the tea. They left her there while they whispered; she could hear them talking as she lay before the fire; she could feel its warmth against the cold skin of her breasts and belly. Between her legs, she felt hot.

Celia wanted to whip her, that was what the whispering was about: whether they would whip her now or wait for tea. She could hear them; the things that they were saying made her shiver. She was still stretched on her side, just as she had been put.

'She needs it. Look at her – look at it,' whispered Celia, but the words carried in the small empty room. 'Did you ever see a bottom more deserving? And her cunt – see how it pouts. You can see it from behind. And have you noticed – look – there is a ridge of skin, like a string beneath the surface, connecting it to her arse . . .'

Justine curled up and hid her face under her arm. Her cheek was pressed against the warmed skin of her breast, which felt sore because of the punishment and because she was overdue. And because she was overdue, she felt excited by this talk, and she felt warm inside, because of this attention. These women had done nothing but touch her, kiss her, punish her and play with her since last night. And now that she was aroused – that her clitoris was poking hard and waiting to be sucked – they would just keep touching her and punishing her and making her harder still. They would keep toying with her, and if she were to come, that would be an accident. It would merit punishment, she knew, which would bring her on again, like last night, when they had smacked her till her bottom contracted hard and it had felt as if her climax would just keep coming and never stop.

The women were now on the floor, behind her, and Justine's pulse was thumping. Celia began to touch her cunny; Justine's leg slid up to give her access and Celia examined the thin rope of skin that crossed the narrow band of muscle separating Justine's cunny from her anus. The skin had gathered up tightly in the cold. Celia kept nipping it and smoothing it and touching. She tugged at it as if it were a rope that was slipped into Justine's anus. But this rope would not pull out: the muscle of the anus seemed to tighten round it hard.

'What if you were to wet it?' asked Elizabeth. But then the pot of water came to the boil. It spilled over, sizzling through the wood coals. Elizabeth started to brew the tea, but now Celia wanted to whip Justine, so the pot was temporarily taken off the fire.

They tied her wrists up to one of the beams in the low part of the ceiling. By drawing the rope up, they could make her hang, but they adjusted it until the balls of her booted feet could touch the floor. Celia whipped her with the birch twig across the front of her belly. She directed the whipping upon the lower part of the belly and above the lips of the leather boots at the front of the upper thighs. From the reaction, she decided that Justine had not been whipped this way before. She whipped until the toes had reached the backward limit that the tether would allow, and the muscles of the belly and thighs were fully rigid. Then she stopped, and for the first time since the whipping had started, Justine breathed. The gulps of breath were like those of a woman drowning. Celia made her spread her legs while she examined her. Despite the sobs, the pubic lips were wet and open and the clitoris was hard. Neither of these had been caught by the lash, because Justine's cunny pointed downwards and was set well back. Celia made her stand on tiptoes; applying the pressure of the narrow wooden cylinder above the pubic lips, she stretched them upwards; she made sure the clitoris remained exposed. Then she whipped her from behind. She whipped across her lower buttocks until the narrow wooden cylinder had slipped and the curvature of Justine's body had changed, so that Justine appeared pregnant with her heavy breasts pushed out before her and her belly formed into a small round bulge which Elizabeth could now massage and gently hold for the rest of the while that Celia whipped. Elizabeth, kneeling between Justine's legs, could hold her cunny open with her thumbs, which she could gently press

114

into the flesh while the birch strokes urged it forwards from behind.

'Her rope . . .' said Celia. She put the birch down. 'Her string of flesh – it is gone.' She touched the mouth of Justine's bottom and below, and the skin between the struggling legs felt warm and smooth; there was no longer any seam that joined her cunny to her anus.

But it felt good to Justine, when Celia supported her between the legs and touched her; it felt to Justine as if everything between her legs was held in a sweetly pressing sling into which she was distending; her cunny felt aroused and swollen and the mouth of her bottom tickled where Celia touched it. In due course, Celia's hand turned wet and then Justine was left tied and hanging, open and moist, stinging from the tracks of the birch, while the women went to brew the tea.

When Elizabeth came back, her hands were warm from the mug; they touched Justine's breasts as Elizabeth drank her tea, and they explored the shape of her underarms. Her fingertips were enquiring. She kept staring into Justine's eyes. She touched Justine's lips and Justine could smell her own underarm scent on Elizabeth's fingers, which Elizabeth then licked as she stared at Justine. Since Justine couldn't move, Elizabeth lifted the mug and fed her the tea. It tasted strong but smoky and sweet; she had put no milk into it. It left an astringent taste at the back of Justine's tongue and a feeling in her throat as if something intruded there and held it open. As the tube of warmth slid down her throat and spread inside her belly, her empty belly ached.

Elizabeth put the mug down. She took a chair, placed it before Justine and sat on it. She had turned the chair around so she had to lift her skirts to sit astride it as she faced Justine. The empty feeling turned to a deliciously sexual weight in Justine's belly.

Celia took her tea and went over to the window behind Justine. She looked out. The blizzard had lifted. It was late morning and the sun sloped down and sparkled on the snow; it glistened on the sheet of icicles hanging from the rocks. She heard a low gasp and turned. She could see the girl's back. The legs inside the long boots were bowed out and were trembling. She could see the chair legs beyond them, and Elizabeth's skirt, gathered up to each side, then Elizabeth's feet, planted squarely on the floor. Elizabeth was whispering but Celia could not hear her words. The girl's arms were straight; she seemed to hang; all her weight was taken by her wrists. The straightness made her waist seem even more narrow. The outbowing of her legs made her buttocks look rounder and tighter; they looked like twin eggs, angled to rest against each other, and cupped in leather eggcups. Between her legs, the bulge of her cunny was split, like a slit peach. Elizabeth's fingertips tested the inner surface, touched the peach-stone, and the gasp came again. The middle finger slipped beneath and touched the anus. All of Elizabeth's touches were gentle. The finger slipped back and began to massage the weeping peach.

Justine moaned again; there was a gnawing feeling pulling downwards in her belly; she found it hard to keep open, hard to keep still. Elizabeth kept wiping the tip of her finger round her clitoris, and the fingertip was moist. She kept touching her labia lightly, then pressing her fingertip against her anus, which wanted to contract, but Elizabeth had forbidden it. She had told Justine to remain completely still. Everywhere that Elizabeth touched became sensitive: Justine's nipples and her navel; the skin at the tops of her legs; the outside of her cunny – with the fingers brushing its silk lips then pressing to the velvet of the anus. Elizabeth used the rod to comb the lips back and open; she rubbed it upwards at each side, until the area around Justine's clitoris formed a wet projecting knot. Then it happened. Justine groaned. 'Oh, no. No . . .' she whimpered. 'No . . .' Because she knew, from the sinking, slipping feeling and from the warmth.

'Shh. . . .' Elizabeth wiped her fingers on a handkerchief. She wiped Justine. But she did not stop what she was doing. She closed the labia gently; they remained together now, held by the viscid stickiness, with the clitoris still projecting at the top. They felt warmer and more silky on the outside. She lifted them to one side and tickled the

116

skin beside the crease of Justine's leg. She used the closed lips to masturbate the clitoris, making them slip around it with the gentle pressure of two fingers, one from each hand. To Elizabeth, all of these things were new and exciting. She liked the thought of having a girl to do with as she would, to play with in various ways, and to keep sexually excited. And she liked the idea that she could forbid this girl to come and the girl would behave as if her whole world centred upon compliance with this one instruction.

Celia came across. Elizabeth showed her the stains on the handkerchief and Justine closed her eyes. 'She is due back at any rate by noon,' Celia said. Her thumb explored the open split of Justine's bottom. It found the mouth and tested it. The thin rope of gathered skin had formed again. Celia plucked it with her fingers. 'Take her down,' she said. 'Let her warm by the fire.' Celia left them and stepped out of the shelter.

When she came back, Justine was on all fours, her cunny pouted out behind her. Her cheek was pressed against the rug. She was breathing deeply; Elizabeth was again examining her. Her knees were so far apart and turned in such a way that the soles of her boots were almost touching. Elizabeth was stroking the sensitive skin in the split, the darker skin around the anus, the skin that forms an ellipse full of nerves for soft fine fingertips to tease, the skin that carries downy hairs that can be stroked or individually plucked out, the skin that cannot relax when it is tickled, but tenses and puckers into wrinkles in the centre. This skin, to Elizabeth, felt very dry and slippy, but the skin that hung below felt hot and wet. She repeatedly pressed her fingertips to this hanging swelling, pushing its hood back.

Celia placed the cloth on the rug. She unfolded it. In the centre was a thick, stubby icicle. It was wet, already melting. 'Her anus must not contract,' said Celia. She bent down close to Justine's face. She touched her cheek and the bareness round her ear, which seemed small because of the way her hair had been cut. 'It must not contract,' she repeated, very softly, with her face approaching Justine's upside down as it lay, cheek against the rug.

Justine could feel the warmth of Celia's breath and she could see the wide pupils of her eyes and she could feel the heat of the fire down one side of her body. The shivers kept coming between her legs, above the grip of the leather boots; the fingertips stroked the soft skin, sweeping it outwards, coaxing the cheeks apart. Her belly tingled as it hung; her nipples brushed against the rug. She felt a fingertip and thumb hold the cheeks of her bottom open; from their spacing, she judged the thickness. The icy wetness touched her; she contracted. 'Push your knees up; open it; offer it,' whispered Celia. Justine offered up her bottom; the icicle touched it; she contracted. Celia licked Justine's lips, because they were trembling. 'Open your mouth,' said Celia. 'Keep it open to me. Close your eyes . . .'

Celia's tongue entered Justine's mouth; it delved inside; it tasted Justine's shuddering, open-mouthed breathing as the round tip of the icicle opened her anus and the freezing wetness began to slip inside. Justine's mouth stayed open while Celia's fingertips slipped under her belly and found her clitoris and rolled it like a nipple. Celia's tongue withdrew. The freezing wetness bedded home. Justine wanted to reach for her and kiss her, to trap her tongue. But Celia held Justine's cheek down against the rug. 'Open-mouthed,' she said. She kept rolling Justine's hot wet clitoris as she bent towards her again. 'Open-legged, open-cunnied, open-cheeked . . .' The shudders came; the nostrils dilated – they stayed dilated through the grunts and the soft wet stroking of the icicle back and forward through her anus, the gentle rolling of the clitoris and the sliding of Celia's tongue around the rim of her open mouth.

They left the icicle in her until it necked and the melted stump came free. 'See how thick her string is now,' said Celia, and she touched it. Justine's string had never been thicker, or more cold.

They made her walk back nude through the woods. They made her sit astride a snow-covered log while Celia kissed her, holding her head and not wanting to let her go. Celia gathered up snow and rubbed it on her breasts and belly. When Elizabeth finally protested, she said, 'But my darling – I may never get another chance.' Elizabeth watched her playing with Justine. She watched her toying with her cunny through the snow, which was turning pink where the cunny pressed against it. She watched her kissing the shuddering body that acquiesced and never murmured, that suffered the pleasures and the hurts, and she watched her touching the beating, open heart that bled its warmth gently into the snow.

10: A CHANGE IN LEASEHOLD

The flat was Justine's own little world; she had chosen its furnishings; she had filled it, crowded it, made it soft, like a cocoon. Julia had smiled when she saw it, but she had been pleased. It was to be private – Justine's retreat during the time that she was resting – Julia had promised her that from the start. And now it was to have an intruder.

Justine, in her freshly pressed nightgown, sat upon her thickly pillowed bed, with her cherished things about her, close, so she could shield them from the night and they could comfort her against the aching knot that tightened in her womb. Beside her was the leather G-string, which she was afraid to touch now, as the minutes ticked away, because it represented him.

The telephone rang again, making her jerk with fright and knock it over. This time, she could not speak into it; she listened with the earpiece trembling against her ear and the mouthpiece held too closely. The smooth confidence of his voice was punctuated by the rasping echoes of her crowded breathing. She had seen him only once, but she remembered him so clearly. Above all else, she remembered the greyness of his eyes and the coldness of his words – *Keep her chin up, I want to see her face*, he had said, and he had watched her caned for tears.

'I am coming up,' the voice now said. He did not even speak her name. 'I expect you to be ready.' Justine looked again at the leather, then her eyes closed against the cramping pain. She must have murmured; he must have heard her. 'You have not taken anything?' The cramping ache became a shiver. 'Well? Have you?' Julia had told her that she must not – that he had insisted – and Justine could hear that insistence in his tone now. It frightened her, the thought that he seemed to want her to suffer the pain.

'No. Not yet, no. But – '

'Don't.' Then he said, less abruptly, 'And don't worry about the door – I have a key,' and he rang off.

It was her own world no more – it was his now, and she was his, his words had said it all. Her eyes were smarting. When she rubbed them, her fingers became wet. She kissed the knuckle, bit the skin, and she could taste her tears. Then she picked up the leather and took it with her into her bathroom. She rolled her nightgown up and washed herself again. But she would not keep washing herself for him. When she dried herself this time, there was no stain, but the low ache was still in her belly. Then she fitted the leather in the way that Julia had shown her, so deeply that it could not be seen from behind, and the lips of her cunny were split – 'kissing split,' Julia had called it, kissing split about the smooth bulge in the rope. Soon, Justine would bleed again, her body would bleed about the rope and she would be ashamed when he witnessed it, but it might put him off her altogether and that would make it worth it.

She stood in front of the washbasin, looking in the mirror. She lifted her nightgown up above her breasts and held it there. Her skin showed only faint marks now, but her breasts were tender. She pressed her aching belly against the coldness of the basin; the leather rope tightened and the lips of her cunny kissed it. She lifted her ankles; the cold line of pressure slid down to her thighs and her cunny lips touched the edge of the basin. Justine shivered and closed her eyes. She felt Rachel teasing her nipples, kissing her neck, soaping her, putting smooth, slippy things inside her.

A key sounded in the front door. Justine couldn't move until the hot wave of nausea had taken its course and passed, leaving her trembling, prickling with sweat. She heard footsteps moving down the short hallway and hesitating at her bedroom door. When it finally opened, Justine was in her bed, shivering, the film of sweat turned cold on

121

her skin. She could not look away from the face that stared at her so searchingly.

Philip did not move. His hand remained on the door-knob. His gaze flickered, took in the contents of the small room, then returned to the figure watching him from the bed. Then he noticed that the bathroom door was swinging slowly shut: a small movement of her eyes had given him the clue. He closed the bedroom door quietly, then walked deliberately to the bathroom, his boots creaking across the polished floorboards, then shedding melting snow upon the carpet. He glanced at her again before pushing the door open. She moved uneasily; she had noticed the parcel under his arm.

In the bathroom, the air was humid and sweetly scented and there were droplets of water on the side of the bath. There was a glass on the shelf by the washbasin; he checked it; it was dry, but the basin was wet. And there was a flannel that was moist and warm. He returned to the bedroom.

She was still watching him; her lips were open and she was taking slight, quick breaths. Her anxious gaze followed his to the bedside table. The only things on it were a book, a lamp and a group of small china animals. There was no glass from which she might have drunk. Now she was looking again at the parcel. He put it down on a chair of his choosing. Step by step, he took her apartment and made it his. There was a larger table in the room. In its centre was a bowl of dried flowers sitting on a small crocheted cloth, but there was an inkstand too, with pens arranged neatly, on a cloth to the side. He moved all of these things aside, sliding them slowly towards the back edge. The bedcovers rustled, but she gave no other audible signal of the mounting disquiet that he had seen so very clearly in her eyes. He therefore examined the polished surface of the table minutely, taking his time, touching it with his finger-tips and tilting his head to the side to alter the angle of the light. When he turned to look at her, her eyes said it all again, before they flinched and the paleness of her cheeks acquired a deepening flush of pink. He watched those eyes widen as he slipped from his inside coat pocket a thin stiffened whip which was black. It was smaller and finer than a riding crop; it was not made for horses, and in the hand it balanced like a knife.

'We might not need it tonight. We shall have to see.' They were the first words he had spoken to her since entering her room. They were his greeting to Justine, that she might be clear as to his intentions for her. He placed the whip in the middle of the space he had cleared on the table.

Her bed was small and it looked cluttered. She was surrounded by pillows and embroidered cushions and soft toys, mainly animals. Philip unfastened his coat and sat on the side of the bed. He moved some of the things to the foot of it. The fingers of her right hand were slipped through the looped, knotted braid of a velvet lion's mane. They were moving, seething slowly, pressing into the lion's skin. When Philip touched them, they became still; they felt weak and seemed to have no strength to grip. He prised them easily from the shelter of the loops, then took the lion from her and placed it on the floor. He edged it away with the toe of his boot.

'You have not taken anything? Shhh . . .' He could see her wide eyes liquefying. He smoothed her thick soft eyebrows with his thumb.

'It hurts . . .' she whispered. Her eyes were pleading. Her eyebrows were so soft and blonde, her hair was so short, with curves of perfect nudity encircling her ears.

On the tips of two fingers, he raised her chin. She tried to swallow. The movement of her naked, pale soft throat made him want to kiss it. A tearflow struggled down her lifted cheek. He lifted her chin higher and tilted it to try to make a pond of her tears in the corner of her eye, but her body suddenly stiffened, her eyes closed tightly and the tearflow escaped. It took a short while for him to realise that it must be because of the pain of a contraction. But he held her chin until her eyes had opened. Then he unknotted her fingers from the sheet and spread them.

'Unfasten your gown,' he whispered, and he saw the fingers tensing again. 'No – look at me,' he said. He lifted her chin so she could, so her head was tilted back and her

123

eyelids, half closed, were made to appear heavy. 'Open your mouth – Justine.' And she shuddered when he said her name. He stroked her neck below her chin. 'Justine . . .' he whispered. 'Sweet, perfect creature – open yourself to me.' Her open lips trembled; her fingertips searched weakly for the smooth pearl buttons. Philip touched the lobes of her ears, rubbing them lightly, crossing his hand over the hand that held her chin, back and forth from lobe to lobe and brushing across the trembling lips. The lobes became hotter as he rubbed. There was a gap in her gown extending almost to her navel. 'Now take it down,' he said. Her hands crossed above her breasts, her nervous fingertips lifted and the gown collapsed from her shoulders to her elbows, burying her hands, leaving her belly crowned by the creamy folds of soft fresh linen, leaving the girl breast-naked and defenceless, ready to be kissed.

He sucked her breasts and kept them wet and blew his breath upon them, so that they gathered. He kept them moving, rubbing two fingers to the sides of them, up and underneath her arm and down again, following the gland, pressing gently but stimulating it inside, then lifting the nipple on his fingers, pinching it gently while she murmured. Her nipples continued to engorge; he noticed there were tiny stretch-marks round them. His fingertips smelt of lavender. 'In future, you will use only water,' he told her. 'I want your breasts to smell of breast, not soap.'

He made her roll her nightgown up from her thighs until it formed a band around her hips and her G-string was exposed to the point where it split the warm pink pubic lips that were sprinkled with yellow-blonde hair.

'Sit back,' he whispered. He made her lean back on her hands. It imprisoned her hands, so they would not be tempted to try to stop him. He wanted no hindrance; he wanted to admire her youthful beauty intimately and in peace. He pushed her rolled-up nightgown up above her bulging breasts. Then he drew the cover back and moved aside her feet. She had feet that looked long until he lifted them; then he could see that what they were was slender. His hand could enfold them; the toes were perfect and slim.

He bent her knees and the bulge of her cunt pressed down into the sheet; the leather rope traversed the blonde curls and dropped straight down; it seemed to bury itself in the sheet. It was as if the rope passed down through the bed and was fastened underneath it, to the floor.

He lifted the front of the roll of nightgown over her head, but did not take it off her completely: it formed a tight band round the back of her neck and under her arms. It seemed to make her breasts larger and more beautiful. He placed his hand against the thin collarbone and pushed and she moved back, sliding down on to her elbows, her breasts slipping to the sides and touching the material rolled up under her arms. And because he kept her feet in position by her buttocks, her belly became distended as her cunt pushed down. He pressed her knees apart and down. The bulge of her cunt lifted, the rope moved deeper into the split and the pubic lips sealed round it. It was as if her tissue had grown over the leather and taken it to itself.

Philip took a hairbrush from the dressing table. He began brushing the blonde curls back from her cunt, exposing the smooth shiny bareness and the velvet lips that sheathed the leather. Then suddenly, she groaned; her belly turned hard; her legs shook. The long slim muscles he had seen that first night, rooted deep between her legs, it seemed, deep between her buttocks and up inside her, now began to tremble. Philip put the brush down. He put his hand against her belly and contained it until its iron hardness had softened and he could press his fingers deep into it. Then he continued brushing back her pubic hair until the trembles in her legs had gradually disappeared.

There was perspiration in the polished grooves at the tops of Justine's thighs. Philip licked it, then he sucked the soft pink lips of her cunt. They did not smell of lavender; they tasted strong, ammoniacal. Through the lips, butted against them, he could feel the rope. He licked the lips and wetted them until the seal between them split; she shuddered and the tip of his tongue tasted ammoniacal hotness before it touched the oily rope. When he sat up again, she was trembling. Her whole body trembled as she leaned

125

back on her elbows, and he found the way she trembled terribly exciting, when all that she wore was this rope between her thick and wetted pubic lips, and the rolled-up nightgown, twisted and secured about her shoulders like a yoke. The tightness and the tremblings in her breasts and belly made him want to take things much more slowly.

Philip turned her round, placing her on her elbows again, crouched on her front with her belly pushing down between her widely splayed knees. He gripped the roll of nightgown that crossed behind her shoulders and he pulled it back. Her belly curved sharply down and her breasts stood out to the sides. He touched them, one by one, changing hands, cupping the breast, milking the nipple as it protruded, while her pubic bulge stood out behind her and her belly almost touched the bed.

But when her pain came again, he massaged the low part of her back and kissed her spine. He fed his thumb beneath the rope, between the cheeks, and there, below the anus he could feel a definite ridge of skin, whose touch he found unusual and interesting. He pulled the rope down and allowed it to slip out from between her labia and to one side, so he could take her fully in hand to masturbate her. And he could clearly see the ridge of skin. His thumb explored it, then moved up again to divide the cheeks and press against her anus while his fingers executed a slow, rhythmic masturbation of her clitoris and the lips of her cunt. He persisted, using all four fingers but keeping the pad of the thumb pressing firmly to the small round place. It would take time and he could tell that she resisted. But he had the time, and it would come: already he could feel the gentle trembles. Even through her pains, her clitoris stayed bone-hard.

With his free hand, he massaged her back again, then her belly, keeping it moving up and down against the steady hand that cupped her cunt. Then he traced the glands again from underarms to nipples. He kept this free hand moving while the other hand contained her. And without warning, the point was reached: her crouched body turned rigid and she was terrified to move. Philip rubbed the bone-hard stub of her clitoris with the tip of his middle finger, very gently and very slowly, and all her rigidity burst: he could feel that she was coming in his hand. Her fingers clawed convulsively at the sheets, her cheek thrust and twisted against the bed, forcing her mouth so open and awry that Philip had to touch it. He teased the gasping, open fullness of her lips throughout the time that Justine came, which seemed to prolong the coming and help it to progress, with Justine's perfect cunt contracting, then opening to his searching hand, then the rapid pulsing coming through his slowly rubbing fingers and, behind, against his firmly pressing thumb, and the base of her spine turning sticky with sweat, and his hand turning warm with her blood. When her shudders had subsided and his fingers had allowed her rest, there were bright red drip-stains on the sheet. But beneath the hot, sticky fold of skin, the clitoris was still bone-hard. Philip lifted her knees apart and lowered her hips; she murmured when her cunt touched the sheet. She was frightened of soiling it and tried to lift herself away. He kept the leather rope pulled to the side and opened her, then pushed her hips firmly down until her labia spread against the sheet. And he held her but she kept murmuring, and her face remained averted and half-covered with her hand. Yet Philip felt a calm of perfect satisfaction.

He found a soft white towel in the bathroom. He used it to wipe his hand. Then he placed it beside the bed. He freed her arms from the yoke of the nightgown, leaving her naked apart from the leather that lay loosely between her legs. Justine was on her front, on her elbows, breathing heavily. She kept her head turned away from him. Whenever her head moved, he had the sudden urge to kiss it. It looked so round, so smooth, with the short hair extending down her neck to make two soft points, like drifts of wind-blown powdery snow, and her ears so starkly naked. Philip kissed her neck and ears now, sucking them – not just the lobes – but sucking the ear into his mouth so his lips pressed against the warm bare skin around it, until he could feel the beat of her pulse through his lips and could lick inside the folds and taste her bitter beeswax on his tongue.

When her pain came again, he kept her on her front and massaged the place where the hollow of her slim back met the round swell of her buttocks. He pushed a hand from behind and underneath and pressed his fingers up against her belly. And he felt the liquid warmth again, on the heel of his hand and on the smooth skin of the inside of his wrist. He wiped himself with the cloth, then made her lie fully down, open-legged, on to the bed. And again she protested weakly. This time, she began to cry. He came close to the face on the pillow. Her lips seemed fuller and redder and warmer and softer when she cried – he discovered it then, and he would confirm it later, when he would make her cry, for the pleasure of feeling their soft full warmth against his skin. But now she was crying because of the mess she was making: with the cruel hand of nature fastened round her belly, squeezing her life blood out of her, she was concerned about the sheets.

Philip covered Justine. He went into the small kitchen and found that she had a stove for gas. He put her kettle on to boil. He made tea and he filled the stone water bottle. When he came back, she still lay in the same face-down position into which he had put her; he could see her knees beneath the sheet, open and to the sides. Her legs formed the shape of a horseshoe on the bed; there was a smooth, flat expanse of sheet between them, where he could have sat and laid his head upon the pillow of her buttocks and, through the thin sheet, felt their warmth against his cheek. Her head was turned away from him but her body stiffened when he came close. Her hand closed tightly when he knelt on the bed. He slid the discarded nightgown from under the sheet. The tip of his finger traced her hairline – the downy drift of snow – around the back of her head to the nape of her neck. Then he took the nightgown and wrapped it round the water bottle and placed the warm soft weight of it in the hollow at the base of her spine. He covered her up again and left her.

Justine lay with her eyes closed. When she breathed in, she could feel the water bottle lifting. When she breathed out, it was like a large warm hand pressing against her, pressing her belly to the bed. Fingers of warmth reached round her spine and down through her body and blunted the ache in her womb. But they did not make it go away. And the flushes of heat were stronger; her face and neck and breasts turned hot; fine sweat prickled out of her skin. He brought her tea, and took the bottle off her back, but she was ashamed to lift her belly up and turn. And when she did sit up, she was afraid to drink the tea because that would only hasten her requirement for the bathroom: she could never get out of bed with him watching. She begged him to leave – now. He just looked at his left hand; there was blood – her blood – dried between his fingers.

'Why would I want to leave you – ever?' he said. He stared at her with his cold grey eyes and Justine started crying. He didn't speak again, but took her head in his hands and held it back, until her tears welled into blinding pools which spilled down to her ears. Then he kissed her lips and murmured so softly that she could not hear the words. Then he took the untouched tea away and made fresh. When he brought it the second time, Justine drank it.

He started to undress. She had seen men naked before, but even so, she felt the pain coming again, triggered by the fear of what he would do. Nobody had ever made her do it with a man. When he turned to face her fully, she saw he was erect. His penis was curving up, the head exposed, the foreskin drawn fully back, the testicles tight. He walked to the bed. 'Take hold of it,' he said.

She could feel her belly cramping – anxiety turning to pain. She remembered what had happened at Celia's, when they had put her, blindfolded, on the table – the hot spurts against her lips, the tremblings, the stickiness, the taste. He took her hand and put it round it. It felt hot; the skin was velvety and brown; the top was polished. He made her touch his testicles; the warm skin crawled away from her fingertips as if it were alive. Then the pain came on so strongly that she felt faint. Her hand dropped away from him and she doubled over.

Philip fell to his knees beside the bed. He spread his

129

hand up and against her belly and held it, kneading his fingers into her skin. But her pain appeared undiminished. 'Turn over. Lie down.' He slipped into bed behind her. He took the bottle wrapped in the nightgown and held it to her belly. He tucked her knees up against the bottle and rubbed the base of her spine. When her pain came on strongly again, he held her, then continued to massage her. Then he refilled the bottle and returned. When the pain had eased a little, he massaged her back from her shoulders to her buttocks; when he rubbed the backs of her thighs, he felt warmness there and moisture. At the front, her pubic hairs felt sticky. She pleaded for the towel; he wouldn't give it to her, but he removed the leather rope altogether and began to rub the flat of his fingers between her buttocks. She stayed tight there; he kept massaging, keeping the round cheek moving in his hand while the fingertips probed deeper, testing the hotter skin. Then he licked his fingertips and reapplied them, keeping her buttocks moving all the time, keeping the rubbing smooth and rhythmic. When she murmured, he put his other arm around her and held her breasts, tickling the nipples while the smooth wet fingers slid against her anus and touched her string of skin. When she murmured again, he turned her on her back, but he kept up that wet-fingered rubbing all the while. While he climbed over her and knelt between her legs, while he eased her feet apart – he kept stimulating the small round place which was becoming softer and more open, a soft, warm, deeper, more accessible well.

He kept probing it while he instructed her to hold her knees up tightly, and probing it while his cock stroked against her cunt, pulling the sticky lips open. The blood was dried into her curls and creases. Her pubic lips were soft, and the entrance was tight yet slippy; she kept murmuring as he pushed. The mouth of her bottom formed a small well for his finger, which tickled the wetted skin, trying to make it close. But it stayed open to the tickling, while the mouth of her cunt stayed tight. He pulled his cock out; the head of it was wet with blood, which turned sticky and tight around him. He turned her on her side, with her head across the bed. He tucked her knees against her breasts and lay behind her, then introduced only the head of his cock into the mouth of her cunt. He put one hand at the back of her neck and pulled her body down into a tight curve. And when he thrust this time, it was as if a burning wet slippery glove had swallowed him; he was bedded to the hilt. The flared base of his cock formed a plug inside her; the blood welled into the seam and dried and the two of them were sealed. Philip wrapped his arms around Justine. He held her with her knees up, her slim back pressed to his belly, and the roundness of her belly accessible to his hands, which rubbed it and touched beneath it, repeatedly applying saliva to keep her clitoris wet and hard until her belly arched out against his hand and tried to push itself through the tucked-up knees and the seal around his cock was broken. New blood welled down over his balls, only to become sticky, then to seal again as her belly subsided sufficiently for Philip to begin the slow re-masturbation of Justine.

It was the feeling of control that he found so sweet, and the sounds and small movements that she made when she was close to her climax: her breathing turning from deep to shallow and then to trembling; her belly turning hard and tight; the way her back arched and her knees came up so far that her cunt appeared displaced down and back behind her legs, like a mouth sucking deeper round his cock; and the way the gap opened between their bodies, presenting a space for his fingertips to slip down between her buttocks and touch the warmth of her anus while his other hand played with her clitoris until the first gasps came, when both hands could withdraw and fold about her belly, before the stimulation moved upwards, to her nipples. Philip did not come and neither did he let Justine, and her arousal kept him hard. Eventually, he broke the seal and took his cock out of her, climbed round to face her and lay between her legs, her full breasts pressed against his chest and his warm wet cock resting against her belly. When her pains came on again, he turned her on her back and kneaded her belly and rubbed the insides of her legs.

He filled the hot water bottle many times that night. He attended her while she slept. She felt his naked penis touching her back, her legs or her belly every time she was awake; it bobbed against her while he rubbed her; it seemed to stay hard. She was thinking of the way his penis and his balls had felt, the strangeness of the texture of the skin, and the way that his living flesh had felt inside her, filling her while she was masturbated but was not allowed to come.

In the morning, she awoke to the sound of running water. He had run her bath for her. Beside the bed was a tray with tea and marmalade and hot, buttered toast. He sat on the bed, then passed her the cup and saucer and watched her drink. Then he gave her two small tablets. 'I want you to take these,' he said. He placed the bottle on the tray. Justine looked at him. 'They will help with the pain. They are very effective.'

His thin forefinger lifted up and pressed across her lips. His left hand slid the sheets down, then moved her elbow back. He took one of the tablets from her hand and touched it to her nipple and gently rolled the tablet round it while his forefinger rubbed across her lips until they opened. 'Put your tongue out – there. Now drink.' Then the second tablet was rolled around her nipple and placed upon her tongue. 'Don't you trust me?' He waited until she had swallowed them. Then he touched her under her arms and rubbed his fingertips upwards under her nipples. 'Your bath is ready.'

He allowed her to bathe herself alone. When she came back into her bedroom, he had stripped the bed and replaced the sheets from the bundle he had brought. 'I'll have these laundered,' he said. When he stood up, she could see that the bed was perfectly made. He stepped across to her. His body briefly pressed against her through her robe and Justine experienced an extraordinary feeling when she looked up into his eyes. It was as if a finger, sliding up, had touched Rachel's place inside her. The feeling continued while he held her chin and kissed her. Then his hand slipped inside her robe and the backs of his

132

fingers brushed the skin hairs on her breasts and whispered against her nipples.

He stood back and smiled at her. 'Here, I have a little something for you.' He waited until she opened the small purple velvet box that he gave her. It contained four silver rings that resembled earrings; they were connected in pairs by short chains. 'Put them on.' He showed her: they were finger-rings which fitted tightly round the two middle fingers of each hand. The chain was slightly loose between them and when he held her hand up, the fine links moved against the joining skin. He twisted each hand very slowly in turn and watched the chain moving, then opened her fingers until the chain was stretched and slipped the tip of his finger under it and stroked the sensitive skin. Then he walked across and picked up the thin black crop. Justine's breasts prickled; the endless sinking feeling started coming between her legs. 'Kneel on the bed, Justine,' he whispered.

'Oh, God,' murmured Philip, when he had finished. 'Let me feel it. Let me just feel. Shhh . . .' He threw the crop down and kissed her hot bare lower back and touched again the wet hard ball that protruded between the slippery pubic lips. 'Shhh . . .' He painted her moisture across the thin red marks transecting the softness of her pubic mount, and the tip of his thumb slipped up and down across the tense skin of her anus. Justine was kneeling with her robe pushed up, her breasts pressed to the bed, her clitoris trembling against his fingers. Then he took his hand away and her climax was postponed. He fitted her G-string tightly – he had to open her knees to attain the tightness across the tense skin mouth and the depth between her pubic lips and the pressure against her clitoris that he wanted. Then he replaced the crop on the table and left without saying when he would be back.

Her sheets were returned two days later, on the Monday. She had been afraid to venture out in the meantime in case Philip were to return and find her missing. Julia had told her she must not leave without express permission. Each

133

morning, she put on her leather string – the last thing that he had done before he left had made it clear that he wanted her to keep wearing it even at this time. She wore it under her panties. She experienced the feeling of arousal when it slipped between her legs, and it aroused her when she sat down and when she moved. On the Monday afternoon, a tradesman called.

'There must be some mistake,' she said.

'No . . .' He examined the written sheet, then showed her the address and the name of the client. 'Mr Philip Clement – he's the owner, isn't he?'

'No . . . He can't be . . . Can he?'

The man looked at her strangely. 'But you do know the gentleman?'

Justine sank into the chair. When she didn't answer, his manner changed and his tone softened. 'Happen you could contact him, Miss – find out if there's been a mix-up? But mind, it does look right, from this note . . .' She still didn't answer him, but stared at a spot in the ceiling, over the table. 'I could always come back when it's been sorted out. Mind – it'd be another journey – we'd have to charge. And then I don't know what the gentleman would say. He seemed – well, he seemed to want it done today, if you understand me.'

It did not take him long to find the beam beneath the plaster. The crop still lay where Philip had put it, in the centre of the table. Justine hadn't moved it; she hadn't been near it. And now she was obliged to touch it. Having picked it up, she did not know where to place it and her fingers held it fearfully. Her nervousness was communicated to the man, who averted his eyes from the crop and looked at her with that same strange, concerned expression – in the way you might look at a beautiful, wounded creature that was suffering in a way you could not comprehend, that was failing quickly and that you knew you could not cure.

He could not complete the fitting without dragging the table aside, then standing on a kitchen chair. He worked in silence; Justine listened to the clang of metal and the slow screech of driven screws. When he had finished, he dragged the table back. 'That's it, Miss – all done. And paid for.' He tried to smile, then bit his lip. She saw that he had kind eyes.

Long after he was gone, Justine sat on the bed, staring at the thick iron stemple in the ceiling.

11: THE STEMPLE

Philip arrived at eleven o'clock that night. Justine was in bed but her light was still burning. This time, Philip wasn't alone – he had with him a young woman who had long brown hair and dark eyes. She seemed to know who Justine was. Philip offered no explanation as to why the girl had been brought there. The first place he looked was to the ceiling and the iron stemple that made Justine so afraid. But he didn't seem to notice that she was upset. He acted very coldly towards her. He made a point of commenting on the girl's hair – how attractive long hair was and didn't Justine think so? 'I used to prefer short hair,' he said, staring at the girl and combing her tresses with his fingers. Justine sat on the bed, numbed by his cruelty.

He threw her a glance. 'Go and wash,' he told her, in a tone that made her feel dirty. She ran to the bathroom. 'And get undressed,' he shouted after her. She stood before her basin, trembling – because even now, she was hoping that he would come to her, and hold her and tell her that he wanted her, but she could hear him whispering to the girl. Justine washed herself with shaking fingers. She was still bleeding. She didn't know what he might want to do with her and she was frightened of the stemple.

When she had finished, she stood in the doorway of the bathroom. He was still looking at her as if she had done wrong, but she had done everything he had asked her to – everything. And now she was nude and that was what he had said he wanted. Justine wiped her eyes. The girl was sitting on a wooden chair. The bodice of her dress was open and her breasts had been taken out. Philip was holding them and stroking the nipples with his thumbs. He turned to face the girl and lifted her chin. Then he continued to play with her nipples. 'Where is your leather?' he said, still staring into the girl's eyes. Justine suddenly realised he was talking to her.

'I . . . I still have my . . .'

'Your what?'

'I'm still bleeding,' she whispered. And now the girl was staring at her, and Justine was choking up inside.

'Put it on.' He was pinching the girl's nipples.

She crept back into the bathroom. 'And remember it in future,' he shouted. When she returned, the girl was bare to the waist. He was tying her arms to the back of the chair. She wore a dress which fastened down the front. When he unhooked the rest of it, Justine saw that she wasn't wearing any panties. He slid the dress from under her, and all she wore now were her buttoned calf-length boots and short silk stockings. 'Come here. Take them off her,' he told Justine. The girl stiffened. She had seemed unworried while Philip touched her, but now her legs – with the right foot bent beneath the chair, the knee rocking very slightly, and the left leg stretched across the floor – suddenly became still. Justine was aware of this; she was aware of the dawning anxiety in the girl's eyes when Justine obediently crossed the room, with slow, silent footfalls, bare toes treading softly in the carpet, leather rope between her legs, nudity of skin.

Philip was holding the girl's shoulders gently down, even though her hands were tied. She had an expression that told that she wanted escape, and it had a strange effect on Justine. She knelt quietly on the floor and looked up at the girl. Philip said nothing, but his eyes yearned as they met Justine's; he stood behind the girl, holding her shoulders lightly, the two middle fingers of his hands stretching down across her dusky skin.

When Justine touched the leg that stretched towards her, the girl attempted to pull it away. Philip whispered to her and the girl stayed still. Justine unbuttoned the boot; the gap opened slowly down to the ankle, and the tiny silver chains between the rings on Justine's fingers clinked. The girl was breathing quickly. Justine teased aside the satin tongue and she could smell the rich sharpness of the inner leather instilled with the scent of female feet. She slid the tip of a finger inside the tongue; the skin felt warm and damp and nervous through the thinness of the stocking. The tip of her finger found the vein on the crown of the foot; it lingered there, then pressed, stopping the flow of blood. Justine looked up at the girl – she must know what was being done to her, and what it meant; she could surely sense these tiny feelings in her feet. When the fingertip lifted, and the blood coursed again, the girl made a barely audible murmur, as if the stopping of the vein had hurt her. Justine slipped one hand round the heel of the boot, the other round the back of the calf, and she lifted. The boot slipped off. She rolled the short stocking down. The foot was naked; it was small, and the skin was much darker than Justine's. Her toes were shorter. Justine could smell their sweet acridity. She placed her cheek to the floor; she allowed the tips of her breasts to dab against the carpet and she licked the sole of the foot, which trembled as the moistened point of Justine's tongue licked salt-sour lines along it.

As Justine rocked gently on her knees, the leather rope was drawn into her split; her cunny was wetting – she checked it with her finger – she was lubricating, in the way she used to do with Rachel, and it made her cunny itch. She sucked the salt from each toe individually and left it wet. Then she dealt with the other foot. She had to coax it from under the chair. When it too was naked and wetted and drying, the girl was already trembling. Her legs had fallen open, but the muscles of her thighs were tense. Justine knelt up. Philip moved away and the girl's eyes followed him across the room, her hands gently twisting about the pivot-points where her wrists were fastened. Philip sat on the edge of the table and lit a cigarette. The girl swallowed. Justine lifted the girl's feet and tucked them under the seat and hooked them round the front legs of the chair. She placed her hands around the girl's hips and drew them towards her; the girl's knees opened and the dark lips of her cunny projected beyond the edge of the seat; they were fringed by shiny black curls.

When Justine took the girl's head in her hands and pulled it down and kissed her mouth, the lips of the cunny pressed a line of warmth against the top of Justine's belly, and in that warmth was wetness. Justine held the girl against her; she put a hand between their bodies, to touch the girl's nipples then to stimulate the girl's wetness by keeping the lips pressed lightly together and stroking her own belly against them while they were closed. Then she slipped her thumb behind her rope and pushed it against the girl, whose labia split. Justine touched her gently with the oiled rope while she sucked the dark nipples, drawing deeply, then gently, always wetly, keeping the nipples hard. She sucked the sides of the breasts and their underneaths. The labia stayed open when the rope was drawn away. She tickled them with her fingers and touched them with the inside of her wrist. They tried to press against her inner wrist and kiss it, skin to skin.

Justine's lips moved further down; she licked the inside of the navel. She could smell the young woman, but there was also another smell, like bleach. It was on her dark, curled hairs; it was in them; they were impregnated. The smell was on her cunny – the smell of semen everywhere – but Justine closed her eyes and kissed it. The girl groaned and pushed to meet the kissing lips. The scent of bleach was in the back of Justine's mouth, but on her tongue was the taste of the girl – faintly animal, faintly roasted, faintly fish – and on her lips was a thickly coating warmth, like melted gelatine. And Justine too was lubricating.

Then she felt a hand behind her, on her back. Her naked legs were lifted as she knelt and a tiny round tripod stool was slid between them. Its smooth, dished surface took her belly and supported it. Her cunny projected back between her tucked-up legs, and while Justine sucked the girl, Philip touched Justine. She felt him touch the tautness of the leather string across her bottom. The tip of his finger searched for access, then moved down to touch her swollen lips which were sealed about the wet bulge in the string. She felt their substance move below the surface of the skin, and the string being rubbed against her clitoris, then the fingers gathering her, string and all. And she felt the girl's clitoris in her mouth, playing touch with the tip of her tongue, which pushed into the tiny hole beneath it and tasted bitterness. The girl murmured and tried to pull away from this kind of penetration. Justine kept her tongue in place and slipped her middle finger up inside the girl; it slid freely. She took it out and rubbed the wet around the clitoris. Then she held the cunny open and kissed it and her lips were coated with the thick wetness. There was a runnel of escaping liquid that she caught on her tongue. Then she used the tip of her tongue again to probe the tiny hole. And all this while Philip's fingertips slowly squeezed Justine between her legs and rubbed the string across her bottom with his thumb.

When she released the girl's feet from round the legs of the chair, her knees automatically lifted and spread, and her hips rotated, offering up the small brown button between the lifted cheeks. Justine squeezed the cunny till the liquid trickled down to wet this small brown place. Then she licked it, then shuddered, because she felt her leather string being stretched aside to expose the well of her anus. She felt the tip of Philip's wetted finger touch her, while the string still pressed against her wet hard clitoris and her tongue-tip touched the girl. Only the tip of Philip's finger pushed inside Justine. Then it slipped out while he rubbed the string about her clitoris in a slow massage that made her want to pee. Then he slipped the wetted tip of his finger back inside her. And during the time that Philip's finger explored her anus and taught it how to suck, Justine knelt immobile, with the tip of her tongue pushing like a rigid fleshy spear against the girl's brown wrinkled button, and with Philip gradually edging Justine's knees apart so her weight was delivered only through her belly into the polished, dished surface of the stool.

The girl's breasts and belly suddenly trembled, the small

brown button expanded and Justine's tongue was enveloped in warmth; her lips sucked moistly about the pouted ring. But the fingertip kept slipping out of Justine, to be re-wetted and to slip itself back in, as if it had all the time in the world, while Justine's tongue held the tight tube of the anus open and her clitoris, gasping to be taken and provoked between the fingers, pulsed against her leather string.

When the girl was on the verge of crying out, Philip took his finger out of Justine and drew her away. He left her across the stool and put the girl on the bed, then returned to Justine. He never spoke to her to give her any comfort, or any reassurance that what she had done with the young woman had satisfied or pleased him. He unfastened her G-string and pulled it free, then pushed her head to the floor but left her belly supported on the stool between her knees. He took his handkerchief out and began to wipe her, and she realised what had happened. 'No . . .' she murmured. And she shuddered every time the handkerchief touched inside her, soaking up her leakage. He still didn't say anything, but applied the handkerchief meticulously; she kept her face hidden; she kept whispering her protest against the shame that she felt inside.

And now, he used her coldly. He spread his hand out over her lower back and leant his weight against it, pushing her belly down into the bowl of the stool. Then he opened her with one finger. He pressed the finger down while he masturbated her clitoris with his thumb. The girl on the bed was watching. When Justine began to gasp, the downward pressure of his finger lessened and the finger and thumb were used instead to hold the lips apart, until after an interval the downward pressure and the steady masturbation resumed. When her gasps began a second time and again his finger lifted, he did speak to her – instructing her to keep herself open – then waited until the pressure had eased on the finger and thumb that kept her lips apart, before he used that same finger and thumb to touch the tips of the nipples that hung down, stimulating them to painful hardness with the gentleness of the touch and his murmuring, 'Keep open,' which were the only words he

141

spoke to her, and kept repeating, as if he felt it very important. And again the finger slipped inside her, pressing down against the front wall of her cunny while the thumb tip lifted her hood of skin and rubbed its short nail over her clitoris until it ached as much as her nipples. Her contraction came again; it lifted his finger and sucked it as it would a penis. 'Keep open.' Justine groaned; the finger slid freely; the thumbnail continued pushing back the surrounding skin. 'We must do something about this; we must keep this clitoris free – exposed for kissing.' Then he whispered, 'And for pricking . . .'

Suddenly, she shuddered; her breasts shook; her nipples tingled. 'Shhh . . . Is that what she did to you, Justine? Did she prick it?' Philip pushed her knees forward. He spread the wet lips of her cunny. He reached through the legs of the stool and smoothed the wetness round her nipples, then he held her clitoris between two fingers and a thumb. He held it until she was on the point of climax, then he suddenly let go. While she shuddered and groaned, he pushed her head down and made her forehead touch the floor. 'Did she prick it with a pin?' he taunted.

The girl on the bed was shaking. She watched Justine, still moaning, being lifted on to the table and being made to kneel while her wrists were fastened to the stemple in the ceiling. He used a thick red braiding, looped through the stemple and wrapped flat for several turns around each of Justine's wrists. Then he pushed her body forward until her hands were far behind her head and her back formed an arch. Her breasts were drawn up and out, her belly curved sharply and the stiff ridge of her labia pointed down. He pushed her knees apart until she felt the tightness across the tops of her legs. He rubbed the tendons, then laid his fingers alongside her labia and rubbed until they opened. When he took his fingers away, her labia fell gently back together, so he forced her knees apart until she winced with the pain of stretching. Then he touched her labia even more gently than before. He slipped a fingertip underneath and rubbed her anus, sending feelings of arousal deep inside her. Then he touched her labia again, while she was stretched – they were becoming thicker and more heavy, and they now stayed slightly open when his fingers moved away. He told her to stay in this position and not move – but he had a leather strap and it was lifting. Her belly jerked away and her knees closed up in fear.

'Justine, Justine,' he whispered, 'how often must I tell you? When will you learn?' And he waited till her belly projected again, till her knees had moved apart, till the arch across her inner thighs was tight, and her labia hung like a ripe, split fruit. 'So many places from which to choose . . .' Then he smacked the leather sharply, once, across her belly.

'Ahh!'

'Shhh . . .' He took her labia and softly fingered them as they hung. The skin of her belly was burning. 'Good. Keep it pushed out.' The stretching made the burning worse. His fingertips slipped away. The smack came again, on her belly.

'Ahhh!'

'Try not to cry out, not to murmur. There . . .' The fingertips slipped around her, pulling the glutted lips, avoiding direct contact with her clitoris, which kept moving as the lips slipped. He kept smacking her belly and making it burn, then touching the lips, opening them wider, keeping them moving, keeping her clitoris aroused, then laying his middle finger along the line of gathered skin that led up to her anus.

Philip left Justine stretched; even from across the room, he could see her pubic lips individually protruding into the gap below the red diagonal marks across her belly. The young woman on the bed sank down on her heels and became very frightened and still. Philip still ignored her. He lifted the stool on to Justine's table, then walked round the bed and began to search. He found what he was looking for in the same drawer in which the crop was hidden and he took it to the bathroom. He returned with the wetted and oiled lawn chemise, tightly folded now and wrapped around itself to form a padded ball about the size of his fist. He placed it in the centre of the stool, then pushed the stool towards Justine. She whimpered as he made her rise. When he lowered her, the padding pressed against her open cunt. The surface of the padding had been oiled; it would cling to her and the oil would squeeze out slowly as the weight of her body pressed. He left her, stretched and aching, and took the strap to the girl on the bed.

All her fears having suddenly crystallised together, Roxanne burst into tears before he even touched her, thus giving strength to his hand – and oh, how she reminded him of Charlotte. He pushed her out on to her belly and knelt on the bed beside her and smacked her till her buttocks bounced. The small bed sagged with the strain of his exertions. Roxanne sobbed loudly, but he kept smacking – and in a way she was like Charlotte – because she never really moved to stop him or to get away from the blows that he dealt. He pulled her on to his lap to smack her; she cried feebly, but he never lessened the strength of those smacks upon her naked skin. She tried to keep her bottom cheeks together; it made no difference. He kept smacking her till the muscles of her bottom had lost the will to resist and her legs fell limp, her knees slightly open, the cheeks of her bottom apart. Only then did Philip put down the strap. When he turned Roxanne to face him, her cheeks were running wet with tears. He placed his left hand palm-uppermost on the bed and nodded. Roxanne laid her cheek upon it. He moved aside the strands of hair which had become wet. He touched her nipples, crooking his forefinger and rubbing it upwards underneath them, as if they amused him with their pertness, as if they were his toys. Then he played with the dark hair under her arm, curling it round his fingers. He whispered to her and she began to cry again, but she turned over. There were deep red marks across her buttocks, separated by the deeply incised gap. He took the strap and smacked the marks again, not spreading the pain, of course, but smacking the same marks.

On the table, Justine shuddered, because she knew that pain. Witnessing it made Justine's cunny throb and stretch against the tight wet ball of cloth. Again the smacking

144

continued until the cheeks of the bottom fell open, unre-sisting.

Philip put the strap down again and touched the place between the cheeks, which he was holding open with one hand. The sobs immediately stopped. He touched the place that Justine's tongue had tasted. He stroked it with his middle finger. Justine watched the girl in tension; she watched the middle finger stiffen, the girl murmur, then the middle finger slide inside. Philip whispered to the girl again; she edged her legs apart and the middle finger slid in to the knuckle. The other hand released the cheeks and began to pinch the places that were marked by the strap. The girl began to sob very quietly. Philip whispered to her, turned her head until she faced him, then continued the pinching, working systematically across the welts, from the outside towards the join between the cheeks, where his middle finger was buried, but pausing when he reached some particularly sensitive part of punished skin and there pinching the flesh minutely before proceeding any further. Her legs began to squirm. Her feet wriggled their protest as much as they dared, but he seemed to be identifying the parts of the cheeks that were the most sensitive of all. Then he pinched these while he masturbated her. He had to take his finger out in order to be able to do the two things at the same time. But he used something – he put something into her – to keep her bottom open.

Seeing him do this, hearing the girl, watching the way she moved, caused a funny feeling in Justine's belly. It made her feel very strange inside to see him do this to the girl, and it made her think of Rachel. It made her press her cunny down against the round pad on the stool, making it stretch her, making it hurt. *Beg me to hurt you* – Rachel used to say to her. *Beg me to make you come*. It made the feelings come now, in her bottom, the awful sensations that Rachel would induce with the things she would put inside Justine before making love to her, to make the climax so intense that she would think that she was drowning. She had never had the feelings come as intensely since those times with Rachel. But the memories of them were vivid

145

as she watched the girl on the bed being stretched and pinched and masturbated.

Philip seemed to want the girl to keep still, with her body limp and this thing inside her, holding her open. She was trying to breathe shallowly; her arms did stay limp, but when her fingers tried to grip the sheet, he stopped what he was doing and waited until they loosened. When her toes began to curl, he explained to her that he did not want this to happen. After that, the only sounds she made were tiny whimpers. Philip was propped against the head of the bed and the girl was across his knee. When she began to shudder, he lifted her leg, so her cunny pulsed freely against the air, and he teased the thing that protruded from inside her anus. Then he lowered her leg again and continued the pinching. He lifted the leg four times that Justine counted, before the girl could bear no more and climaxed with her leg in the air and the object holding her anus open being turned. Philip took her quickly; he didn't bother undressing, or taking the object out of her and it made her moan when he entered.

When he had done, he came to the table and looked at Justine. Then he lifted her carefully up and took the stool away. Between her legs, the oiled pad adhered to her open lips. He eased it away from them and placed it on the table. Then he dragged the table aside. It was heavy and would only move gradually. Justine, still fastened to the ceiling, had to edge sideways on her knees. One knee slipped over the edge; he kept pulling, determined to take the support away. Her leg dropped down; her toes touched the floor but her arms ached from the stretching. The table slid away; her other leg dropped and she was balanced on her toes, her arms still aching. She had to take tiny steps to bring her feet in line with the axis of her body. Even then, her heels could not reach the floor. Philip watched her teetering gyrations. He came close to her. Stretched, she could not move; she was balanced on the balls of her feet; the muscles in her arms were burning, aching. He came so close that his jacket brushed against her nipples. But where he touched her was under her arms, in the soft damp hair.

Then he walked around behind her. She felt a fingertip tickle the small of her back, and a booted toe separating her feet, which edged stiffly apart, arching up, making the muscles of her thighs stand out and the divide of her buttocks steepen. The tip of the finger stroked across the mouth of her bottom. 'Open it, relax the muscle.'

Justine gasped: she felt something smooth and round being pressed against her, probing. Then it was taken away. The fingertip tickled her anus again, then the smooth thing returned, wet and slippy now.

'Shh . . .'

'Ahh!' Her bottom could not resist the pressure. It opened her. At the same instant, something metallic slipped between her legs. It felt like stiff wire. When he touched the wire, the thing inside her anus moved; they were connected. He pushed the thing in deeper; the muscle of her anus gripped it. The wire was in a narrow loop which curved up to press against her labia. Philip stretched it open and pulled her labia through it. When he released the spring, it gripped her. It squeezed the lips together and made her clitoris stand out. When he touched her, she contracted; her contraction moved the lips, the anus and the wire as one. Then he left her, hanging, aching, sexually aroused with this thing inside her anus and gripped about her cunny, while he took the girl for a long hot bath.

When they returned, he put the girl on the bed and played with her, then left her with her breasts partially covered but her legs open and bare while he sat in the armchair and watched Justine. He moved the chair closer, then directly beneath her. He allowed her to kneel on the arms of the chair while he sat in it and examined her while she was aroused. He wetted the swollen edges of her labia projecting through the clip, then touched her where the instrument kept her open, in the crease of her bottom, permitting the contractions of her anus to bring about the stimulation of her clitoris through the medium of the wire. When her clitoris began to throb, he touched it with the underside of his tongue, allowing this to press against her labia and touch her clitoris, tip to tip, until her climax was

147

almost delivered. But at the very last second, he steadied the wire and said: 'Wait . . .' And he kept teasing her clitoris as he slid underneath her and out between her legs. Then he spanked her with the device still in place – toying with her cunny lips and spanking – until her climax came. When he put her to bed, she slept, exhausted, in the girl's arms while he covered himself with a blanket and watched them from the chair. In the morning, he took the girl away.

Late the next night, Philip returned without Roxanne. He suspended Justine by her wrists again and fitted the device. He played with her more slowly. When she was aroused, he went to bed, setting the alarm, declaring he would check her every hour. After the first time, he found that she was very excited when he came to kiss her – that she was already trembling and that the wire was wet. But then he did not wake again until several hours had passed. Justine seemed asleep and her body was stone cold. He took her down and rubbed her wrists and put her to bed and warmed her with his own body. When she came round, she behaved very strangely, whispering to him incoherently, touching him, wanting him to hold her tightly, kissing him demandingly, making him aroused. The following morning, she did not want him to go. The same urgent need was in her. And where her breasts pressed against him, their points seemed thick and soft; they laid a tender trail upon his chest. He kissed her nipples, licked them clean, and she wanted to be penetrated, wanted to be fucked. He turned her round and took her from behind and she climaxed quickly when he rubbed her clitoris and pumped her nipples.

Afterwards, Philip told Justine: 'I have had a telephone call from Julia: it seems a lady wishes to borrow you.' Then he explained – that the lady had said she would want to treat Justine cruelly, and that he had acceded to this request.

12: THE MARE IN HARNESS

The rising scent of soft sweet hay mixed with the warm pungency that drifted up from the stalls where the horses sighed and gently pawed dulled thuds into the deep-littered earth floor of the stables. Celia had wanted hay up here – away from the doors and the snow and close to the stove and pipework – because straw would have been too harsh against the knees and the sensitive skin of the breasts protruding through the open loops of the thin leather halter. For that skin and the nude belly skin and the thighs, there was reserved this different spread and intensity of harshness, which Celia now delivered while the other three looked on, and the deliciously perfect girl – Justine – writhed upon the yielding heap of hay. Her body was twisting sweetly, her slim limbs catching the softened light, the rapid smacks of the short leather crop causing raised heads, anxious eyes, flared nostrils. The long rein that secured her prostrate body to the post snaked in quick whiplashes through the green-dry strands of grass hay as her slenderness tried to spin frantically back and forth while Celia calculatingly followed every little movement – smacking sharply but always waiting for the breasts to show, smacking them while Justine lay upon her back or on her side. Then, while she lay upon her belly, she smacked ever more deeply into the crease of her naked buttocks, until the area around the pole was a circle swept smooth, with the hay strands combed out by those tantalising gyrations, and Justine's breasts were leather-reddened but her belly was milk-white and the gap between her buttocks felt burning hot when Celia touched it. And Justine's mouth stayed open as she gulped for breath – her lips looked red and thick and dry because of all this excitement, all this luscious effort, all this sexual need – and the tears slid in smooth, unconditional surrender down her cheeks.

'Elizabeth,' said Celia, and once again, Elizabeth came and bent over the girl and kissed her and the girl's full lips took Elizabeth's cool lips frantically. Her arms tried to lift as if to take Elizabeth, to wrap around her and to love her, but they could not, because her wrists were tethered and her arms were stretched and Elizabeth only offered her lips tentatively, while the young girl was straining to keep her head lifted. The muscles of her arms were tight, her underarms were bulging. James, standing next to the pole, could smell that underarm scent above the hay, above all else – unperfumed, driving-strong – and he shuddered when Elizabeth lifted her lips away from the trembling face and gently kissed the round bulge of soft wet underarm hair that Justine offered, with her shoulders tightly back and her eyes now closed in a lassitude as sweetly heavy as if the kissing of that warm place were a drug.

Then Celia, creeping up to James, touched him. She traced the line of his cock down the left side of his trousers and to the upraised, straining tip. She did this while her husband, Robin, stood across from her and leaned against the wooden stall. But Robin was watching the girl – and waiting his turn. It would come soon, but that decision was for Elizabeth. Celia's fingertips found the form of the cap of James's cock and held it. Her fingertips, through the material, were cool against its warmth. The tip of her second finger found the small mouth and pushed against it to keep it open. Celia waited.

Elizabeth, skirtless and astride the girl's body, gradually moved up. Her opalescent stockings slid palely against the perfect skin. Her knees touched the striped, weighted redness of the punished, haltered breasts, which lifted slightly, turning, so the nipples shone with their overextension, which Elizabeth now encouraged by gentle flat-handed pressure and wetted fingertip squeezing. She continued until the nipples responded by a more secure and visible erection through the shiny film of spittle which Elizabeth carefully distributed in smoothly flowing spiral patterns into the down-covered surrounds, making the breasts appear to have been kissed by wet, pushing lips or dipped in thin milk which had clung to the soft blonde skin hairs. Elizabeth left this film to dry and, spreading her legs, moved up.

Celia, on her knees before James, touched him, teasing the opening, pressing the tip of her finger against it through the cloth and rotating, sending tiny rubbing, buzzing feelings to the inner skin as James watched his wife preparing to kiss Justine with the stretched soft cloth, the warm thin cloth of the knickered lips pouting down between Elizabeth's legs – split fullness through the thin material, straining to be kissed. He watched Justine taking them open-mouthed and trying to swallow them through the knickers, and Elizabeth's belly shuddering from the sucking drawing touch, then the split bulge of the crotch left dark with wet, but the tongue pushing out again and up and entering the open cotton-covered sac – as the fingertip touched the inside of the mouth of James's cock through the cloth of James's trousers until the fingertip, too, encountered wetness.

Then Celia left James leaning against the waist-high pole, with the cloth cupped into the tiny hollow of this tender inner skin, sticking there, pulling downwards, while she slipped Elizabeth's knickers gently to her knees and drew the thin wet gusset back. She held it and she pushed Elizabeth down until her pouted, naked sexual lips were taken by Justine, who sucked and licked and nuzzled the weeping wet until Elizabeth whimpered. Celia used one hand to free the hooks of Elizabeth's brassiere. She ran her fingers underneath it then up and over Elizabeth's nipples, which were larger and darker than James had ever seen them. Celia stretched them, then moved her hand down and under. Elizabeth lifted and Celia's fingers entered her. She looked at James. The hand between Elizabeth's legs continued moving, continued probing, opening Elizabeth, progressing deeper. Small gentle whimpers issued from Elizabeth's lips; her belly rippled as the muscles tried to relax; her breasts hung down; her cunt lips opened to the hand; the reaching tongue beneath her licked and kissed the back of the hand, which withdrew shiny, with a small thin streak of whiteness between fingers that were tightly bunched together.

Celia stood up. She carried the hand as if it were coated with the preciousness of life. She made Robin kneel, then she fed this precious oil to him, and he sucked upon it greedily while Celia's booted toe rubbed up and down his inside leg. Celia turned. Elizabeth, open-legged, lay upon Justine. Celia reminded her that it was time again for the leather. Her toe left Robin's leg and edged across the floor. 'It is time for you to smack her cunt,' said Celia, toeing the brass-ferruled handle of the strap, but watching James's eyes. 'Smack it – make it red, Elizabeth. Redden her up for your man,' said Celia, glancing at the pulsing bulge still trapped inside James's trousers.

Then Celia came across and caressed the cone of his cock and carefully pulled the stuck material free. 'May I take it out?' Celia murmured. 'May I take him out, Elizabeth – and drink his gorgeous prick?' Elizabeth smiled like a cat. She picked up the beautiful instrument that Celia had had crafted for Justine. She stroked its dense brass ferrules and its fan of smooth, tawny leather. 'Smack it, my dear, then oil it – then smack it again,' said Celia.

The trousers fell away; Celia felt the bare warm cock bob upwards and strike the curve of her waiting hand. 'While I suck this gorgeous fucker – shhh . . .' she whispered. 'Mmmm . . . It's so hot and thick and . . . Mmmm . . .' she murmured, edging him over, steadying his buttocks against the pole, allowing the cheeks to spread. 'Uummm . . . Stay still – let them open. Mmmmmm.' Celia sucked him, trapped against the pole, as Justine writhed on her back at the end of the long rein while Elizabeth smacked her naked cunny, which Elizabeth kept exposed. She wanted every smack to land there; she wanted no leg or thigh to get in the way, no swing of her arm to be stilted; she wanted that cunt to be precisely and brightly reddened and to smack it until it throbbed and burned with ungratified sexual need.

James saw Elizabeth's breasts shake every time she smacked the leather down; he saw Justine's belly jumping. He saw Elizabeth take the slender feet and push them back and round until the smacked lips pushed out, red, so Elizabeth could smack across them from the side. And he felt the head of his cock slipping deeper down Celia's throat and the tips of Celia's fingers probing up into the seatings of his balls until he felt the urge to spurt against the back of Celia's throat.

But Celia left him bobbing and she sprawled across the hay to Justine. 'Robin!' she cried and she kissed Justine's mouth and lifted one of Justine's legs open while Elizabeth held the other and Justine's bottom was lifted off the hay, with Celia holding the leg up through the smacks and kissing the sweet mouth through the whimpers – 'Robin!'

She made her husband kneel above Justine and offer his cock for her lips to drink. She told him not to come – to hold it in whatever Justine did. Then she supported Justine's head and stroked the front of her neck as if it were an extension of his cock. Her hand moved up and down it, controlling it, stroking it, stimulating the reflex to swallow, then kissing Justine where the shaft entered and lifting Justine's head back so the cock could slip deeper and be absorbed. And during this time, Elizabeth stopped the smacking and she opened Justine's pubic lips. She found that the flesh inside was almost cooler than that outside, and the colour was no different, though the flesh inside was coated with a scented wet that made her want to drink. She explored it with her fingers and she touched the small red knob. Justine was breathing fiercely through her nose; the muscles in her neck moved strongly; Celia coaxed them with her fingers. Robin started to groan and plead, and Celia relented. She eased his cock from Justine's mouth and asked him to pass her the birch, which she would use upon him most severely.

She made him kneel across the low pole and she secured him there, with the smooth wood pressed below his chubby belly, and his arms stretched out with the wrists strapped down, so that, should he choose to lift his head, he could see Justine, whom Elizabeth had turned upon her side to face him while she masturbated her slowly with an oiled, sponge-coated dildo, which Elizabeth slipped into the entrance of her vulva from behind. Celia touched Robin's short, stubby, downturned cock which throbbed against the polished wood. She slid her hand around it and squeezed. She pressed the flexible tip of the birch across the entrance to his bottom then opened the cheeks and whipped it once, then left him for a little while to contemplate his fate.

She asked Elizabeth for a special favour with regard to her husband James. She said it in a whisper that he could hear. 'I would like to finger-fuck him – to try to make him come through penetration,' Celia said. 'I understand it works with some men – provided they are kept restrained.'

Elizabeth slowly nodded, but her eyes never left Justine: she was watching Justine's belly moving as the dildo was gradually introduced, and the oil was expressed against the red, gripping lips of Justine's swollen cunny and ran down her inside leg towards the hay. James did not move while Celia finished stripping him – he could not move; there was a buzzing in his ears and a fluttering in the pit of his stomach and below. Celia reassured his cock with gentle pressure between her fingertip and thumb, slight pressures which she kept repeating. She showed him the two fingers she would use. She whispered to him, 'Kneel down. I shall fuck you and you will come.'

She stroked his nipples, then touched his cock, then pressed her fingertips to the sides of his sac, high up against the creases. She made him kneel with his back to the upright pole. Then she bound each wrist individually in front and drew the ropes down between his legs and fastened them behind him to rings attached halfway down the pole. When she pulled his knees forwards, he teetered. His legs were spread and his cock and the balls beneath were trapped between his wrists. His cock had never softened since the first smack had resounded from the tightness of

Justine's breasts. And it did not soften now, because nothing would let it: not Celia, not Justine, not Elizabeth, who had left the dildo in Justine – with its fat ball-sac filling out the space between her legs, which could not fully close when her knees were tied together – and had now rolled her on to her belly, so the balls protruded behind her, invitingly, so that anyone free to grasp might tug the smooth oiled dildo out of her. But those who had the strongest urge to do it were tied. The restraint only made the urge come even stronger.

'James – you are sweating,' whispered Celia. She licked the droplets from James's chest while Elizabeth smacked Justine, smacking the place above the balls that were squeezed between the legs, that is, smacking the buttocks, with her bare hand dropping quickly to make the buttocks bounce. Then Elizabeth slipped one hand down between the tied-together legs and under Justine and smacked again with the other hand and everyone stopped breathing, because they were listening for the sounds – between the smacks – that would tell what Elizabeth's fingers were doing to Justine. And those sounds came: they were rending pulses of shattered breath from deep within an open gentle throat – like the warm soft breath that comes against your belly when she comes the first time, with your cock inside her open mouth, and you are straining to hold because you know that if you keep kissing her in that place she will come again and then she will be so very soft inside when finally you enter.

Celia leisurely oiled her fingers until the oil ran down between them and over her palm. James was straining. He was tense, so tense, when Celia moved behind him. Justine was on her back. There were strands of hay between her legs and stuck upon her nipples; her lips were trembling, her back was arching, offering her breasts up as Elizabeth pulled the sticking strands away. And with every little pull, Justine's nipples lifted.

Suddenly, James groaned and Elizabeth stopped and looked at him. 'Shhh . . .' said Celia. Her wrist moved; James shuddered and moaned. Robin moved uneasily.

Elizabeth's fingertips wavered, stroked the slightly sticky nipples, then moved up to her mouth. James gasped. His cock throbbed as if its core were filled with a curving stick of wood that Celia directed upwards from behind. But she did not touch it. She touched him from inside. 'Shhh . . . He is unused to this, Elizabeth. But that is better – it comes quickly. See . . .' While Elizabeth began again to masturbate Justine, she watched him. James's knees were moving apart. The tips of Celia's fingers touched the place inside him and they pressed. His knees jerked outwards; his back arched down; his cock thrust out and swelled. 'Shhh . . .' said Celia. 'I can't touch it; it must come this way, from the penetration. Open. Open it . . . Shhh . . .' Her fingertips slid freely, rubbing, pushing downwards through the rim. Then the tips of her fingers touched again, and a low deep moan issued from his throat and his cock pulsed in the air. 'We are there.' Celia nodded softly. 'We are there . . .' Her fingertips stayed there, pressing faintly, deep inside him, all the long while that he spurted. 'Ohhh,' she whispered, touching his nipples. 'Oh, you poor thing, and so much that you have been saving up, so much to be thrown so far away . . . What a gorgeous, fucking waste.' And she pressed her fingertips against him until the last yield of his semen had slid down the underside of the shaft. 'And now, to deal with Robin.'

She held Robin's cock while she caned him; she kept it pointing down. When he was near, she pushed his foreskin back and held it so it could not move and nothing touched it other than her fingertips pulling it back towards the base and when his climax came it seemed to hurt him; it seemed difficult for the semen to spurt and afterwards, the cock stayed rigidly hard as if there had been no satisfaction. Celia left him tied.

'And now, gentlemen, I fear the ladies require their privacy,' she said. 'Elizabeth – we shall take her into the large stall. We shall need the footmen to assist.'

'Quiet . . .' whispered Celia, placing her finger to her lips and opening the door. Elizabeth craned her neck and stared inside; there was a movement in the straw. 'She is

156

frightened,' said Celia. Elizabeth's mouth fell open when she saw the eyes appear above the blanket. 'Oh, and she has waited so patiently.' Celia tiptoed in. 'She has waited here for love. And we are here to love you. Shhh, my sweet . . .' Celia lifted the horse blanket back. 'Is she not sweet, Elizabeth? Is she not freckled?'

She had hair that was long and fine and pale orange-red, that flowed through Celia's fingers. She had breasts that were small and cuspate; they reached out to concave pin-points long after they were touched; they had the resilience of hard jelly beneath yielding skin. Between her thighs were soft white clinging panties, and within these, orange curls which Celia pointed out and stroked.

Elizabeth never learned her name; Celia never told her and Elizabeth never asked. She only spoke when Celia insisted that she wanted to know what the young woman was feeling – whether it was hurting her, whether she might come. Celia only seemed to ask these things to tantalise Justine.

At the start, Celia said: 'She is here for you, Justine.' And although she was never allowed to touch the girl, Justine was to be able to see what they were doing to her, and those sights, and the soft interrogations, would keep her wet. They reminded her of the things that Rachel used to do to the other young women while Justine was forced to watch.

And it helped so much – it made it sweet – that Justine was now to be restrained. She was to be fastened to the wall, on the wall, in fact – Celia showed her the three hooks. And she explained that Justine would witness all that happened between the two older women and the younger, who was tethered by a single long leash attached to her ankle. It made Justine excited, that she and the girl were to remain tied, and the women were free to touch them where they liked.

Celia now instructed the footmen to lift Justine and hold her legs open. In Celia's hand was the flat strap that she had had made for punishing Justine's cunny. Celia toyed with the brass rings set into the polished leather handle.

One by one, she pushed them through the circular hole that she had formed with her forefinger and thumb and Justine's legs automatically tried to close but the footmen held her open. They held her only by her thighs so Justine's belly trembled as she tried to balance while she faced the two women. She saw the young woman watching from the shelter of her blanket.

Elizabeth began admiring Celia's footmen. 'So tall, such long legs.' She nervously touched.

Celia using the soft lint cloth to wipe the oil from Justine's cunny, whispered, 'I'll lend you one if you like, Elizabeth.'

'I'd like to borrow both.'

'Shh! What if your husband should hear you?'

'Celia – I should require my husband to watch.'

'Elizabeth!'

And a response was elicited from the footmen. Elizabeth gently stroked them. 'So big,' she whispered. Then she stared wide-eyed at Celia. 'Would my feet ever touch the ground?'

Celia smiled. 'My darling – later: we are here to please Justine.' And she instructed the footmen, who twisted Justine's legs open until the place between them bulged. Celia wiped it with the cloth until it opened; then she wiped inside. Elizabeth moved behind and continued to touch the men, but Celia kept looking over her shoulder and watching the girl, who had crouched into the shelter of her blanket, so the only parts of her that projected were her tethered foot, her freckled face with its large brown eyes, and the tightly pinched trembling cusps of her nipples. 'Is not the process of learning sweet?' asked Celia.

Elizabeth did not reply; she was trying to extricate a hard shaft of pink from the narrow slit that she had opened in one pair of trousers. Then she slid her fingers underneath and levered out the sac, which swelled and shone from the pressure of confinement. Celia waited until Elizabeth had completed the same operation at the other side. 'Now, we can compare the two,' said Elizabeth. She did not touch them further. Nevertheless, they continued swelling

158

through their narrow constrictions – as Elizabeth observed, 'Like forcemeat through a sausage' – while Celia smacked Justine.

'Keep her knees open. Keep her cunny lifted. There!' Her arm swung down. Justine's belly lifted. *Crack!* 'Her hairs get in the way; they soften it.' But it did not seem so to Justine. *Crack!* Her labia were on fire. 'Keep her still.' *Crack!* 'Did you see it? Oh, Elizabeth, did you see it?' *Crack!* 'Watch.' *Crack!* 'She's letting down. Oh, my dearest fucking darling . . . It's as if she's giving milk.' And Celia touched Justine between the legs and Justine shuddered and her clitoris pulsed like a nipple being squeezed as Celia smacked her over and over again, and through Celia's searching fingertips ran an opalescent liquid with the consistency of milk.

Justine was slumped, her legs wide open, her cunny pushed forward, punished, burning. 'We must keep it coming, Elizabeth, keep her on. Get me the cloth, my dear.' Celia kissed Justine's belly while Justine was so aroused. She slipped her finger under, and up and down the groove of Justine's spine. 'We have so much to do to you, Justine,' she whispered. She crumpled the cloth and inserted it, gently working it in until Justine's labia were held apart by the bulge of cloth between them. Then she instructed her footmen: 'Put her on the wall.' The men moved stiffly. There were three hooks – one high up, to which her wrists were tied, and two large projecting padded ones lower down. These latter hooks were spaced widely apart. Her legs were draped over them. She was to be supported at these three points only: at her wrists and behind her knees. When the footmen moved away, her back slid by stages down the wall. She murmured as the tension in her arms and legs increased. 'Shhh . . .' said Celia gently.

Elizabeth watched the thick cocks pulse and harden as Justine's belly curved, and the weight of her body gradually stretched her open until the hollows of her arms became bulges and the muscles of her thighs stood out. When the hooks had locked under the bends of her knees, her body could move no further. 'Another cloth,' said Celia. She shook it, crumpled it and slowly inserted it beside the other until the lips of the cunny seemed so stretched apart that they would never again be able to close. Then Celia dismissed the men, saying, 'Madam Elizabeth will require the services of both of you tonight.' She turned to the blanketed girl. 'Elizabeth – shall we begin the lesson?'

They brought James in to witness it and they made certain he was firmly tied. 'It will give him strength, my dear, for tonight,' said Celia. They took away the girl's blanket and moved her as far out from the opposing wall as the tether round her ankle would permit. Elizabeth lifted her to her knees and knelt behind her. The girl was able to lean back against Elizabeth while Celia attended to her. At first the girl was stiff from fright and her body was unwilling to cede itself to pleasure. But gradually, she was rendered pliant. In between times, Celia paused to masturbate James – touching him only until he started to move against her hand – and to punish Justine. All of these things were part of Celia's lesson to the girl – that she might become aware not only of the immediate pleasure, but also of the pleasures that reside in prolonged attention during arousal, the pleasures of curtailment and of weepage and of gently pricking need.

Celia returned to the girl. She slipped her cupped hand down the front of the soft white panties. She watched her fingers moving, gently stroking, through the thin cotton, the tips of her fingers grazing the warmth of the closed bare lips and tickling the orange curls round the narrow crotch. The girl was yielding; Celia could see it as a lazy glazing of her sweet brown eyes; she could taste it in her thickening nipples. Celia's hand reached down and under and the girl shuddered with the shock. Celia lifted up her chin and kissed her as the tip of her middle finger pressed against the small warm cup of her anus. She kept kissing, and gently pressing, and when her hand withdrew, the eyes that looked so pleadingly upon her were as black as liquid night.

There was a low murmur from Justine. 'Elizabeth, hold this one. Just hold her. Put your hand here. Slip it down

her panties. Now hold it. Save it for me. Keep it warm.'
The young woman gently gasped, then sighed as the curves
of Elizabeth's slender fingers were outlined through her
knickers. Celia moved across to give attention to Justine.

She took the strap and used it. *Smack!* 'Look at me,
Justine.' She touched her chin; she smacked again; Justine's
belly lifted. 'Let it down,' Celia whispered. *Smack!* The
strap kept falling between her legs. 'It must come; let it
down. So full – it must be hurting.' She touched each waxy
nipple and rolled it. *Smack!* She traced the centre line of
Justine's belly. 'Feel it running down inside you.' The
fingertips gently stimulated Justine's clitoris. *Smack!*
'There . . . Oh – *there*. Oh, God – Elizabeth, see it running.' Justine moaned; the milkiness was exuded; the cloth
inside her cunt was wet. She wanted Celia to lift her belly
from the wall and suck her. But Celia only watched the
liquid welling from Justine. Below the bright red pubic lips
was the narrow string of skin, which Celia now took hold
of while she smacked the cunt so comprehensively that,
several times, the leather stung her fingers. But she was
fascinated, because accompanying every smack was a tiny
throbbing spurt of liquid from between the open lips. Celia
watched this a few more times, then joined Elizabeth and
the girl.

They tried to locate the girl's clitoris through the material
of her knickers; they demonstrated her shape to James
through the stretched, thin cotton sheathing; they held it
tight against her till it moistened, dark at first, then lighter
as the colour of her skin showed pink. Then the clitoris
appeared as a tiny bump. Celia nibbled it through the
knickers while Elizabeth played with the girl's nipples.
Then they made her kneel. They folded the knickers down:
the loosened waistband dangled at the back; at the front,
the thin wet gusset clung. Neither woman freed it. They
kept her kneeling with her legs slightly apart and the
material of the waistband tickling the backs of her thighs
while they kissed her back and belly and Elizabeth's fingers
roved across her buttocks and slipped into the crease. The
girl murmured into Celia's mouth while Elizabeth's finger

smoothed across the warm dry lip of the well, debauching its innocence slowly, until the wetted knickers dropped to the knees.

'Oh,' said Celia. 'Ohhhh . . .' The girl sank backwards on her knees against Elizabeth, and Celia's mouth moved downwards, over her breasts, over her belly, to take her between the legs. 'Her beestings, Elizabeth. Oh, they taste like honey.' And as the nude round belly pushed itself to suckle, beneath it, deep between the open cheeks, the smooth light strokes of Elizabeth's fingers took every last nerve of innocence from the warm brown mouth – gently brushing it, teasing it and kissing – until the small hot cunny came in stabbing wet pulsations that seemed to reach for Celia's throat.

Then Celia arose. 'It is your turn now, Justine.' The streams of drying liquid had formed sinuous glazed lines running down from Justine's cunny. The cloths between her legs were fully wet. Celia touched her wetness with the handle of the strap; she coated the round, polished tip. She showed Justine the three thick brass inlaid rings so conveniently spaced for gripping between the fingers: the rings increased in size progressively from the tip. Then she took hold of the narrow string of skin between Justine's cunny and her anus. She placed the wetted tip of the handle firmly to the mouth of her anus. She moved it gently. Then she suddenly nipped the string of skin. Justine's anus tightened; Celia thrust the rod. Justine whimpered as it entered to the first and narrowest ring. 'Steadily . . .' Celia nipped again, Justine tightened, Celia thrust and the ring entered. Celia used this procedure – nipping the skin, then forcing the ring through against the cramping tightness – until the widest ring was set in place and the strap hung freely below Justine, supported by the muscle of her anus, which closed, below the widest projecting ring of brass, around the smoothly polished handle.

Then Celia pulled the saturated cloths out of Justine but held her labia open and masturbated her to the verge of climax. Then she twisted the handle of the strap until it moved, and she masturbated her again. She kept masturbating her and stopping, then twisting the handle, until the point was reached where Justine's anus was in spasm and the handle would not move. At this point, Celia wetted her palm and smacked Justine between the legs and pulled firmly down upon the handle of the strap and Justine came. Celia left the handle inside her.

It was still inside her an hour later, when the girl's discarded knickers lay threaded on the tethering rope that was still fastened to her ankle, and James's semen glistened across the girl's toes, which Celia had now taken up to suck because it was Elizabeth's turn to masturbate Justine and to keep her on, by alternating the masturbation with the smacking, until that evening, when Justine would be stretched more fully.

Elizabeth was restive in the night because it seemed that Celia would never come for her, although it had been promised. 'I want it, I want it so,' she whispered. James stroked her naked body. When he kissed her nipples, Elizabeth became excited and whispered to James that she loved him and that he was so good to her. Elizabeth was crying when Celia crept in through the door; James tasted the salt tears on Elizabeth's lips, then Celia led her away. He lay on the bed, listening, hearing no sound, but counting the minutes, and tasting the bittersweet imaginings – the surges of arousal and the drain of jealous fear. But his penis was rock hard when Celia returned.

'She wants you to witness it,' she said to him. 'It will make her pleasure sweeter if you watch but take no part.'

She allowed him to take his robe. She led him along the landing and up the stairs. The door of the bedroom was ajar and he could hear Elizabeth's shaking whispers and the murmurs of the men. Celia put her finger to his lips; she ushered him in. But nobody had noticed either of them.

The first thing that he saw was the young woman on the end of the bed. Then below her he saw Justine, her breasts still in their harness. She was spreadeagled, face-down, tied by her hands and feet. Robin stood beside the bed. Elizabeth was across the room, kneeling up on a cushioned box.

The two footmen were with her. Everyone was nude, but for Justine in her harness and the young woman in her pure white panties. Her orange-red hair had been brushed until it glistened. She was crouching between Justine's thighs and reaching underneath, manipulating something curved and curling, some narrow flexible coiling object, which she was introducing into Justine's cunny while Robin directed her by stealthy whispers. Every so often she would stop and spread apart the pubic bulge and Justine would moan and Robin would whisper, then Justine would arch her back downwards, which would lift her cunny very slightly and the insertion would progress. The young woman's hips moved with the intricacies of this slow insertion; each time she bent forwards, her small jellied breasts were drawn to points and the tight cheeks of her buttocks were outlined through the clinging cotton panties.

Celia nodded to Robin. He suspended the operation on Justine by picking the girl up; James saw that she had reached up and put her arms around Robin's neck to facilitate the lifting. Then Robin carried her to the armchair and lowered her; her small tight cotton-covered buttocks sank into the ample pink bowl of Robin's lap. Her cheek pressed against his chest; her fingers moved across the dense curls and tickled Robin's nipples.

Celia led James across and sat him on the bed, next to Justine. When his dressing gown fell open, he attempted to cover his erection. Celia smiled. She lifted the robe aside and touched him, and she turned his head so he was looking at Justine. Between her legs was the fine tubular twitching coil that resembled an open spring. 'A catheter,' whispered Celia. 'Shhh . . .' She put her finger to her lips. 'Only a little way – but it excites her. It takes away her self control and delivers it to me.' Celia's eyes were wide and black as she looked at him. 'Did you like it with my fingers up inside you, James? Ohh, but I can do exquisite things to make you come . . . and to prevent it.' She wrapped two fingers round the most sensitive part of his cock and let them slide down under the weight of her hand. She held him while she spread open the cheeks of Justine's bottom.

The anus looked distended and reddened. 'Would you like it, James?' Her hand slid up, her fingers formed a cone and pushed down and the head of James's cock pulsed. 'Would you like to go inside it – with this?'

Justine moaned. Celia, still holding Justine's anus open, now released James and reached under Justine to grip the narrow tube and push. Justine gasped and James shivered. 'Shhh . . .' A pulse of liquid spiralled down the tube and leaked from the end before Celia retracted the tube enough to make the flow stop. 'Oh, she wants it dearly, doesn't she? Mmmm . . . And would you believe it, James? Julia told me that this was what Justine's teacher used to do.' Her finger and thumb jerked open; for a second, the anus formed a dark well which suddenly nipped shut again because the fingers were not holding it. 'And this is why she likes it, isn't it, Justine? Would you like to go inside her – push it up her, let her nip your tip? There.' Justine whimpered as Celia touched and stretched the reddened rim. 'Oh, but look, James, see how your Elizabeth is getting it. Mmmm . . .' When he turned, Celia's lips descended to close around the cap of his cock and suck it.

His wife was kneeling, nude, on the cushioned box between the two young footmen, one at her front, the other behind her. Both men were naked and erect. The one in front held a round ruby-coloured glass flask which glowed in the light. He glanced at James; Elizabeth's eyes followed; James felt the sweet surge of arousal. Her eyes looked frightened and excited. The young man took her chin and turned her head back and now her head stayed still, looking at the man who stared into her eyes while James burned. His pulse raced. Celia sat up and looped her fingers round the wet head of his cock. She whispered: 'She must do as they say – that is the condition. She cannot change her mind now.' Celia turned James's head and looked at him. 'They can do anything that they care to, James, anything they like.' Celia took his fingertips and placed them on Justine. Her back was warm, her skin very smooth and naked.

Elizabeth moaned. The man behind her was supporting

her. The one in front withdrew his hand from between her thighs then rubbed it up and down his rigid cock, which shone with the smeared-out liquid. Then he refilled his hand from the flask. Elizabeth, her breathing coming quickly, turned her head away. Again her chin was held, then the hand was reapplied; Elizabeth's legs stiffened, her breasts shook, the cupped hand moved, making tiny squelching sounds as the creamy liquid extruded between his fingers and dripped to the cushioned seat.

'Giving and receiving, James – is not pleasure sweet?' murmured Celia. The flask was passed to the man behind. He whispered to Elizabeth while the lotion spilled into his hand. Elizabeth tensed again; she glanced at James before her head was turned to face the front. Then her hands slid down her buttocks. The man in front of her held her chin up while he masturbated her, but even while she was gasping with the slowly mounting pleasure, her slender hands were behind her spreading apart her cheeks. Celia drew James's fingers down Justine; she placed the tip of the middle one on Justine's anus, which felt hot and clung to his skin. Elizabeth kept shuddering, but her fingertips kept the cheeks wide open while the hand from behind moved smoothly, reaching down and underneath her, slowly probing each critical point from her cunt to the tip of her spine. Celia pulled James's fingertip away and slipped it into his mouth. 'So hard,' Celia murmured, squeezing the cap of his cock. 'So round and thick to stretch Justine.'

On the armchair, Robin groaned. 'Raunchy little bitch,' said Celia. The girl had lifted up; there was a flash of rigid pink as she manoeuvred to face away from him, then she rolled the waistband down at the back and Robin was in her panties. When she closed her legs and sank back down, the bulge of his cock appeared between her thighs, poking through the cloth. She twisted her head round and kissed him while she fingered him through her knickers. When Robin came, her body was lifted by the thrusts of his hips and the fiery cap of his cock burst out of her panties, flinging strings of dense white liquid which splashed upon her naked skin and dribbled between her fingertips to soak into her knickers.

Both shafts entered Elizabeth at the same time, pushing hard and lifting quickly. Elizabeth cried out; she tried to steady herself with a hand on each man's shoulder as the force of the double penetration lifted her off the box. She was supported on the cocks. Then her legs were lifted almost horizontally and the cheeks of her buttocks were stretched apart but there were always two hands free to masturbate her, one beneath her and the other searching for the top of her cunt. When Elizabeth started to writhe and moan, she was shaken up and down, then touched again above the entrance to her cunt. Then her knees were lifted up and held. Her breasts, squeezed out sideways, were rubbed continually upwards to make the nipples lengthen. Then she was shaken while her nipples were held, then she was rubbed between her legs while she writhed upon the cocks until she climaxed.

Celia took hold of Justine's harness, twisted her shoulders round and directed James's fingertips to the swollen breast that thrust through its leather ring. Then she opened Justine's buttocks again. 'But will it be tight enough, James?' she asked. 'Will it squeeze?' And she began smacking the anus with the small leather ornamented strap, whereupon Justine's nipple hardened in James's fingers. Celia gently pushed the narrow tubing; Justine leaked; Celia collected the golden drops of yield and smeared them round his cock, then directed the tip to the pouted cup of Justine's anus. The moisture provided insufficient lubrication; the anus formed a clinging sucker around the cap of James's cock while Celia slowly worked his shaft. When he shuddered, she held the foreskin steadily back and waited, then resumed the slow massage, and the cock sank slowly in. Then she stretched one hand down between his buttocks, pushed the thumb into him, and she felt the wrenching tightness round the thumb, and the powerful force of the spurts being delivered inside Justine.

After watching the footmen complete their pleasure, Celia declared the men to be spent, and she dismissed all

167

of them, James included. 'The girls are only beginning,' she said. They kept Justine in her harness, on the bed, or in the chair, or on the box or the floor. And they kept the catheter in her in every position where this was physically possible. Even while they sucked her, one of them would press it up inside her to cause a trickle of warm liquid, which was directed through the tube on to some part of her skin. They gave her drinks to compensate for leakage; her climaxes came more strongly with her bladder full. They stayed strong even when Celia took the catheter out of her and encouraged her to dribble. Afterwards, they washed her belly and bottom and the insides of her legs and put her to bed. They left her with the young woman, who snuggled up to her, sucking Justine's swollen nipples until she fell asleep.

Celia and Elizabeth later returned to the room. The girl sat up, looking frightened on account of Celia's expression. Celia said: 'Julia needs her back tomorrow, and she hasn't been fully stretched.' She held something cylindrical and metallic which had a handle.

'Oh – not you my darling. Shhh . . . Not you . . .' whispered Elizabeth, sitting on the bed, putting her arms around the girl's waist, protecting her, while Justine was made to kneel on the floor and her anus was stretched progressively while her clitoris remained exposed.

'Do not fight it; let it open,' whispered Celia. 'It will make the muscle swell and burn at first, but afterwards – for a few days – it will feel so tight.' She teased the clitoris and turned the handle notch by notch, while Justine's moans came deeper and deeper and her knees slid out across the carpet until her belly touched the floor.

While Elizabeth gently rolled the girl's knickers down and bared the nude soft labia to the smoothing pressure of the back of one finger, Celia twisted Justine's head round. 'Give me your tongue. Mmmm . . .' And Celia sucked it numb while Justine's anus stretched and opened and her vulva bulged behind her, its lips open, its clitoris a wet, red ball.

And the girl's clitoris too was carefully exposed. Then it was fitted with a minute waxed cone of leather, porous on its inner surface, and the moisture on the clitoris sealed it tightly to the leather. Elizabeth toyed with this small shiny waxed projection while Celia now feathered Justine's clitoris and, in between times, continued turning the handle until Justine screamed and came with a spasm so pronounced that Celia could feel it through the handle.

Celia left her on the floor and joined Elizabeth on the bed. The girl was passed back and forth between them and masturbated by tongue-tip touch and finger-sharing, but always with the waxed leather cone in place and kept dry by dint of holding the labia open and ensuring that the tongue-tip was dry, so the seal stayed firm and she could experience the sensations entirely through the cone, which, when her climaxes were triggered, moved like a tiny weight forever lifted and pushed by the stabbing pulses in the clitoris behind it, while the two wetted fingers slid in turn up her inner thighs to be gloved individually and alternately inside the cunny or the anus, or sometimes simultaneously in both.

In the morning, when the instrument was removed from Justine, the predicted reaction occurred and within a very short while, the anus, so stretched before, would accept no object any wider than Celia's little finger.

Elizabeth and James dropped Justine at her flat. When she opened the door, she found Philip waiting. His face was pale and he was standing at the window overlooking the street. Justine took her coat off quietly.

'Who was the man?' he asked abruptly. Justine told him. 'He looked young,' Philip said. 'Did you sleep with him? Look at me.' He ran across and took her by the shoulders. 'Answer! Did you?'

'No!' She turned her head away. 'I. . . ' Her lips were trembling. 'Oh, Philip – please?' He had wanted her to go there – he had watched Celia take her.

He shook her like a limp doll. 'You loved it, didn't you – with him? You little slut. What else did you let him do?'

169

She had never seen his eyes so wild. 'Take your dress off. Take it off. Take everything off.' He dragged it off her, its buttons springing to the floor. She was naked underneath it. She stood shivering, her hands across her breasts until he pulled them away. 'Shut up. Shut up!' He flung her into the armchair. 'Get your legs up. Get them open.' She lay there shaking while he opened her. 'Turn over. Shut up!' He spread her cheeks and he turned silent. She burst into tears even before he touched her there and she continued crying while his shaking thumb-tip rubbed across the still-distended rim. Finally, he murmured, 'Why? Why did you let him do it, Justine?' Then he whispered, through her whimpers, 'I would have been gentle. I would have been kind.' He kissed her back and stroked her hair. And when she turned and looked at him she saw that he was almost crying. 'I waited for you – here. I couldn't leave. As soon as you were gone, I wanted you back – so desperately. I love you, Justine . . .'

She took him in her arms and pressed her naked breasts against his shirt and kissed him hungrily, sucking his breath away.

She kept on kissing him while he lifted her up and fastened her to the stemple. Her body surged with so powerful a wanting that she could not breathe. His eyes were still wet when he took the crop from the drawer and whipped her. And in the stinging whip-strokes across her thighs and belly, Justine found atonement. She found a sweet catharsis in the warm, throbbing afterpains as Philip lay with her upon the bed – her bed – and held her in his arms. She offered him her mouth, her sex, her anus. And though his cock was stiff, he would not take her. He kissed her face and lay against her neck and she could feel his heart beating steadily against her breast when he was asleep.

When Philip woke up, she was wearing the linked finger-rings and the G-string that he had given her. He lifted her belly off the bed and up into the air so high that her shoulders dug into the mattress. Then he sucked her between the legs and her climax came on so intensely, with

170

the leather string across her clitoris, that she felt that she had peed. 'I love you, Justine,' he whispered.

She didn't see him for the next three days. He had said that she could go out, but she waited. On the Sunday, most of the snow had gone when she ventured on to the street, not really knowing where she was going. But she found herself passing the park, then turning back and going in. She stopped by the bridge over the narrow part of the lake and watched the swans. And when she turned round again, her heart stopped, because he was there, walking towards her. But he was not alone. He kept walking, not changing his pace, until he passed her. But the woman on his arm had seen her. She turned confidently, her secure brown eyes fixing on Justine, then she whispered to her man, who took her arm gently, shrugged perceptibly, but did not turn to look, or to acknowledge by any sign, other than this shrug, that the pale girl on the bridge existed.

13: THE PREPARATION OF THE BRIDE

Philip came to her next morning. 'I've brought you something to wear,' he said, and tossed a parcel on the bed, but Justine wasn't interested. He was behaving as if nothing had happened. 'Your eyes are beautiful,' he told her; he didn't even seem to realise she had been crying. Justine pulled away when he tried to kiss her. He stared at her for a few seconds, then he edged on to the bed where she was kneeling, breathing quick defiance, but afraid. When his hand stretched out to her, she pulled back. The hand hovered, then lowered, and the tips of his fingers touched her knee. Then the heel of the hand, placed against it, pushed. That one knee slid across the bed; her body was twisted, and the top of that one leg hurt. But he pushed until the space between her legs was sufficient. 'Open your mouth,' he said. She kept her head turned away, but her neck, her smooth pale neck, was bare and her mouth was open when he touched the tops of her legs and the pouted, split lips of her cunny.

'Where is your leather string?' he said softly. 'I want you to wear it.'

'Why should I?'

His half smile made her want to gouge her fingernails into the corner of his lip. 'Ah – I see. You want me to talk about what happened yesterday? Is that it? You want me to explain myself – to you.' He stood up, his eyes staring wildly, but his voice a chilling whisper: 'Since when is it your prerogative to question with whom I spend my time and what I choose to do?' His hand shot out and grasped her wrist as she lifted it to protect herself. He used the

172

other hand to drag her nightgown over her head. But he would not let go of her wrist, and the crumpled nightgown bunched around her forearm. Justine was crying; Philip dragged her till she fell stretched along the bed. Then he let go of her and took his necktie off. Her tears kept coming while he wrapped it tightly round her wrists to leave a short length in between them. He looked round, then he picked her up bodily and, ignoring the stemple, carried her across the room and suspended her from the heavy hook high on the back of the door. Then he unfurled a leather strap and smacked her bottom, while she danced on her toes, and the cheeks of her buttocks tried to seal together, while her knees knocked against the wood, and her belly tried to push itself through the door. He smacked her till her toes could not support her, and her buttocks, cramped and burning, succumbed and softened and shook with every smack that accompanied the slow slide of her belly down the door. Then, from behind, he touched her between the legs. She was hot there – she knew it; she was erect. He played with her until the deep moan started in her throat. Then he smacked her bottom again, with her legs kept apart.

Suddenly, he threw the strap down and fell against her, kissing her shoulders and her neck. 'She could never, *never*, love me as much as I love you.' And he kissed her again and again. But Justine's tears kept coming; they would not stop and now she did not want them to. Her tears were her exoneration for denying him and turning away.

He lifted her down but did not untie her when he put her on the bed. She was face down while he took her. She wanted him hard and deep. He kept her legs wide apart and he kept touching her while he moved inside her, thrusting to reach her womb, but masturbating her slowly, until she felt her buttocks spreading their burning skin across the coolness of his belly. When the mouth of her bottom kissed his skin, she came. His fingertips squeezed the come right out of her clitoris; it kept pulsing and he kept squeezing the wetness and the waves of pleasure came again, with her warm dilated anus sealed to his belly skin. He ran his

173

fingers upwards from the nape of her neck and through her short blonde hair.

Justine heard a voice above her. 'Are we ready?' She hid her face and tried to pull away from Philip. When he turned her back again, she hunched her shoulders and tried to avert her eyes from the man staring down at her. Philip stayed inside her while he rolled her on to her side. He moved her fastened wrists away and Lawrence Jesber stared impassively – but she knew he was staring at her breasts, exposed now and bulging with the quickness of her breathing. Then Philip opened her legs. He brushed the hairs back from her labia, displaying her wetness, displaying that she was tight about his penis.

'Has she tried her clothes on?' asked Lawrence.

'Not yet,' said Philip. He slid out of her and sat up. Justine didn't move from the position where Philip had put her, but her eyes were closed now. She became more and more frightened by the tone of Lawrence's voice:

'Hadn't she better wash first?' he said.

'I suppose so.'

'Where's the bathroom?'

'Through there.'

Philip didn't stop Lawrence. A part of him wanted to, and a part of him didn't. And it was the coldness of giving that won. He looked at the wall, but from the corner of his eye he saw this much younger man take her by the tether between her wrists and draw her from the bed – it was a drawing rather than a lifting action, the act of taking some slim and flexible thing whose resistance is measured in weight alone and is inadequate – and he heard the weight-less faintness of her pleadings. To cruelty, to arousal, they were the cooing sounds of love. He watched her being swept across his distant vision and disappearing. He checked his watch and he finished dressing, completely but for his tie, which was still in use, fastened round her wrists. He dressed silently and stealthily, moving like an interloper, listening.

The door had swung shut; there were words that he could only hear as hollow sounds, coming in loud rapid bursts; Lawrence was instructing her. And there was the sound of running water – the basin being filled. The instructions came again, then silence, then the dripping sound of water. Philip heard the faintest whisper – her voice. He heard faint splashing sounds; a murmur – her voice again; light smacking sounds; a catch of breath – Justine's; an instruction from Lawrence; a gasp; a pause; a cupboard being opened, bottles being moved (which bottles? Philip tried to recall); another instruction; silence; then a low moan, building, waning; a wrenching gasp, cut short – muffled by what, a hand across the mouth, a kiss? – but continuing to a gagged groan of deliverance.

Philip sat on the bed. He heard the basin being emptied, then refilled. He heard sounds of splashing. He crept across and pushed the door, which swung silently on its hinges.

She was standing at the basin, facing it. In the mirror, he could see her breasts; he could see that her nipples were hard, as if they had been pinched. Lines of wetness funnelled to their tips. He could see that she stood on tiptoes, that her hands supported her as she hunched forwards. But her head was back and she was gasping. Her legs formed the shape of a horseshoe, but it was balanced above the rim of the bowl; she was almost sitting in it. Lawrence stood beside her, masturbating her. He was using one hand to cup her from the back and the other to masturbate her. He poured something from a bottle into the hand that cupped her and her thighs squirmed open. The hand at the front moved rapidly, then stopped, then moved rapidly again. Her toes lifted from the floor and she was sitting in the palm of his hand when he lowered her into the bowl. The door swung shut. Philip returned to the bed. He heard splashing, then gasps, then the gurgling sounds of water draining, and Justine climaxed again – he heard her above the sounds of water sucking past her open pubic lips and draining from the bowl.

A few minutes later, Justine emerged with Lawrence behind her. He appeared as cool as ever but Justine's face and neck looked flushed; her eyes evaded Philip's gaze; her nipples still stood out, but they were dry now, and between her legs, the pale blonde pubic hair was fluffy.

Philip showed her the clothes he had brought her. She unfolded them warily. Then her fingers began to shake.

'Are they not your size?' he asked her.

'They . . . they are boys' clothes.' She looked at him with an expression that was innocence and pleading. Philip wanted to kiss her.

' "Are they not your size?" was what I asked.'

Her lower lip was trembling.

'Put them on.'

It seemed to terrify her that she was asked to do it. She never stopped shaking. Philip kept glancing at the strap on the table; his fingers itched to take it up, but he had no cause to do so. He needed a cause, a reason to do it. She was moving the things on the bed. There was a boy's worsted suit, with knee-length breeches and a waistcoat, and there were long stockings, a shirt and buckled shoes. Where would she start? What would she put on first?

It was the shirt. It reached her bottom. She stood bare-legged in this shirt, which was short, so her bottom projected. Philip's fingers itched. There was no underwear and she wanted to use her own, her panties. 'No,' he said. 'No underwear.' Naked is accessible. He watched her legs slide into the trousers, the small feet reappearing, then the calves, then the worsted sliding over her buttocks. The fit was tight and her pale blonde fluff erupted as she struggled with the fly. She fastened the belt, and the straps below the knee, then pulled the stockings on and tied them, folding the tops over. When the shoes were buckled she looked like a boy from the waist down. But the shirt was thin. Her breasts moved underneath it and he could see the conical shapes of her nipples. He lifted her breasts to make her nipples slide beneath the material. Under her arms already felt warm. Suddenly, Philip was anxious: about the way her sex and bottom were enclosed, about the number of belts and buttons and straps, about the time it might take to reach her in a hurry.

'We make time,' said Lawrence. 'And we undo only what needs undoing.' He stepped behind Justine and unfastened one button of her shirt, making an oval gap which he slid across to her right nipple. He pulled the nipple and part of the breast through until the gap was filled, and he rubbed the nipple with his thumb. Then he pushed it back, closed the gap again and fastened it. But Philip became concerned again when Justine's waistcoat was fitted: it was tight and the buttons were close and the eyelets small. However, it flattened her breasts, and that was the intention. Philip buttoned her collar and knotted her necktie; the fit about her neck was perfect but the cuffs were slightly wide. He put the jacket on her and asked her to walk to the mirror.

When Justine moved, she felt the worsted rubbing against the insides of her legs and the shallow crotch invading her split, pushing her labia to the side. The peaked cap was slightly large; Philip lowered it gently, but it sank to her ears and rested there, turning them outwards. In the mirror, Justine saw a pale, gangly boy with large eyes, in his brand new Sunday suit.

At the door, Philip suddenly stopped her. 'Quickly – hold her.' He hurried to pick something up from the table. Then Justine saw the strap and realised what was coming – and she couldn't breathe. Lawrence grasped her by the waist; she hid her face against his coat. 'Quickly, Lawrence, quickly.' She felt him unbuckling her belt, then wrenching the buttons. 'Quick . . .' She sucked her belly in, the trousers fell to her knees: her bottom was bared. The smacks fell quickly and without a pause; a hand began pinching the insides of her thighs; she opened her knees and the hand found what it was looking for. She gasped; it kept pinching it. 'Yes?' said Philip. Lawrence grunted. 'Hold it,' said Philip. 'Keep hold of it.' The smacks kept coming; her clitoris pushed between the wetted thumb and pinching finger; her belly sagged forwards; her clothes slid up her back and her breasts burst out and touched his shirt. Her bottom writhed, trying to shake the pain away, trying to rub the lips of her cunny against Lawrence's pinching fingers, but the smacks kept coming until her legs gave way.

In the carriage, the two men seemed pleased that the driver had called her 'laddy'. 'Drive into town,' was all the instruction that Philip had given. The men sat opposite her. There seemed to be no feeling in their expressions – in that sense, they were alike, although physically, they could scarcely have been more different. Lawrence was not much older than Justine, and was tall, large-framed and muscular. He was blond and his eyes were bright blue. Whereas Philip's voice had a quiet, secure strength, Lawrence's had an edge of arrogance.

They were talking about her. They seemed concerned that she should be able to continue to pass for a boy. 'She looks awkward,' said Philip. 'There's something . . . I don't know.' The clothes were uncomfortable: she could feel the roughness of the unworn wool against her legs, making them itch. 'Cross your legs,' said Philip. Her body shivered as the seam, hot and rough and clinging, was drawn into her split.

'She's keeping them together too much,' said Lawrence. Justine let her foot drop back to the floor. 'Open them – that's right. Let them go wide. Sit back. Slouch.' He leaned forwards quickly, placing his feet between hers. His elbows rested on his knees and his hands hung poised above her thighs. The seam was tightly against her; it was into her. She was breathing quickly, wanting to pull back, expecting him to touch her through her clothes, to touch the seam where it pressed into her cunny. 'It's the gap, Philip – between her legs. There's nothing there – no bulge.'

'We could have the trousers refitted, lower the crotch, even put something in there – have it made properly, and she could wear it.'

Lawrence's finger touched her. 'Unbutton your fly.'

'Go easy, Lawrence – here, I mean.' But Philip did not press the protest.

'Do it, girl. Quicker. Lie back! Keep your legs open.' But that kept the buttons tight and more difficult to undo. 'Do it!' She felt waves of heat and coldness washing against her belly. She could see carriages passing in the street, people glimpsing. Philip shaded the side of his head, but his eyes stayed with Justine, whose hands lay limply against her crotch, which now lay unbuttoned, gaping. Lawrence's

hand came across. 'Hold it open. And lie back, right back.'
Philip never intervened. Justine's hips moved; she murmured and her knees began to close around his hand.

'Open,' Lawrence told her again, but she was already
open. His fingers were cold, so cold, opening her cunny,
pushing up inside her, distending her as he had done with
her in the bowl. 'She's wet, Philip, so hot and wet. God
help me – I want to fuck her here and now.'

'Have a care, Lawrence – her new suit, remember.' Justine's head slumped back, her mouth fell open and her
belly started to strain against the belt. Lawrence's fingers
stayed inside her. Her clitoris was against his thumb. 'It's
her mouth, you know,' Philip was saying. 'She has lips that
are too full, too red, to be a boy's.'

The two men walked into the barber's shop with Justine
between them.

The barber asked: 'Shall it be each of you gentlemen?
I'm closing soon for a bite of lunch.' There was already
one man in the chair and another waiting.

'No, just our young friend here.' The barber glanced at
Justine, then at Lawrence, then looked quizzically at Philip,
who added: 'Our friend is of a delicate and rather nervous
disposition.'

'He'll be all right here sir.'

Philip beamed. 'I know it.'

'Then if you'll take a seat, sirs, I'll be with the young
gentleman soon. Oh . . .' He apologised as he squeezed
past Philip, locked the door and pulled the blind down.
'No assistant today you see, sir, so I have to close.'

'That's fortunate – that we arrived in time, I mean.'
The barber looked at him rather strangely, then bethought
himself and returned to the man shrouded in face-cloths.
The newcomers sat on hard narrow chairs, with the barber
eyeing them at intervals while trying to keep up a cheerful
banter with his other customers. Justine sat stiffly between
Philip and Lawrence; her knees were together. Lawrence
whispered to her and her knees fell open, but stayed tense
as they touched the legs of the men to either side. Lawrence

whispered again. Nervously, her thumbs tucked into her belt. The conversation turned to women; Philip interposed some questions which appeared to unnerve the barber. Eventually, the queue was dealt with and the other customers had gone.

'Right then, young sir.' The barber smacked the cloth over the seat and headrest then shook it with a flurry. 'What will it be?' He looked at Justine. Her eyelashes flickered beneath the peak of her cap, then she looked at Philip. The barber looked puzzled.

Philip interrupted his gaze. 'Trim it short. Short about the ears and neck.'

'Then you'll need this off.' The barber laughed, a little curtly. He put the cap on a vacant seat. Justine's hands gripped the arms of the chair. Her fingers looked narrow and small, delicate and frail. The barber tried to make the lad speak – using small talk, asking about school, asking if it was his first visit to town and so forth – but it was always Philip who answered. The barber seemed nervous, too, that Lawrence hadn't spoken audibly, and he kept looking towards the locked door as if he hoped someone might knock and break the embarrassment of this scene. But his confidence returned when he started cutting.

'Fine hair,' he said, almost to himself, as if resigned to the thought that nobody was listening. But everybody was: every snip seemed to have a meaning. The slim cold scissors snipped about her ears and tickled the back of her neck. The finely clustered cuttings of hair trickled down her skin and caught beneath the cloth at the nape of her neck. The nerves in that skin became excited by the tickling. The barber tilted her head gently; the coolness of the scissors slipped. He made small nervous coughing sounds which became more frequent; the scissors slowed, then stopped completely. He tilted her head and stared into her eyes. He lifted her fingers from the arm of the seat. 'Why . . . This is no lad. It's a girl . . .' But it was clear from his tone that he wasn't certain, and that he was challenging Philip to deny it.

'Did I say it was a lad?' asked Philip.

180

'Yes . . . Well . . . no. But look how she's dressed.'

'And so?'

'And her hair. You've ruined her, made her look like a boy.'

'Is that what you think?' Philip stood up, not raising his voice, but sounding angry. Justine slumped down into the chair. 'You think she looks like a boy, do you?' The barber stood aside, looking worried, staring from one man to the other. 'A boy, is it?' Philip stood over Justine as she sank deeper into the chair. He pulled the cloth off her, grasped her waistcoat, wrenching it till the buttons gave. Then he ripped her shirt open. Her breasts spilled out; the barber gasped. 'You think she's a boy, then?' repeated Philip. The man stuttered, turning deep red and his scissors clattered to the floor. Justine was slumped deep into the chair, her shirt pushed out of the way now and the fullness of her breasts exposed. Their paleness was stark against the material of her waistcoat. Her nipples were up, the circles dark around them, soaking up the weak light in the room. Philip stared at her. In the fixity of his gaze was a cold obsession.

Philip stared at the girl in boys' clothes, a girl with short blonde hair and neck completely bare – with a nudity around her ears – and breasts that were so full and perfect, and eyes that seemed so large, and skin with the flawless smoothness of youth. He touched the darkening firmness of her nipple. He slid a hand beneath the neckline of her shirt and across the collarbone, feeling the thinness of the skin across her bony shoulders, sliding his fingers up beneath the tie – but still touching her nipple, holding it – and drinking in the breast-swell of her breathing as if it were young red wine. 'How can you say that this is a boy?' he whispered. 'How can you even think it?'

Lawrence got up quietly and checked the door. He tested that the blind was secure. Then he spoke to the barber, who protested feebly. His eyes looked worried. Justine's looked afraid and her lips began to form the refusal. Philip placed a fingertip across them.

He kept touching her nipple while her body lifted and

181

readjusted as the belt around her waist was unfastened and slid out; as her fly was unbuttoned from the top; as her hips were supported on Lawrence's hands and her trousers peeled down while her shirt was pushed up and she was left belly-naked, her bottom against the leather of the chair, her peeled-down trousers turned inside out, so they hung down bell-shaped, like the base of a heavy, hobbled dress, from below her knees. The barber gasped again: from her waistcoat to her calves, she was naked; she was in his leather chair. Lawrence tried to draw her legs open; he had to lift them over the polished arms of the chair; he couldn't open them properly, because they were fastened below the knees, but her joints were flexible and her knees reached out and apart.

The joys of arousal are manifold and sweet. Philip cupped a breast anew and touched the nipple, feeling a greater hardness there, then pulled the shirt more open, revealing the hollow beneath her arm and the tightly curved bony slimness of her ribcage. He touched the ridges that the ribs made in the skin.

Lawrence used only the tips of his fingers to hold her knees apart. 'Can you do it?' he said to the man. When Justine murmured, Philip's hand – which had slipped under her arm and touched the curls, now sticky-damp with fear and femininity – pressed against her mouth, the lips of which were swollen and warm and slightly open, and his fingertips slipped in to touch and to stay the tongue that wanted to protest. 'Five guineas, if you do it,' she heard Lawrence say. Her eyes stayed closed.

'I don't know, sir . . .' But she heard the money clinking its inducement. 'But it's not possible like this. You'll have to take the trousers off her.'

Philip, over by the door now, glanced around the blind and into the street, then turned and saw her in the mirror. Her legs were open; the barber was combing the hair between them. In his hand were the scissors. 'No scissors,' Philip called across abruptly. Her pubic hair was fine. He wanted to watch it disappear in smooth, sweeping shaves of the razor.

'But I can take the most of it off with scissors.'

'No scissors,' Philip repeated.

He watched it being slicked back against her and dissolving in the thick, creamy foam. He watched the way the barber's fingertips moved gently, precisely, lifting her labia to one side with a pressure so gentle that it was causing them to swell, so when he released them, they moved; they tried to lift. 'Shave her to her navel,' said Philip. 'I want nothing at all on her belly. And shave her thighs – just the insides.' He wanted the skin there to be naked where it touched her cunt. He wanted that skin to be able to glide over the newly smooth mount when he pushed her knees up, with them pressed together. And he wanted to be able to see the way her skin varied in colour and texture; he would see that only when her cunt was naked.

When he had finished, the barber wiped her. Philip inspected. The skin became pinker, then more velvety, then polished, but the inner lips were a ruby matt. It was the intensity of the pinks that was exciting, and feminine, even with her in her waistcoat, even in boys' clothes. 'Hot towel,' said Philip.

'What about this?' Lawrence lifted aside her shirt and pointed to the hair under her arms.

'Don't touch it,' said Philip to the barber. 'To touch it with a razor would be sacrilegious.' And he lifted her shoulders and pushed the shirt up and open and kissed the curls that he had saved, and touched the new bareness between her legs, the smoothness beside her pubic lips, and with his eyes, caressed the textural change where the nudeness of her mount became more velvety and the skin turned deeper pink.

Justine's belly lifted when the hot towel touched it. The barber placed it carefully, his fingers moving quickly, lifting it and readjusting. It lay, a hot heavy flowing weight on her belly and between her legs, drawing the blood to the surface of the skin.

'Towels for her thighs,' said Philip. 'A little hotter.' She whimpered when they touched the skin, then the pain turned softer, like the afterthrob of smacking. The heat

183

seeped into her; beneath the towel, the lips of her cunny turned soft. When the towels were taken off, her legs and belly were red; the lips of her cunny were burning hot. The men stood her up and fastened her shirt and waistcoat. They didn't put her trousers on her, but first made her walk. When she took a step, she felt smooth: everything between her legs felt smooth, as if she had been powdered with talc. She was aware of the lips of her cunny hanging down, weighted with arousal and sliding against the smoothness and the nudity of her thighs. It was an awareness that was most intense then, on that first day, the first time she was shaved, and it stayed with her even when she was made to put her trousers on, because she now felt so completely naked underneath them.

The awareness was also shared by the men; that day, they seemed less concerned with smacking her than usual and seemed to want mainly to touch her. Still in the barber's shop, they kept her fly unbuttoned and took turns to touch her. Her clitoris was up; they kept it up. Philip told her that he wanted it kept that way. He said, 'I shall find a way to have it done. Look at me, Justine.' And he turned her head towards him, held her chin up and touched her naked clitoris until her throat arched out and her breathing came shallowly. 'Lawrence,' Philip whispered. Philip watched him take his turn with her. Lawrence was the crueller. He kept her standing up, whispering to her and playing with her; her legs were shaking and the tips of his fingers were painting her wetness down her inner thighs.

The barber had wanted to be rid of them at first, but his attitude had now changed. While Lawrence stood with Justine, allowing her to lean against the frame of the door while he touched her inside her trousers, Philip asked if he might bring Justine back on a regular basis. He explained that he wanted her kept permanently bare between her legs and that that would require repeated shaving, for preference by an expert, in order to avoid the possibility of damage and resulting flaws, or even a rash on the skin, which might prove an annoyance to the fingers.

184

But there could be difficulties, the man replied – even now, his shop should be open.

Justine gasped as the slow massage of her clitoris restarted, but Lawrence spoke coolly. 'Is there another room?' he asked. 'Perhaps in the back, where the problem would not arise.' Justine gasped again; the tips of his fingers held her.

There was a room, it seemed; the fingertips released her clitoris and pressed against her inside leg. Philip offered the man a small retainer. 'May we see it?' The man took him into the back. Lawrence brought Justine.

It was a stone-floored room with a number of boxes and crates and an old barber's chair. There was a stove, and a table where the man took his meals. Philip examined the back of the room. 'Where does this door lead?'

'The street, a side street.'

Philip nodded. The man began tending the stove and putting something on it to boil. Philip, still looking round, came to a place where a heavy chain was set into the low ceiling. There was no obvious function for this chain, which was rusted. It might once have been something to do with the loading of goods: it was by a small window whose panes were rendered milky with accumulated dirt. Philip said, 'The room will serve our purpose admirably.' The barber stared at them, puzzled. 'We wish to use it now.'

'But – '

'We shall not inconvenience you in any way, my man. You may go about your business uninterrupted.' He strode across and pressed a coin into the barber's palm. 'You shall not hear – a sound.' The final words were whispered as his eyes met Justine's. Her gaze lowered. She felt a terrible chillness slipping down inside her. In Philip's hand was a thin silk scarf. Lawrence slid his hand around her back, beneath her jacket, and the chill, slipping feeling came again.

Then the doorbell jingled; the barber stared at Justine then turned and went into his shop, leaving his pot on the stove. There was the sound of voices – two or three people – and the barber did not come back.

It was the first time that Philip had gagged her. The scarf was thin, like gauze, and it trapped her tongue. Lawrence took her jacket off, rolled her shirtsleeves to her elbows, took her tie off and used it to fasten her wrists to the chain. Then he pulled the chain and locked it and she was stretched. 'Tighter . . .' whispered Philip. Lawrence jerked the chain again; her cry was muffled by the gag; a gap appeared between her belt and belly; her buckled shoes tiptoed on the floor. Lawrence unfastened her belt; her trousers stayed up, held by their stiffness. Lawrence took hold of them and dragged them to her knees.

Philip moved closer, positioning himself with his back to the light, between the window and the couple – for so he thought of them: she as the bride, and Lawrence as the young man to whom he had given his blessing to take her and to sow his oats inside her as he pleased. Her body was illuminated clearly: it was palely naked between waistcoat and knees. But between her legs, her nudity was perfect and he could see her labia glowing with the same liquid ruby heat as in the picture he had painted in his mind.

Lawrence pulled her trousers back and through her legs, which bowed out and remained so while he touched the naked insides of her thighs and the smooth slight swell of her belly. He pushed her waistcoat up around her breasts and held it lifted while he touched her labia, nuzzling his clenched fingers against them, then stretching them slowly down until their weight had increased and displaced to the outer edges, which looked gathered into rounded, polished lobes. Philip moved round to the back and could see them dangling between her open legs. Her legs moved; the trousers dropped further and the muscle tightened up the back of each thigh. He saw the narrow band of gathered skin that fed into her anus. Then he saw Lawrence's finger-tips open Justine's labia from below. She trembled on her toes; he heard her gasping through the gag as Lawrence's cock tried to enter her, and the narrow skin band tightened. It made him want to touch it. Philip moved round to the front; he positioned himself by the cloudy window. The cock had edged back; it was thick enough to make the balls

186

look small. Philip tried to imagine that cock slotted up through the gap between those slim, bare, bowed-out legs; he could not picture it being accommodated in the space that was available in Justine.

But Lawrence pushed her waistcoat up again, and her belly stretched and she whimpered her arousal. He held her belly taut and rhythmically stretched her labia down, tightening the skin round the ball of her clitoris, wetting the hood and thinning it until her clitoris was visible through the skin. 'She's a tight one, all right,' said Lawrence, 'but she's getting there.' Philip nodded, but did not answer. Her legs were making tiny jerking movements every second or third time that the fingertips moved down.

Her labia had become soft. Lawrence was able to fold them up inside her, then to close the outer lips to make a single smooth-sealed split, which resembled a fine ink line across her naked skin. He gently squeezed it and her labia stayed inside her. When he pushed the head of his cock up against the line, Justine moaned and lifted on her toes. He kept pushing; she kept moaning. The head of the cock entered, but the head was not the widest part. She was balanced on tiptoes. He touched the point at the top of her split: it was shielded by the labia pulled round it and it had the form of a polished arrowhead sculpted in bas relief. He used his wetted fingertip to touch the hard ball in the arrowhead through the skin. He wetted the naked area round her cunt and rubbed this wetted place, but did not wet his cock where it entered her. When he touched her shielded clitoris again, her cunt pulsed and his cock entered her and lifted her.

Justine was pivoted on this rod of flesh which had pushed her labia into her. Her waistcoat was lifted up again and held – to stretch her belly, which stretched the skin around her clitoris, made it ache, made it push. Then Lawrence put his hands against the insides of her legs and lifted them open and her belly opened, his cock bedded deeply and her toes lifted from the floor. He began to bounce her on his cock; her naked belly buffed against his curls; her clitoris touched the base of his cock; his fingers, underneath her, held the cheeks of her bottom apart. Her cunny was bumping against the base of his cock and he was holding her in the air. She was breathing hard against the gag, wanting to come. But he stopped moving inside her and allowed her toes to touch the floor. Again he touched her clitoris, rubbing it and stretching back the skin.

The pot on the stove began to simmer. Philip used the cloth to lift it aside. He heard the murmur of pleasure-pain from Justine, then turned to see her being lifted on the cock again. Lawrence's hands were round her waist. Her lower body hung; her toes did not touch the floor. With each thrust, her unsupported buttocks shuddered. He eased her down again, spread her legs akimbo and began touching. Philip moved back to watch: the hand moving very gently up and down between her legs; the back of the other hand pressing into her belly; the fingers of the first hand being wetted and reapplied; her legs slowly buckling; her waistcoat being pushed up, baring her from waist to ribs; the hand rubbing up and down this bareness, touching again the place between her trembling legs; then both hands moving round her ribs and up and Justine being taken under the arms and lifted, gasping through the gag, her clothes pushed up, her buttocks bare, her legs kept open by the width of the cock. Philip walked across and touched her. He touched the place where her buttocks split. He opened the cheeks and touched the burning skin of her distension; it clung to the tip of his finger. Then he traced the line of gather. 'Bring her on,' he whispered. He watched the hands that held her under her arms relax, and the weight of her body bed itself on the cock, and the tips of her toes touch the floor. Then the two hands moved to the front.

Philip held the cheeks of Justine's bottom open through her trembles. He took out his silken handkerchief and stretched it round the tip of his finger and he stroked her anus with this soft silk fingertip glove. Her orgasm came quickly, with her anus pulsing against his finger in tiny nervous starts, as if she were trying not to squeeze with her cunt, as if she were frightened that Lawrence would come inside her.

Philip replaced the handkerchief in his pocket. He examined his watch; it said one o'clock. The time had moved on quickly. He begged to be excused.

He had luncheon with Charlotte, but his mind was elsewhere. She told him as much. Her face was full of concern for him. Philip took it in his hands and he kissed the warmth of her lips. Charlotte was embarrassed; her cheeks coloured at the knowing nods from the nearby tables. 'I don't care who knows it,' said Philip, 'I love you.' And he took her hand. 'I love you,' he repeated. Her eyes were shining. 'Shhh . . . Don't cry . . .'

Charlotte shook her head, looked away for a second, then looked back. Her eyes were filling up with tears, but she was smiling. 'Harsh, cruel man,' she whispered. 'Don't look at me so . . .' But her hand had closed around his and squeezed it with a strength he had not expected.

That night, in the small flat, he kept Justine dressed only in the waistcoat while he touched the places that were shaved and he asked her about the things the housemistress used to do to her in the school. She wouldn't tell him. But some of it, he knew already.

He bent her across the table and smacked her with the flat, short leather. Then he opened her waistcoat and pulled it back, so her breasts pressed to the surface while he smacked her. He continued smacking until her breasts splayed out across the table. Then he touched her naked cunny from behind and said, 'Justine, tomorrow I shall take you to see a man. I have told him that I want your clitoris permanently exposed.' When she protested weakly, he spread her legs astride the corner of the table and pushed her forwards until she was sitting on her naked cunny and her toes were off the floor. When he smacked again, her cunny opened, her clitoris kissed the surface of the table and she came.

14: A STRING OF BEADS

The next afternoon, Philip took Justine to a large house in a quiet avenue. They were admitted to a small reception room, where they were kept waiting for a few minutes before being ushered into a spacious office where a large man in a suit and waistcoat sat behind a desk. There were a few heavy, leather-bound books behind glass in a case against one wall. On the other main wall were several country and riding scenes in oils. There was little else in the room apart from a couch. The man had a florid complexion and a port-coloured mark across his jaw and down his neck. He leaned across the desk and extended his large pink hand in greeting to Philip, who took it and shook it once.

'Please, have a seat. Er, Mr Clement isn't it? Please . . .' said the man, pointing with a large, precisely directing finger. Philip sat down. It seemed to be assumed that he knew the name of the man behind the desk, who had not introduced himself. Nor had Philip attempted to introduce him to Justine; she still stood, in the absence of any invitation to do otherwise, and nobody attempted to bring her a chair. 'Well.' The man with the large hands looked at her. 'And what can we do for you, Mr Clement? How may we be of assistance?'

Philip was impatient – his eyes turned away and looked at the blanker of the two walls. His voice had a quick, cutting edge. 'The problem has been explained, has it not?' When his eyes struck back, the large man flinched and Justine's heartbeat quickened.

'Well . . . I take it this is she?'

Philip pointedly looked away again, but when his eyes met hers, Justine suddenly felt that he was blaming her for the way that this other man annoyed him. She knew from his expression that he wanted to punish her again, for this inconvenience, just as he had punished her for seeing him with that woman. She knew that he would do it for her as soon as they were alone.

'Well,' the man kept saying. 'Yes . . .' When it was obvious that no answer would be forthcoming, he finally stood up and said tentatively: 'The young lady will need to undress.' Then he pulled the bellcord. Philip nodded to Justine.

The man began to discuss the weather. Philip stared sullenly at the wall, but kept looking back at Justine, who stood with her blouse unfastened but not removed, half-sheltering the bareness of her breasts and nipples, which stiffened against the gently sliding material and against the fact that he was making her undress before a stranger. She fumbled with her thick-buckled belt and the man was looking at her as he kept saying, 'Yes . . . Well, yes . . .' in a low voice and Justine was so aware that beneath her skirt she was naked and shaved and he would see every contour of her shape between her legs. And he would see her labia protruding, because Philip had played with her in the carriage.

When her skirt fell away, the assistant appeared with a notepad and a pencil, and her presence – because she seemed prim and businesslike with narrow eyes and dark hair tied tightly in a bun – was more embarrassing than that of the men. The large man conversed with the woman in a low voice while her sharp eyes criticised Justine and her small tight fingers gripped the pencil and wrote things down on the pad. Then the woman said one word that was terrifying to Justine. The word was 'doctor'. She called the man 'doctor'. Twice, she used the word. Justine felt dizzy and faint. She put her hand to head.

'Get undressed,' said Philip, coming over to her, swirling across the turning room, then catching her as she overbalanced. 'Get undressed!' Then to the man, he said, 'Doctor, do you want her on here?' She went limp at hearing that word again; he had to lift her on to the couch and she felt unsteady because it was narrow and backless. Philip's annoyance was intense, but she couldn't do anything. She was drowning in her mind, drowning in the terror of her memories of what they had put her through – the doctors – when her lover had died.

Philip lifted Justine by the shoulders, pulled her blouse off, and she was nude. Her breasts shook but he didn't want to touch them. He held her ribcage gathered and almost contained within his hands. She was very beautiful and frail, so slimly boned, with her breasts so swollen, pressing out against the unresisting muscle of her slender upper-arms. And now, with her belly so naked, she looked more exquisite still. She lifted her hands and tried to protect her breasts in the soft crooks of her elbows, but Philip moved her arms away. She would have to get used to being displayed and being touched and used by other men, as he would have to come to terms with giving her. He made her open her legs. Then he allowed her to be examined by the quack.

It was afternoon and the light was already failing. The assistant brought a lamp. The large man washed his hands in a bowl, then dried them meticulously and for too long. The scent from the bowl was of carbolic; it gradually diffused into the air as his skin warmed while he touched her. He was thorough with her. He whispered to her gently when he wanted her on her side. He reassured her through her shame. He used cushions on which to lift her and he took her slim feet gently in his hand. He communicated some of his findings to Philip. Once it had been established beyond doubt that the breasts themselves would require no attention, the physician, as he was now seen (for he gradually gained promotion in Philip's esteem, through the delicate precision of the placing of those large, ungainly hands, and through his manner, and the wisdom of his words), explained the options while the assistant, hunched on a hard chair of her choosing, took occasional notes.

'All of a woman's body is sensitive,' he said. 'Yes – every

part of her skin. We are trying now to see that sensitivity enhanced. Is that not so? And there are many methods. Shaving is a simple one, but it can be very effective – will you keep her this way?'

'I expect to,' said Philip.

The physician nodded. He touched the outer parts of Justine's mount and gently stretched the swell of skin. 'And it has the advantage of being reversible.' He waited, but no reply came and the soft spatulate tips of his fingers kept testing the belly skin for smoothness where it became more velvety and changed to a deeper pink. 'The warmth extends to here, you know, further out than you might think.' He pressed most of the width of his hand against it, covering the broad band of deep rose pink, collecting her in the middle of his palm.

'I know,' said Philip, but he allowed the doctor to demonstrate.

'And all this area here – shhh . . . Gently, my darling.' The tips of two fingers palpated the anus and the red, dilated rim. 'I see that you have been a little urgent with her.'

'No!' Philip's gaze stabbed at her and Justine flinched.

The doctor shook his head. 'As you wish,' he whispered. Then he tested the line of wrinkled skin that traversed the perineum and connected to her vulva. 'But I would advise that we proceed with caution in the other matter.'

'Caution?' asked Philip.

'Not everything that could be done would necessarily be appropriate: not everything can be reversed. For example, you might not like her appearance afterwards; the sensations . . . they may not be quite as you expected. There are many factors to consider. Things could go wrong.'

'You mean, I might have paid my money and then be disappointed?'

'Exactly.' He opened Justine's legs a little wider again and pushed the supporting cushion further beneath her. It seemed to be difficult to get the angle right. The assistant moved aside while they turned Justine completely round, with her hips now on the headrest of the couch. Her knees remained bent, suspended in the air above her belly. 'Show me again the problem.'

'I want her hard, doctor. Whenever I put my hand between her legs – whenever I look at her, in fact – I want to know immediately that she is hard.'

The doctor moved Justine's knees gently apart, rotating them so her feet came together in the air, wavering and touching at the toes, and the naked skin between her legs was stretched. He took the tip of the prepuce between his fingers, which did not appear to move, and yet Justine murmured and her toes pressed together in the air. A low, soft moan escaped her lips. 'She is hard now, in fact – her clitoris is erect.' He drew the prepuce back to show Philip. 'She has been so since she lay upon this couch. I checked that when I examined her. I would guess that she was erect before she came into this room. It is simply that it does not show.'

'No. How can we make it show, doctor?'

The doctor kept rubbing the skin back, exposing the clitoris, which was a shiny blister, then allowing the skin to fall back slowly, only to be rubbed firmly up again. Then he pinned the skin back with the tip of his finger. 'We could reduce the prepuce surgically. It is akin to a foreskin on a man. We could remove it altogether.' A murmur escaped Justine's lips, and the shiny blister pulsed through the tautness of its skin. 'She would be sore at first, of course, but the sensations in the clitoris would be enhanced.'

'They would?'

'In suitable undergarments, even walking.' The doctor rubbed his fingertip quickly across the clitoris while he held the prepuce pinned and the clitoris appeared to retract and pulse repeatedly in tiny gulps. 'And, as you say, it has the advantage that her state of arousal is never secret.'

'And the disadvantage?'

'You are cutting away a part of her that is sensitive.' He sleeved the skin down and touched its exterior very lightly with his finger, stroking until the wrinkled skin rippled and contracted. 'It has its own nerves, its own arousal. Perhaps it should be utilised rather than discarded.'

'You would not recommend the knife, then?'

'I did not say that, Mr Clement. We use it to enhance sensitivity, just as you might spank a girl before you masturbated her. But in general, we prefer to add rather than take away. Let me demonstrate . . .' The assistant put her notebook down and brought him a slim box on a stand. It appeared to contain jewellery, mainly small items in gold. His thick fingers delicately picked up one of these and put it in the middle of his palm, where it rolled about, because it was a tiny gold ball. He added to it other gold shapes, some larger, some smaller, to make a small collection. 'We use metal because it is hard – its presence can be sensed by touching. We use pure gold because it is heavy. Even small things, when they are heavy, respond to gravity: they make their wishes felt. And gold is inert; it causes no additional irritation other than that of its presence beneath the skin.'

Justine murmured softly. The doctor reached across and touched between her open legs. Then he picked up a small gold ball which was about half the size of a pea. 'We could slip this into the prepuce,' he said, 'between the layers of skin, to make a nodule. It would press against the tip of her clitoris – its weight would adjust and move against her when she walked.

'And I would advise that she is pierced. The optimal place is here – just small incisions – through the lips immediately below the clitoris; then these holes can be used as anchorages for a variety of constrictions. It is often desirable to have the clitoris constricted with the foreskin stretched around it. And these anchorage points could also be used to solve your problem – to keep the foreskin back. We can arrange it so it can be pulled back and fastened. We would also embed a small securing ring here.' He touched the place where the nose of the prepuce merged with her lower belly. 'You could fasten it back with a miniature stirrup-iron fitted through the two incisions. I could have it made up.

'And in her case, you might wish to consider this.' He drew across his palm a short string of gold beads. They were equally spaced along a fine thread.

'Where?' asked Philip.

The doctor pointed to the line of gathered skin that extended from her vulva to her anus. 'Here.' He laid the beads alongside it. 'Why not?' Each bead was the same size and about as wide as the fold in the skin. 'It will fill it out. Then, when she sits, the small bumps under the skin . . .'

'How is it fitted?'

'A special needle – short, so it can follow the contour easily; thick, so you can feel it as you work it through; and not too sharp, so it does not pierce the skin prematurely and emerge too soon.'

'What about the thread?'

'It will break – dissolve away and be absorbed – in time. It should not cause a problem. But as with any treatment, you bring her back if it does. Eventually, you might wish to do so in any case.'

'Why is that?'

The doctor showed him. He took another string of beads which were larger than the first ones. 'They come in different sizes. You might wish that she progress. The skin, you see, stretches – with manipulation, it adapts.' Then he showed him a string of beads that were almost the size of marbles.

'But the disfigurement?'

'But this takes nothing away. It adds. The sensitivity is not lost – it improves.'

Philip straightened up. He walked over to the other side of the room and stared out of the window. Then he walked slowly back. Justine's eyes were closed. He took hold of her feet and pushed them apart. Her naked sex opened; her string stood out, snaking across to bury its head in the swollen ring of her anus. 'Which are the largest beads you would recommend?' The anus tightened. 'For a first insertion?' Philip added.

The doctor pursed his lips. 'In her case, these. For a first time – with this girl – I would hesitate to go any wider than

196

these.' They were the size of small peas. He pinched the raised line of flesh. 'She will need only a short string; the distance is not far.' He measured it between his finger and thumb, which pressed against the anal ring.

'Could she be threaded a little deeper?' asked Philip. 'Perhaps a little up inside?'

'Inside?'

'Yes. At the back.'

The doctor's thick brows knitted. He pinched the gathered skin again and gently pulled it as if it were a cord which he was trying to draw out of her. He pulled until the anus tightened. He pressed the broad tip of his thumb against the opposite side of the ring and pulled again. The wrinkles tried to shrink together, but the cord itself was drawn out a little through the ring. He nodded his head. 'It should pose no problem. You do not want it very far?'

'Just one or two beads within the influence of the . . .' Philip searched for the word.

'The sphincter?'

'Yes.'

'I think that can be arranged.'

'Can you arrange it now? I have a rather busy week.'

Philip attended Justine in the small room with its bright lights, its smell of antiseptic and its large adjustable chair. He pinned her hands back against the headrest. And although her breasts were to be spared the knife, he wanted them lifted and exposed. He wanted her naked from her underarms to her feet, so he could see her body tighten and her toes curl-up to the point of cramping. He wanted to be with her at this time of pricking torment and of fright, this time of small adjustment. He kissed her nipples gently while her labia were pierced and the short joining rod was slipped between them. He stifled her murmurs with his mouth while the small gold pip was inserted then worked to the tip of the nose of skin that sheathed her clitoris. He touched this bedded pip while the small gold ring was fitted into the place where her belly became her cunt. Then he held her knees while she was threaded on to her beads.

Guided by stout, precise fingers, the short pilot needle burrowed from front to back along the line of gathered skin. Two thick fingers reached up through the oiled, distended ring, and searched. Justine whimpered softly; Philip kissed her. Then the needle was retrieved on its thread and the string of beads was drawn through – 'Gently, so the cord does not snap before we have the beads in place.' The small incision stretched round each bead and swallowed and the beads slid visibly under the skin. When the first bead had disappeared completely through the ring, the thread was cut at each end. The only visible attachments now were the gold rod passing below her clitoris and connecting her labia, and the anchoring ring fastened at the base of her belly. But it was the buried beads that drew the attention, one at the tip of her prepuce and the others forming a line of bumps in the tube of skin that connected to her anus.

'May I?' Philip's fingertips, browsing, brushed across the buried beads, pressed the skin between them, investigating the interconnections, the movements and the shapes.

The patient was placed on the couch again while the collection of trinkets was made up and displayed in a small boxed tray. 'I will have the stirrup-piece ready by tomorrow. You must be careful with her – take it gently until she heals.'

'Of course,' said Philip.

Then the physician went to the couch. 'Justine . . .' He whispered something to her. She hesitated, then closed her eyes and pushed her knees out widely, so her cunny opened, and with the tips of two fingers, she folded back the skin of its lips. The clitoris stood out harder than ever, pushing between the rod and the round ball under the skin. 'Stay still.' The doctor slipped his middle finger up into Justine. There was no need to lubricate it. He turned it to each side and pressed and the small ball began to move against the clitoris. Justine moaned with pleasure; her cunny contracted and her head turned to the side. 'She has a small pad of skin – just here.' The finger continued pressing and moving and Justine gasped out loud; her legs opened until her cunny was lifted and her knees were projecting sideways from the couch. The finger slid out wetly. The physician nodded. His finger extended, its tip curving up as if to press. 'She is very responsive – unusually so. You are a very fortunate man. But remember – you must take it gently.'

'Of course,' repeated Philip.

15: THE PLEASURE-PANGS OF GIVING

She did become more sensitive, even before the tiny punctures had healed. But with the constant attention, her flesh became irritated by the small gold balls under the surface of the skin. The doctor said that it happened in some cases, with certain skin types: if Philip wished, he could have them taken out and that would effect an immediate cure.

'The question is, I suppose, does it prevent her . . . ?' the doctor asked.

'No – quite the reverse,' answered Philip.

'Then perhaps we should leave well enough alone. One might even venture that a small amount of irritation is beneficial in this case.'

Philip used to take Justine to his barber at lunchtime every day. He made her dress in boys' clothes for these visits. He would instruct the barber to take his time. Sometimes, she would climax while she was being shaved: she could not control it; it was because of the beads. Philip would light a cigarette and watch; the barber would put her on the table in the back room and carefully remove her ring and any other items that Philip might have fitted that morning. But the heavy bead would still be there inside her hood of skin. She would be soaped while she was kneeling, and the soaping would be prolonged because this was what Philip would have requested. Then the barber would make her lie back with her feet still tucked beneath her. He would touch her soapy labia very lightly while the edge of the razor was drawn across the tightness of her skin. Her labia would be swollen. He would hold her clitoris nipped against the bead inside the hood and, as the razor rubbed away from it, the pulling sensations and the pressure of the bead would make her come. Nothing was ever said about it; Justine tried to hide her climax but the barber always knew. Once she had come he would finish her quickly, wipe her and Philip would take her away.

If Philip then became very intense, very excited, Justine would know that he meant to punish her. She never knew whether he would take her back straight away or wait and punish her later, in the night. But on the day he took her to the doctor, he made her change into a skirt for the visit; then in the afternoon, he took her somewhere else. In the carriage, he explained briefly to her what would happen. On the seat was a leather case.

They drew up at a large, well-appointed hotel. Philip picked up the case, paid the driver off and hurried her past the doorman and inside. There were many people in the lobby and several uniformed attendants. Philip sat Justine on a large leather couch while he spoke to the man at the desk. Then he took her upstairs and into a large, sumptuously furnished suite where Lawrence was pouring champagne for a man she had never seen before; this man watched her from the moment she came in. He seemed distinguished and well-spoken; he was much younger than Philip, yet Philip seemed to treat him deferentially when he introduced him to Justine. He referred to the man only by his first name – Alec – and he seemed at great pains to please him. Lawrence continued pouring, laughing, and the men continued drinking, with Alec never taking his eyes from Justine. They talked of business, some venture that Philip wanted Alec to become involved in, but its nature was never made clear.

After a while, Philip told Justine to take her hat off. The conversation halted and the three men turned to watch her as she stood by the table fumbling with the brim. 'Put it down, Justine,' Philip said gently. Her heart began to thump as he explained to Alec about her beads. 'I must be back at the office soon,' he said, finishing his drink. He placed the leather case on the table, then took the small jewel box out of his pocket, showed it to Alec and said: 'She is at your disposal for the afternoon.'

Alec did not reply, but the tip of his index finger sifted through the contents of the small box while Justine waited where she had been put, beside the table, facing the three men, facing into the room, clothed but with her legs naked to the tops and beyond. And Alec was looking at her again. Beneath the innocence of her long plaid skirt, her belly was shaved to a smoothness that was perfect; her prepuce was drawn back fully from her clitoris and was fastened by a tiny stirrup to the ring. Her labia felt hot against the cool shaved skin of her thighs. And her clitoris was so swollen that it hurt her. In the short walk from the doctor's to the carriage, she had almost come. Philip had known how excited she was, and he had made her remove her knickers. He had made her ride in the carriage with her skirt pulled up and her clitoris exposed. It had hurt her when he touched it. And it hurt her now, while the men were talking about the tiny instruments in the box and the ways in which they could be applied.

Justine leaned back, in the way that Philip had told her to do; she pressed against the table edge and moved her toes apart. Alec watched her every movement. She could feel the edge of the table pressing into her buttocks on a horizontal line; the cloth of her skirt was poised to brush against her anus. This was the way that Philip wanted her to pose in front of men – her toes apart, the cheeks of her bottom pressed against the table. He had told her that he found her anus more attractive now that it was dilated; he had touched it in the carriage and told her that he wanted to kiss it; he had touched it with his wetted fingertip and Justine had wanted to come. He hadn't let her, but he had exposed her breasts and touched the ring above her clitoris, where it threaded through her skin, and he had explained to her that he would introduce her to a man whom she must please; that it was very important to Philip that she please this man. Philip's eyes were upon her now; he nodded slowly and Justine felt a wave of warmth coming deep inside her, and a throbbing between her legs as if her

202

cunny had already been smacked and now it was being sucked. Her toes edged further apart; she pushed back; her labia felt swollen; her clitoris was distended hard; it hurt her. She pushed back until her anus kissed the table through her skirt. Lawrence was opening the leather case. Philip extended a hand in Justine's direction, inviting Alec to take a look for himself, while Philip moved away and Lawrence investigated the things in the case. Justine knew that it contained whips and ropes, but she was more frightened and excited by the contents of the small jewel box, which contained the tightener for her clitoris.

Philip lit a cigarette and watched. It burned with a quickness that sizzled – Justine could hear it. She could see him taking deep, intermittent draughts. She felt Alec's hands open her jacket and lift up her ruffled blouse and perch its soft folds high upon her naked breasts. Her nipples were excited, but he had not touched them. The cigarette smoke wreathed round Philip's fingers. She felt her skirt being hitched; in the mirror she could see the small smooth dimple of her navel below the hem now. Philip took a deep draught. Justine gasped; the strange hands spread across the bare cheeks of her bottom and opened them and pushed, and the edge of the table kissed against her naked anus, which adhered to it because the skin of her anus was sticky clean from the soaping. It would stick to a finger that was wetted then wiped; Philip had repeatedly proved this in the carriage. The skin of her belly was bare and milk-white, but between her legs she was red; she had felt the lips open when Alec had spread her. The stirrup around her clitoris could be seen, she knew; the beads underneath her could not. They could be felt: his fingers touched them and tested them and moved them and traced them to where her anus kissed against the edge of the wood. Her skin itched; the small beads moved beneath it; the pad of his thumb was touching her clitoris; the tip of his middle finger was against her anus, testing the bead that was balanced on the rim; and she could feel the next bead, which was inside her, where the muscle of her anus trembled as it sucked against the wood. But there was a sweet sexual feeling of abandon welling in Justine's throat. Her blouse slipped down over her aching breasts. Alec lifted it and balanced it above them. She pushed her shoulders back, arched her neck, and the feeling in her throat went deeper, sinking down inside her, spreading her, filling her all the way to the place where she was suckered to the wood.

Alec lifted her up and broke the seal, leaving her sitting on the table. Her legs were trembling. He released her stirrup and began attaching the small gold butterfly-shaped tightener through the punctures in her labia, so the droplet of gold that was inserted into her hood was captured with her clitoris and the two parts moved as one. Justine moaned with pleasure as the miniature instrument was tightened. Her breasts shook and her belly pushed out above the edge of the table, to present her captured clitoris for wetting. It poked out below the droplet like a shiny ball.

Philip's cigarette was almost gone. Lawrence was assembling on the table an assortment of oiled leathers and whips that he had taken from the case. Philip looked at Justine one last time before he left her. Her nipples were pink and thick, her eyes were closed, but her mouth was open. And she was sitting on her string of beads, which pressed into her as the man controlling her edged her haunches apart, until her buttocks spread on the table and her labia projected moistly, with the small gold tightener sealed around their upper tips.

At the office, that afternoon, Charlotte came to visit. It was so unusual for her to do this that Philip knew something was wrong. She did not offer her cheek; she wouldn't look at him for longer than a second at a time.

'What is it?' he asked her.

She stared at her hands and spoke in a low voice: 'Yesterday, I saw you in town, Philip. You were with someone . . .' Charlotte looked at him. 'A boy,' she said.

'My nephew,' he said quickly.

'That's what uncle George said; that's what we assumed – a relative. But it wasn't, was it?' She searched his eyes. 'Tell me . . .'

Philip was casting about for clues. 'Tell you what?'

There were tears forming in Charlotte's eyes. 'That it wasn't a relative – that it wasn't even a boy. Oh Philip, I recognised her face. I knew that I had seen her before: the other day – she was on the bridge. Wasn't she? Why did you tell me then that you didn't know her? Don't lie to me now, Philip – please.'

He said nothing. He looked at her with sad, grey eyes and waited until she was forced to look away. Then he extended one hand and gently touched the ring upon her finger and she broke down into tears. 'I did not want to hurt you, Charlotte. But I could not just put her aside . . .'

Charlotte's head was against his jacket; his fingers were searching her soft brown hair. 'Tell me her name,' she sobbed.

'Justine . . .'

There was a pause in which he heard her swallow. 'Do you . . . Do you love her?' she whispered.

Philip sighed. 'I think she loves me. I think that is why she followed us into the park.'

Charlotte's head lifted. She studied his face. She touched his cheeks apprehensively, her fingertips moving softly over his skin. 'Philip, I do not know what to think, now. I want to trust you, but . . .'

'But what?' He stroked her long, soft hair.

'I want to meet her, Philip. I want to talk with her – alone.'

Philip returned early to the hotel room. The door was unlocked and he entered quietly. Justine was naked on the couch. Both men were naked too. Alec had noticed Philip, who merely nodded. Justine had not seen him. She was kneeling up, with her arms behind her back. Lawrence held her wrists but she was facing Alec, who sat on the couch, his hand between her legs and rubbing the shaved, facing surfaces of her thighs, but avoiding the naked labia, which dangled, overfull and red and wet. Justine, turning, saw Philip and froze. Alec turned her head back. He held her jaw and took the red wet droplet in his fingers and

205

masturbated it very slowly, until she shuddered. Then he slid his hand round the back of her head. Though she resisted, he pulled her down. Lawrence took up the masturbation from the back, spreading her legs to obtain the access. In his fingers was the stirrup-clasp. Justine's lips hesitated above the thick shaft of Alec's cock; she was breathing quickly as Lawrence's fingertips moved her closer to the point of coming. Her face looked small; the cock looked broad and solid; its conical cap was short.

When Alec pulled her down, her hands came forward to stop herself overbalancing. Her slender fingers touched the base of the cock; her small fingertips pressed into the balls, then moved away. Alec brought them back. He whispered to her. Nervously, her fingertips gathered his balls and her small hand weighed them. He whispered again; her full lips pouted to a cup above the solid conical cap. His knees moved further apart; her nipples brushed across his thighs; his hips lifted and her middle finger extended down and slid between his buttocks. For a moment, Alec closed his eyes, then he murmured as he lifted higher. Behind Justine, Lawrence fitted the clasp to her swollen labia and hooked it on to the ring. Justine shivered; her clitoris protruded through the stirrup. Then her pouting lips spread about the cap of the cock and the hand around her head pushed down. As she swallowed him, her nostrils flared to cope with breathing and her middle finger reached so deeply into him that her inner wrist spread his balls. The fingertips behind her kept wetting her exposed clitoris while she grunted with the cock inside her mouth.

Alec murmured again; he eased her head up a little, eased her finger out of him and forced her to lie down on her side with the cap of his cock still in her mouth. Her slim back made a curve; the soles of her tucked-up feet were visible and the cheeks of her bottom were marked with bright red welts. Lawrence's hand lay against those welts; his fingertips pinched them as she sucked. He opened her legs and touched her at the front. He tucked her legs up tightly, so that her labia could now be seen again, as could the beads bulging through the string of skin connecting to her anus. Lawrence stared at Philip while he touched this string and measured each small skin-coated bead between the tip of his finger and thumb. Justine became very still while he toyed with her beads: her head did not move; her lips stayed fixed about the cap of Alec's cock but her hand writhed slowly, and the finger that had been inside him stayed lifted and separate from the rest.

Philip moved like a shadowy figure away from the door and around the periphery of the room. He reached the cabinet and silently poured himself a drink. He looked at the case on the table; there were several items missing. There were marks, faint marks, on Justine's back. And when Alec turned her over, Philip saw that there were also marks upon her belly, which Alec was now touching while Lawrence held her legs. The clasp was removed and she was smacked between the legs; they used a small oiled leather on the lips. Alec kissed her, Lawrence whipped. Then, in place of the clasp, the tightener was fitted, which was difficult, with Justine being so swollen now, because she had been smacked. But they persevered while Justine, her legs held apart, gently whimpered. Her legs looked even slimmer when they were apart and the space between them at the top looked wide. It was dominated by the pink shaved bulge of her mount and the bright protrusion of the smacked lips of her cunt. Where the lips were joined, the tightener glinted like a small gold butterfly that had alighted there to suck. Philip settled into a chair and lit a cigarette.

Alec made her stand up. He smacked her bottom with one of the other leathers. He smacked her with her legs apart. Then Lawrence tightened the small gold butterfly and Alec smacked her again, until her hips thrust forwards and her labia pushed between Lawrence's waiting fingers. Alec made her kneel on the floor while he played with her from behind. Then he made her crawl into the bathroom. Lawrence accompanied him, taking the leather. Philip did not follow; he knew well enough that Lawrence could cope. He put his glass down, put his cigarette down and watched it burning away. He looked at times towards the short corridor and the blank, partly open door, then his gaze returned to the whisps of smoke while he listened for the sounds.

In the bathroom, Justine stood naked before the full-length mirror, the tightener gripped around her pulsing clitoris, her legs and bottom burning from the smacking. The men moved quietly, their cocks curving upwards, smooth as bones. Alec told Justine to open her legs. He kissed her while he touched the small gold tightener and his cock brushed her naked belly and the pleasure-pain of throbbing made her tremble. He stroked her smooth nude inner thighs and wetted her tightener and gently masturbated her again. She heard the tap being run, the glass being filled.

'No . . .' she whispered. They would make her drink again. Alec continued masturbating her, and the feeling came between Justine's legs, that she would pee.

Lawrence held the glass to her lips while Alec knelt in front of her – and his kneeling there made the feeling come again. She felt the water sliding down inside her empty belly, which Alec's fingertips pressed where her naked skin turned pink. Justine's legs progressively opened; Alec licked her belly ring, which hung loose now and could move inside her skin, then he sucked her naked cunny. Three fingers opened her vagina and pressed against her bladder from inside while the gold butterfly that constricted her clitoris was loosened, then retightened and the feeling came on very strongly, that she wanted to pee. Then she was turned around to face the mirror fully and Alec's fingers, reaching underneath her, slipped inside her cunny from behind. Lawrence was filling the glass again. She knew that this time, they would make her do it. 'Bend down,' Alec whispered. He made her stoop and close her knees across her belly while her cunny projected down between her legs and his fingers probed and rubbed ever deeper inside her from behind. Then they made her stand with her legs together while she took the drink.

'Lift her, Lawrence.' She was edged astride the rounded corner of the sink, facing the mirror, so that her belly thrust forwards, her cunny pouted out above the edge and she was sitting on her beads, with the tightly clenched mouth of her bottom projecting behind her, available for touching. The freezing, glass-like surface of the enamel was pressing against her smoothly shaved thighs. Alec turned on the cold tap. Justine moaned: the wet tip of Lawrence's tongue had pressed against her anus; Alec's fingertips flicked freezing droplets up against her open cunny. Two stone-cold fingers entered her and lifted; Justine gasped; the warm tongue stretched the anal ring and a thimbleful of hot liquid squirted into Alec's hand, which closed around her cunny while he turned her head and kissed her. Justine's small wet tongue thrust deep into his mouth.

'Quickly . . .' They lifted her down and placed her astride the lavatory seat, facing forwards, facing Alec, trembling, with her belly pushing out towards him. Lawrence held her arms behind her while Alec licked the burning droplets that had spilled when she was lifted and were gathered round her cunny. Then he sucked her clitoris through the tightener and she whimpered because she could not use her hands to hold his head against her. Her arms were being held so tightly behind her that the pressure in her nipples hurt. 'Open her legs.' And when they spread them even wider, Justine leaked. Alec reached below Justine and pulled her buttocks forwards, so the gap narrowed between her cunny and the front edge of the seat and she was slumped, with her legs wide open and her cunny pointing upwards so that nothing that leaked would escape. Then Alec smacked her with the leather. He smacked between her legs: he smacked her cunny while she was bursting. He smacked until the leather was wet with her leakage, then he sucked her. When he smacked her again, she started to pee. It came slowly, then surged. She gasped and moaned; her belly trembled. Alec held her open and the liquid formed a sturdy fountain which tumbled back across her clitoris, restrained so perfectly by the gold. He tried to trap the flow in his hand; the liquid spurted through his fingers and ran across her thighs.

In the sitting room, Philip heard Justine's gasps and sobs of desperation turn into a prolonged and rending moan.

The cigarette in the tray in front of him had burned to a snake of powdery ash, warm to the touch of a finger. He sat back silently; he did not move. Justine emerged from the bathroom, with Lawrence behind her, then Alec, drying his fingers on a small white towel. His cock was still erect; it stood out like a thick curved staff. Justine's thighs were wet; down each inner thigh, she was wet to her knees. The area round her cunt was wet. Philip could smell it – a faint sharp bitterness in the air, like the smell of water on still-warm coals, like the smokiness of burnt wood. Alec picked her up easily. Her body was limp and her breasts slid gently outwards. The backs of her thighs were wet across his forearm. His cock, curving up beneath her, touched her spine. He lifted her and opened her legs; the tip of his cock pressed against her labia, which opened and clung about the cone.

The two men carried her to the bedroom; Philip remained in the chair. Through the open door, he saw her being smacked, face down, while the tightness of the butterfly sucked the place between her legs. He saw her buttocks opened and one leg being bent and lifted to the side while her head was placed upon a pillow. He saw Lawrence, kneeling close to the pillow, crowding Justine's perfect face, holding it between his hands. Then the door was closed. This time, the sounds were less distinct, but more prolonged. Philip lit another cigarette. It took a long while before the men reappeared and closed the bedroom door, leaving Justine still inside.

Philip poured them a drink before they left. Alec was pleased with Justine.

'We shall be having a small gathering on Thursday evening at the club,' he said. 'Just a few invited friends, you understand. One or two girls for company. You would be very welcome, Philip – very welcome.' Alec glanced towards the bedroom door.

'I could bring Justine,' Philip offered.

'I would like that very much.'

Philip cleared his throat. 'I was wondering, Alec, whether you have had any further thoughts about that financial matter I mentioned, things being a bit tight now at the firm?'

'We could discuss it at the club.'

When Alec had left with Lawrence, Philip went to Justine. There were dried starchy marks on the sheet and pillow and fresher marks that were wet. He took out his handkerchief and wiped her lips and neck. He traced the line of every welt upon her bottom. He opened her legs and unpinned her butterfly. He wetted her clitoris. When he moistened his fingers again, his fingertips tasted salty bitter; he could smell the burnt wood scent strongly, though the moisture upon her legs was long dried. He covered her nudity with a sheet. When he slipped into bed beside her, the skin of her breasts and belly and legs was burning where it touched him.

He opened her legs and lifted her knees. He kissed the whip marks on her belly, then drew the hood back using the stirrup, exposing the clitoris while he traced the string of beads, wetting them one by one, while Justine stayed open, with her legs up and the smooth nude skin between them fully stretched. 'The woman in the park,' he whispered, 'she has asked to meet you. I want you to tell her the truth about us. I will tell you what to say.' Justine did not move nor answer. The liquid tip of his finger touched the bead that was poised above the lip of her anus, and a droplet of his saliva ran into the well.

Then Philip lay behind Justine and pressed the head of his penis against her anus, which opened out to take it. He kept it at the entrance, keeping the ring fully dilated while he played gently with her exposed clitoris. 'I had to do it,' Philip whispered. 'I had to see you used by other men.' And suddenly, Justine began shuddering, gripping his fingertips and pressing them around her clitoris, then turning her head and kissing him deeply, moaning, while Philip whispered into her mouth, 'I had to give you away. Shh . . .'

'Aghhh!' And his fingertips turned wet.

'Shhh . . . Your tongue, Justine.' He sucked it and nipped it with his teeth and held it. Then he felt the ring of her anus moving into spasm, and the bead inside it pulsed against his penis when she came.

16: A STUDY IN AROUSAL

Philip spent the whole of the next day with Justine, and that was very unusual. He did not go to the office. He behaved very secretively when he took her to be shaved, and afterwards he took her home – to his own house – where she had never been. He took her upstairs to his study. There was a large leather chair in which he put her to sit. Opposite the chair was a small round table. Philip seemed nervous with her. After a short while, he had a visitor – Alec. Justine was afraid to look at him. She knew that Philip was jealous of Alec touching her – he hadn't said it, but she knew – so why had he brought him here? Alec stood by the small round table, touching its surface, which was polished to a mirror finish.

'Alec would like to get to know you a little better, Justine,' said Philip. When he said it, she was aware that he was watching her to see how she would respond. She did not look at Alec, but she could feel her cheeks colouring. The linked silver rings made small sounds as her fingers moved across the leather arm of the chair.

'Has she been shaved again?' Alec asked. Philip nodded to Justine; slowly, she obeyed. She got up. She kept her face turned away, looking towards the window. But she lifted the hem of her dress up to the tops of her stockings and then across the paleness of her thighs.

'Justine,' whispered Philip, and he was looking across to the small bare round table that was positioned between the two men. It was bare for one reason, Justine knew, and it was positioned there for her. The tips of Alec's fingers touched it and it felt to Justine as if his fingertips were touching her. The feeling, the full, stretched feeling, was coming in her throat. She was the reason for this meeting. 'Justine.' She moved across and the room turned completely silent. She had kept her dress lifted; now she took it up above the cheeks of her bottom and to her waist. She turned round; the tops of her stockings touched the edge of the table behind her. She opened her legs; she heard Alec gasp. And the fact that he had gasped excited her – but she must not make it known to Philip, or he would smack her again. She spread her cheeks and sat, with her legs kept open, so her weight was taken against the beads, which pressed into the skin below her cunny. She held her dress above her navel. Her cunny was red because Philip had smacked her in the carriage. Its lips were faintly sticky because she had become wet; they swelled as they pressed against the table. Her fingertips trembled as they stroked the foreskin back, exposing the shape of the droplet that was sealed inside it and moving the ring that nipped through the naked skin above it in two dark, pinched pits in the pinkened white, deepened these last few days by the repeated toying, repeated pulling at the ring, repeated movement.

'Take everything off,' said Alec – Alec had said it; it was as if he were taking over with Justine – 'and stand at the window.' Philip placed the jewel box on the desk. Alec had another box that was larger. He showed Philip what was in the box, and Philip approved. Justine was now nude; her dress and stockings were on the floor. 'Go on,' said Alec. She crept across and stood to one side, close to the curtain and half facing into the room. Alec got up. 'Stand against it. Face it. Spread.' And the feeling came to Justine, as if ice had been put inside her – because of those words and because of the people down in the street and because he clearly knew what Rachel had done to her. He made her press her hands against the sheet of glass that reached below her knees. He made her spread her legs and turn her knees until their insides touched the glass. And he made her stand in this open, stilted way until the cramps came up her inner thighs and up her buttocks. 'Will you feel them? Hard . . .' he whispered and with the pressure of the hands upon her buttocks, her nipples touched the freezing glass and Justine gasped and shuddered and her buttocks tightened while they were held open and the men became more interested in touching. She caught sight of figures moving in the street, and the feeling came again. She felt fingers against the beads and against the fleshy ring and then her breasts being lifted so the nipples pointed upwards and the undersides lay upon the glass. Then she felt the hand between her legs unfastening the gold ring and rubbing the punctured skin. 'She is better without it for the present,' said Alec. 'It is better that we keep it nude.' And his fingertips collected up the metal droplet sealed inside her foreskin and nipped it while his other hand moved down again and back between the cheeks.

'You give her plenty of this, I take it?' asked Alec. The fingers moved across the swollen surface of her anus, searching gently, fitting to the mouth.

'Lately,' said Philip, 'yes. I find I can keep her on for longer – and that way, you still have all the rest of it to hand.'

'Mm . . . She was good yesterday – I enjoyed her. But I like this idea of keeping her on.' He squeezed her breasts and rubbed his hand all the way down her belly, then rubbed the lips between her legs and shaped them into an 'o'. He turned her round and kept her legs open. 'Oh God, Philip – look . . .' Her pubic lips had stayed open, formed into the 'o' which trembled as Alec lifted her foreskin back, and Justine's eyes closed as her buttocks gradually opened and their inner skin touched the pane of glass.

When she opened her eyes she saw that the larger box was now on the polished table. The men retreated; Philip sat on the desk and Alec on a chair close to her. Alec asked her to go to the table. His expression when he asked her made her afraid – she was naked in this room and they were clothed and they were using her as their plaything. Justine reached the table. 'You must keep your legs open,' Alec said. 'Wider. Put your hands on the table. Now move forward.' Her pubic lips grazed the surface of the table. 'And stay still.' Her pubic lips were balanced. She heard

215

him get up, then felt his fingers sliding underneath her, teasing the lips apart again, so the edges of the insides touched the table and trembled, because her knees were open. He walked round to the front and opened the box. In it was a perfect replica of an erect penis. He made her rest on her elbows and he put it in her hands, the stem in her left hand and the balls in her right. The two parts moved independently. They were heavy; the balls were soft and the cock was not perfectly rigid. The whole thing was covered in smooth soft skin that slipped against the stiffness inside. When Philip saw it, he wanted it put into her but Alec told him: 'No – put her in the leather chair.'

She was much more aware of the softness of the leather now that she was naked, and because the surface was matt, it was warm against her skin. The cushioned seat yielded; Justine sank into it, her arms along the soft chair arms. Alec drew up his chair. He said he wanted to know about the things that Justine had done with Rachel at the school. He took from his pocket the letter that Julia had made her write. While he glanced at it and waited, Justine sank deeper into the chair. Alec then explained that they had the time – plenty of time – and that he wanted to know. He gave the letter to Philip, who then moved back and sat on the desk. Justine's eyes darted round the room. 'We have lots of time, Justine,' Alec said again. 'I want you to tell me what happened.'

Justine's hands retreated from the arms of the chair and into her lap. Alec lifted them up and put them back. He opened her legs. He formed her pubic lips into an 'o' again. 'I want to hear about the others.' Justine turned her head away, but saw only Philip gazing calmly. She felt Alec's hands against her inner thighs, pressing, and she felt the small 'o' opening more fully, stretching the skin around her clitoris and making her aroused. 'Philip, I think she wants it smacking.' Justine moaned. 'Oh yes,' said Alec, 'I really think she does.'

Philip used a thin leather on the outer lips of her cunny while Alec held her knees apart and the inner lips formed

216

a broad 'o' whose edges gradually softened as Philip smacked the bald red pubic skin on either side.

'Open your mouth, Justine,' said Alec. Then he played with her. He allowed her to keep her eyes closed while he touched her cunny and opened out the softened lips. He lifted her foreskin back and masturbated her, very gently, and with one fingertip brushing the velvet deep depression of her anus throughout, until Justine's mouth opened so widely that Alec touched it with the fingers that had touched her cunny. Then he moved away. Justine's breathing gradually slowed and her eyes flickered open. Alec held the replica penis. 'Get something round her wrists,' he said.

But they didn't restrain her legs, which lifted up, her feet sliding on the seat, her toes in the soft matt leather, her belly bulging, and the leather wristbands taken back and held while the slippy penis was introduced through the stretched 'o' of her pubic lips, leaving the weight of the balls hanging down. And Justine's mouth stayed open while Alec kissed along her lips and two curving fingers pushed the last part of the penis up inside her and the head of it touched her womb. Then he moved back again and looked at her. 'Keep her wrists fastened back.' Her eyes opened lazily. 'Give me the small strap.'

He walked to the side of the leather chair. 'Justine – we want to know about the others. Lift your legs over the arms. Close your eyes.'

She cried out. Her legs and arms jerked as the leather smacked her nipples. 'Keep her tight, Philip.' Then Alec dealt with each breast individually, holding the nipple turned up and smacking the belly of the breast, the smacks increasing in urgency and frequency until Justine's legs splayed open and the loose weight of the balls between them lifted and rolled against the well of her bottom. Alec held the balls up and touched her bottom while Philip smacked her breasts until Justine cried out that she would tell them. They took the penis out of her and lifted her up. The ties hung loosely from her wrists. Her head stayed down. Then her voice came in a whisper:

'I was her favourite; she always told me that – always.'

217

Her hands moved across her breasts, the wrist ties trailing; her fingers dug into her arms. Then the words spilled quickly. 'When she was with the other young women, she always wanted me there. She would take me into her bedroom first; she would undress me and kiss me. Then she would tie me in the chair and go into the other room. And I would hear her with the other girl. It would go on for a long time. Then Rachel would bring the girl in, make her lie on the bed and she would kiss and touch her. And when she was aroused, Rachel would make her watch the things she did to me.' Justine hesitated. 'She would keep her partly dressed, sometimes nude, but mostly, wearing just a blouse.' Justine's eyes closed. 'Rachel had a tall stool that she would make her sit on. If the girl got excited by what she saw, Rachel would take her off the stool and stand her up and smack her. But sometimes, she would ask the girl what she would like to do to me . . . She had pins and other things – instruments she had taken from the clinic.' Again she hesitated.

'Tell us about the pins,' Alec said.

Her voice was trembling. 'She used to put pins through my skin, then play with me until . . .'

'She used to put pins where? Show us.'

Justine whispered, 'Through here.' She lay back and touched herself and shivered. When her hand moved away from her pubic lips, Alec caught it. He brought her fingers back.

'Show us where she put the pins, Justine.' The tips of Justine's fingers held her pubic lips apart. She turned her head away. 'On the inside?' Alec touched it. Justine shuddered. He lifted back her foreskin; her clitoris protruded. 'Philip, pass me the box, would you?' He took from it a fine chain with a fastener at one end and a gold ball at the other. He slipped the thin rod fastener through the hole in the top of her left pubic lip and secured it with a stud, which nipped the lip. Then he stretched the chain upwards and dropped the weight into the hollow of her navel.

Then they asked her about the instruments Rachel had used. Justine didn't know what they were called but she told them that they had been put inside her to stretch her and to keep her open. 'She used to use them on me, and sometimes leave them in me, then make love to the girl.'

Justine closed her eyes, and she could see Rachel's mouth making love to the girl who teetered on the stool, her left leg wrapped around it, her right leg in the air. And then it was as if she could feel Rachel's tongue again, sliding round the pearl-beaded heads of the pins that she had pushed through the lips of Justine's cunny.

'She won't answer . . .' Their words were becoming distant to Justine. She was sinking down into the softness of the leather chair, sinking deeper while her cunny opened wider as her legs were drawn apart. She could feel all of these things but she was somewhere else. Her wrists were taken back and held in their leather straps behind the chair while she was masturbated with the ball and chain. The ball would be lifted, the chain slid across her clitoris, then her clitoris would be rubbed, the ball would be dangled against it, then lifted up and held so one lip was drawn open while the other one was gently smacked.

They played with her until her limbs felt heavy and unresisting in their hands, her jaw fell slack and her head rolled to the side, so her cheek was pillowed on the soft arm of the chair. Then they lifted her down on to the floor. The thin chain dropped between her legs and the small gold ball bounced on the carpet. Alec sat on the arm of the chair. He stroked the back of her neck and ran his fingers up into her hair; he cupped her chin; her head fell back. He rubbed his thumb back and forth across her lips to make them open.

Philip opened out her legs and lifted aside the ball and chain and Justine's belly rotated and her naked cunny pushed into the softness of the carpet. Philip rubbed a hand across her breasts and slapped the insides of her thighs, making the ball beside her labia jump. Alec got up and examined the dildo that had been inside Justine; then he picked through the box of jewels. He found what he was looking for – a curved gold rod shaped like a miniature penis, about an inch and a half in length, with a strong, flanged head and a fine short chain attached to the other end, which was shaped into a solitary ball. He said that he wanted the gold ring refitting to Justine. She was leaning back with her elbows behind her on the seat. Alec rolled his sleeve up, came across and, kneeling, kissed her, lifting up her breasts on his naked forearm and holding back her head and kissing deeply, then running his fingers down her body and rubbing the red naked pubic skin until her toes turned and pressed together as Justine's cunny opened and his fingers tasted warmness and soft wet. His thumb, stretching up, pressed into the perfect hollow in her belly and his tongue reached ever more deeply into her throat.

'Give me the ring, Philip.' Justine murmured as he pulled the skin above her cunny and threaded the ring through. When he touched her belly, the ring stood out and moved. He put his head to the floor and kissed the ring, pushing his tongue through it and lifting, so her clitoris became exposed and rubbed upon his wetted lower lip.

Philip watched Justine's expression: her eyelids becoming heavy, the blonde-gold lashes trembling in the light, her head thrown back, and her belly lifting. But most of all he watched her mouth – staying open, her breathing becoming quick and distracted. Philip crept across and sat upon the chair arm. Her head, hanging back between her shoulders and her elbows, dangled like a doll's head – china pale, with bright red lips. Her skin was shiny where it stretched round her bony shoulders, and her breasts were round and full and her nipples looked dark and large. While he touched them, he put two fingers to Justine's lips and she took them in her mouth and shivered; her knees jerked open. Alec's head lifted; the gold ring pulsed between her legs; the bead inside her foreskin had been drawn by the suction to the front, so it hung from the stretched skin like a droplet. Alec rubbed her open thighs until Philip could withdraw his fingers from her mouth. Then he took the gold ball that was attached by a chain to her left pubic lip and fed the chain down along the outside of the lip. 'Lift, Justine,' Alec whispered and as she moaned and once more took Philip's fingers deeply in her mouth, her anus opened and the chain was stretched as the small gold ball was taken up inside her. Alec returned to the desk and the box; Philip stayed on the arm of Justine's chair.

A servant came in and looked at her as he whispered to his master; Justine turned her head away; Philip turned it back. The servant's eyes slid down to her belly. Philip lifted Justine's head up. He reached down and touched the ring and chain, pulling it to the side, gradually increasing the drawing feeling inside her bottom until the red, shaved place between her legs contracted, with that one lip drawn open, its lower edge pressed moistly to the carpet. When Justine opened her eyes again, the servant had gone, but Alec was in front of her. He had brought the tiny curved gold rod on its chain. And while he spoke to Philip, he put his arms around her waist and pulled her belly forwards.

'In the bathroom yesterday – I think she liked it,' he said, and Justine became frightened again. 'Do you think this will be effective?'

'I think so,' answered Philip. Justine felt the end of this new chain being fastened to the ring; she felt her foreskin being lifted back, and the trapped gold droplet that was inside it being lifted away. The tiny flanged head of the rod touched her clitoris, then moved down a fraction, pressing, searching. Justine caught her breath; Philip had to hold her; she gasped; the head of the rod found the tiny tender hole below her clitoris, pushed in and stretched the tube and made her cry out with the pain.

'It's tight,' said Alec.

'I imagine tight is better – easier to control the flow.' And Justine gasped again. 'Wait – try this.' He had found a small tin of lubricant in the box. This time the rod slid up the tube, the head pressed against her bladder and Justine wanted to pee: that feeling came on very strongly.

'Relax, Justine.' Alec pushed her legs apart and now the rod began to be expelled. He pressed it slowly with the tip of his finger; Justine's belly tightened; the curved rod slipped and the feeling came again. He continued pressing. She gasped. 'Relax . . .' And when the head pushed through inside her, a tiny spurt of liquid sprayed against his finger, but the instrument stayed in place, with the short tube from her bladder filled with gold, the head locked into her and the ball drawn up against her, pressing below her clitoris, keeping it aroused. 'Ohh . . .' Alec murmured, 'ohh,' touching it, as Justine's head twisted to the side and pressed into the soft leather of the arm of the seat and her lips opened and the tip of her tongue protruded as her belly writhed, with its chain drawn down to the side of her labia and this small curved rod inside her, opening her, making her leak a little every time it was moved and keeping the feeling there all the time – arousal combined with the inescapable, uncontrollable feeling of wanting to pee. Alec played with Justine until the sight of her open lips and the feel of her soft wet vulva moving against his fingers and the scent of her burning liquid drove him on.

He used a cushion in the middle of the seat to support her head and raise it. While he undressed, Philip continued the slow masturbation of Justine. When she came to the point, he smacked her thighs with the leather until she was ready to be masturbated again, with the ball inside her anus gently pulled and the rod inside her bladder pushed to bring about a leak.

Philip watched Alec rise above her, kneeling on the arms and facing the back of the chair. He watched him crouch and push his cock down, vertically down, so the ball sac was divided. Justine's lips reached up and took the crown and sucked it while the tips of her fingers tickled up the back of the shaft and came to rest in the dark hollow where the base of the cock was rooted. The leather ties still hung from her wrist. Philip held her soft pubic lips apart and masturbated Justine; he felt her cunny tighten round his fingers. Her knees tried to lift; he pushed them down and took his fingers out of her but touched the small protrusion of the rod. Justine moaned through her nose; the cock slipped deeper into her mouth; her fingers curved into the hollow between the cheeks above her and Alec groaned.

The ties about Justine's wrists shook gently. Small droplets of yellow were balanced on the carpet between her legs; Philip's fingertips were warm and wet; the smoky scent was in the air. He slid the soft-skinned heavy dildo slowly across the carpet, so that the balls trailed out behind it. He opened out her pubic lips. When the head of the dildo touched inside, her knees lifted again. Philip pushed them down; he slid a hand underneath her; her belly bulged as her shoulders took the strain. As the pad of the middle finger pressed against the slim chain that fed into her anus, her cunny lifted and the dildo slid inside her. And even as it was still sliding, Philip heard her muffled breathing and Alec's gasps. He saw Alec's dangling balls drawn up his shaft, which pulsed as Justine's lips pushed up it, and her fingers opened his anus in that delicious, nervous way. The muscles of her neck rippled as she swallowed in perfect time with the shudders that shook her own belly and the quick spurts that sprang from between the pubic lips that Philip's thumbs held tightly closed now, with her vulva still lifted, supported between his hands, and her legs rigidly open, though trembling, with the ball sac of the dildo between them, resting in a pool of her liquid that balanced on the floor.

When Alec had finished and dressed, Philip asked again about that pressing matter.

'We can discuss it at the club. She will be there?' Alec said.

'Of course.'

Justine had been lifted into the leather chair. Alec bowed his head and kissed her. 'She is perfect,' he whispered. His lips moved down her body. Justine's legs moved open. Alec kissed the small protruding gold ball below her clitoris, then pulled it with his teeth and Justine emitted a tiny cry that was a mixture of pain and pleasure as the rod came free. Her cheek pressed into the soft arm of the chair and with that pressure, her lips opened to make an 'o' that was so sensual and perfect that Philip wanted to kiss it.

There was a small room off Philip's study. He put Justine in there that evening. He kept her naked and he tied her hands to the wall above her head, where a brass ring had been fitted. He explained to her that she would have to keep very quiet because he was expecting a guest. And he spent the time until his guest arrived masturbating Justine. Justine became aroused quickly, because she was fastened but was free to move her legs, which Philip made her open while he smacked her. The smacking was restricted to her inner thighs, which helped the masturbation progress quickly to the point where he could fit the curved short rod up into the tube to her bladder. He dried his fingers on her labia and began to play with her again. But his guest arrived. Philip gagged Justine, turned off the light and closed the door.

It was a woman – Justine could hear her, although neither voice was distinct. But she could tell from Philip's tone that this was a woman he was treating very differently. She knew it had to be the woman on the bridge. But Philip had told her that the woman wanted to meet her, and she suddenly became frightened that he would show her off in this way, while she was tied, and might do things to her in front of the woman.

The conversation continued long; she heard glasses chinking. The woman laughed, then the voices became lower. She heard other sounds, then whispers. Then the door opened. Philip started to come in, but instead turned back, leaving the door open. Justine waited, terrified.

The leather chair had been moved and the woman was sitting on it. Justine could see her in profile. She turned and seemed to stare at Justine, then turned back without making any acknowledgement of her presence. The study was brightly lit. The small room that Justine was in was dark and she was against the far wall. The woman must not have been able to see her. Philip went across and locked the study outer door. The woman seemed nervous. But when Philip came back and bowed his head she kissed him. He knelt in front of her, unfastened her boots, took them off and kissed her stockinged feet. His hands slid up her legs. She gasped, but still her leg lifted and she bent her head towards him and kissed him passionately. Then his hand moved to the buttons at her breast.

And Justine watched it all; she did not even close her

eyes; she watched every moment of this seduction, and she knew from the tremors of excited fear that this woman had not done such things before tonight. Philip did not take her stockings off her; he left her knickers round her feet and her bodice open at her breasts, which had the darkest nipples that Justine had seen. From her breasts to her thighs, the woman's skin was now exposed. Justine watched him kiss it. She watched the woman's fingers curling and digging into the soft arm of the chair, fingers that were too afraid to touch his head and guide it, so her first pleasure came too quickly – like a knife that Justine felt too, as if the short curved rod was twisted inside her. Then she watched him penetrating her and making love to her slowly, touching that expanse of skin, touching her between the legs, making her climax strong.

It was the way that she reacted – the way that she enjoyed it – that terrified Justine, because she knew then that Philip did not need her. When they had done, they kissed like lovers and he, still kneeling, lay in her arms and she suckled him with those dark nipples. Then she bowed her head and took his tongue into her mouth. Afterwards, Philip closed the door, leaving Justine in the darkness. She heard them leave.

It must have been a long time after that when light flooded into the room. She had slept. Her shoulders and her wrists were racked by excruciating pains. Philip still wore his cloak. It was cold where the sleeve brushed against her skin, making gooseflesh spread across her belly.

'You saw her?' he whispered, removing her gag. Justine bit her lip. A tear spilled down her cheek. He lifted her chin. 'Is she not a beautiful woman?' She could not see him properly for the tears. 'I had her maidenhead tonight . . .' Her chin slid off his fingers; her eyes turned away. 'I did it for you, to show you – to make the passions flow, Justine.'

Her first climax came while she hung there; it was delivered by his fingers, which wiped her wet against her legs and returned, and when they touched her open softness, Justine came. He lowered her to the floor and massaged her wrists and shoulders and turned her over. He opened her anus with his tongue. When his fingertip touched the gold protrusion under her clitoris and the rod moved, with his tongue still inside her, stretching her, her second climax came. Then he carried her to the leather chair and lowered her, head down, on her back, so her legs fell open round the chair back and her head hung upside down, and he made love to her in that position. He made fully-penetrative, long-lasting love to Justine's mouth and throat. She could taste the woman on his penis, which was harder and hotter than she had known and it kept pushing for her throat, making the gagging feeling come. But she did not try to pull away; she wanted him to fill her throat. Her heavy breasts hung downwards and he milked them. When he hunched, her belly rubbed against his chest and the bare red liquid lips of her cunny reached to suck upon his mouth and suddenly she could feel him tense, begin pumping and try to hold back. And Justine's throat opened round him and swallowed, her top lip touched his balls, pushing them back, and the tip of her finger touched his anus and he spurted.

When he was finished, he lifted her up and took her in his arms and told her that he loved her. He made her keep her legs open while he detached the rod and pushed it part way into her again. He told her that she was special and that he did not want to have to lose her, and between the kisses, he used the rod to keep her on the point of coming, wetting it and rubbing it round her clitoris, then pushing it into her mouth again, and making the shivering, shuddering feeling come inside Justine. He pulled her up as she began her climax and his hands made a sling for her cunny. And in this sling her body was lifted and bounced until her legs ran wet and her climax was completed.

17: THE CLUB

'Miss Lessing, Mr Lessing – please make yourselves comfortable. Justine will be here directly.'

'Thank you, Miss Norwood.' Charlotte perched herself uneasily at one end of the ample settee.

Her uncle, glowering by the fire, waited until the woman had gone. 'I shall do the talking, Charlotte. One must be firm.'

'Uncle, please, I don't want her upsetting.'

'And what about you? And that . . . that . . . Oh – if I were a younger man I'd – '

'Uncle, I love him. He's my fiancé. You do not seem to understand.'

'Pah! He's a womaniser, Charlotte. He's after your money: I've said so all along.'

'*Hush . . .*'

The door opened; the girl came in, glancing across at them then closing the door behind her and walking nervously across the room. She bowed her head a fraction then, looking up, seemed suddenly very frightened. Her large eyes stared at Charlotte's uncle.

'You are Justine?' he said imperiously.

Her lips were trembling; she frowned, then glanced at Charlotte before she nodded.

'Please, uncle, let her sit,' whispered Charlotte and Justine's eyes grew wider as she stared again at him and he stared back at her with a look of utter disdain. 'Justine,' said Charlotte gently, 'please sit down – we wish only to speak with you. Nobody will harm you.' And the perfect, wide blue eyes met Charlotte's. 'Do you know why we are here?'

There was a long pause before Justine whispered, 'He told me that he loved me . . .'

'There!' declared the uncle. 'What did I tell you?' Charlotte lifted a hand to quieten him. He turned and glared at the two women through the mirror over the fireplace.

Justine edged forwards on the chair. She glanced up at Charlotte. 'He said that he wanted me – that he desired me – but that he had chosen you . . .' She had to force herself to go on. 'That he loved you much more deeply, because you had never asked for anything in return, and he would never do anything to hurt you . . .' There were tears forming in both women's eyes. 'And . . . and that is why he is giving me away.'

'He is giving you up?' whispered Charlotte, but the other couldn't answer, because the tears were streaming down her face. Charlotte fell to her knees beside Justine and comforted her. 'Please – I would not have you sad, Justine,' she whispered. She was moved by the expression on that perfect countenance. 'I know that you are warm and good; I would not wish upon you any sadness, nor any blame. You need only ask and we shall help you in any way we can.'

But Justine, overcome with emotion, apologised and hurried from the room.

Charlotte's uncle held her back when she tried to follow her. Then the lady of the house returned and closed the door.

'She will be all right, Miss Lessing, once she is rested. I shall take care of her. And yet I fear that she is still very much in love.' She sighed. 'Young girls are impressionable – they read messages that are not there.'

At the front door, Charlotte thanked her.

'I am sure, my dear Charlotte,' said her uncle, 'that the young lady is in safe hands. And that Miss Norwood will keep us informed?' His eyes sparkled.

'Indeed,' Miss Norwood answered, as she handed him his lacquered stick and grey kid gloves.

Julia kept Justine chaired and open-legged for the rest of the afternoon, with Caroline in attendance, toying with Justine's nipples, kissing her clitoris, moving the buried nodule against it with her tongue, and between times – with Krisha's assistance – tying Justine's knees back and smacking the lips of her naked cunny and the line of buried beads.

In the early evening, Justine was dressed and taken to the downstairs drawing room to meet her escorts. The gentlemen stood up. Philip hardly acknowledged her, but the other two were watching her. Philip introduced Alec to Julia, who smiled disarmingly as he took her hand.

'And who is this handsome flower of our youth?' she asked him, and in the same breath, she dismissed the girls who had had the new arrival cornered.

'My nephew – Robert,' said Alec. The young man, though well-spoken and perfectly mannered, had appeared overawed by his surroundings even before Julia had embarrassed him, and now he was blushing furiously, and speaking to her falteringly. Once seated, he didn't move a muscle but continued watching Justine until their gazes met directly, when he glanced away.

'Where is the other one?' Philip at length asked Julia.

She seemed deliberately to hesitate, looking at Justine before replying. 'Roxanne? Ah, yes . . .' Then she cleared her throat. 'Roxanne is delayed. She is with Lawrence. She is visiting a gentleman. Lawrence told me to explain that she would meet you later – at the club, was it?' She looked to Alec.

He nodded. 'My club, madam,' he said. 'We shall have to leave word at the door, Philip, if she is to be admitted.'

'How will she find it?' asked Julia, examining her nails.

'Lawrence knows it,' said Philip.

'Ah,' said Julia, 'good.'

Then Alec showed Julia the small jewel box. 'With your permission, madam, we would like to make her ready.'

'Certainly.' Julia then seated herself beside Robert while Philip remained standing. Alec brought the small box over to Justine. He opened it: the tiny things inside it glinted; Justine's nipples tightened and she could not breathe.

'Lift your skirt,' Alec whispered. She wore no panties. Her eyes darted round the room for help. They came to rest upon the young man, who earnestly edged forwards on the seat until Julia drew him back.

'Such urgency,' she declared, and the older men smiled. 'So brave a head on such young shoulders. Shhh . . .' She held him back and forced him into a kiss. 'You must not intervene,' she whispered, playing with his sandy hair. 'Justine is taken.' She kissed him again and touched the place between his legs and he became very still.

'Stand up, Justine.' Alec sat down in front of her and placed the box of terrors open on the couch.

'It will be easier if she sits astride the arm,' said Philip. Justine's legs and hands froze. The young man turned pale and open-mouthed as Alec lifted up Justine's skirt for himself, exposing her slim, white legs and, round the back, lifting it higher still above her buttocks until she was half turned and the furrow of her backbone could be seen. Then he moved her stiff, frightened body round again. Perfect paleness descended to the junction of her pressed-together legs and the thin slit in the rounded pink.

'Sit upon the arm, Justine. Lean back,' Alec said, 'I want to look at it again.' Then he said, so only she could hear: 'I want to touch you where you pee.' His eyes met hers and the feeling came between her legs. She edged back. Her buttocks touched the padded arm; her knees moved open then her ankles lifted and her buttocks spread about the round, stretched velvet. Alec encouraged her knees apart and the thin slit of her cunny opened. Her cunny lips were thin because Caroline had played with them until they were too soft to be smacked any more; instead, Caroline had smacked the mouth of her bottom with her fingers.

'She is very beautiful,' Julia observed to Robert as he turned paler and began to tremble. Then she whispered, 'She is nineteen; how old is your uncle?' Then Philip coughed and Julia kept quiet.

Alec made Justine hold her skirt up. He hooked the

small forked stirrup-clasp through each of the tiny eyelets in her labia and drew it upwards, lifting back the foreskin with its nodule trapped inside it and attaching the clasp to the belly ring. Justine felt as if her flesh had been turned inside out. Her clitoris stood out like a tiny cock. Alec then selected from the box the short curved gold rod attached to its minute chain. He clipped the end of this chain to the ring attached to Justine's belly and began rolling the tip of the rod around the well surrounding her clitoris, then rubbing it point to rounded point against the wet fleshy tip. He made her lift her blouse up. Philip came across and unclipped her brassiere at the back. He did not remove it but raised it up above her breasts and stood behind her, lifting her proffered nipples while Alec masturbated her with the small curved gold rod that was anchored to the ring above her naked vulva.

Justine began emitting tiny noises – short gasps, light grunts. The young man was pale and mesmerised; Julia held his moist, cold hand and touched him gently between the thighs. 'Take her skirt off completely,' Julia said. 'It spoils the line.'

Justine was now naked to the shoulders. Her knees were open and her booted feet were balanced on the arm of the couch. Alec wetted the rod and fitted its tip into the narrow hole below her clitoris. Justine whimpered and her knees lifted. Philip gagged her with his lips as the rod was gradually introduced inside her until nothing of it could be seen but the rounded base that anchored to the chain, which hung in a loose arc, pinned at each end now, above and below her clitoris. Alec gently pulled the rod; it would not retract; he squeezed her flesh round it; Justine gasped into Philip's mouth; then Alec pressed the rounded tip, and a droplet of her golden liquid was delivered into his hand. He wiped it round her clitoris and pubic lips. Then Justine's brassiere was refastened, and she was made to stand while Alec displayed her clitoris, with its gold adornments, standing proud of the junction of the warm nude pouting lips.

'You might need to replace her skirt,' said Julia, 'before

you take her out.' She smiled again at Alec and said casually, 'And is the journey far – to your club?'

'Not far, madam,' he answered vaguely. 'And she will be safe with us, I do assure you.'

'I do not doubt it. But may I at least offer you my carriage for the evening?'

'You are kind, madam, and most considerate. But I have one already waiting at the door.'

Julia tipped her head and smiled.

At the door, Miss Norwood's butler was most apologetic; it seemed that an oversight had occurred and that the gentlemen's carriage had been dismissed.

'Then it seems I must call upon your most generous offer after all,' said Alec, 'though I fear the inconvenience this might cause you.'

Julia smiled again. 'I insist that you take it. I had proposed in any case to spend the evening quietly at home, where I shall be available, should you need me.' She gently offered him her hand. 'If myself or any of my ladies can be of any assistance, sir, you have but to call.'

Julia watched the party leaving; the young man still appeared in a daze, mesmerised by Justine.

The place to which they took her was unimposing from the outside: a large stone building with the windows so heavily curtained that it appeared to be in darkness. The air inside the lobby smelled smoky; portraits of racehorses crowded the walls; the furniture was heavy leather; the doors were thick and had large round polished brass knobs positioned in their centres. Alec and Philip spoke in hushed tones to a steward who had appeared from behind a desk to intercept them. There was a book to sign. Then he pointed up the stairs:

'The Oak Room, sir. You are expected. I shall see that you are not disturbed.'

Philip hesitated. 'Oh – I expect a young lady . . .'

The steward nodded. 'And I shall send her up, sir . . .' He glanced at the page. 'Mr Clement? Yes, directly she arrives.' He resumed his place behind the desk.

Justine stared up the wide staircase, which turned and disappeared after one flight. She could hear voices up there. Then a door clicked open opposite. The door was so heavy that the sounds had been absorbed and she hadn't realised how many people were in the room. There were distinguished looking men and young, attractive women – far more men than women and all the women were either scantily clad or nude. Some of the women were laughing, but others looked very nervous and afraid. She could hear music coming from an adjacent room.

'Welcome to the club where the whores rub shoulders with the daughters of the gentry.' Justine watched Robert's eyes as Alec was speaking. The young man seemed trapped – a victim, just as she was. 'It's a kind of coming out for some of them, a learning process, an erosion of the inhibitions. Isn't that so, young Robert?' He slapped him on the back. 'Come on – you take her up, Philip; I'll introduce him here then join you.'

Philip led Justine upstairs. But she had seen the young man's quiet eyes fall wistfully upon her before Alec closed the door.

At the top of the first flight was the source of the voices. There was a girl, and she wasn't one of the whores to whom Alex had referred. But she wore neither shoes nor stockings and she was bare down to the waist. She turned to hide herself, and Justine saw that she had been fastened to the balustrade by a bellrope round her middle. Two men drinking from bottles emerged from a room; there was laughter from within. Justine glimpsed other men and women – a girl being lifted, naked, on to a couch by two older men, and another girl on the floor with a red-faced man who began waving his arm to the two on the stairs. They closed the door behind them. Philip greeted them, then moved Justine along. But when they reached the next flight, he stopped her. They could hear the girl murmuring. Philip placed Justine with her back to the wall.

She could see what the men were doing. Philip unfastened her blouse; he unclipped her brassiere; he exposed her breasts as fully as the girl's breasts were exposed; and he watched Justine breathing. Her arms remained clothed to the wrists, as they had remained on that first night. He moved her arms out until her hands pressed against the wall, seeking fingertip grips within the texture of the paper, while her breasts projected, full and naked, but her arms stayed fully clothed. And Justine watched the girl, and listened to the soft sexual sounds as the two men kissed her breasts and opened out her skirts.

Philip lifted Justine's breasts and touched the nipples with his wetted fingers, then touched beneath her arms. He made her open her legs. That was the pose in which Alec found her when he returned without Robert.

'Alec,' Philip whispered, 'help me . . .' He raised Justine's skirt and moved aside. He pinned her leg open with his knee. And she was nude of any panties. Alec tucked the lifted skirt into her waistband. He stood to the side and pinned the other knee. Justine closed her eyes. Her hands were pinned against the wall. She was bare-sexed, open and excited. She heard a murmur. She looked. The girl was being lifted up; Justine shuddered; Alec touched her. The girl was being lifted astride the corner of the balustrade with her cunny lips suspended above the round dished surface of the wood. She was kneeling in the air, balanced precariously on the men's arms, the bellrope still around her waist, and she was being masturbated. And now she was lowered, open-legged, until her cunny touched the centre of the dish. But they did not lower her fully; they kept her poised with her cunny lips tightly pressing to the polished surface.

Alec's fingers teased the gold chain that irritated Justine's clitoris; Philip touched her nipples; both men pinned her knees apart, against the wall. The girl on the balustrade was making soft mewling sounds, because she could not bring to bear the pressure that she needed, and a hand was against her belly, imparting tiny guiding movements to the open lips that barely brushed against the wood.

They decided to pour champagne into the dish of wood where she was almost sitting, but when they let it gush down on the split of her cunny, she kicked her legs and

234

came. Justine whimpered; a trickle of her wet ran down Alec's fingers.

'Philip, the crop,' Alec said and Justine gasped with the deliverance of that lashing, across the front of her naked legs, until they burned. Then Alec gently masturbated her again until her clitoris stood against its chain, and he kissed her while he pulled the chain which tugged upon the tip of the rod that fed into her bladder, and Justine's cunny lifted even though her legs were held against the wall. Philip's fingers, searching underneath her, rubbed bead by itchy bead up to her anus, and when the final bead was rubbed, she almost came.

'It's when you whip her – she gets so . . . Shh . . .' Alec whispered and he rubbed the naked legs that burned against his hand.

They took her skirt off and refastened her jacket after removing her brassiere and blouse. The jacket fitted snugly, moulding to her waist, so the junction between the clothed and the naked skin was sharp and the two parts appeared to move as separate entities. When they made her walk along the corridor, her buttocks could be seen rising and falling smoothly, freely, below this pinched, clothed, narrow waistline and above the slim long legs, with the perfect gap between them looking wider now that she was shaved and also more precisely vee shaped about the down-bulge of her naked cunny.

Justine shuddered as she was pushed against a door. The large round brass knob in the centre pressed coldly against her belly.

'Lift her,' Alec said.

'Nnn . . . Ahhh . . .' Her feet left the floor; the toes of her boots scraped up the door; the tips of her fingers clawed upwards on the smoothness of the wood; her belly touched it; her buttocks opened; her cunny spread about the shaft behind the knob of cold smooth brass.

'Hold her.' But they couldn't manage her – with having to support her on this pedestal, they couldn't get the required swing. They had to lower her again while Philip went to get assistance. He came back with a steward, who also supplied a larger strap, and Justine was lifted up again and, balanced in the air, her fingertips against the wood, the lips of her cunny open to the brass, she was leathered with this larger and more effective strap across her buttocks, which tightened at first, but then gradually opened, so the string of love beads could be seen, and below them, the nude lips spread about the shaft of the doorknob, which was becoming wet and the wet was coalescing to a heavy droplet dangling from the polished brass.

Philip stopped smacking her, not because she was moaning, but because her anus was pulsing steadily now, like a mouth that was trying to swallow. But he took his time. Alec and the steward held her. Philip reached round and touched her clitoris and simply held it lightly through the chain. Then he pressed his fingertip against the pulsing mouth of her anus, which swallowed it greedily until it touched the bead inside her, when she came, with her legs open, held in the air, and her fingernails clawing the perfect polish of the wood. Her clitoris was like a wet, chained stone that stabbed against his fingertips as the captive bead inside her was repeatedly squeezed against his finger to the bone.

They sat her in a heavy upholstered tub chair. Justine's body was slumped. Alec wanted to take her boots off. Philip wanted to keep them on her – he said she looked more sexual like that, with her boots on and her legs open and her cunny shaved naked but the top part of her body clothed. They lifted her arms over the back. Philip held them while Alec smacked her legs, then tested the state of her erection. Then he smacked her again, with two fingers slipped into her cunny, curving upwards, pressing, and Justine started to become very excited. Philip and the steward had to hold her legs as well as her arms while Alec slowly masturbated her. They were able to keep her on until the upholstery between her legs was wet. Then they pushed her knees up tightly and held her. They kept her doubled up with her bottom lifted in the air for many minutes. Philip said he would be happy just to keep her like this all night, but Alec wanted to take her into the Oak

Room. Justine wanted somebody to suck her cunny while she was in this position and could not move; she wanted somebody to make her come, to stretch a tongue right up inside her, because she was wet and open now. She wanted the tip of a tongue to press inside against the place that Rachel had branded on the night that she had died.

They decided to smack her. Philip held her knees together and still doubled up while Alec smacked her labia. He used the crop and the strokes were delivered from the side, across the labia, which projected. But he avoided the area of the clitoris itself, which remained hard while the labia, striped with red marks, burned.

The corridor being relatively public, the snapping noises of the crop and the gasps of supplication attracted a certain amount of attention, so it was decided that they really ought to move. When they made her stand, her legs could hardly support her. They made her close them so the red lips of her cunny burned against her thighs; when she walked, the gap between her legs was very much narrower than before. Before they had got much further, Philip stopped her. He turned her round to face him and took her cunny in his hand. And to Justine, it felt large and hot and swollen; he kissed her and his middle finger slid inside and touched the place that was so special to Justine. It was as if he did not want to give her up, but wanted to keep touching her forever. Justine moaned; her knees bowed open and Philip's middle finger slid deeper and his other fingers, separated by her naked labia, pressed to either side. His free hand moved round the back and played with her beads, counting them one by one, all the way up and inside her, in the way that he did each night before she went to sleep. Justine's mouth opened and her tongue thrust deeply as he kissed her. She tried to squeeze her legs together round his hands. He lifted her on his fingers and she moaned. He pressed his thumb against the chain across her clitoris and she peaked.

They reached a room at the end of the corridor and Alec opened the door. It was quiet, but Philip could see people moving in the shadows. The atmosphere was warm and heavy with the scent of women – that was the most notice-able thing, that the scent was of women – their perfume and their sweat. The room was large and low, with polished heavy wood walls and free-standing carvings. The pervasive red glow from the fire was reinforced by the reflections of candlelight in the panelling. Then he realised that parts of the carvings were moving – there were women fastened to them.

The clients were waiting. Philip's heartbeat quickened as he watched Justine, her eyes moving round the small group, alighting very briefly on each one, then moving on – beauti-ful eyes, rendered perfect by their width and depth and crystallinity of fear. He saw the fleeting terror in them as he moved away: she was like a creature drowning in the sea of other men's desire. He watched her sit – the way the leather pressed against her naked thighs, the way she shivered because that skin had been whipped, the way she trembled when Alec explained about the small curved rod that was fitted inside her. He made her open her legs and sit forwards. Philip watched the way the men were reacting; the way they were gathering round, hands reaching gently to touch Justine and to spread her legs and tease this mys-terious rod inside her.

When they raised her legs there was a small dark pool on the leather. Alec showed them the clasp and chain and beads and explained to them in graphic detail the things that Justine liked. He explained that she preferred women but that she liked to be punished and used by men; he made it clear that Justine would be shared between them. Then he slipped the chain sideways and made her sit for-wards again to the point where her naked clitoris touched the leather through the pool of wet. He made her excite herself by rocking her hips. The men opened her jacket so they could see her breasts moving. And while her clitoris rubbed against the leather, she would be fighting against the feeling of the rod inside her, pressing, and making her want to pee again. Philip turned away and left her to the men's attentions, but when he heard her moan, he turned back briefly and saw that her legs had been lifted in the air

238

while her wet, chained clitoris was being gently held, and that her climax had been prevented.

He moved deeper into the room, passing the carvings and the women fastened there, roped in positions of vulnerable exposure, or wrapped – flesh to polished wood – in positions of explicit love. He passed a table where a naked woman was strapped with her legs open; there were two other women with her; she was being examined with a speculum while she was kept aroused with a feather.

Against one wall were two girls, one standing, the other crouching. Both were fastened. The one on the floor was attached to the wall by a thin rope; she was nude apart from a string of pearls round her neck. There was something about the line – the way that she was crouching, the curve from her back to her buttocks to her legs – that attracted Philip. And there was something of the deliciousness of inexperience in her eyes. She was waiting her turn. The girl who was standing wore stockings, nothing else, and she was tied to a heavy post. A young woman and a man were masturbating her. There was a short leather whip on a hook nearby. The young woman's hair was jet black and as short as the man's and it was cut to a point at the nape. She wore a long thin shirt without buttons, and brief black leather panties. Her nipples stood out against the thinness of the shirt.

She stopped what she was doing and looked at Philip. He waited. The girl at the post murmured. Her stockinged legs moved; there was something dangling between them. Her hands were fastened back above her head; her lips looked swollen and dry; her slim lithe body sagged. She looked as if she had been fastened there for a long while, but the black-haired woman appeared in no hurry. She moved in concert with the young man, who crouched and held the stockinged thighs apart while the woman attached something else between the girl's legs, which forced her belly to buckle outwards so that the woman had to steady her. Then the woman straightened up and kissed the girl. Their nipples touched through the thinness of the shirt. The girl took the woman's tongue and the woman touched her between her open legs. The girl's moans were gentler. Philip could see the metal weights glinting between her legs and moving as the woman touched her. The girl who crouched beside her looked frightened and sweetly innocent.

A little beyond the group was a wooden bar extending part way across the room. Philip went round it and continued. He could hear sounds. Around a corner to the right, he came upon a woman suspended in a rubber sling hanging from the ceiling. The seat of the sling was between her legs and her toes were off the floor. Her breasts had been taken to the outsides of the rubber sling and her labia had been pulled through a slit in it. There were hands tugging at her breasts and there were fingers pushing up between her legs and spreading apart the slit. There was a girl nearby, tethered by one hand to the wall behind her. She was half squatting with both feet on a stool. Her free hand held her vulva open. It looked swollen and inflamed and the girl was still moaning. A woman knelt beside her with a crop.

Philip went back and examined the wooden bar. It was coated with velvet that was soft at the sides and downy underneath, but worn shiny on the top, which absorbed the light in cloud-shaped patches of polished darkness that were hard and slightly oily to the touch. Above the velvet bar was a simple wooden one; below it were two parallel smooth grooves in the bare floor. Philip looked back at the first girl – the one in pearls, who was crouching, perfect and smooth and naked and waiting. She was watching him. He walked back and stood above her. Her toes were small; they gripped the floor where she crouched, the candlelight softly kissing her skin.

He unfastened her rope and took her, though she murmured. He put her arms around his neck and carried her to the bar and lifted her astride and felt her shudder when the velvet touched her. He rearranged her string of pearls. And he could smell her skin; she was sharply aromatic underneath the arms. Her fingers were small; they clung above her head to the plain wooden bar as Philip held her belly and her back between his hands. Around her ankle was a thin chain. He made her lift her knees up and grip upon the sides of the velvet as if she were riding; he made her ride. Her pearls swung against her breasts; the chain around her ankle moved like a shaken thread of falling liquid. He held her breasts up on his hand and he cupped her belly as it pushed forwards. Then he stretched her foreskin upwards and made her open her legs and drop them down. The chain around her ankle swished. He made her lift her legs and drop them, lift and drop while he held her foreskin stretched until people began to gather round. But he held her breasts up and made her keep on doing it until he saw it in her eyes and felt it in the shudders in her belly – that she had never before been brought on in this way. Then he turned and saw that Robert was back in the room and standing over by the door, close to where the group of men were attending to Justine.

Philip left the girl astride the velvet bar. He told her to keep her toes stretched down; they brushed against the floor. He brought down her arms and made her fold them behind her back, so that her body wavered gently as she tried to balance. Then he spread the cheeks of her bottom quite fully. He wanted the tenderest inner skin sealed to the polished velvet. 'Reach down,' he whispered, and now her toes could bend and press against the floor and her belly and bottom looked so round and sexual and so close against the velvet.

Philip then went over to Robert. He stood with him and watched Justine. She was fastened between the ceiling and floor so that her body formed a cross. In front of her stood Alec and, behind her, a young man holding a short length of rope on a handle. The rope was oiled and had been formed into a smooth egg-shaped knot at the end. But it seemed there was some problem. The man was opening the cheeks of her bottom, but with her body being upright, the cheeks would not remain open when he released them. He tried slapping her legs and lifting her on her toes.

'Use a belt,' said Philip. There was a wide one on a chair. Philip passed one end under her belly and got someone to hold the other side. 'Pull it,' he said, and when the strain

241

was taken, Justine's body curved, her hips were drawn back and she moved up on to her toes. Her buttocks were now presented correctly, open as required. Her breasts hung down and her belly was supported in the tight sling of the belt. And below the belt, her cunny was naked and pierced and adorned with its fine gold clasps and studs.

'She has such slim thighs, but such thick, full nipples,' Alec said, taking up a cloth. 'And such a perfect cunt – the skin around it feels like velvet.'

'I know,' said Philip. They were distracted by the first dull snap of the smooth knot against Justine's pouted anus. Alec folded the cloth and oiled it. The snap came again and Justine's naked belly bucked above the belt and Alec held the oiled cloth pressed against her open cunny. The drumming snaps of the knotted rope sounded steadily against her anus, and the oiled cloth pressed against her cunny till it dripped. 'May I?' asked Philip. He gave the end of the belt to the man behind him. 'Lift it, slide it up,' he said to the men holding the belt, and it was now drawn up her body till it lifted up her breasts. 'Now smack it again.' Philip spread his hand over her belly while Alec held the cloth against Justine and the man behind her opened out the cheeks with one hand and smacked the oiled knot steadily between them. 'Oh God,' Philip whispered, 'I can feel it . . .' And as he kissed her, he could feel those smacks coming through Justine in tiny thuds of her belly against his hand. Alec paused to oil the cloth.

'I am concerned about Robert,' he said, when Philip's lips released Justine. 'I left him downstairs but he seems to keep drifting back here – and then just standing about.'

'I'll keep an eye on him. I think it could be that he's shy.'

There was a steward at the door, so Philip asked about a room: 'Nothing special. Just the two of us and the girl.' He slipped him a coin and pointed to the girl on the bar and the steward nodded. Philip went to collect her and, for the first time, Robert's eyes moved from Justine. 'Help me,' Philip called, but Robert wouldn't touch her. He followed at a distance as Philip and the steward half carried, half dragged her reluctant body, her belly pressed against Philip's hip, her legs dangling, dancing intermittently along the carpet, all the way along the corridor and up the stairs.

In the room – which turned out to be much larger than Philip needed – the steward lit the lamps and the candles then discreetly left. Philip allowed the girl to slump to the floor. When Robert, suddenly shaken from his dreaming, stooped to help her, Philip pushed him into an armchair. 'Relax,' he whispered. 'She's here for you, remember that.' Philip sat on the bed. 'Get up,' he told the girl. Then he whispered to her and nodded towards the armchair. But he knew that she was too afraid to make it work.

He watched her move across to Robert and kneel before him, her hands upon her naked thighs, her breasts rising and falling, lifting the string of flawless pearls. The carpet was so deep that it buried her knees; around her ankle was the chain, thin and fragile. Robert hadn't moved. 'Go on,' whispered Philip. Her hands moved up uncertainly and hovered in the air a fraction above the young man's knees, then moved out and came to rest on the arms of the chair. Her breasts, thrown forwards, grazed his knees. 'Touch her,' Philip said. Robert stared at her face. Then his right hand lifted and the tips of his fingers touched her cheek, but immediately retreated. She in turn tried to stroke the fingers that had touched her, but they pulled further away. Her rejected hands returned to her thighs and she sank back on her knees.

Philip sighed. He got up. He undressed quickly. The girl was watching him while pretending to look at the floor. She had seen his erection. Philip, naked, strode across in front of the large mirror and took her by the hair. It was black and long and wavy; she gasped when he pulled her slowly backwards. He did not hurt her, but he knelt and drew her head down to the floor, so her body was arched and her belly was pushed out and her breasts were drawn open. Then he pulled her slowly across the deeply piled carpet, so she was crawling on her elbows and her heels, and the slim chain round her ankle made a sweet metallic tinkling. He made her kneel before him in front of the mirror while he sat on the bed. He opened his legs. She was breathing quickly, and it made her more inviting. He did not look even once at Robert, but he knew that he was watching. He concentrated on the girl.

He asked her name: it was Alexandra. He asked her age: she said eighteen. There was a dark, sweet sensuality in her eyes, so large and heavy lidded – Alexandra of the dark eyebrows, the tinkling anklet, the pure white pearls. Philip touched Alexandra's breasts; her eyelids closed; Robert stirred in his chair. There were marks of punishment around her nipples. Philip bent forward and whispered, 'When I put you to the bar, you liked it?' Her nipples were turning hard. 'Oh, Alexandra, open your mouth.' Her eyes stayed closed. Her head was tilted back, her mouth and throat aligned. Her lips were trembling, stretching wide. Philip slid his hand around the back of Alexandra's neck and guided her lips against the base of his cock, against his balls and beneath – open-lipped kisses against his skin, open-mouthed breathing, licking. Philip fell back on his elbows. Alexandra's fingers closed around the top of his shaft and pushed down. 'Your tongue, Alexandra,' Philip whispered.

He looked in the mirror on the ceiling, at the slim hand moving up and down his cock, the fingers round his ball sac, lifting, the open mouth searching, and the moist tongue slipping out; he felt it dabbing, finding, pointing upwards, opening him and lifting, sliding thickly through the ring of his anus. The slim hand gently masturbated; the fingers kept the ball sac lifted; the wriggling wet tongue stretched the ring. Philip groaned. He pulled her head away and drew her up his body so her breasts hung down and slid across his cock, which pulsed a small premature emission that left a thread of liquid silk between her nipples.

Philip pressed Alexandra face down on to the bed. He kissed the breasts that pushed out to the sides. He touched the cleft of her buttocks and her breathing changed. He opened them and he could smell her. The well of her bottom was small and deep; the skin was drawn in tightly; she shuddered when he touched it.

There were a number of toys on the dressing table, but

Philip selected the spoon. He warmed it in the candle flame, wiped it, tested it, then quickly opened Alexandra's buttocks and pressed it to her anus. She gasped with the sudden warmth of contact and her buttocks tried to close. Philip held the belly of the spoon in place until it had cooled. Then he made her hold her buttocks open while he warmed the spoon and reapplied it, pressing it gently to the anus, then using it to smack. Her anus warmed and stretched; the skin made gentle smacking sounds; the chain around her ankle trembled. He kept wiping the spoon and warming it and pressing it against her, then smacking softly until she had spread sufficiently that when the bowl of the spoon was against her anus, the stem was touching her to the tip of her spine and he could feel her cunny underneath, soft and moist, pushing down against his fingers, driven by the steady pressure of the spoon. Then when he lifted it, the belly of the spoon adhered to the skin, which formed a ridged ring now, but not so thick nor so perfect as it did in Justine. But he kissed it and closed his eyes and thought of his lover being whipped and masturbated by those other men and Alexandra murmured as his tongue pushed into her, distending her, penetrating to the root while his fingers, underneath her, held her open. Her clitoris was larger than Justine's, but there was no means of constricting it while it was sucked, and no captive bead to irritate it while she was punished.

Philip moved a pillow down the bed; he laid her cheek upon it and turned her on her side so she faced the lad. He bent her overlying leg until it touched her breasts, leaving the other leg with her cunny lips against it, and the roundness from her belly to her buttocks accessibly exposed. He held the bent knee pinned against her, then wetted his fingers in her mouth. Then he wetted his thumb and held it pressed against her anus, with the first two fingers against her labia, exactly on the join. He held her leg up tightly, while he bent across and kissed her and gently moved his hand. She began to breathe rapidly. It was a beautiful feeling; he could feel her breath against his lips between the kisses. His fingers tightened towards his

245

thumb. She gasped into his mouth – his fingers and thumb were inside her, sliding up until the web between his finger and thumb was pressed against her bridge of flesh and his thumb could rub the separating wall of inner skin into the groove between his fingers. Alexandra was leaking; there was a clear paste that slid across his knuckles to her leg. Her eyes were closed and her cheek was pressed against the pillow and the pressure had pushed her lips open to form a ring.

'Robert,' he said. He wanted him to make love to her mouth. He wanted to see that soft ring open to the pressure of a cock while Philip held her body trapped in this special way, her anus open, his thumb inside it, pressing down to meet the juice-slicked fingers which were pushed into her cunny, tightly pinching the separating skin, holding it through her climax – with her clitoris exposed – while the cock slid until her nostrils flared and the soft ring of her sweet lips pressed against the balls.

Robert jumped; the door opened. Justine came in with two people; one was Alec, the other was a very obese man. She walked with tiny, stilted steps – she was hobbled with leather cuffs above the knees clipped together on a short chain. She was moaning. Between her legs was the soft, thick dildo. They had made her walk with it inside her; only the balls were visible, hanging between her legs. Alec pushed her against the door and made her close her legs more tightly so that the balls squeezed out between them at the front of her thighs. Then he smacked her with a leather. He did not make her turn but smacked her while she faced into the room. Her hobbled legs jerked and the balls between them lifted; above them, at the junction of the naked slit, were the gold irritants fastened to her clitoris.

The fat man began to check the contents of the room. He carried a glass and a bottle of champagne in the same hand, leaving the other hand free to explore. 'Alexandra,' he said, pausing by the bed. But he did not touch her or come near her and said to Philip, 'Please, do not let me disturb you; she must learn.' He transferred the bottle to the other hand and drank from the glass, then moved back to watch Justine gasping as her legs were smacked. The chain between her knee-cuffs had been unclipped to allow exposure of the more tender skin. 'She is there, she is,' he said to Alec. 'Just hold her.' Alec stopped smacking and the man knelt unsteadily and put the glass down and Justine started coming even as the dildo was being taken out of her and the bottle was being lifted: her legs were open and her stretching fingers clung to the door. She was breathing in sobbing gulps. 'Shhh . . .' The nose of the bottle was brought to bear. And now Justine's gold-chained clitoris was lifting and pulsing in tiny gulps as her labia gently sucked upon the glass nose of the bottle.

Philip's free hand accepted from Alec the dildo that was wet with Justine's juices, and he fed it into Alexandra's mouth. He left it in her, smoothed his hand across her cheek, then touched her thickened clitoris and she moaned and her head curved down, pushing deeply along the dildo, trapping the slippy balls against her breasts. He slapped her nipples with his fingers, then took her clitoris again and continued moving his fingers back and forth between these places, slapping and squeezing until the muscles in her neck went rigid and the dildo did not move. Then he felt her contractions pulsing steadily round his buried hand and her clitoris jerking between his fingertips like a tiny cock, and there was a warm wetness coming out of her that had the stickiness of come.

Robert suddenly jumped up and stood trembling before the two men holding Justine. 'Leave her!' he shouted. 'Leave her alone.' Justine's blue eyes met his as she stood there, her shudders coming on again. Alec said nothing and continued to toy with her imprisoned clitoris; he wiped his fingers across it, then he pressed the body of the bottle which was still inside her to the door, holding it in place between the unclipped shackles above her trembling knees, and he continued to wipe the clitoris, and to wet the naked vulva with his fingers until Justine's belly suddenly shuddered uncontrollably and she came. And throughout the time that she was coming, he held the bottle so it did not move, and he held the outer lips of her cunny lifted while the inner lips freely sucked and Justine closed her eyes and turned her head away.

Robert's face was drained of colour. Alec now quietly asked him to wait downstairs.

'You can wait for Roxanne,' said Philip. 'Bring her up when she arrives.' Robert left without a word. Only then did Justine's eyes open.

'I worry about him,' said Alec.

There was a special seat from one side of which rose a single stem that bellied out and was shaped like a lyre which had supports for the breasts but became very narrow below the place where the bellying was greatest. At this place the polish was pale and stained. They made Justine sit astride it. When they pushed her against it, the lips of her cunny split about the place that was smoothest and narrowest and most stained. Because there were no other bars but this one, they could open her legs until the sides of her cunny were exposed in a smooth and naked double bulge while her breasts were lifted over the shaped top of the bar. There were whips and leathers in the drawers and on the dressing table. Alec found an instrument that had a tap-shaped handle connected by a short rope to an egg-shaped wooden weight at the end. He placed it next to Alexandra on the bed and Philip could feel her shudder through the bridge of flesh still trapped between his fingers and thumb. He took his fingers out of her and took the dildo from her mouth and he played with her nipples, which again became hard as she watched Justine. It was as if Alexandra had never seen a woman properly smacked; her eyes had a look of frightened excitement. Philip asked her if she wanted it, and Alexandra couldn't answer. He placed the rope and wooden egg against her belly and Alexandra shivered.

Alec chose a narrow leather for Justine. He moved behind her and drew her shoulders back, pushing her belly forwards while her stirrup was replaced by a fine chain used to fasten her labia around the bar. Then he smacked the naked bulges at the sides of Justine's cunt. He smacked, while the fat man watched and drank, until Justine's shoulders, which Alec had formerly had to pull back, slumped back of their own accord and her slim back formed so tight an arch that her breasts projected upwards and he had to support her shoulders while he smacked her. In between the smacks, the fat man rubbed his wetted fingers on the chained naked lips that bulged around the narrow part of the bar. When her legs jerked open the first time, Alec dropped the leather and held the soft weight of Justine's body and caressed and kissed the nipples that projected out so far. And the sexual moisture that had been inside her, mixed with her involuntary leaks of wet, had made the stained wood shiny.

They unfastened her and lifted her to the floor and sat her with her back against a large soft leather cushion. Her elbows sank into it, making her body curve out strongly as her head fell back. Then they opened out her legs and kept them straight. Her naked cunny, bright red from the strapping, pressed into the carpet. Alec sat behind her, his weight upon the cushion throwing Justine's shoulders back, so her head could now be cradled in his lap. He took his cock out and the underside pressed into the soft skin behind her ear, then below the lobe and round to throb against her cheek. The other man knelt between her legs and pressed his thick pink fingers to her belly; her swollen labia lifted from the carpet and the chain across her clitoris glinted. He pressed her thighs further apart and Alec drew her shoulders back, and the open split could now be seen. The man took his gold watch off and hung it from its chain. When it touched her labia, Justine moaned, and when her labia were opened and the watch was slipped inside, she gasped, and when the man closed the lips and stretched the chain across the carpet, Justine's head turned and her mouth opened and she took the cap of Alec's cock, with the other man gently stretching the chain as her belly shuddered and Alec held her breasts restrained with her nipples poking through his fingers.

Philip kept Alexandra on her side. He lifted her leg out of the way and lubricated the cap of his cock between her labia. They were soft and thin and clung to him despite the fact that they were oily; they moved with his cock as the warm weights of his balls slid across her thigh. But when he pressed his cock to her anus, Alexandra baulked. Philip pulled her head downwards again towards her breasts and held it, sheltering her, coaxing her, touching her precious pearls, and Alexandra opened and the tight skin of her anus sealed to the cap of his cock and the straight deep groove between her buttocks was now punctured by this 'o'. Then he drew her shoulders back to make her curve in the way Justine was curved. He held her arms behind her back and pulled, and when her belly turned to tightness, he felt the small skin cap around his cock squeeze and he saw her clitoris, fully enlarged again, projecting through the soft wet lips. Philip lifted the top lip to expose the clitoris. He trapped it with his finger and again he felt the tightness round his cock. He rubbed the clitoris slowly; Alexandra's head arched back; her cheek slid over the pillow and her lips, compressed against it, opened to an 'o'.

'Alec,' said Philip, and Alec knew. He lifted Justine forward and left her with the other man. Her legs were still open and the watch chain was stretched out between them and along the carpet. Alec undressed fully and joined Philip on the bed. Philip steadied Alexandra's head. Her eyes stayed closed while Alec pushed against her face still resting on the pillow, sliding slowly into it while Alexandra's sweet lips took him to the balls and Philip rubbed her belly gently, held her enlarged clitoris, then opened the lips wider and held it again. When he took it the second time, Alexandra climaxed so intensely that she brought him on. He pulled his cock out of her and pressed it against her jumping clitoris and watched his semen extruding thickly to fill the space between the lips. Then he forced her knees open and played with her clitoris through the slippiness until Alexandra moaned and her hand slid up between Alec's legs and pressed against him underneath and Alexandra came again. Alec tried to pull out, but his semen spurted over Alexandra's mouth and chin and ran down to her necklace.

Philip left them on the bed. Justine lay arched across the leather cushion, gasping sweetly, the gold watch now dangling wetly just above her belly. Philip watched it touch the chain across her clitoris. Her heels dug into the carpet.

It was one of those times when the first time drives you on; Philip felt his cock harden and the dull ache inside him told him there was more. When he touched her arching body, there was a buzzing in his head. She was so sexual when she had been repeatedly used; he could smell it on her face and belly. He wanted to possess her in this way, when her cunny had been buttered by several other men; he wanted to possess Justine completely and forever. And you do not have to be with someone all the time in order to possess her; you have only to tell her you will think of her and then give her to be fucked by other men. Philip kissed Justine. 'I love you,' Philip whispered.

He put her on a firmer stool and held her from behind and kissed her while the fat man smacked her naked cunt. He lowered her head and shoulders back to the floor, leaving her hips upraised so that the highest point of her body was her pouting vulva, which shook beneath the smacks and shuddered beneath the kisses, then trembled as the fat man's semen filled the split.

Philip kissed Justine and wiped her with a cloth and turned her round. He made her kneel across the stool and spread her legs. He touched the small gold rod that protruded on its chain; he found her clitoris to be hard. He lifted up her knees so her cunt projected out behind her and the pressure of her tightness caused a leak; drops of her moisture spread darkness into the fabric of the seat. Philip crouched down and took her salty labia in his mouth; he pushed his tongue inside her; he licked her beads and sucked her anus and held her clitoris in his fingers. Then he took the wooden egg upon its rope and pushed it into Justine; she gasped; the muscle of her anus closed about the rope. Philip held the handle, took the strain and gently played with Justine's clitoris. He listened to her breathing. He watched her breasts rub gently against the sides of the cushion, her fingertips reaching deep into the carpet. Then she froze; her anus opened and the polished egg showed, with the small bead inside her pressed against it, a small sharp pain against the dull ache of spreading and the swollenness of pleasure. Philip touched the rod and Justine squirted. Her anus tightened and the egg slipped back. He released the handle; he placed his hand against her back and masturbated her very gently till she grunted. Then he took hold of the handle again and pulled and Justine was stretched and her clitoris protruded with the pleasure-ache of squeezing. Philip rubbed the backs of his fingers underneath, across her naked belly, drawing her labia away until she contracted and the egg slipped back inside. Then he masturbated her again to the point of balance, and when the distension happened this time, Justine's climax came, with her clitoris pulsing against the air, and her anus gripped about the egg and Philip slapping her thighs on the insides, then her breasts, then drawing the egg out through her anus and first kissing the newly stretched flesh then, as Justine shuddered, nipping it with his teeth. Then he lifted Justine up and made her stand against the wall. He kept her with her legs apart and whipped her.

At this point, Robert opened the door. Philip turned, then couldn't move.

'Charlotte!'

She saw the whip in his hand, and she saw Justine, naked, the cuffs still above each knee. Then Charlotte's hand came to her mouth and she began to tremble.

'Charlotte – please . . .' As Philip moved towards her, Charlotte turned and ran. Philip burst past Robert and ran after her.

Justine was on the floor. The door was still open. A hand was pulling her up, but the room was a blur of tears. Philip's parting words were still ringing in her ears: 'She's just a whore, Charlotte,' he had shouted.

When Philip came back, having failed to catch Charlotte, Justine was already gone. Robert had taken her. Alec had let him. 'It will do him good,' he said.

In the small room above the inn where they had fled, he made love to Justine with the quick intensity of youth.

252

Then he stayed inside her while her arms lay stretched across the bed and her cheek lay turned against the pillow. And while the flickering light of the candle was reflected in her eye, he promised her things that she did not wish for, and that could not come about. These desperate promises disguised as love fed the slow swell of her tears. He said that he loved her and that he would marry her, and that they would run away to a place where his family would never find them. She felt him hardening up inside her as he spoke; she felt that all of these words, though spoken softly, were to do with this hardness. But she pressed her lips against the smooth skin of his chest and felt his body arch, his nipple pushed between her teeth, and then the desperate urgent truth of all his promises burst inside Justine.

When he was asleep, she slipped from the bed. She took his cloak and crept downstairs. The landlord made the call for her. Ten minutes later, she was in the carriage, asleep, her head in Julia's lap, Julia's gentle fingertips caressing every feature of her perfect face and sliding through the short soft bristles of her hair.

18: BEWARE HER NEEDS

It was beginning to snow again, but Philip hardly noticed. He banged the doorknocker for the third time, then stepped back and looked up at the darkened windows. A light finally came on in the hallway and the door opened. Philip strode forwards, but the butler did not move aside. Philip cleared his throat. 'Mr Philip Clement, to see Mr Lessing's niece.'

'Sir?'

'I know she is here, damn it!'

'It is late, sir.' The butler arched an eyebrow. 'I shall see if Miss Charlotte is at home.' He stared icily for a second, then pointedly closed the door again, leaving Philip on the steps.

When the door reopened, the butler was not alone. George Lessing stood there, red in the face and glowering. 'How dare you, sir? How dare you show your face at my door?'

Philip stared back stonily. 'I will speak with her. She is my fiancée and I will speak with her tonight!'

'Is that so, sir? Then let me tell you this – from your fiancée.' He puffed his chest out. 'Charlotte is not at home to you, sir – not tonight. And she will not be at home to you again!' The arm shot out; Philip dodged. The ring bounced down the steps and rolled a trail through the thin new snow. Then the door slammed shut. Philip picked the ring up, examined it, then, squeezing it until the diamonds dug into his palm, turned and hurried into the night.

Half an hour later, he was at home. In one hand was the telephone, which was ringing, but there was no answer. In the other hand was the crop. He smacked it down across the table. Then he tried another number.

'Julia – is she with you?'

There was a short delay: 'Philip?'

'Is she?'

'Philip. You have to understand: Justine is upset. She does not want to see you now. Give her time and I am sure that – '

'I am coming over.'

'No – ' But he cut her off.

Julia opened the door to the Yellow Bedroom. Justine had been sleeping. 'I am expecting a visitor soon, Justine. I want you to put this on.' In her hand was a leather G-string.

'Damn it, woman! Where is she?' Philip careered up the stairs, with Julia running after him, then overtaking him and barring the door. 'Get out of my way!' He burst through the door then stopped as if struck by a thunderbolt. Justine was on the Yellow Bed, wearing the leather G-string. But there was a hand there, touching the nakedness unbelievingly, and the ring through which the string was threaded.

'Charlotte?' Philip whispered weakly.

'How could you?' Her eyes cut through him. 'How could you do these things to her?' And he saw the tears flood Charlotte's eyes and Charlotte's arms enfold Justine.

'Perhaps you had better leave now,' Julia told him. 'She does not need you . . .'

He looked across at Charlotte and Justine and knew that it was true. And for the first time in his life, there was no action that he could take, and there were no words that he could muster to redeem the situation.

That night, Justine unburdened many secrets. She told Charlotte of her love for Rachel and explained how she had died.

'But, Justine, it was fate – a stroke coming like that, so

quickly. There was nothing that anyone would have been able to do.'

'They told me afterwards that it was a punishment for what she and I had done.'

'Shhh . . . Oh no, you must not believe it – what they said was wrong. It was so wrong of them to say that.'

But the tears were forming again in Justine's eyes. 'I sat there with her in my arms and I was screaming – screaming. I was screaming and she was dying . . . I never left her to get help and nobody came. In the end it was too late. They dragged me away from her. By then, she was already dead, and I was still screaming. They wouldn't let me go to the funeral; I didn't know that it had happened. I never even had the chance to say goodbye.'

And now there were tears in Charlotte's eyes as she held Justine and did not speak.

Late in the night, two men in dark clothes called at the house. Julia admitted them and ushered them up the stairs. She pushed open the bedroom door silently. Justine was asleep at Charlotte's breast. Both women were naked. The first man in black took out a photograph and examined it, then showed it to Julia:

'You know this likeness?'

Julia nodded. 'Miss Charlotte Lessing.'

'And the woman with the girl?' he asked.

'The same.'

The two men looked at each other and nodded. The second man wrote something down.

'Must I wake them?' whispered Julia.

'It is not necessary, madam. The testimony of witness will suffice. And your name need not be disclosed in public unless it comes to a denial.' But he shook his head and looked with sad eyes at the sleeping couple. 'But to have to sacrifice so much – for this. How can she deserve it?' Then his eyes met Julia's and he looked away.

'Do I detect a heart, sir?' Julia whispered. 'Is the plight of innocents now your mission?' Julia closed the bedroom door and ushered them out.

On the evening of the Saturday after Christmas, the snow came again in wide papery flakes slanting through the air, deadening the sounds of the carriage-wheels in the street. In the lobby of the hotel, a dark-eyed woman was sitting on a large circular couch. Beside her was a beautiful girl in a lemon-coloured jacket. The gentleman who had been standing at the door shook the snowflakes from his cloak and ventured forward. The woman had seen him, and she smiled; the newspaper that she had been reading was immediately placed aside and she whispered to the girl, who stared once at him before looking down. But in that one glance, he saw eyes of melting blueness, and lips that seemed to tremble, and a visage that would forever be ingrained into his mind.

Julia made Justine stand for the introduction. She placed the loop of leather in his hand. Then she watched his eyes follow the thin line of the leash, down below Justine's jacket, to the narrow, barely visible slit in the side of her skirt. 'Pull it,' Julia whispered. His hand tightened; Justine's mouth opened to a soft moan. 'She has a ring above her clitoris,' Julia whispered. 'She likes to be tethered; she likes to be whipped . . .'

Once the arrangements had been made clear, Julia watched the couple at the desk. Then she looked down at the newspaper beside her. Her eyes again perused the double column which was headed:

Heiress Disinherited
'Questionable Moral Standing' – Trustees

Miss Charlotte Lessing, only daughter of the late Sir Charles Lessing, yesterday suffered public rebuke in a hearing of the trustees of her father's estate, which declared her behaviour 'thoroughly reprehensible' and 'a disgrace to her good father's memory.' It is reported that, on hearing the verdict, Miss Lessing collapsed and had to be assisted from the chamber.

Although the estate was due to pass to Sir Charles's daughter on her thirtieth birthday, or on earlier marriage, the will included the proviso that the recipient 'Should uphold the family name and at all times conduct herself with such propriety as

becomes a young lady of her station.' On these grounds the
bequest was challenged by evidence put before the trustees,
alleging that Miss Lessing had for some time been engaged in
a tribadistic relationship with a girl more than ten years her
junior, with whom she had allegedly been discovered in flag-
rante delicto *at a house of ill-repute.*

*Under the terms of the will, the estate now passes instead to
the unfortunate lady's uncle, Mr George Lessing . . .*

Julia put the paper down. She opened her handbag and
looked at the fat manila envelope bearing her name. She
would have to visit the bank again, first thing on Monday.
And by Monday . . . She looked across at the man who
was already oblivious to anything but Justine, who was
looking past him, through the doorway, at the heavy white
flakes slanting in perfect contentment through the blackness
of the night – Justine, a victim of this long atonement. For
when you wake to find your lover dying in your arms,
and there is nothing you can do to save her, then all the
compassion, all the words of kindness in the world, can
never take away the anguish in your soul, and the only love
that counts for you – the only love that can ever have a
hope of helping – must be expressed through pain and
pleasure, hand in glove, with Julia watching over you,
safeguarding you, choosing lovers for Justine.

NEW BOOKS

Coming up from Nexus and Black Lace

Displays of Innocents by Lucy Golden
April 1999   Price £5.99   ISBN: 0 352 33342 1

The twelve stories in this collection reveal the experiences of those who dare to step outside the familiar bounds of everyday life. Irene is called for an interview, but has never been examined as thoroughly as this; Gemma cannot believe the demands made by her new clients, a respectable middle-aged couple; Helen learns that the boss's wife has an intimate way of demonstrating her authority. For some, it widens their horizons; for others it is an agony never to be repeated. For all twelve, it is a tale of intense erotic power.

Disciples of Shame by Stephanie Calvin
April 1999   Price £5.99   ISBN: 0 352 33343 X

Inspired by her grandfather's memoirs, the young and beautiful Amelia decides to begin her own erotic adventures. She soon draws all around her into her schemes as they help her to act out her most lewd fantasies – among others her best friend, Alice, who loves to be told what to do, and her shy aunt, Susan, who needs to be persuaded. All her friends take part in her increasingly bizarre games, before the final, most perverse drama unfolds.

The Institute by Maria del Rey
April 1999   Price £5.99   ISBN: 0 352 33352 9

Set in a strange institute for the treatment of delinquent girls between the ages of eighteen and twenty-one, this is the story of Lucy, a naughty young woman who is sentenced to be rehabilitated. Their disciplinary methods are not what she has been led to expect, however – they are, in fact, decidedly strange. This is the third in a series of Nexus Classics – dedicated to bringing the finest works of erotic fiction to a new audience.

Brat by Penny Birch
May 1999   Price £5.99   ISBN: 0 352 33347 2

Natasha Linnet is single, successful, independent and assertive – the ideal modern woman. But she has only one wish, and not one that she could ever admit to her smart friends. She wants to be spanked, and not just by a girlfriend or any of her male admirers. Instead she needs proper, strict discipline, and from someone stern enough to see her not as the aloof young career woman she appears to be, but as what she is underneath – a spoilt brat.

The Training of an English Gentleman
by Yolanda Celbridge
May 1999   Price £5.99   ISBN: 0 352 33348 0

When Roger Prince enjoys an educational summer idyll in Surrey, he learns the hard way that the female is indeed deadlier than the male. His voyeuristic host, his insatiable wife and their perverse step-daughter Florence conspire to humiliate him by imposing severe corporal punishment entirely at whim. His obedience to them and other ladies earns their adoring respect, and thus encouraged he chooses total submission to a Mistress as the true mark of an English gentleman.

Agony Aunt by G.C. Scott
May 1999   Price £5.99   ISBN: 0 352 33353 7

Harriet is unlike any other agony aunt, helping clients to live out their perverse fantasies of bondage and domination. When her servant Tom finds her tied up one day he decides to reverse roles, leaving her perplexed about her real desires. When he then goes to the continent to learn the art of correction, she decides to experiment further with subservience and humiliation, reaching surprising new extremes of pleasure. Harriet's friends want her to satisfy her fresh passion for servility with Tom, but she is still suspicious of her former lover. Will they ever find contentment in correction together again? This is the fourth in a series of Nexus Classics.

BLACK
lace

Stand and Deliver by Helena Ravenscroft
April 1999   Price £5.99   ISBN: 0 352 33340 5
It's the 18th century. Lydia Fitzgerald finds herself helplessly drawn
to Drummond, a handsome highwayman. This occurs despite the fact
that she is the ward of his brother, Valerian, who controls the
Hawkesworth estate. There, Valerian and his beautiful mistress initi-
ate Lydia's seduction and, though she is in love with Drummond,
Lydia is unable to resist the experimentation they offer.

Haunted by Laura Thornton
April 1999   Price £5.99   ISBN: 0 352 33341 3
A modern-day Gothic story set in both England and New York.
Sasha Hayward is an American woman whose erotic obsession with
a long-dead pair of lovers leads her on a steamy and evocative search.
Seeking out descendants of the enigmatic pair, Sasha consummates
her obsession in a series of strangely perverse encounters related to
this haunting mystery.

Village of Secrets by Mercedes Kelly
May 1999   Price £5.99   ISBN: 0 352 33344 8
A small town hides many secrets, and a contemporary Cornish fish-
ing village is no exception: its twee exterior hides activities such as
smuggling, incest and fetishism, and nothing is quite as it seems.
Laura, a London journalist, becomes embroiled with the locals – one
of whom might be her brother – when she inherits property in the
village. Against a backdrop of perverse goings-on she learns to in-
dulge her taste for kinky sex. Nothing is obvious and all is hidden,
in this erotic exposé of small-town living.

Insomnia by Zoe le Verdier
May 1999   Price £5.99   ISBN: 0 352 33345 6
A cornucopia of sexual experiences is explored in this collection of
short stories by one of the best-liked authors in the series. Zoe le
Verdier's work is an ideal reflection of the fresh, upbeat stories now
being published under the Black Lace imprint. From group sex, SM
and spanking, to dirty talking, voyeurism, virginity and love, there's
something for everyone, and all the stories are sexy, hot and imagin-
ative.

The Black Lace Book of Women's Sexual Fantasies
ed. Kerri Sharp

May 1999   Price £5.99   ISBN: 0 352 33346 4

This book has taken over one and a half years of in-depth research to put together and has been compiled through correspondence with women from all over the English-speaking world. The result is an amazing collection of detailed sexual fantasies, including shocking and at times bizarre revelations guaranteed to entertain and arouse. This book is a fascinating insight into the diversity of the female sexual imagination as we begin a new millennium.

NEXUS BACKLIST

All books are priced £5.99 unless another price is given. If a date is supplied, the book in question will not be available until that month in 1999.

CONTEMPORARY EROTICA

AMAZON SLAVE	Lisette Ashton		
BAD PENNY	Penny Birch		Feb
THE BLACK GARTER	Lisette Ashton		
THE BLACK WIDOW	Lisette Ashton		Mar
BOUND TO OBEY	Amanda Ware		
BRAT	Penny Birch		May
CHAINS OF SHAME	Brigitte Markham		
DARK DELIGHTS	Maria del Rey		
DARLINE DOMINANT	Tania d'Alanis		
A DEGREE OF DISCIPLINE	Zoe Templeton	£4.99	
DISCIPLES OF SHAME	Stephanie Calvin		Apr
THE DISCIPLINE OF NURSE RIDING	Yolanda Celbridge		
DISPLAYS OF INNOCENTS	Lucy Golden		Apr
EDUCATING ELLA	Stephen Ferris	£4.99	
EMMA'S SECRET DOMINATION	Hilary James	£4.99	
EXPOSING LOUISA	Jean Aveline		Jan
FAIRGROUND ATTRACTIONS	Lisette Ashton		
JULIE AT THE REFORMATORY	Angela Elgar	£4.99	
LINGERING LESSONS	Sarah Veitch		Jan
A MASTER OF DISCIPLINE	Zoe Templeton		
THE MISTRESS OF STERNWOOD GRANGE	Arabella Knight		

ONE WEEK IN THE PRIVATE HOUSE	Esme Ombreux	£4.99	
PENNY IN HARNESS	Penny Birch		
THE RELUCTANT VIRGIN	Kendal Grahame		Mar
THE REWARD OF FAITH	Elizabeth Bruce	£4.99	
RITES OF OBEDIENCE	Lindsay Gordon		
RUE MARQUIS DE SADE	Morgana Baron		
'S' – A STORY OF SUBMISSION	Philippa Masters	£4.99	
'S' – A JOURNEY INTO SERVITUDE	Philippa Masters		
THE SCHOOLING OF STELLA	Yolanda Celbridge	£4.99	
THE SUBMISSION OF STELLA	Yolanda Celbridge		Feb
SECRETS OF THE WHIPCORD	Michaela Wallace	£4.99	
THE SUBMISSION GALLERY	Lindsay Gordon		Jun
SUSIE IN SERVITUDE	Arabella Knight		
TAKING PAINS TO PLEASE	Arabella Knight		Jun
A TASTE OF AMBER	Penny Birch		
THE TEST	Nadine Somers		Jan
THE TRAINING OF FALLEN ANGELS	Kendal Grahame	£4.99	
VIRGINIA'S QUEST	Katrina Young	£4.99	

ANCIENT & FANTASY SETTINGS

THE CASTLE OF MALDONA	Yolanda Celbridge	£4.99	
NYMPHS OF DIONYSUS	Susan Tinoff	£4.99	
THE WARRIOR QUEEN	Kendal Grahame		

EDWARDIAN, VICTORIAN & OLDER EROTICA

ANNIE AND THE COUNTESS	Evelyn Culber		
THE CORRECTION OF AN ESSEX MAID	Yolanda Celbridge		
MISS RATTAN'S LESSON	Yolanda Celbridge		
PRIVATE MEMOIRS OF A KENTISH HEADMISTRESS	Yolanda Celbridge	£4.99	
THE TRAINING OF AN ENGLISH GENTLEMAN	Yolanda Celbridge		May
SISTERS OF SEVERCY	Jean Aveline	£4.99	

SAMPLERS & COLLECTIONS

EROTICON 4	Various		
THE FIESTA LETTERS	ed. Chris Lloyd	£4.99	
NEW EROTICA 4			

NEXUS CLASSICS
A new imprint dedicated to putting the finest works of erotic fiction back in print

THE IMAGE	Jean de Berg	Feb
CHOOSING LOVERS FOR JUSTINE	Aran Ashe	Mar
THE INSTITUTE	Maria del Rey	Apr
AGONY AUNT	G. C. Scott	May
THE HANDMAIDENS	Aran Ashe	Jun

Please send me the books I have ticked above.

Name ....

Address ....

....

....

.... Post code........................

Send to: Cash Sales, Nexus Books, Thames Wharf Studios, Rainville Road, London W6 9HT

Please enclose a cheque or postal order, made payable to Nexus Books, to the value of the books you have ordered plus postage and packing costs as follows:

UK and BFPO – £1.00 for the first book, 50p for the second book and 30p for each subsequent book to a maximum of £3.00;

Overseas (including Republic of Ireland) – £2.00 for the first book, £1.00 for the second book and 50p for each subsequent book.

If you would prefer to pay by VISA or ACCESS/MASTER-CARD, please write your card number and expiry date here:

....

Please allow up to 28 days for delivery.

Signature ....